Praise for Books by L.V. Ditchkus

L.V. Ditchkus's *The Sasquatch Series* won first place in the Sci-Fi category for the Colorado Authors League 80th Annual Writing Awards.

"Her character development is excellent, with the reader quickly feeling he/she *knows* these people."

—Arlene Shovald, Book Review for *The Sasquatch Series* in *The Mountain Mail*

"I thought this was a well-crafted and enjoyable tale and imagine that the sequel will be just as entertaining."

—Judge's feedback for *Crimes of the Sasquatch,* Writer's Digest Book Awards

"The author's ability to put readers in astonishingly creative settings is nothing short of delightful."

—Laurel McHargue, Award-Winning Author

"I was immediately hooked."

—David Kramer, Author of *Entering the Real World: Timeless Ideas Not Learned in School*

BY L.V. DITCHKUS

Chrom Y
Returns

Book I of The Chrom Y Series

Chrom Y
Returns

Book I of The Chrom Y Series

L.V. Ditchkus

Pinon Press

Colorado

This book contains an excerpt from the forthcoming book *Primogenitus: First Born, Book II of The Chrom Y Series* by L.V. Ditchkus. This excerpt has been set for this edition and may not reflect the final content of the forthcoming edition.
Library of Congress Control Number: 2021918279
ISBN: 978-1-7342125-4-9
Subjects: 1. Time travel 2. Cloning 3. Artificial intelligence 4. Gender
Cover design by Rafido.

To: Val and Leida

Chapter 1

DENVER—OCTOBER 11, 2026
ENGINEER SOFIA ANDES7

At precisely 1:14 A.M., my wife Dr. Briana Memphis7 and I stepped from our time capsule. We stood in a manicured backyard with our Defense 43 pistols drawn. As predicted, the night was dark with clouds covering the waxing moon.

After a blink to confirm my internal thought-directive, the low-light vision inserts in my ocular implants engaged.

Time travel had its share of perils, and boots on the ground over two centuries in the past made my heart pound so loud Briana could probably hear it. Nothing moved except leafless branches rattling in the stiff fall breeze.

"We're good." I mouthed the words. "Follow me."

Briana's implant lip read my message and transmitted to her earpiece. She nodded and became my sweep.

While scanning for potential threats, I moved toward the back porch.

I wrapped my fingers around the antique door handle on the screen door. Breaking in would be easy without a voice-activated entrance. The screen opened with a squeak. I wedged it with a painted cement frog from the adjacent mulch-covered garden.

Did the Pierces trim their own shrubs? No landscape bots in their time, but maybe they hired someone to help with outdoor chores.

Stay focused on the mission, Sofia. Easier said than done with so much to question about life in the past.

I slid the lock neutralizer from my waist pouch. With a quick insertion and twist, the deadbolt opened.

After giving Briana a wink and plastering on a confident smile, I pushed open the door.

Despite the skintight Hipposkin enviro-suit covering my fitness-junkie body, the temperature difference between the chilly fall evening and the warmth inside the house made me flush. Within seconds, the garment responded to compensate.

"Wait," I mouthed as I paused with my arm outstretched.

Silence. No barks or frantic toenails skittering across the floor. Historical records about domestic animals in 2026 were virtually nonexistent. I released a long slow breath—no pets to complicate the mission.

The kitchen island was devoid of food remnants or dishes. A box with slits across the top sat on the counter near a sink. I recognized it from historical images—a toaster. Next to the toaster, the Pierces had placed an old-fashioned, oil-based plastic and glass device with a blue light that flashed 12:00. Funny, they had so many mechanisms that performed one function apiece. Did they know how inefficient the machines were?

The room smelled of fish and spices. Was Megan Pierce a good cook? Or perhaps her husband Luis prepared the family meals. Either way, the couple's nightly routines would remain undisturbed if Mission Y went well.

With a nod from me, Briana holstered her weapon and slid a hand into her harness. Like the times we'd practiced in simulations, Briana removed a black vinyl medical case full of tools for the extraction. Two compressed vaccine injectors, or CVIs[1], of sleep cocktail nestled in the case. At least that's what I called the serum. Back in the lab, Briana would have encouraged me to remember its pharmaceutical name—something with too many letters and too few vowels. Knowing my wife was a stickler for accuracy, I usually played along.

Briana gripped one CVI and offered me the other. Before taking it, I stroked her outstretched hand. I wasn't here with just any Human Continuance Coalition, or HCC, doctor. We were a team—now and back

---

[1] See the Glossary at the back of this book for acronyms and definitions

home.

As trained, we held the CVIs with the injector tips pointed upward, thumbs poised on the plungers.

"Time to go." Briana's voice blasted in my earpiece even though she'd only mouthed the words.

I grinned. Briana reserved her assertive side for work. Our family—especially her domineering mother—viewed Briana as accommodating, almost deferential. Seeing her taking charge of this mission showed me why the HCC continued to promote her.

"You're amazing," I mouthed.

She raised a finger to her lips and snapped her head toward the bedrooms.

As we inched forward, Briana followed so quietly I could scarcely hear her breathe.

My low-light vision inserts helped me avoid a scattered pile of blocks and a toy truck while we made our way to the main bedroom where Luis and Megan Pierce, our carefully researched targets, would hopefully be sound asleep.

At the door, I motioned for Briana to stay on the other side of the opening.

Next step—assess their sleep status.

Two sets of sounds came from the bed. The lighter rhythmic breathing likely came from Megan. Sometimes Briana's night noises were imperceptible, and at times I'd fear she'd died in her sleep.

A sharp gargle tone overrode Megan's breathing, making me tense. I'd never heard a man sleeping and considered whether Luis' louder sounds might, sometimes, keep Megan awake.

"Are you daydreaming?" Briana's voice burst into my earpiece.

I gave a firm head shake and mouthed, "Now or never."

We entered the bedroom and tiptoed to either side of the bed.

Just when I lifted Megan's CVI—ready to press the injector into her neck—something moved under the covers between the couple.

Briana must have seen it, too. Her CVI tip was an inch from the vein in Luis' neck, but Briana mouthed, "Stop."

We locked eyes and pulled away.

With a thought directive and confirming nod, I switched to heat-seeking vision. A child's outline nestled between them.

Briana must have switched as well. She stared at the lump, and her shoulders drooped.

My job was to attend to tactics and engineering, not medical decisions. I waited for Briana to consider alternatives. We had two CVIs, each with a single dose, but three people were in the bed. We knew the Pierces had children but didn't expect to find one with the adults.

Briana's lips pressed into a thin, straight line. I could almost hear her brain noodling out a solution. With the help of her implanted medical info-base, she likely calculated the time needed against lower doses spread among the three people.

Whether from our subtle movements or the tension in the room, Megan's breathing quieted.

We froze.

Megan stayed silent, rolled over to her other side, and cuddled the pillow. Precious minutes elapsed. Neither of us moved until Megan resumed her rhythmic pattern.

"Just the adults." Briana mouthed as she jabbed her CVI toward Megan and then Luis.

Without a dose for the child, it would undoubtedly awaken during the extraction. What if the child later talked with their parents about what happened? Our protocol called for no witnesses.

Briana narrowed her eyes and repeated her signal, pointing the CVIs at the adults.

This was no time to disagree.

I confirmed with a nod.

With a glance toward Briana, I leaned over Megan and held the injector tip to the sleeping woman's neck. My thumb poised over the inject button, and I waited for Briana's three-finger countdown.

Briana stared at the child and then the father.

She stepped back and shook her head. I pulled the CVI away from Megan and stood motionless, waiting for Briana's guidance.

"Switch places," Briana mouthed.

This was a significant change in plans, and I wanted to hear her rationale. But I knew I wouldn't get away with it. In our time, I led a team of engineers who collaborated on important decisions, but as the medical operative in 2026, Briana's decisions were sacrosanct.

I moved to the other side of the bed, next to Luis. A deep breath drew in his scent—an unfamiliar, musky fragrance. A flutter skimmed across my chest and hardened my nipples.

What's that about?

I rolled my shoulders and shook my head to clear it.

Once Briana was in place, she held up a finger, asking for a minute. She leaned across Megan to inch the cover from the child. When its head and neck were exposed, Briana pressed the tip under the child's chin. Briana barely tapped the inject plunger before she pulled the CVI away. As the tot went slack, I released a slow breath.

We had no options—this place, this man, this day. Our instructions were clear.

After the signal from Briana, we injected Luis and Megan. The sleeping couple's already relaxed bodies sagged.

"There's not enough room to work with that child here," Briana mouthed. "Take it to another bedroom, and I'll get things set up."

I lay across Luis' chest to slide my arms under the sleeping tot. Ever so gently, I lifted the babe off the bed. The body smelled of talc, lotion, and a hint of urine. The child's onesie was covered with emblems I knew but had never seen on clothing. Miniature brown footballs and the message, "Mommy's little boy," confirmed he was male.

Straightening, I cradled him against my body.

I could barely breathe. No one on Earth had held a baby boy for 180 years. This mission would change all that. We wouldn't fail.

He wriggled against my chest and extended an arm, hitting me in the chin with his tiny fist.

"You're a tough little one. There's no boxing in 2240, so it's good you're alive now." I stroked his downy head and walked from the room.

Nightlights illuminated each outlet along the hallway, and my low-light inserts automatically adjusted to compensate. I found the children's bedrooms near the end.

In the first room, a fixture on a pink desk rotated flecks of light toward the ceiling. Orion, the dippers, the familiar W of Cassiopeia—the same constellations as the night sky in 2240.

So much had changed, yet so much hadn't.

As I crossed to the bed, I spotted a half-uncovered little girl curled against a wall plastered with a dozen posters of female superheroes, action figures, and manga. She must be the boy's sister.

A pang of grief gripped my stomach, knowing what she'd endure in a few decades. But burdening her with news of the future wasn't my remit.

"Enjoy your life now—while you can. You'll need to be strong." I mouthed my message to the girl, hoping Briana wouldn't pick up my transmission from a room away.

Once I'd adjusted the limp boy on my shoulder, I carried him down the hall. The next room held an empty bed shaped like a race car with a yellow body and bold red stripes. With my lips near his ear, I whispered, "I'm guessing this one's yours."

He must have tossed his comforter on the floor when he'd abandoned his bed. After laying him down with his head on a pillow, I fluffed the coverlet and tucked him in.

With a tentative finger, I stroked his cheek and the fine hairs on his head.

Sleep well, sweet boy.

I stepped into the hall and returned to his parents' bedroom.

Blazing lights had transitioned the Pierces' bedchamber into an operating arena. My low-light vision inserts responded, and I rubbed my eyes as they transitioned.

Briana had been busy. Light-blocking film covered the windows, and luminosity strips spanned the ceiling above the bed. She had removed Luis' sleepwear and connected monitoring disks on his arms, chest, and belly.

He lay there naked, legs apart. I drew a quick breath as my ribs constricted. My gaze locked onto his penis. What an oddly shaped appendage. HCC videos showed full frontal nudes, but those images hadn't prepared me.

"What took you so long?" asked Briana. "We don't have much time."

Her voice broke the spell. I crossed to where she stood and placed a firm hand on her arm. "Sorry for not hurrying. He was so precious. Imagine, a healthy baby boy. Will the sedative hurt him?"

"The serum has self-dissolving bots to increase his oxygen efficiency and monitor vitals while he's out." Briana jerked her arm free. "Get your head back into the mission. If we succeed, we'll have our pick of five baby boys in a few months."

"I know. But he's here now." I stroked her arm and chuckled when she didn't pull away. "When I put him in bed, he took my finger. His grip's strong. It took all I had to wriggle free."

"Really?" Briana tilted her head, no doubt to hide a smile. She loved kids as much as I did—probably more, as she'd already cloned once. "Was that his physical strength or your emotional weakness?"

I shrugged.

"Here." Briana handed me a foot-long metal cylinder. "Take this and extract the spermatogonia while I harvest my eggs."

I stood next to the bed to take in a full view of Luis' body. I ran the back of my hand along his arm, switched to the top of his hip, and continued down his body to his ankle.

My pulse quickened.

"Have you lost your mind?" Briana snapped. "Start the extraction. The machine needs at least a minute to accelerate the maturation and create viable sperm. My eggs should be ready by then."

I half heard her.

"They're remarkable." I traced across his ribcage, below his well-defined pectoral muscles. "So much denser and hairier than we are."

"Stop gawking and get to work." Briana placed a fist-size machine on the floor and twisted a ten-inch post into the center of its dome. She separated her protective suit's bow-to-stern fly and lowered herself over the device.

I winced. Was the post pre-heated? Lubricated?

Turning from Briana to Luis, I stared at the bumpy rows of muscles between his lower ribs and pelvis. No number of sit-ups would give my abs that definition.

Something primal triggered.

I wanted to feel his body next to mine.

After three years of marriage, making love with my wife had become routine. In less than a minute with Luis Pierce, I flushed with heat I hadn't felt in years.

Had my original attraction to Briana felt as strong as what Luis Pierce did to me in that room? My sister Phen swore she could never fully love a woman. What if I was like her?

"Sofia?" Briana's curt voice shattered my thoughts.

I knew that tone. If I ignored Briana, all hell would break loose.

"Fine." I moved to his groin.

His penis lay motionless and limp against his thigh. At first hesitant to touch it, I grasped it between a finger and thumb and moved it to lay on his belly.

It fell back into place. It must've had a mind of its own. I tried again with the same result. Had it become larger? Probably my imagination. I tucked it to the side and held out my extraction cylinder.

When the suction nozzle entered his testicle, he twitched.

I stopped.

Had he felt discomfort? With no males to test the procedure, our engineering and medical teams guessed the extraction would be painless. If distress counteracted the sleep serum, he might awaken too soon.

Again, I looked to Briana for guidance. "He moved when I pierced his testicle. Do you think he feels what's happening? I don't want to hurt him."

"Don't worry about it. I'm guessing the spasm was a normal reaction to jabbing a place filled with nerves. Continue with the procedure." Briana shrugged while she sat on her heels, skewered by the shiny metal post inside her vagina. "We'll be out of here in a few minutes, and if he's got a body ache tomorrow, who gives a crap?"

"You're in charge." I gave her a confirming nod.

Briana looked down between her legs. "I can feel the optic fibers swirling inside me. They're finding the healthiest eggs in my ovaries. I should be done in a second."

I placed an empathetic hand on Luis' arm. *If it hurts, I'm not doing it on purpose. Forgive me.*

Once I extracted Luis' single-celled organisms destined to fertilize Briana's eggs, I brought the cylinder to her. "This would be so much easier if we could take his sperm to our time."

"Tried and failed a bajillion ways. This method *will* work." Briana tapped the extraction cylinder against her open palm. "My extraction isn't finished but should be soon. The timing seems slower than the simulations."

Shortly, the egg harvesting apparatus issued its final tones, and Briana stood to slide from the post.

Briana screwed together the two mechanisms. Inside, bots would destroy sperm without Y chromosomes and force fertilization.

We both stared at the device's blinking lights. It whirred and hummed. After a full minute, a long beep sounded.

"It's fertilized and prepared the five zygotes." Briana's face wore a grin like I'd not seen in all the years of our marriage. "Let's make me pregnant."

I placed my hands on either side of her face and kissed her hard. "The next few months will fly by, and then our little Latrice will have a baby brother."

Briana nodded and situated herself on the post once more. "Please, let me hold all five to term."

"I'd settle for one we can raise as our own." I squeezed her arm. Decades of sacrifice were culminating at this moment. If we were successful, men would again walk the Earth.

The machine released a final tone. "We're finished." Briana stood and slid the mechanisms into her medical case. "Time to clean up and go home."

"Well?" I grasped her hand in both of mine. "Do you feel any different?"

"Not yet." Briana beamed. "I love that you're here with me."

I agreed and turned to remove the luminosity light strips while Briana inventoried her medical equipment and returned the kit to her waistband.

We worked together to dress Luis and roll him and Megan onto their sides. Afterward, we stood at the door to survey the room. Stored comparative images taken when we arrived ensured nothing was out of place.

I checked the time on my visual readout. "We have a few minutes to get to the capsule. Head there, and I'll meet you."

"Absolutely not." Briana grabbed my arm. "I'm not going without you. You'll be stuck if they start the transfer and you're not in your seat."

"Don't worry. You can strap in and set the signal for the five-minute countdown. I'll make it." The hallway beckoned. "I want to be sure I didn't move anything in the boy's room."

"What could you have changed?" Briana tilted her head. "You just laid him in bed, right?"

"I want to take one more peek at the boy." I winked at Briana. "We won't see ours for months."

"You're incorrigible." With a huff I'd heard many times before, Briana left for the backdoor while I dashed to the boy's bedroom.

As expected, nothing was out of place, but my feet wouldn't let me leave. At the boy's dresser, I touched an assortment of neatly folded clothes, a rash cream, and his hairbrush. The black enamel brush had a bright green dinosaur logo and a name stenciled on the back.

"Milo," I whispered aloud.

A snort escaped, and I clasped a hand over my mouth. Hopefully, Milo was the boy's name, not some cartoon dinosaur popular in 2026. Scribbled drawings tacked on a board convinced me that Milo was his name. Why else would someone put *Milo* on his artwork?

I knelt by the boy's side. He was lying in the same position I'd left him. His slow breathing mesmerized me.

Thankfully, there was no noticeable reaction to the drug Briana gave him. But she would have known how much to inject. We had no access to the HCC computers, but the scaled-down medical info-base inside her neural implant would have guided her.

"Beautiful boy. You have no idea what the future has in store for you." I cringed to imagine him facing the deadly virus in a few decades and stroked his ear.

I glanced over my shoulder toward the main bedroom and recalled my physical reaction to Luis.

"Maybe I'll find a way to save you and your father."

Chapter 2

Strapped inside the time capsule, my body shook with the voracity of prey in a wild bitch's maw. I succumbed to the motion and enjoyed an adrenaline high. We weren't traveling on a linear road or a corkscrew path like a rollercoaster. The capsule spun us on a jaggedy journey to overcome quantum gravity and proceed along the closed timeline curve.

Firmly secured in the other zero-gravity recliner, Briana clutched the chair's arms with a white-knuckle death grip. Her eyes remained pinched closed, and I wished I could reach her hand to hold it.

"It'll be over soon." I tried to calm her. But her eyes stayed shut.

We'd broken exhilarating boundaries. But Briana would consider time travel a means to an end—like a trip to the store. She'd acquired what was on her list, and it was time to go home.

Shaking made the control panel unreadable, so I blinked to confirm my internal thought directive and connected my vision inserts to the onboard computer. Numbers, symbols, and words scrolled. I nodded, satisfied we were on track.

"Only two more minutes, and we're home."

"Uh-huh."

The veins strained in Briana's neck and jaw. My throat tightened, knowing the brief time would feel like an eternity to her.

The HCC had arranged targeted athletic training for Briana to handle the mission's physical demands. But I'd played at the cliff edge my entire life and was more prepared—physically and mentally. If only I could share my confidence with her.

Despite our preparation and testing, something could go wrong.

Every year since 2200, the HCC sent one or two women back to 2026. We retrieved sperm and immature spermatogonia. The cargo unsuccessfully rode back to our time in containers made from dozens of materials inserted in our bodies—under our skin and buried in organs. Ultimately, nothing survived the journey. But the only positive results came when male cells did the jump inside the traveler's uterus.

On this trip, we tried a new process. Briana carried the fertilized eggs in vivo. It worked well in simulations. I was guardedly optimistic we would keep the eggs safe during time travel and isolated from the voracious Human Androgen Virus, or HAV, that plagued our time.

A yellow light on my console blinked once.

What the hell?

When it didn't advance to orange or a catastrophic red, I took a calming breath.

For yellow warnings, the team in 2240 would handle any adjustments on their end. Back in the control room, my engineering team would be glued to their stations, collaborating on how to respond to the alarm.

I flexed and unflexed my fingers on the armrest. If the team failed to correct the problem and the warning advanced to orange, I'd take control to stabilize the trajectory interface.

I pulled my focus from the control panel to Briana. With jaws clenched tight, it seemed like the muscles in her neck were tethered to her recliner.

Should I warn her?

Briana was already stressed, and heightened anxiety might affect her new pregnancy. Could increased tension prompt a miscarriage?

Better to let her believe everything was proceeding without complications.

Five more slow yellow blinks.

Come on team, respond.

The sixth flash came. Then a long gap.

I stared at the indicator and hoped the break wasn't a pause. If it started again, I could recalibrate the interval stabilizers or manually fine-tune the horizontal shift distributor.

I held my breath.

The seventh appeared in green, and I forced a slow exhale.

I smiled at Briana, who was none the wiser for our foray into the yellow zone.

The next ninety seconds passed without mishap. Readouts reported normal levels, and status lights remained a comforting green.

Abruptly, the shaking stopped.

"One more minute of that, and I'd barf." Briana slowly opened her eyes and adjusted to look at me. "We made it—all seven of us." She beamed.

"I know you hated it, but part of me is disappointed the ride's over."

Briana rolled her eyes.

My gaze traveled to Briana's belly. *Please let them be alive and healthy.*

Once the control room crew opened the door, Briana and I would be the first time travelers to return alive with viable cargo. Fingers crossed.

With only two seats in the capsule, the HCC planned to double male infant production by sending back two doctors next time. I'd seen a draft schedule, and the next jump coincided with Briana's due date to ensure the process worked before impregnating more women.

In the future, engineers like me would remain in our time, remotely handling technical challenges. My opportunity to time travel was over. It would be decades before I'd see an adult male again.

As I recalled Luis' naked body, a flush of heat spread from my groin. I squirmed in my seat and shut my eyes tight. Was it him specifically or any male that caused my reaction?

After grounding my grip on the armrests, I forced a look toward Briana. Her familiar grin confirmed our love, and I appreciated the 214 years separating me from Luis Pierce.

The hatch opened with a crack. As expected, frigid vapor poured in. When we transitioned to the present, the chamber's external skin temped out at absolute zero. While the outer surface froze, the internal compartment stabilized at 40 degrees. Once past the nadir, the outer shell warmed quickly, vaporizing any ice crystals that formed.

I rubbed the Hipposkin emblem on my suit's forearm. The manufacturer named the brand after the bulletproof skin of a wild animal that roamed Africa's devoid-of-humans grasslands and rivers. I had never seen such creatures except in virtual reality arcades, but its namesake synthetic fabric kept our bodies comfortable through the wild temperature swings during time travel. The nearly impenetrable fibers also protected us from most projectiles.

I shivered when the control room crew fully opened the hatch.

Two engineers and two doctors crowded around the entry. They greeted us with applause when they saw us tightly restrained and alive. Other travelers had died when their restraints failed. Now we took nothing for granted and tested and retested all safety protocols.

I unclipped my belts and helped Briana with hers before urging her through the exit.

The lead doctor whisked Briana to an examination chair to evaluate her health and precious cargo. I stayed at Briana's side until a physician confirmed both were fine.

As the carrier of five tiny zygotes on their way to becoming embryos, fetuses, boys, and men, Briana was the star of this show.

I gladly stepped to the side while she accepted back slaps and hugs from her peers. The tightness around their eyes confirmed that envy leaked from every pore. They'd have their shot at time travel and motherhood on future trips. Missions like these might become routine if all went well with Briana's babies.

At the far end of the control room, I dragged a hand across a waiting surgery bed and medical equipment. The readout screen on the Vital Signs Elucidator, or VSE, was grayed out. When we were in the capsule, the machine calculated our statistical probability of death. A readout above 9.0 would have told the doctors the cost of treatment to save us would have exceeded the value of our life expectancy.

One of my teammates, Lisa Chicago6, must have seen me staring at the machine. "Neither you nor Briana ever read out higher than a 3."

"I figured as much, but it makes me think about the first time jump in 2200 when Engineer Joffre6 came back near death."

"They had no choice but to let her die."

"The lab crew must have been horrified." I shook my head. "Imagine. Dr. Memphis5—Joffre6's own wife—couldn't do anything when the VSE reached 9."

"Everyone knows the story by heart. But it must feel surreal to travel in her footsteps. And you came back alive." Lisa placed a hand on my arm. "Joffre6 will always be a hero in our history books. But today, you and Briana are, too. If Joffre6 were alive today, she'd be proud of you for continuing her legacy."

I glanced around the room to see if any others might overhear. "Briana's private about her heritage—she doesn't like to brag—but did you know that Dr. Memphis5 was Briana's grandmother?"

"I never made the connection. But it makes sense that Briana comes from a long line of doctors."

"Briana is Tiana Memphis5's clone's clone," I confirmed with a nod.

"I saw Dr. Memphis5 speak at the University of Denver before she died. Her advances in materials transfer are legendary. Did Briana know her grandmother?"

"Nope. Briana's mother waited far beyond when most women submitted for cloning." I scoffed. "You've met Jayla—she's always on her own schedule."

"Seems like most of my friends are going in at twenty or twenty-one."

"Briana cloned our little Latrice at twenty-four. But that wasn't Jayla's way of operating." The thought of my mother-in-law prompted a shudder. "Jayla was nearly thirty before she cloned Briana. So Briana was a baby when her grandmother died at 55."

"Her grandmother died at 55?" Lisa took a step back. "My mother died at 47, and I thought *she* beat the odds."

I pulled close to Lisa. Not everyone needed to know what I'd overheard from Briana. But Lisa and I had been close colleagues for years. She wasn't the type to start rumors. "Briana knows docs working in clone longevity. I try to stay out of those conversations. But despite what you hear in the media, lifespans continue to decrease."

"That's not what official broadcasts say." Lisa cocked her head.

"Not everything you hear in the media is true. Our hope lies with a new crop of males." I indicated a thumb toward the capsule. "Men'll help us repopulate with originals. Without them, our cloned material will keep degrading, and humans won't rule the Earth in the next century."

"Sofia." I jumped at Briana's voice directly behind me. "They're going to connect to the capitals in a few minutes."

Had Briana heard me giving up trade secrets to Lisa?

One glance around the room told me Briana wouldn't have noticed. Dozens of women from the medical and engineering staffs had made their way to the underground bunker housing the control room to offer their congratulations.

Corks popped, and flutes passed among the teams.

A nurse approached us and handed Briana a glass. "Don't worry. It's sparkling grape juice."

"Thanks." Briana took the drink. "I'm not doing anything to jeopardize these five boys." She patted her tummy.

Briana grabbed my hand and squeezed before she pulled away to approach a stark white wall. The lights dimmed, and everyone in the room grew silent. The wall transformed into a screen.

The HCC banner appeared and framed the top in blue and red with their crests on either end. The rest of the screen held a grid of four dark rectangles, one for each leader from the four remaining countries in the world. The capital cities' names blinked in yellow while the frames waited for the designated honorable chiefs from Limassol, Kyiv, Singapore, and Panama City.

One by one, the presidents connected to the video feed. Someone must have briefed them about the mission's success as all the esteemed women smiled from the screen.

I stood at the back and watched Briana glow in recognition of her work.

Even when we'd first met, Briana made her plans clear. She would take a starring role in Mission Y and follow in her ancestors' footsteps.

Men represented half the population when Briana's an-grandmother, her non-cloned grandmother, Joffre6 attempted to bring sperm back from 2026. That destination was nearly four decades before 2060 when HAV spread like wildfire across the planet and inflicted men with Testicular Wasting Syndrome, commonly referred to as TWS or *twas*.

In eighteen months, billions of men died. Every man had succumbed to the tortuous disease except twelve immune but sterile infant boys. The last of those surviving males, Dr. Simon Merlin, died in the control room on the same day as an-grandmother Joffre6.

On this day, the sidewall cycled through images of the pivotal 2200 team and every time traveler in the forty years since. Tiana Memphis5 stared from the wall with penetrating dark eyes. But it could have been Jayla up there. In a few years, Briana would look exactly like them.

I studied Simon Merlin's photo. The shot was taken shortly before his death. The great scientist might not have approved of this particular image with him wearing his exoskeleton, a red and silver mechanical skin that kept him safe and upright. He posed at his science station in this control room.

Simon's team had worked tirelessly to perfect time travel, the necessary step to bring men back into the population. Since he was an original, he lived more than three times longer than the average clone and was 141 years old when he died. As an original, organ regeneration nanobots prolonged Simon's life. But the bots didn't work as well on cloned tissue.

Briana stood in front of the dignitary-filled screen, her shoulders squared and back ramrod straight. No one but me and maybe Jayla would notice the nearly imperceptible shake in her hands.

The Earth's four presidents had connected to the control room to congratulate her. This moment would be recorded and played across the world. Younger medical officers might contact Briana, looking for a position on her team. Future time travelers would seek her advice. She'd earned their respect and praise.

My ocular implant viewer automatically switched from flat to 3D mode. Techs would set the presidents' video streams for the most flattering resolution. Despite their advanced ages, they came across as polished yet amenable—always prepared for the next voting season.

As the HCC's current Chair, President Fuji6 from Singapore spoke first. "Dr. Briana Memphis7, we were informed about your safe trip to 2026 and back to 2240. The HCC and the world are grateful for your sacrifices and the risks you've taken to bring us to this momentous occasion. We thank you."

All the staff in the lab turned toward Briana. They expected something profound. Briana raised her glass and cleared her throat.

She'd practiced her speech a dozen times in front of me. But the prearranged words must have eluded her. "The women in this room and their predecessors deserve the glory for what we've accomplished today. This is only the beginning of our journey. I promise to keep safe the five babies I'm carrying."

She stammered, tipping her glass to each president on the screen. "They're your sons. They'll help us ensure humans, both men and women, will survive into the next millennia and beyond."

Briana's flushed cheeks and white-knuckled grip on the glass betrayed her disappointment at forgetting her lines.

I rushed forward to help. While I couldn't deliver Briana's speech, I could fill in the gaps with a few impromptu words—something to diffuse her mistake.

"As the co-pilot on today's mission, I'd like to add a thought." I slid an arm around Briana's waist, and she leaned into me as if to show she was grateful.

What should I say?

"I'd like to give special thanks to the person who made this day possible. That's the one individual who will be a part of our children's children and guarantees humanity's place on this planet."

I raised my glass to Briana. Her eyes glistened, and we exchanged adoring glances any married couple would recognize.

Turning to the wall of presidents, I nodded. "Let's all thank Luis Pierce and his generous gift."

"What?" Briana's response came out in a whisper. But I knew my stoic wife well. For her, the reaction was a bloodcurdling scream. Briana barely glanced at me and placed her glass on a tray. Without a word, she marched toward her mother, next to the bar.

Surely Briana appreciated Luis' contribution. What did I say wrong?

Keeping a keen eye on the hallway's center, I wobbled to my studio with a tight grip on my fourth glass of champagne.

I'd given up drinking grain-based alcohol long ago. It didn't seem special since the HCC started promoting vineyard reestablishment. Great wine in any variety remained elusive, but the reds grown in the southern America reformatory farms—like where the government incarcerated my sister Phen—were probably the best.

After two ineffective commands to open the entry, the computer finally recognized my voice.

What was wrong with my voice activation?

The entrance panel dissolved to allow access to my private space.

With only one minor stumble, I crossed the room and set my glass on a table against the wall holding the sole real piece of art, an antique tennis racket that once belonged to Steffi Graf, my tennis idol. A grand sweep of my arm slid an assortment of tennis balls and sport gloves off the table. I plopped on the adjacent chair.

It was late. After the presidents' call ended, Briana and her mother left the celebration. Briana was furious, and I still had no idea why.

Shortly after they'd gone, I detoured to Jayla's studio and visited our daughter Latrice until a strange summons called me to the control room. I suspected Briana had sent the message—a passive aggressive move to get our little girl to herself.

To give Briana time to cool off, I returned to the control room festivities. After the party wound down, I figured an uninvited trip to Briana's studio wouldn't be welcome. I imagined her asleep in pristine surroundings. How would she have decorated today? Something in bright reds to match her excitement or gloomy blacks and grays to mirror how she felt about her inconsiderate wife?

I never changed my décor. When I'd turned fourteen, I programmed functional furniture in the five Olympic colors—blue, yellow, black, green, and red—to keep my Olympic dreams front and center. The style stayed with me even after my competitive years. The continuity felt right.

Briana changed her studio every day. Her type of cleanliness bordered on an obsessive-compulsive disorder. No wonder she insisted on separate suites when we moved into the Merlin Building's employee housing. I grinned. There was nothing borderline about Briana's eccentricities. She probably inherited them all from her controlling mother Jayla.

After guzzling the last of my champagne, I moved to the bed and pushed off the pile of clothes I'd worn before putting on my Hipposkin suit in the morning.

Time to get comfortable.

Starting at the neckline, I unclasped the releases down the length of my body. In less than a minute, the suit lay on the floor in a heap of high-tech fabric and microwires.

Dressed in only my sport undies, I bundled the suit into my arms—not an easy task. The semi-rigid arms and legs flopped in all directions, like wrestling an octopus.

"Open cleaning portal."

After I stuffed the suit into the bin, I inventoried my slovenly room. Despite my inebriated condition, I gathered all my discarded clothes and piled them on the suit.

"Shut portal and process cleaning."

Briana recycled her clothes for a fresh and fashionable look every day, and it showed.

While cleaning took more resources, I opted for the old-fashioned approach and allowed a robotic service to refresh mine.

The cleaning portal door disappeared, replaced by a faux window with a nighttime woodsy scene.

"Open window."

A crank turned, and my fake window swung outward. A cool breeze and cricket sounds wafted from the wall.

"Larger."

The entire wall changed into a picture window with an open sliding glass door.

Nice, but not enough. Briana was angry with me for no good reason and shortcutted my time with our daughter. I'd design the rest of my evening around myself.

What setting would my O.C.D. wife find particularly annoying?

Hmm. Something uncontrollable and disorderly.

I snapped my fingers and sat in the room's center.

"Create an outdoor setting. Remove all bedroom furniture and give me a campsite with a fire ring."

The room instantly transformed into a tree-lined clearing with a transparent, flexi-pane dome tent and a fire secured by a rock circle. Wood smoke scent tingled my nose.

"Ditch the tent. I'm sleeping under the stars tonight."

The tent disappeared, replaced by a fluffy sleeping bag on a thick mattress. With a finger poke, I tested the firmness. Perfect.

When a breeze crossed my arms, goosebumps formed. I could have raised the temperature, but the coolness felt authentic. While never having camped, I imagined the mountains would feel chilly at night—irrespective of the month.

Once I snuggled into the bag, I stared at the starry sky and the sliver of a moon. Milo's sister's constellation lamp came to mind.

"Remove the moon and make the constellations brighter."

Cassiopeia flickered in the northern sky.

Only a few hours earlier, I'd invaded the Pierce household.

Seemed like ages ago.

I sighed.

Was Milo having a good night's sleep?

Hopefully, he'd wake in the morning without recalling how he'd moved from his parents' bed into his own. Did children typically wander from bed to bed in 2026?

Latrice had a studio she shared with her robot nanny. Briana and I were confident Latrice couldn't wander out of her room at night. Surely, Milo's parents knew he'd joined them in bed. When they awoke to find Milo gone, they might assume he had abandoned them and be proud of his independence. Why would they think otherwise?

Luis.

A flutter spread across my chest.

I shut my eyes and pictured him lying on his bed.

Our Mission Y profile folder listed his career as a *fitness trainer*. No wonder he had such a developed body.

I touched the space between my breasts and recalled how my fingers caught on the mat of dark hairs on his broad chest.

The carved muscles across his abdomen must have come from a million ab workouts. My hand drifted to my own taut stomach.

Pausing to stroke the soft fabric inside the sleeping bag, I imagined him inches away.

My nipples hardened, breath quickened.

I gripped my hips and slowly moved my fingers downward. My hands became his.

I inhaled long and slow to recall his scent.

My fantasy Luis nuzzled my neck and pressed his weight on top of me, not the heft of my hundred and fifty-pound wife, but nearly two hundred pounds of male flesh crushing my body with force and desire.

In my mind, I brought him into my campsite and deep into my body.

Chapter 3

Jayla's shrill reprimand saturated the airwaves in our family's breakfast room and reverberated inside my pounding temples. I stood by the entrance and mused about whether to leave quietly. Perhaps I'd meet the family for lunch instead.

Our little Latrice, oblivious to her grandmother's rant, looked at me and grinned.

"An-ma." Latrice's truncated version of an-mother, the non-cloned mother, made me chuckle. I crossed to her and kissed the top of her head.

Before heading to my chair, I patted Nanny Tori's squishy, silicone surface.

"Too close, Sofia Andes7." When my hand accidentally grazed one of her 360-degree sighting ports, Nanny Tori beeped the proximity warning.

I glared at Jayla. Had she programmed the robot to keep me at arm's reach?

Jayla ignored me and started in again on Nanny Tori, the human-size, hourglass-shaped robot destined to act as both mentor and teacher to our daughter for the next five years.

According to Jayla, our beloved Nanny Tori had secured the highchair's straps too tight. How would Jayla know? While my mother-in-law had contributed to our nanny's original specifications, actually touching our child had little to do with Jayla's daily routine.

"Jayla, I know Tori's calibrated for machine learning. But maybe you should reprogram her instead of explaining how to tighten the straps?" My smirk aggravated my well-deserved hangover.

Both Jayla and Briana turned toward me with identical piercing stares. They reminded me of a nature film I'd seen with two leopards simultaneously turning to appraise a grazing antelope. Mother and daughter enhanced the image in similar spotted jumpsuits accentuating their toned muscular curves. The sole physical difference between the two women was the deeper lines surrounding Jayla's eyes.

Unable to bound away, I backpedaled. "I didn't mean to intrude on your lessons. Please, continue."

"Nice of you to join us for breakfast." Briana stood to nudge aside her mother and manually adjust Latrice's restraints. "I figured you might decide to stay in bed after the night you had."

Was she referring to when I circled back to the party in the control room or my forest fantasy?

Briana couldn't possibly know about either. Better to assume she was talking about my toast to Luis. Twelve hours of solitude and sleep must not have dispelled her anger.

"I didn't want to miss breakfast with our adorable daughter." I winked at our girl. "What's on the menu? Looks like Latrice has smashed peaches on cereal."

"Something like that." Briana gave the strap a final tug. "I've added new supplements to her meals. Studies show promising results for cell resilience and early development enhancement."

"Only the latest and best for our little girl." I placed both elbows on the table and rested my chin on steepled fingers, giving full attention to Briana. "Thanks for keeping up with new developments about clone longevity. I know you already have a lot on your mind."

"The research was from me," Jayla injected. "More precisely, the underlying research came from one of my advancements in cell pliability. We recently gained approval for the supplement's commercial distribution."

"We all benefit from your breakthroughs, and you're living proof cell degeneration can be slowed." I smiled innocently at my mother-in-law. "At fifty-five, you've beaten the odds."

"Don't you ever think about what you say before it bursts from your mouth?" Her eyes narrowed. "Ten years over the average life isn't unheard of. Some women die sooner, and some much later. I never imagined I'd drop dead on my forty-fifth birthday. But perhaps you'd rather I was more *ordinary*?"

"We're having strawberries and waffles for *our* breakfast today." Briana intervened. "The strawberries were AereoPodded from Chile. Their growing season just started." She looked from Jayla to me and back. "Please, let's appreciate this meal. According to the manual, I'll start morning sickness in a few weeks. If you can't be civil for yourselves, then do it for me."

Sufficiently chastised for taunting Jayla, I sat and shoveled waffles and fruit onto my plate.

As I chewed, Nanny Tori fed Latrice using one of her many available arms. This one mimicked a human limb, with prosthetic fingers holding a pink, rubberized spoon. Probably a visual training tool to simulate human eating.

Latrice repeatedly banged a tight fist against the robot's hand, creating a mess on her tray and face. Another of Nanny Tori's arms quietly discharged from a hidden door to vacuum excess food. Latrice giggled in response.

"I wonder how long it'll take Latrice to understand she'll have a little brother next June?" I mused aloud.

Nanny Tori responded immediately. "On an average day with 643.38 waking minutes, I mention Latrice's baby brother approximately 42.29 times."

"Are you certain about that? I suspect you mention him 42 times on an average day." I chuckled. "On the 0.29th time, do you use one-third of the words?"

"Processing question." The robot's ring of sighting ports blinked with flashing blue lights. "Insufficient data to respond. Sorry for any inconvenience."

"You know," Briana placed her fork on the table, straightening the utensil until it was perpendicular to the table edge. "Aria Harpeth7's family teased their nanny until it needed two days in the repair station."

Translation—Briana said I'd be responsible for any programming bugs my banter caused.

"Okay." I turned to Nanny Tori. "I appreciate that you speak with

Latrice about her new brother. Does she understand?"

"Even though Latrice cannot verbalize a proper response, talking with her about complex topics is effective. At fourteen months, she understands more than you might expect." The robot's sighting ports ran a loop of green lights before changing the topic. "Has the medical team decided upon a firm delivery date? There was deliberation between an eight- and nine-month gestation period. My interactions with Latrice will be modified based on Briana Memphis7's scheduled delivery date."

"The medical team will monitor Briana nonstop." I reached across the table and laid a hand near Briana's place setting. "But with five babies, there's no way for her to go full term. She might be on bed rest for her last month and will deliver a month earlier than for a single baby. I'm guessing June."

Latrice chewed her cereal, oblivious to how her life would change with a sibling. Would her experience be different from other girls who'd only have sisters? Would raising a daughter and son be different from having Latrice and a clone of my own?

I still had years to decide, but I didn't see myself going through the cloning process. If we chose to have another child, Briana could replicate another.

To no one in particular, I asked, "How will our son know how to act like a brother to Latrice?"

"What do you mean?" Briana's brow creased. "He'll probably act the same as a sister. Surely, minor below-the-waist variations won't matter."

"I don't know. But I suspect they could be hard-wired differently."

"That's doubtful." The subject was closed. Briana picked up her fork and touched each pointy tine. "I can't believe I forgot my prepared message last night."

I kept my head down.

"You did an exemplary job." Jayla punctuated her statement by stabbing a finger in Briana's direction. "You spoke of teamwork and safeguarding your five sons."

"The message was mediocre." Briana sighed. "I wanted my words to be memorable."

Before I could stop, I asked, "Do you feel like giving your prepared speech now?"

"At this point, it's irrelevant." Briana regarded her plate. "The moment's gone."

"Please, tell us." Jayla placed her clasped hands on the table's edge. "I'd like to hear it."

"Well, okay. I wanted to say something like…" Briana straightened in her chair. "My babies will be born into a different world from their predecessors. *They* will decide the template for men in this century and beyond. Our accomplishment today gives new meaning to the term *founding fathers*."

"That's perfect, but so was last night's speech." I rounded the table to embrace Briana. When she relaxed into my hug, I hoped she forgave me for my previous night's faux pas.

"That's nice, dear." Jayla's clipped tone didn't sound like a compliment. "When will you decide on a name for my grandson?"

"Sofia and I didn't discuss it before yesterday's trip." Briana shrugged. "We didn't want to hex the mission by picking out a name before we knew it was successful."

"Now that we're back and the babies seem safe and healthy, we can think about it." I stroked Briana's cheek before returning to my place.

"Of course his last name will be Memphis." Briana beamed. "We'll have an original—not a Memphis8 like Latrice but plain old Memphis."

"Maybe he'll be a Memphis½. After all, he'll be one-half original and one-half clone." Seemed logical to me.

"What did you say?" Briana's fists clenched on either side of her plate. "Between the original donor sperm and the fact that I'll carry him for eight months, he'll be a full original."

She was right. Cloned babies developed in synthetic uteruses in a lab until fully formed. Briana was the first pregnant woman since the last live birth in 2060, and that was 180 years ago. Our son would be more original than the fifty percent of his genes.

"I'm sorry." If I could keep my mouth shut, I wouldn't have to apologize so often. "What I said was insensitive. Thanks to you, he'll be one hundred percent original." Was my response sufficient to recover any goodwill?

"What about his first name?" Nanny Tori's unexpected question couldn't have come at a better time.

Jayla scoffed. "After last night's spectacle, I suspect any name—besides Luis—would work." She held up both hands in surrender. "But don't let me be the one to interfere with your decisions."

Briana released a heavy sigh but said nothing. For the last four years, I'd hoped for support or a remark to put Jayla in her place.

Both Memphis women returned to their waffles like breakfast on the Titanic—in pleasant ignorance of any impending disaster. Sometimes Jayla's taunts pushed too far.

Ignorant of the dynamics, Nanny Tori wiped the last bits of breakfast from Latrice's tray.

A long jog would clear my head and untie the knot in my stomach. I stood and nodded to each person. "I'll be in the lab after I take a run."

If I were lucky, Jayla would find new dinner companions.

I stretched my calves as I took the elevator from my seventeenth-floor studio to the lobby. The elevator shot past the other residence floors and gave me a clear view into the Merlin Building's interior atrium, passing Briana's medical crew at six and my engineers on five.

In the lobby, natural light beaming from the skylights made me squint, and I tapped my temple to engage my optical implant's UV dampening mode. I pulled my hair into a ponytail and nodded to the half dozen guards who protected the entrance and supervised the access control vestibule, security scanners, and microbe neutralization stations.

My employer, the Chromosome Y Reestablishment, or CYR division of the HCC, maintained maximum security as some citizens didn't agree with our mission.

Traffic in and out of the building was light compared with the days leading up to our time travel. I suspected most staff stayed inside to pore over results from the previous day's events. I'd join them after my run.

After passing through the access control vestibule, designed to allow one person at a time to either enter or exit, I paused on the concrete steps. The midday October sun warmed my shoulders while I checked out the latest protests.

About two dozen women stood on the sidewalk, chanting and holding signs that blinked messages about our work. "Disband the CYR," "Men are in the past. Don't let them join our future," and "We don't resurrect dinosaurs. Why men?"

I swallowed hard, then pinched my lips shut to keep from calling out to them. This protest group, called the Front, had set up a permanent rallying point at our building. Their messages defied civility. They opposed something I supported to the core.

A lone woman stood on a raised platform with a microphone. Everything about her demeanor said plain, innocuous, and approachable—the perfect person to cultivate a following and lead a revolt.

"Our world is peaceful." When she spoke, the group fell silent. "HCC leaders strive to ensure sound health, advanced education, and meaningful work for all citizens. We haven't experienced war for 180 years. In 2060, we decided to create a future based on collaboration and cooperation. You might wonder how we could change the political rhetoric away from developed nations that kept the best for themselves while taking advantage of lesser-developed countries?" She waited for effect. "One paradigm shift occurred in 2060—all men died."

The crowd cheered, and she pointed toward our building. "The scientists at CYR work day and night to fulfill our worst nightmare. They plan to repopulate our world with men." She paused as they jeered. "Women eradicated warfare, unfair benefits for the wealthy, and pointlessly aggressive activities—like boxing, martial arts, and football. Why would we want to bring men back? They'd re-infiltrate our society with the brutality we've left in the past."

Her audience followed each proclamation with applause. I couldn't stomach her distasteful speech. Disease had robbed our world of the beautiful creatures who added diversity that now only existed in the nonhuman animal kingdom. Men's strength and bass voices were missed—at least by some of us.

I shook my head before walking through a hologram water fountain and away from the spectacle.

A double-lane fitness path snaked between steel and glass multi-use buildings to a green space along Cherry Creek Drive. The trail followed the creek until it ended at Survivors Park, two miles east of Denver's dense city center.

My first mile was the toughest, with erratic heartbeats and gasping breath. After pushing for ten minutes, my body fell into a rhythm I could sustain for hours if I wanted. A physician once told me I had a rough idle that smoothed out when I hit my stride.

Few other joggers were on the path, but two women on Uni-fit striders whizzed by me in the fast lane. Their arms and legs ferociously worked the pedals on the trendy new outdoor fitness device that combined the bicycle, rowing machine, and hoverboard. The shiny steel Uni-fit made these individual pieces obsolete. I had no intention of joining the fad—running gave me a full-body workout to stay in shape for tennis and clear my head.

I passed under bridges designed for pedestrians and Levi-plate riders. Spandrel-supported arcs held signs identifying the byways above for Bannock, Lincoln, and Colorado. Finally, I reached Cherry Street where the path entered Survivors Park.

October's low-angle sun and the fresh, dry air evaporated my sweat before it could saturate my running suit. At the entrance gate, I propped my hands on my hips and slowed to a walk.

After my first loop around the monuments, my heart no longer pounded in my ears. On my second circuit, I stopped at each obelisk to pay homage to the twelve men who survived the savagery of TWS. They were newborns in 2060, and most lived long lives thanks to regeneration nanobots. All dedicated their lives to science and agreed to decades of poking and analysis. They were sterile, and any attempts to clone them failed miserably. Their newborn male duplicates suffered for a few painful days before they died.

Before returning to the lab, I sat on the bench in front of Simon Merlin's column. Without Simon's innovative work to overcome paradoxes and capitalize on wormhole vacuums, my trip to 2026 would have never happened. I was sad to think Simon had died forty years before his dream to resurrect men became a reality. If Luis Pierce had lived through TWS, would history revere him?

Lost in my thoughts, I barely noticed the scruffy dog that came up to sniff my foot. Its bark snapped my attention back into the park, and I bent to scratch behind its ear. I'd grown up with a dog and always assumed I'd have one, but restrictions in the sterile Merlin building banned pets of any kind.

One glance at the person on the other end of the leash disoriented me. I stared, trying to make sense of what I saw. Moments ago, she'd spoken to a crowd on the plaza in front of our building.

"How did you get here so fast?" I asked.

Despite the abruptness of my question, the woman gave me a warm smile. "You must have mistaken me for someone else. This park is a block from my home. I've just arrived."

"You weren't at a rally in front of the Merlin Building? I swear it was you. She even dresses like you." I scanned her from head to toe. "Well, maybe her boots were brown, and yours are black, but her coat was exactly like the one you're wearing."

Perhaps I was thinking too narrowly. This woman could be a different clone—the speaker's family member.

She sat on the bench beside me, near enough to suggest familiarity. I moved a bit to add space.

"My sister's giving speeches today." The woman smoothed her coat across her lap. "I didn't ask where she planned to go. Considering her agenda, the Merlin Building was likely on her list."

"She's with the Front?"

"My sister is Charlotte, and I'm Mia Danube9. We're both with the Front, but don't hold it against us."

Mia held out her hand. Did she expect me to take it?

I stood to leave, but she continued. "Charlotte likes to be in the spotlight, while I prefer helping in the back office. Maybe that's because I have a more balanced opinion about the cause. Generations of my family have worked for the Front. It's expected, whether or not I'm a hardcore believer."

I turned to stare at her hand, still outstretched. "And are you a believer?"

She rubbed her palm against her thigh as if trying to remove the slight I'd delivered by ignoring her gesture. "Not sure. How about you? Were you attending the protest, or do you work in the Merlin Building?"

The Front had tentacles everywhere. She probably already knew the answer. But I responded anyway. "I'm an engineer for CYR. My support to reintroduce men is unwavering."

"I admire your conviction. I've spent most of the last two decades studying the history they don't share with us in school." Mia reached to scratch under her dog's blue collar embroidered with the name *Shampoo*. "The facts they don't tell the public might make you wonder what's true."

In my experience, curriculums doled information about the world before 2060 in snippets and generalizations. Academic programs prepared youths for a future in the current world rather than rehashing past mistakes.

Mia's hint at her data resources made me recall my pre-time jump dossier about the Pierce family. Besides a fact sheet about Luis' medical history and his career up to 2026, it included no further information. Both Luis and Milo had probably died in 2060 or before. Milo would have been thirty-five and Luis in his mid-fifties when TWS swept the planet.

What happened to them between 2026 and their untimely deaths? Any attempt to find out more on the CYR computers would likely set off an alarm and an inquiry I'd avoid at any cost. But I wanted to know more about the Pierce men.

Hmm. Wheels turned in my head.

I glared at Mia. "Does the Front have access to historical information about people who lived before TWS?"

"It's probably borderline illegal, but we have digital copies of books and archives covering millennia of history, both at a country level and an individual level. I could pull up data on the ordnance used for every battle fought in World War II or find the names and addresses of everyone who lived in Denver in recorded history."

She gave me a disarming smile. I could tell she wanted something from me, but I wanted something from her, too. Engaging with Mia after this first encounter could jeopardize my career. I'd have to be incredibly careful to protect CYR from any plots that Mia or the Front orchestrated. Was obtaining historical information on Luis and Milo worth the risks?

I decided to leap. "I might like to check out your information. Is there a way I can contact you?"

Mia pulled a case from her coat pocket. She extracted a small, thin bioplastic square like the card I used for nontraceable calls to my incarcerated sister Phen. "This com-card has a direct line to me. Be sure to adapt it to your voice commands before anyone else can access it, and no one besides you will be able to use it. I'm happy to speak with you anytime."

The card slipped easily into my waistband pouch. When Mia held out her hand for the second time, I immediately took it. I wanted her to trust me. Later, I'd consider whether to trust her.

When I arrived back at the Merlin Building, the rally had dispersed. But a few stragglers remained to shake their signs and heckle me while I approached the entrance. Mia's sister Charlotte was nowhere in sight.

As I waved my hand in front of the security monitor, it read my implanted microchip and the door opened. Consistent with protocol, I stepped inside the access control vestibule while sniffers searched for evidence of tiny microbes or viruses. I'd performed this procedure at least once a day for years without a glitch.

When the alarm sounded, I stiffened in shock.

"Stay calm." A soothing female voice replaced the beeping alarm. "We have detected low levels of Human Androgen Virus on your person. We will begin decontamination protocols shortly. When directed, please enter the neutralization station. The chemicals used for this procedure are non-toxic to humans. Thank you for your cooperation."

How had I picked up HAV on my run? City-wide scrubbers continually cleaned the air, and detection monitors sat at nearly every intersection. Denver's Automatic Point Monitoring machines were probably less sensitive than those at CYR, and Ms. Congeniality said it was a low level. Maybe the quantity was too negligible for the city's detection systems.

Instead of the welcoming whoosh from the building's entrance doors, a side panel opened. Floor lights blinked to direct me to the microbe neutralization station.

I didn't know whether to feel embarrassed or violated.

After I tromped into a blindingly lit chamber, the door slid shut on the isolation bay. An encouraging female voice reverberated from above. "Sophia Andes7, thank you in advance for your full cooperation in this decontamination procedure. Please place any valuables on the tray for separate inert material decontamination." I tapped my foot as a white tray slid from a pocket inside the wall. "Then remove your clothing and store it in the incineration drawer."

With fists on my hips, I called to the ceiling, "The words *store* and *incineration* seem incompatible. May I assume you'll destroy anything I place in the drawer?"

"Your assumption is correct." Her annoyingly calm voice continued. "Please do not place any valuables in the incineration drawer. They will not be returned."

"They wouldn't be returned in the condition I gave them to you. That's for sure." I cursed under my breath.

"Do you need further instruction?" The voice stopped but continued seconds later when I didn't respond. "You have approximately two minutes before the decontamination process begins. You must be completely naked for this procedure. Please place any valuables on the tray. Then remove your clothing and store it in the incineration drawer."

Mia's com-card. I could toss it in with my running clothes and never see it again. That was probably the safest idea. It would burn into dust, and no one would ever know she'd given it to me. If we ran into each other again, I could explain what happened, and Mia could give me another.

What if Mia had something to do with my contamination? Maybe she was testing our sensitivity to small doses of HAV. If I told her what happened, I could be falling into a trap.

Don't overthink.

I pulled her card from my waist pouch and placed it on the tray under my synthetic wedding band and gold hoop earrings. I strained to detect visible signs of cameras but saw none. The walls were smooth except for rows of holes along the floor and ceiling—likely vents.

Off came my clothes and shoes. I stuffed them all in the open drawer before pushing the blinking *Close When Undressed* button.

My composed verbal attendant came alive again. "If you are fully undressed and your valuables are on the tray, step onto the illuminated footprints and raise your arms above your head. While it's not required, you may be more comfortable if you close your eyes."

After I complied, a low hiss came from everywhere and nowhere. I peeked to watch the room fill with steam and intermittent strobing lights. After a minute, the chamber cleared, and another drawer opened.

"Thank you for completing the decontamination process. We have provided a robe for your convenience."

"More likely for the convenience of everyone else in the lobby and along the route to my studio." I grabbed the robe from a tray.

"Do you have a question?" she asked.

"Do you have a sense of humor?"

"Sorry, I am not programmed to answer that question. Would you care to word your question differently? I would like to assist in any way I can."

In a huff, I resecured my earrings and slid on my wedding ring. "No, thank you. You've been extremely helpful and courteous."

"Your feedback is much appreciated. I will pass along your comments to our programming division."

"I bet you will."

As I slipped the com-card into the robe's pocket, I searched the ceiling. A tiny silver dot glistened in the far corner. The congenial voice must have come from the speaker. Would the CYR Internal Investigations Board install a video capture along with the audio?

Maybe I'm being paranoid.

Briana's golden gown clung to her in all the right places as she stood to pull my chair from the dinner table. She indicated for me to sit, but I waited at the entrance to appreciate the moment. Since Latrice came home from the cloning lab, romantic evenings on the residence floor were rare. How did Briana manage to ditch Jayla for the night?

"Sorry I'm late." Had I ever met up with Briana without needing to say those words?

"You're here now, and you look magnificent." Maybe the extra time I'd taken to upsweep my hair was worth being tardy.

I poured a generous portion of wine at the beverage cart and turned to give Briana a long appreciative look. "I assume you don't want any wine, but how about juice?"

"No, thanks." In response to my scrutiny, Briana crossed one leg in front of the other and drew her shoulder back. Parting her lips, she tipped her chin down into a sultry pout. My heart fluttered in response.

Briana stood sentry at my chair until I sat. "What's keeping you late at work?" she asked.

How did Briana figure out my delay was work-related? I hadn't mentioned my meeting overrun in any messages to her. Another engineer had dragged the group into discussing the prep schedule for the next time travel jump. Precision instruments made in EuroRosse from minerals mined in Gulf-Africa were delayed by a week and could cause a launch deferral. Probably a good guess on her part.

"Work *is* the reason I'm late. But let's not talk about those details." I slid off the napkin ring and placed the cloth on my lap. "I've been looking forward to our date night since you messaged me. What's for dinner?"

"I'll need extra protein for the next few months. So for tonight, I've doubled our plant-based polypeptides. They're easier to digest than animal proteins and should give me a better night's sleep. Yours imitates beef and mine's fish. But we can split them and have surf and turf."

"Sharing's perfect. I love eating with Latrice, but we should do this more often."

"Since I had a few minutes while you were getting ready, I preordered everything." Briana tipped her face to the ceiling. "We'll have our soup with the main course. Please serve each course when they're complete,"

A double tone responded to acknowledge the command, and Briana turned to me. "It should be ready in a few minutes. Do you need an appetizer to go with your wine? You must be famished after your long run today."

Hmm. "I don't recall mentioning my run."

"You said you planned to jog when you rushed out this morning."

Something didn't seem right.

"Except for acknowledging your text about dinner for two, we haven't spoken since breakfast. How did you know how *long* I ran?"

Without skipping a beat, Briana reached across the table to place a hand over mine. "You were crazy angry when you left. I thought you'd appreciate a long run. Forgive me if I assumed wrong."

That made sense—why was I suspicious? Maybe my guilt over the previous night's fantasy with Luis had me on edge. I took a long breath. "No, you're right. Jayla's crack about naming our baby Luis irked me. I ran all the way to Survivors Park."

"I need you to be my eyes and ears to what happens outside." Briana fidgeted with the napkin on her lap. "It'll feel strange to be indoors for the next eight months, but it's worth keeping the babies safe." Briana placed her elbows on the table and rested her chin on a fist. "See anything interesting on your run?"

"Nothing out of the ordinary. There was a typical protest out front. The weather's cool and dry, as I'd expect for October. The breeze had a bit of a chill—like winter's coming."

"The HAV detection alarm must have startled you. I helped design the decontamination procedure. Did you have a good experience?"

"What?" How could she know about that?

"I'm a chief physician." She waived a dismissive hand. "I get a notification for every bio-security breach."

"Of course, but they wouldn't specifically identify who brought in the virus, right? It's not like anyone would do it on purpose. Naming names could start rumors. Or maybe reflect on a person's department. Imagine if someone from security brought in HAV, others might believe the security division isn't doing their job well."

"You sound like you're looking for a conspiracy." Briana laughed. "I assure you, none exists."

"Maybe AI could track the identities instead of reporting me to the medical staff. If the same person kept bringing in the virus, AI could notify the Board, and they could send in an investigations team."

"The leadership team wouldn't campaign against someone who accidentally brought in HAV." Briana shrugged. "You probably picked it up from a protester. They're always thinking of ways to sabotage our work."

"You're right." I sipped my wine. "I moved through a group of them on my way toward the fitness path. They could have planted it on me."

"You might want to give them a wide berth the next time you run."

Another tone sounded before the table's center section sunk and returned to deliver dinner. Once we moved our plates from the central server, it returned to a perfectly flat surface covered with a pure white cloth.

"Ahh." I sniffed a spoonful of soup. "Tomato bisque—my favorite."

"I knew you'd appreciate it." Briana gave me her I-know-you-so-well smile.

"It's perfect." I sipped and then replaced the spoon on the saucer. "One of my teammates made a comment today about the history they teach us in school."

"History classes at the university? Do you mean history about bioscience, engineering breakthroughs, or what?"

"That was the point. She said they taught us history related to our career tracks but never about past civilizations—even our own."

"I never thought about it." Briana shrugged. "My history classes talked about the progression of cloning, biology, pharmacology, surgery, with a bit of phytology thrown in. I took a course on current world economics and culture exchange, but I don't remember any classes about ancient world history."

"Until it came up today, I'd never thought much about it either." I propped my elbow on the table. "In high school, we studied about how far we've come in the last two hundred years. But, thinking back, the details about life before 2060 were pretty slim."

"They briefed us about culture and machinery before our trip to 2026," Brianna offered.

"You're right." I tipped my wine glass at Briana. "Funny how single-family homes were the norm back then. I can't imagine living in anything but a high-rise. CYR's simulations helped me understand what to expect back then. But walking through a virtual reality house based on 2026 technology isn't the same as reading how governments succeeded and failed before 2060."

"Sounds like you've come up with a new research project for your free time."

"Yeah." Briana had given me the opening I needed to justify my research about Luis and Milo with the Front. "I think I'll dig into our archives and piece together a historical timeline. Maybe I'll even publish a book about it."

Briana twisted a lock of hair between her fingers. "I'm glad you've found a new hobby. Hopefully, you won't mind if I spend time focusing on the future. I mean, *our* future together."

I came around the table and knelt to grasp Briana's hand. "Sorry for my distraction since we came back. Our trip to 2026 got into my head."

After tilting Briana's chin with a finger, I kissed her before continuing. "Let's enjoy our dinner. We can talk about plans for Latrice and what's his name."

Briana smiled. "Do you have any ideas about a name for our son?"

"How about Simon or Merlin?" I stroked her cheek.

"Great ideas. I'm guessing the presidents will claim both of those." Briana's brow furrowed. "Maybe you'll find a good name in your research."

The idea came in a flash—a name historically masculine and relevant to Mission Y.

"Not sure I have to look too deep. How about Adam?"

"Adam." Briana cocked her head. Her eyes twinkled. "I like it."

I rubbed a thumb across the back of Briana's hand. Rough skin surrounded her knuckles and nails. "Did you miss a manicure appointment?"

"Excuse me?" Briana jerked her hands from under mine and shoved them under the table. Her lips formed a straight line.

"Your hands are exquisite. But I'm surprised they're dry."

Why can't I censor myself? I only wanted to ask if she was too busy at work to take time for herself. Ugh.

Chapter 4

OCTOBER 14, 2240

During my lunch break, I headed to my studio instead of joining the family. All morning, my work lacked the coherent stride of a typical day. Instead of engaging with colleagues about astrophysics and the laws of physics, chemistry, and time, I daydreamed about the two males I'd met in 2026.

Why couldn't I shake them from my thoughts?

"Shut and lock," I commanded while entering the studio and smiling at the unmade bed and its tangled sheets. I lay down and stared at the ceiling. A few hours ago, Briana and I made love here. I caressed the sheet where we'd writhed and sweated.

Had she realized I'd imagined Luis in bed with us?

I snapped upright, wanting to escape from my obsession.

"Enough." Rubbing my hands together, I rose and moved to my desk.

"Screen open. Engage a high-priority security protocol. Connect to external internet sources." A semi-transparent screen appeared. It blinked twice to let me know the security was active and wouldn't allow outside sources to access CYR systems.

"Bring up a historical timeline for all significant events from the present to the year 1950 with the most recent dates first." The request was broad enough not to attract attention if security monitored my activity.

"Define *significant*," my computer replied.

Hmm. Economics? Political regime changes? I opted for a more inclusive definition. "Define significant as any event that may have prompted high variability in death or birth rates."

My slight nod prompted the program to scroll backward through the list. It cited hundreds of entries from the current year through 2060. From 2040 to 2060, one entry included two words, "Cursed Decades." Before 2040 a few dozen lines identified wars, major economic hardships, and periods with voracious diseases.

I stared at the entry for Cursed Decades and blinked to initiate a search for additional data. I expected another page to appear with more detailed information, but nothing happened. I closed my eyes again, this time with determination.

A message flashed in the screen's center. "Accessing this link will be reported to the CYR Security Division. Do you wish to proceed?"

Why would historic periods have limited access? Did CYR assume anyone with an interest had subversive motives? I simply wanted to find out what happened to Luis. Nothing untoward about that. But if CYR forwarded my name to the HCC and I came under investigation, what would I tell them? Pure curiosity seemed like a feeble explanation.

"Delete browsing history and commence shutdown." The computer screen executed my commands. When the display screen disappeared, I reached into my waist pocket and removed Mia's com-card.

I tapped the card against my palm. It had a smooth front side, and the back held a single raised button—to connect with Mia and possibly a career-ending path.

Advertisements covered the illicit cards Phen gave me. But Mia's was plain white and screamed to be noticed. How badly did I want to discover what happened to the Pierce males? Would the information make a difference in my life?

The HCC had scheduled the next time jump in eight months—after Briana's five boys were born. If Briana delivered the babies and they lived, the HCC would send two doctors to 2027 for egg fertilization from a sperm donor named Vladimir Almo in EuroRosse.

Subsequent jumps were planned until we had forty baby boys. While we could get by with fewer than forty to ensure a viable population, the HCC planned to suspend the time travel program after each of the four countries had ten young men. Every president would gain a son with each time jump, and the carrying physicians would keep a baby for themselves and their countries. The draft schedule didn't allow for catastrophes like baby attrition or capsule failure.

Great. The HCC was optimistic. But were their expectations realistic?

With partial HAV immunity from their cloned mothers, repeated vaccine doses, and limited outside exposure, the boys would provide the seeds for the next generation of humans in ten to twelve years.

What about transporting a human from the past? I shifted in my chair.

A transported man wouldn't be immune from the virus. Despite all the scrubbers outside, he'd likely succumb to TWS within moments. Prepubescent youths were not spared from contracting TWS in 2060. So a young boy wouldn't survive in our time either.

The virus lived in nearly everyone outside our building. Our time travelers took vaccines for weeks before jumping to rid our bodies of the minuscule organisms to ensure we never carried it to the past. We filtered the air in the control room and the nurseries where Briana's five babies would start life.

If I could find a way back, I'd give Luis the vaccine and save his life.

I scoffed. What a ridiculous idea.

Except for my animal attraction, I knew nothing about him. What if Luis became a criminal in later life?

I tapped my desktop with a finger. I'd never find anything about Luis with my limited CYR computer access. Without another alternative, the Front's data seemed a likely option.

I came close to pushing the button on Mia's card when I recalled my experience in the microbe neutralization station. If there might be a video feed in that chamber, why not in my studio?

With my lunch break finished, I stood. Whether I traveled back to see Luis one more time, saved him from TWS, or simply quenched my thirst for details about his destiny, connecting with the Front was a crime. If caught, I'd lose my job and probably my family.

On the other hand, Luis' stolen sperm would save the human race. Didn't he deserve a chance to survive TWS? Before risking my career and marriage, I needed to learn more about him.

As if on its own power, the card slipped into my pocket. I'd call Mia on my afternoon break—from outside the building.

Chapter 5

OCTOBER 24, 2240

In any given year, I could count October's rainy days on one hand. Unfortunately, the time my sister Phen and I had picked for our annual talk was one of those. I pulled my rain jacket hood over my head and sped along the fitness path, hoping haste would keep me warm.

With my mouth pursed into a circle, I forced moist air in and out of my lungs. Despite the chilly temperature, sweat leaked from my skin and evaporated through my jacket. I kept my pace brisk and longed for the perpetual comfort of my Hipposkin enviro-suit. Maybe the company should design a cheaper version for everyday fitness use. When I returned to my office, I'd send them my suggestion.

The half-mile run to Confluence Park seemed twice the distance as usual. I had the path virtually to myself, and the solitude gave me time to think about how to pose my questions to Phen. Preparing for conversations was not my strength.

I took the exit ramp into the park and found an unoccupied covered table near the intersection of Cherry Creek and the South Platte River. One glance at my ocular timepiece told me Phen would call in a few minutes.

When the government issued her sentence nearly two years earlier, she'd sent me four encrypted com-cards so we could talk each year until she finished her term.

I'd sat in this same park for our first call—only weeks after our mother died. During that all-too-short, illegal talk, Phen and I shared growing-up memories and regrets for not being closer to our mother or each other.

I jogged next to the table and activated the canopy's heating element with a blink. Lamps warmed the space under the roof and dried the damp bench. I slid onto the seat and thrust my hands deep into my jacket pockets.

A mixture of historic 19th-century brick warehouses and low-rise, modern steel residences surrounded the riverbanks. No one lounged outside on the terraces. But a few condo dwellers sat inside having lunch next to their windows.

My stomach grumbled, and I pulled a protein bar from my waistband.

Before my first bite, the com-card in my pocket vibrated. When I pushed the connection button, my ocular implant activated an overlying encryption program and connected to her call.

Phen appeared on the table's opposite side as if she were sitting across from me. My park and the terrace outside her farmhouse became a blended setting. Mixed with my cityscape, I could see part of Phen's 2,000 square kilometer reformatory farm with giant boxy robots inching down evenly spaced rows.

"Are you planting or harvesting?" I asked.

"Both, Sofie." She glanced over her shoulder. "Once they clear a field, flying drones survey the land and the FART sets the planting schedule. Some fields rotate in a few days, and others lay fallow for a year." She shrugged. "It depends on what they plant."

"FART?"

"Fully Automated Robotic Team."

Her smirking grin told me she was joking, but I had to ask, "Is that your name for the system or the government's?"

"When you're not allowed outside contact for two years, you get creative." Phen motioned a thumb over her shoulder toward the fields. "Repairing defective machines and updating the programs keeps me busy."

"Sounds complicated."

"Not really. The work's fairly routine as long as the harvest yields stay consistent." She squinted. "Is it raining there? You look soaked."

I pulled on lightweight gloves and clasped my hands on the table. "Yeah. It'll be sunny again tomorrow, but today's a mess."

"It's nice to see you—well, anyone actually—it's been a long year. They give me the news, but even that gets boring." Phen pushed a stray lock of hair from her face, and for a moment I felt as if I were looking in a holograph mirror. She drew me back into our conversation. "I assume you didn't want to spend our call talking about the weather."

"No." I flexed my fingers and took a deep breath for courage. "How did you know you weren't homosexual?"

"What?" Phen burst out laughing but stopped short. Perhaps she noticed I hadn't joined her. "You're serious. Are you and the high and mighty Briana hitting a rough patch?"

"Don't assume this has anything to do with Briana." I felt a flush across my face. Had Phen noticed? "We just got back from our time jump to get Briana pregnant."

"Is she okay?" Phen tensed as if bracing for bad news.

"She's fine, and the jump went well. What I need to tell you is that I saw a real man. Up close. I touched him." Leaning forward, I lowered my voice. "I can't stop thinking about him."

"Well, join the club." Phen pulled back in her seat. "I told you ten years ago I could never marry a woman. Just because there aren't any choices, we don't have to ignore how we're designed."

"Don't get me wrong. I adore Briana and crave her company." I rubbed a thumb across my fist. "Maybe I'm bisexual. Tell me how you knew."

"It's simple. Women came on to me, and I never felt the same about them. I tried some physical stuff. But it wasn't satisfying. When I started going to the ARP escort arcades, I found out pretty fast that men offer a different experience—and not only their unique parts. I yearn for their bodies, deep voices, scents, and mannerisms."

"You get all that in an arcade?"

Phen rolled her eyes. "Why do you think I ended up with a five-year sentence monitoring this farm?"

"They transferred you there because you took out illegal personal loans—not because you're attracted to men."

"I don't know what Mom told you before she died, but that's only half the truth." Phen lifted her chin. "Madam Avaritia loaned me money to pay for extra ARP sessions at her arcade."

"You fell into debt from having fantasy sex?" I drew a sharp breath.

"What story did Mom spin? That I took out illegal loans to finance a gambling habit?"

"She did." Why would our mother prefer a daughter branded as a gambler rather than one addicted to fake men? "Thank you for setting the record straight. But tell me how you felt when you first had sex with an ARP man."

"There's nothing like it." Phen gave me a conspiratorial wink. "I can send you a basic program. Mine's nothing like the ones at the arcade—those guys can rock your world. But the simple version keeps me company while I'm here at the farm."

"I'm not sure." Could I get in trouble for bringing an unauthorized program into CYR headquarters? I'd have to design some rock-solid encryption to mask it.

"My ARP relies on the same tech as the décor in your studio." Phen took a breath. "It replicates basic surfaces and interacts with your brain. It might help you figure out who you are."

"I *know* who I am. Briana and I are happily married."

"Sounds like you have doubts or wouldn't have brought it up." Phen reached across the table. If com-cards utilized holomatter, I'd have felt her stroking my hand. "I'll send it to you. I'm a master at encryption. Your ARP will be as private as this call. It's up to you whether you activate the program."

"What does it do?"

"First, you input physical attributes and basic themes, like aggression parameters. After that, internal intelligence modifies his behaviors based on your reactions. While the software engages with your studio's décor subroutines to give you realistic, hard surface settings, the magic comes from an interface connected to your optical implant and your brain's occipital and parietal lobes. I'll include code files—you'll want to tinker with them to suit your needs." Phen waved a hand. "If I know you, you'll be fiddling with the ARP until you can't live without him."

"Okay. Send him." I clenched a fist on the table. "I mean it. Transfer the program via our encrypted card, and I'll find a way to replicate it."

"You're gonna love it."

That's what worried me. Many women must have fantasies—some in their minds and others with ARPs.

I already dreamt about Luis most nights. Unless there was a real person involved, it wasn't cheating. Right?

Chapter 6

NOVEMBER 11, 2240

When I arrived on the front steps of Mia's three-story townhome, I followed the pattern we'd established over the past weeks and rapped twice.

The security screen came alive, and Mia's familiar voice came over the intercom. "Come on in when the door unlocks."

After a soft tone, I placed my palm against a square chrome plate that measured my temperature and took an imprint. Once it recognized me as a registered visitor, it released the lock. Mia waited at the top of the stairs.

The place hadn't changed since my previous three visits. Sturdy fake leather armchairs and sofas in yellow and green sat on faux concrete floors. Apparently, Mia wasn't into making full use of her decorating programs either.

Her artwork made me dizzy, with splashes of color swirling as I walked past. Would the motion slow to a stop when no one was around? Briana decorated with optical art depicting deep space scenes—partially illuminated moons and multicolor swirling galaxies. She'd love Mia's taste.

Still in exercise mode, I took the stairs two at a time. Mia chuckled and gazed down at me from the landing. "It's been more than a week since the last time you came. I wondered if I'd said something to offend you."

I paused when I reached the landing. "Sorry if I don't hug you. I'm dripping with sweat. Isn't mid-November supposed to be cold and damp?"

"Winter's coming, but you wouldn't know it from the temps we've had this week." She held up her hands. "No need to hug. But I'm wondering if we're okay."

"We're fine. I've been crazy busy at work. Anyway, if I came more often, Briana would wonder why my jogging routine is taking precedence over our family lunchtime."

"I didn't realize you made a point of spending lunches together. Do they have a cafeteria in the Merlin Building or only private dining rooms?"

Her question might not be as innocuous as it seemed. To keep our meetings cordial, I shared some personal information about my wife and child. But I drew the line at saying anything specific about the building's layout or CYR processes. "It's not about the meal. We enjoy our time together during lunch. Sometimes I review learning modules with Latrice, and other times we play games. There's no set program."

Mia lowered her gaze to the floor. Had she noticed I didn't answer her question?

I stepped back to stretch my calves on the stairs and waited for Mia to invite me into her office. She moved inside and crooked a finger at me to follow.

"I appreciate you letting me research earlier societies." I followed Mia into the room that took up the entire top floor of her and her sister Charlotte's home. "It's opening my eyes to how we've arrived where we are today."

Like a launch control site for the space program, the Danube9s had decked out their office floor with high-resolution computer screen paint on every wall. Some screens included grids with live feeds from major cities around the world, and others were blacked out.

Mia directed me to my usual place in front of a sleek black desk devoid of clutter. Two other workstations sat against the wall. Piles of folders and Holo-tablet computers teetered on both. I assumed one station belonged to Mia and the other to Charlotte.

On my first visit, Mia told me she and Charlotte were single and shared this modern townhome in tony Cherry Creek, a well-to-do, close-in Denver suburb. Their home sat on the city's outskirts, several blocks from the decaying, vacant mansions that represented suburban life two hundred years earlier. Nearly everyone lived in urban centers near cloning clinics and health care.

The townhome had been in their family since 2065, when Frida Danube, an original, bought the house after she cloned Danube1. Frida was forty-seven, and the cloning process was in its second year. A framed photo of Frida sat on Mia's desk. At least, I thought it was Frida. She could have been anyone from the Danube line. The woman was an older version of Mia.

As I sat at the desk, Mia said, "Screen open. Mask security protocols. Connect to all historical external internet sources." She looked at me and glanced away. "Do you plan to search for historic periods again, or is there something special you'd like to see?"

With her staring over my shoulder, I didn't want to look up anything about Luis. That could wait until future meetings when she might leave the room for a while or even allow me to search alone. I'd told Mia I was here to research world history. How many sessions would it take before she made her pitch for me to work for the Front?

"Reading about the wars in the eighteenth through twentieth centuries has been interesting. It was a violent world back then with hundreds of countries vying for power and stealing each other's stuff." Mia nodded, and I continued. "This is all new to me, but I assume you're an authority. Maybe you could fill in the missing pieces."

"You mean what happened during the Cursed Decades?"

I crossed my arms. Would Mia's picks be unbiased if she steered me to sites that described what happened? I needed to stay vigilant about what she let me see and whether I should believe it.

"Sure." I mustered a neutral tone. "I'd be interested in reading about those times. In school, we learned women didn't play a substantial role in politics or business between 2040 and 2060. It seems like there was an economic reason for women to step aside and allow more men to enter the workforce."

"You've got the gist but not the magnitude of the situation." Mia wheeled her office chair next to mine, close enough for our thighs to touch. "In the mid-2030s, technology companies made substantial advances in AI and robotics. Within a few years, robots performed most agricultural, manufacturing, and resource extraction jobs."

"Sounds like what we have now." How would advancing technology oblige women to become redundant?

"It all happened at warp speed. Jobs in the military, construction, transportation, and purchase fulfillment disappeared next. Then law enforcement, firefighting, accounting, banking, and so it went. Worldwide unemployment went from seven to over fifty percent within five years."

"Wasn't there growth in sectors that supported technology?" I grappled to find mitigating conditions. "There must have been offsetting jobs."

"Some. But retraining costs a lot. Countries focused inward to preserve resources, particularly for the wealthy." Mia touched a finger to her chin as if considering. "Change started first in smaller countries but quickly spread across the globe. Back then, the heads of the military were mostly men. The armed forces in each country gained influence. Misogynous rulers took over, changing laws and legal processes. They directed women to work at home—to raise children, support their families, and allow men to take women's abandoned jobs."

"Like that would happen." I scoffed. "Wouldn't women refuse? And what about the men who didn't want the change? Didn't they fight to keep women in the workplace?"

"Some tried, but the new leaders grabbed power fast. With military and religious leaders behind them, they took control. Anyone who fought them risked prison or worse."

I focused on the blank computer screen and half-believed what she'd told me. Surely, women would have resisted, and men would help them. How could the entire world become duplicitous? "Now that you've told me the story, what do I need to review?"

"You should see firsthand what went on." She glanced up toward the speaker chip. "Allow access to underground news sources from 2050 through 2055. Scan pages via voice command, Sofia Andes7." Mia turned and slowly smiled. "My computer recognizes your voice from your earlier visits. Say 'next' when you want to advance the screens."

Mia moved her chair back to her desk and left me to stare at the screen in horror. Articles with blurry photos described re-education programs where non-compliant women trained to become servants in homes and businesses to perform menial tasks deemed unsuitable for robots. Others told stories about uncooperative women and sympathetic men sent to prison camps. When they became overcrowded, the inmates were considered expendable and executed. Photos and video clips of malnourished people and stacked bodies lined the pages.

While repulsed by the images, I couldn't stop looking and reading. Finally, the timer in my eye insert told me I needed to leave.

I turned to Mia. "Why don't they teach kids about this? Can't we learn from past lessons to prevent this from happening in the future?"

"Nature already took care of the problem." Mia bit at a cuticle. "It won't happen again."

I cocked my head and puzzled over her words.

She continued. "Men caused the Cursed Decades, and nature created the Human Androgen Virus to stop them from ever doing it again."

As I jogged away from Mia's home, my thoughts churned, solidifying arguments against Mia's narrow-minded view about men. My pace started slow but increased with my anger. I'd be late returning to CYR headquarters, but I didn't care.

Let them wonder where I've been. I can't go to the office in this state.

I took an extra lap around Survivors Park and stopped in front of Simon Merlin's obelisk. Long shadows combined with the crisp autumn wind and made me shiver.

I did a couple jumping jacks, then rubbed my upper arms.

"You weren't all a bunch of sadistic monsters!" I shouted at his obelisk, thankful no other visitors were within earshot.

For all my life, Dr. Merlin's legacy sprinkled into my training. His advancements in time travel were legendary, and he'd worked shoulder-to-shoulder with women until the day he died. He was respectful and kind. I wanted to believe Dr. Merlin represented his gender. Who were the men in those articles, and how did they become powerful enough to enslave half of the population?

The HCC kept this part of our history hidden. Once we'd lost our men, the leadership looked forward. They didn't need to take stock of the past because no one was left to penalize or forgive. Countries joined to consolidate resources and capitalize on strengths. In 2061, our founding women knew cooperation would forge a path to preserve humanity's existence.

Over the past month, I'd read about centuries with brutal behaviors from religious crusaders, agriculture and sex slave traders, and war criminals. These people were vile, but what about those on the sidelines who allowed these crimes to happen? Without impotent bystanders, these dark times in history may not have occurred.

After reading about men at their worst, how did *I* feel about reintroducing them?

Milo was a baby when I saw him. Where had he and Luis stood? In the 2040s, would they have been part of the male-dominated movement or fighters behind the lines for women's rights and freedom?

I pictured my new ARP from Phen's program—so willing to accommodate me. While the ARP wasn't real, Simon Merlin lived his whole life helping women. Was the Luis I'd seen in 2026 like Simon?

Luis' images in the HCC's files didn't hold the malice I'd seen in pictures of angry men from the 2050s. In my heart, I knew he'd come to Megan's defense. Or if not hers, then a champion for his mother or sisters.

His physical strength could have intimidated other men and helped women retain some level of equality. But if Luis had come to their aid, security forces would have sent him to a re-education camp.

Bracing against a swirling breeze, I balled my fists.

"Luis was kind and helped the women to fight. He was like you." Simon Merlin's obelisk stood as a reminder—men deserved a place on this earth. "You would want me to help him."

I turned toward the Merlin Building and started to jog, determined to find a way to save Luis Pierce.

Without announcing myself, I silently stood at the entrance portal to Briana's office and leaned a hip against the frame. With her back to me, Briana moved her hands with the fluidity and grace of an orchestra conductor. She simultaneously operated three semi-transparent screens, dragging data between them. Her intensity with medical irregularities rivaled any of my temporal engineers when they attacked time travel incongruities.

"Simon," Briana leaned into a screen. "Compute the predicted cloned fetus abnormalities and neonatal death rates with the stipulated nuclear reprogramming redistribution."

She's alone. Who or what is Simon?

As seconds passed, I shifted my weight. Perhaps I should've told Briana I was watching, but curiosity forced my silence.

"Simon, did you understand my instructions?" Briana glanced up from her work but didn't turn to the entrance.

The longer I stood there, the more I felt like a voyeur. The game had gone on long enough. "Who's Simon?"

Briana jerked at my voice.

"You startled me." Briana squirmed in her chair before smoothing the front of her tunic. "Don't stand there. Come on in. You never visit the bio-lab. Has your team run out of time-travel puzzles?"

Briana closed the screens with a swipe of a hand. A slight tremble shook her fingers.

In a rush, she stood and crossed the room. Briana pulled me into a firm embrace and rubbed the small of my back.

Why couldn't she look me in the eyes?

It might be guilt, or maybe I was transferring my shame for the ever-growing pile of secrets between us. Mia, Phen, and ARP Luis—no wonder I was paranoid.

"I'm serious." I pulled away—far enough to draw Briana's chin toward me and kiss her cheek. "Nobody else is here with you in the lab. Who's Simon?"

"Okay, you caught me." Briana cleared her throat. "I'm testing a new AI program to simplify my database interactions. I give it the parameters, and the system calculates the results. It's still in a beta version and not ready for distribution, but the early tests seem promising."

Her words were plausible, but why the initial secrecy? I'd been in trouble a lot lately—better to drop it.

"Sounds sophisticated. Let me know after you've put it through all the test scripts. We might be able to use it in engineering." I chuckled. "Of course most of my engineers will re-calculate the answers—even if we have an AI do it first."

"We'll have the same challenge. Nobody wants to turn their jobs over to AI." Briana took my hand and led me to the conference table in the corner. "Tell me why you've come to visit."

"Can't I take a mid-day break to see what you're up to?" I gave her my disarming smile.

"Any time. Want something to drink? The chiller has plenty of choices, or I can order something hot from the dispenser."

When I asked for sparkling water, Briana pulled two softpacks from the chiller. She handed one to me, and I popped open the ecostraw before taking a sip. Briana motioned for me to join her at the conference table.

"You must have had a great run today." Briana focused on her drink. "You were gone longer than usual."

Again. How did she know details about what I'd done?

"I had an extra-long one today. I was working through how to speed up a procurement issue we're dealing with." I pressed a hand firmly on the table. "Tell me how you know I was gone longer than usual."

"Every afternoon, the medical staff gets a fitness report. It lists how long the staff leaves the building to work out."

"I can't imagine." I searched her face for signs of deceit but saw none. "There's at least a dozen joggers in my section and probably a few hundred in the building. You review stats on every staff member who runs?"

"No." Briana waved a dismissive hand. "The report has the longest runs first, and your name is usually close to the top."

"Seems weird, but okay. Maybe I'll get a promotion for staying fit."

"You're stewing about something." Briana patted the table. "What's on your mind?"

"You're right. I've been scouring the archives for information on pre-2060s history for that book we talked about."

"Have you uncovered anything worth publishing?"

"Nope." I shrugged. "There's not much beyond what's already out there."

Briana raised a brow. "So you came here to tell me you're looking for a different hobby?"

"Yeah. It turns out there are plenty of historical accounts already available." I leaned toward her. "But I found something you could help me with."

"Great." Briana relaxed into her chair. "Tell me."

"I've read about scientists and medical experts who worked nonstop in 2060 to find a vaccine to prevent the spread of HAV. They also created anti-viral drugs to counteract the progression of TWS. But there wasn't time to finalize a drug for effective prevention or treatment. All the men died too quickly except for the twelve immune babies."

"That's right." Briana gave a solemn nod of agreement. "It swept the world at an unprecedented rate, starting in urban centers in emerging market countries and spreading to developed countries and rural areas. Once the virus became airborne, there was no stopping it."

"They dosed us with the anti-HAV vaccine for weeks before we left. I'm guessing the vaccine was perfected long after it could have helped anyone."

"Years too late." Briana motioned a thumb toward the door. "I'm not the one working on clinical trials, but the team next door is."

"There aren't any men." I drummed my fingers on the desk. "How do they conduct trials?"

"Not on people—on male cells we harvested from people who died and the twelve little boys who didn't contract the virus. We haven't stopped working on the vaccine. HAV has unique attributes. It's small enough to go airborne but not typically spread through the respiratory system." Briana's voice ramped up to full speed. When she talked about her discipline, there was no stopping her. "The virus's spikey outer coat has an acid component that can penetrate the skin. It also mutates like crazy. We add nanobots to the vaccine to manage the mutations." Briana patted her belly. "We'll use cells from Adam and his brothers in our trials once they're a bit larger."

"Isn't it dangerous?" Briana and her team surely wouldn't do anything to compromise the fetuses.

"No. We use highly specialized nanobots to retrieve minuscule samples. The babies are dosed in vitro with small amounts of vaccine. If all goes well, they'll develop full immunity before they're born."

"So Adam will be able to have a life outside of this sterile building?"

"That's the plan." She reached across the table and gave my shoulder a shove. "Don't start to imagine you can put him into a jogging stroller once he's born or that he'll play tennis at the park with you or Latrice as soon as he can hold a racquet. We won't expose them to outside air until we're certain they're immune."

"You can let me dream, right?" My stomach clenched before asking for the information I'd needed all along. I'd make a terrible spy. "And we store the vaccine here in this lab?"

"Of course." Briana pointed to her belly with both hands. "The babies are here. Why wouldn't the vaccine be close by?"

I came around the table to stroke Briana's tummy. Leaning in to talk directly to our unborn sons, I whispered, "You guys are miracles, and you better take care of each other in there. We'll keep you safe but stay strong and do everything on your end to join us in seven months."

Briana put a hand over mine. "They'll be fine—all of them."

"Of course they will." Jayla's harsh voice boomed from the doorway to disrupt our moment. "We have the best minds in the world watching out for you, my darling daughter."

When Jayla swept into the room, we moved apart like magnets with repelling poles. Jayla's bright yellow lab coat billowed around her.

"Good to see you, Mother." Briana gave her attention to her mother as if I'd never been there. "Did you come to review the latest results? I've input the calculations and the data, but I've not seen them yet."

"That's no wonder." Jayla looked from Briana to me. "It's difficult to get work done when people interrupt you with personal conversations."

I pressed my fingernails into the flesh of my palms.

Without looking at me, Briana leaned in and whispered, "Please ignore her. It won't be worth the aggravation."

She was right.

I kissed Briana full on the mouth, hoping Jayla would cringe.

"It's been wonderful to take a break with you." I spoke louder than necessary. "Don't work too late."

As I neared the entrance, Jayla's voice echoed behind me. "Sofia's not the type to stop by for a friendly visit mid-day. Engineers are singularly focused on their work. What did she want?"

I'd gotten what I came for. But what was Jayla after?

Briana didn't know, but our vaccine discussion advanced my plan to save Luis. I needed time on my own to work out a strategy. The projects I'd planned to address that afternoon flew to the bottom of my list.

Another jog was out of the question. Thanks to tracking reports I didn't know existed, Briana and all the medical staff knew how often and how long I left the building. I decided to find another vigorous activity to help me think.

I stopped in my studio to grab supplies. Before changing, I glanced at the ceiling. "Book court time, starting in fifteen minutes. Use program Serena Williams and set to eight out of ten as the difficulty level."

"Limited use program Serena Williams is currently engaged. Would you like to select another program?"

Damn, I'd helped to develop that one. "Can you run Cori Gauff?"

"Yes, the Cori Gauff program is available. Set to eight out of ten?"

"Perfect. I'll be there soon."

As I hurried to the building's indoor courts, I mused about challenging Cori Gauff9 to a real game.

Like she'd have the time or inclination to play against me.

We'd crossed paths in the 2236 Olympic trials. Cori went on to win gold, and I was out in the first round. According to Mia's files, the original Cori Gauff was one of the few people who didn't change her last name when women regained their freedom in 2061. Most wanted to leave their family names buried in the past and adopt new ones to honor a river, mountain, or city near where they gained independence. Cori must have figured she'd worked hard to make a brand out of her name and kept it.

The top fitness floor overlooked a grid of cubicles filled with women playing racquet sports. Some played against another person but most against a programmed character. After I logged on with the AI attendant—a speaker box sitting on a desk—I found my assigned court and warmed up.

When the program switched from warm-up to actual play, my conversation with Briana distracted me. I couldn't concentrate on the game. AI Cori beat me handily in two sets, and I left the court exhausted and covered in sweat.

Our pristine locker room smelled of grapefruit and lavender. I inhaled deeply. A shower would help me think.

Standing in front of an unoccupied shower stall, I commanded, "Steam room for twenty minutes, followed by a 115-degree shower for ten minutes. Allow for extensions if asked. Supply sandalwood soaps, conditioners, and lotions. Make the formulas appropriate for mixed skin types—Spanish and American indigenous heritage. Heated towels, please, one sheet size and two bath size."

After a sixty-second wait, I stepped inside to the sounds of faint guitar music and thick steam. A tiled bench offered the perfect place to relax and consider my strategy.

What if I could travel back and inject the vaccine into Luis and Milo to keep them safe from HAV? They wouldn't need to know why they were immune. The virus would ravage the male population, and the two Pierce men would survive. Once the newly formed HCC discovered the miracle, they'd move Luis and Milo to Panama City, a coastal city in a country long ago known as Panama, where the Americas established their new consolidated capital in 2064.

The Pierce men would join the twelve immune babies, and the HCC would protect them while they studied how their bodies had fought the disease. Milo could become a big brother to the infants, and Luis might act as a father and mentor.

While I had discussed possible time travel anomalies with my engineering colleagues, we had no idea about the ramifications of tinkering with the past. But if the Pierce men lived up to 2060 without knowing they were immune to HAV, I wouldn't have compromised the timeline. After 2060, the father and son would help raise Simon Merlin and the other eleven male survivors. Could that significantly change history?

I mopped sweat from my head and arms. How could I gain access to the vaccine? It must be locked up behind fifty layers of security. Even if I found a way to take some, how could I transport it to Luis' time?

This crazy idea had too many moving parts, and I was getting ahead of myself. To ensure I was saving the right guys, I'd continue researching with Mia to uncover Luis' choices after 2026.

Since the HCC chose Luis to be Briana's sperm donor, I knew he had robust family health, but what about Milo's mother Megan? I knew nothing about her and added her to my list of people to research at Mia's.

How could I keep Mia in the dark about why I wanted this information?

Maybe I could first research Vladimir Almo, the EuroRosse sperm donor for the next scheduled time jump in June. Since Mia wouldn't know my true purpose, she might help me with that. Once familiar with the process, I could investigate the two Pierce men on my own.

In the meantime, I needed an excuse to have the time capsule prepared to take an immediate second jump after the doctors' return from collecting the next set of sperm in June. Once they came back and the recovery team focused on the newly pregnant physicians, I could slip inside the capsule and jump back before anyone noticed I'd gone. A million details still needed addressing. But I had an overall plan.

Making sure the next jump came on the day Briana delivered would keep her out of the lab and out of my way. There were already delays eating into our built-in slack. I'd need to keep the team focused on the June date. If the schedule slipped and CYR delayed the jump a week or two, Jayla and Briana might both be in the control room. Then I'd lack the necessary autonomy to make my move.

"Prepare to switch from steam to shower mode." The computer-generated voice nearly jolted me off the bench.

"Give me five more minutes of steam. Then proceed without another notice."

"As you wish." A final blast hissed into the room.

I leaned back against the tiled wall and drew a long moist breath.

How to gain access to the vaccine? If the babies got small doses throughout Briana's pregnancy, she'd have appointments for those procedures. What if I asked to join her in the examination room?

Briana would want me to be with her. Why would she refuse?

Cleaned and refreshed, I turned the corner to my studio entrance panel and nearly collided with one of Briana's colleagues.

"Dr. Nile8, it's good to see you." I summoned an engaging smile. "Do you have a minute?"

She glanced up from her Holo-tablet, opened her mouth and quickly shut it.

"I won't keep you long," I assured her before she could excuse herself and leave.

"I only have a sec. I'm already late." Nile8 glanced past me and down the hall.

"It's a quick question about fitness reports. The Engineering Section has considered modifying one of the building's entrance tracking protocols. But we're worried about compromising existing reports. Do you receive a daily log of staff who leave the building to exercise outdoors?"

"Absolutely not." She laughed. "How would we know if someone went out to run versus shop? Do you notify the computer about your destination when you leave?"

I shrugged. "The system could judge based on what we wear at the exit. Like tracking those who go out wearing athletic clothes or shoes."

"And the purpose of using up all that storage with irrelevant data?"

"Monitoring staff fitness?"

"Really?" She gave a dismissive wave. "We monitor what you eat, track weights in the bathroom floors, and measure the four primary vital signs with sensors in your bed. We have enough data from other means without tracking what you do outside the building." When she turned away, she gave a final suggestion over her shoulder. "If you want to log your fitness activities, ask your personal computer to track them. You're an engineer. It might take you all of ten minutes to write a program."

"Good idea," I called to her retreating figure. "Thanks for your help."

I flexed and unflexed my fingers. Briana lied to me about the reports. But worse, someone was feeding her information about my comings and goings from the building.

It had to be Jayla—that meddling hyena. Who else would want to breed Briana's mistrust of me? I thumped a fist against my palm.

Chapter 7

DECEMBER 15, 2240

Mia placed a chai latte on my desk before returning to her own cluttered space. After more than a half dozen visits in the past two months, Mia finally seemed to trust my motives for being there.

I'd limited my searches to historical records from obscure databases. These dark places were not accessible from my lab computer, and if there were any attempts to find such sites, the CYR security system would likely send a crew to my door. I had no plans to lose my job or serve time in a remote outpost like my sister—repairing and monitoring crop robots.

I checked on Mia before changing the screen to allow a single word or name search. She leaned into her screens and seemed to be working without any attention to me.

As soon as I tapped in "Vladimir Almo," Mia scurried across the room to look over my shoulder. Did a corner of her work screens hold a video feed of what I accessed?

"Who's Vladimir Almo?" she asked.

"He lived in 2027 in what's now EuroRosse." I kept my voice even, hoping Mia wouldn't realize I was researching him as a cover before I found a way to look up Luis without her watching.

Mia leaned toward the screen. When her chest touched my back, I inched forward to gain more space.

"Why is he relevant to your historical research?" she asked.

"One of the articles I've read mentioned he was involved in low-level politics with the movement to gain control in the early 2040s. I wondered about the full extent of his role."

"I can help you with that." Mia retrieved a chair and slid it next to mine. "We have detailed personal records in a separate database."

Mia tipped her head toward the screen. "Continue to mask security protocols. Connect to the organization's private historical files related to personal histories. Security certification Mia Danube9. Include legal, financial, medical, and miscellaneous files. Give this station full access." She glanced at me before she gave the next command. "Extend access indefinitely."

Mia placed a hand on my thigh and squeezed. "Let's make sure we have time to talk before you rush out today."

When she returned to her desk, I swallowed hard. Was this the day Mia would ask for a favor in return for giving me access to their resources? I wasn't prepared to betray CYR or compromise my colleagues. I'd deal with that if it came up.

Multiple forms filled the screen about Vladimir Almo, including photos from his youth until immediately before his death from TWS in 2060. The final shot included an emaciated Vladimir in a hospital bed with hoses connecting him to machines that likely kept him alive longer than his pain should have allowed.

In earlier days, Vladimir was a healthy specimen of manhood. Like Luis, he had an olive complexion and brown eyes. Would Vladimir's offspring look like the babies Briana was carrying? Of course Vladimir's progeny would be a fifty percent mixture with eggs from two doctors— one from Asia and the other from Gulf-Africa. So the mothers' physical characteristics would weigh in. But if the infants were male, the father's looks might dominate. Later, I'd ask Briana about that probability.

Vladimir's financial records reflected a middle-income earner who worked as a professional sports trainer. Did the HCC have a criterion for choosing sperm donors? Luis and Vladimir were moderately but not highly educated and worked in the fitness field. Briana may have been privy to the selection parameters. I'd ask her about that, too.

On the personal side, Vladimir was married and had two children. In 2027 both would be under five. The dossier included one sentence about his wife, "Marina Almo was born in 2004 and died in a prison camp during a riot in 2043."

While I wanted to know more about Vladimir, my curiosity drew me to Marina. I tapped her highlighted name to bring up her records. Much of her early financial and personal details mimicked Vladimir's history, but in 2042 everything changed. Authorities arrested Marina for actions unbecoming of a wife and incarcerated her in a facility several hundred miles from their home.

Actions unbecoming could have been anything from wanting to work outside their home to attending a public protest. Did Marina ever see her children again?

I turned toward Mia. "What do you know about the prison riots of 2043?"

She crossed the room and sat next to me. "They were coordinated efforts by women's movements across the globe. While locked away, the women found ways to communicate through sympathetic guards or illegal radio transmissions."

"I assume they were broadcasting the conditions to other women and male sympathizers."

"It was impossible to incite outrage when the military had a stranglehold on the populace." Mia's voice grew solemn. "Many were afraid to take a stand, and others were in denial that the situation could be as bad as the prisoners claimed. The jailers said the prisoners had open channels for complaints and hadn't brought forward any grievances."

"Hard to believe no one did anything to help them."

"When officials exposed the riot instigators, they executed them without a trial." Mia pulled up a screen with several dozen women wearing stoic faces and shaved heads. They leaned like zombies against walls with gradient lines to designate their heights. "Here are a few of the murdered ones. The riots went on for a couple of years but stopped when the prisoners lost hope. There was no record of riots in the 2050s."

"No record or no riots?"

"No records." Mia shrugged. "Some jailers might have dealt with insurgents internally and never reported them."

"That's outrageous."

"I'm glad you're beginning to see how the Cursed Decades soured women on the male species." Mia reached over and put a hand on my knee.

I glanced at her hand and nodded, feigning my charade of converting to her side. While those with power misbehaved, they didn't represent all men.

"What did you find out about Vladimir Almo?" she asked.

"He was a mid-level player. Maybe I misread where he served in a higher role."

"You can always go back to the original article."

"I'm not worried about it." I gave her what I hoped was a sincere smile. "Most of my searches are random, and he's not important. I've noted a few other arbitrary names to check into before I go."

Mia left me, and I stared at the screen. Should I look for Luis or Milo? Since Milo was a child, his search seemed less risky. I'd start with him.

Three records came up for Milo Pierce in Denver, but two were adults in 2027. The other was a boy born in 2025. I tapped the one for *my* Milo.

The photos showed the boy's progression from his first baby photos—likely from a hospital as it had no toys or other personal articles—to a snapshot from a few months older than when I met him. The final picture might have come from his parents' collection. He sat on the floor in his room, surrounded by toy trucks.

My breath caught when I recognized his race car bed in the background. I tapped the screen to show the photo's reverse side. A message in a cramped script appeared. Had someone written it in haste or stress? It said, "Milo Pierce. December 2026."

The file included articles from Denver publications at the time. They spoke about the tragic kidnapping of Milo Pierce by an unknown female assailant. Later clippings talked of suspicions surrounding possible involvement by Megan Pierce. In 2027, authorities formally questioned her despite initial protests from her husband. They immediately released her, but some articles suggested the timing may have been due to Megan's mother being the Denver Police Chief. Had Megan played a part in her son's abduction?

I kept reading through the file, mesmerized by the evolving story of Megan Pierce. Within months of Milo's disappearance, his parents divorced.

Officers must have continued working on the case because in 2041 Megan was arrested and charged with Milo's death. Authorities sentenced her to a work prison, where she died two years later. There were no details about how Megan disposed of the body or whether she worked alone or confessed to her crimes.

After the final lines, I sat back in the chair, exhausted, as if I'd been physically running between the press offices to read the stories.

What kind of mother kills her child?

I wished I'd taken a better look at Megan when we jumped to 2026. Would I have seen telltale signs of her evil side while she slept? Luis must have been devastated. First, to lose his baby boy and then to find out his wife masterminded the boy's death.

Briana would never hurt our children. Perhaps mixed-gender marriages held more uncertainty and risks. How would we ever know?

I was about to input Luis' name when the alarm in my eye insert told me it was time to go. I cleared my throat, hoping to alert Mia. "You asked me to save time to talk, but I need to leave. Is it something that can wait?"

Mia came near and leaned a hip on the side of my desk. "Nothing urgent. I thought it would be nice to get to know each other better. I have no idea what you do at CYR, and you don't know what I do for the Front. We might surprise each other."

"Let's make a plan to talk on my next visit."

She paused as if considering options. When she agreed to the delay, I released a long breath and hoped she hadn't noticed.

While the Holo-screen in front of me was blank, Milo's image remained burned into my sight. The boy had a tragic end. Were his circumstances common?

Maybe I could spare a *few* more minutes. Mia's perspectives might help me understand.

"I never hear of mothers murdering their cloned children. Have you?"

"Why would you ask that?" Mia cocked her head.

"I read a story about a mother who killed her son."

"Maybe…" Mia's gaze tracked to the ceiling, "there's a different relationship between a parent and a cloned child."

"That's what I wondered." I drummed my finger on the desk. "While both types of children are part of their mothers, cloned babies are one hundred percent from their mothers. Would killing your child feel like you're murdering yourself?"

"You'd be killing your family line's future."

I stood and pushed my chair against the desk—time to leave.

"Are *you* planning to be cloned when you're twenty-five?" Mia shifted her weight.

While I'd never longed for a baby, I'd always enjoyed being Latrice's an-mother. I had all the cloned mother benefits and responsibilities but subtly fewer rights in case of divorce. My role with Adam would be the same. Would that be enough for me?

"I'm undecided. You?"

"I think it's important for a child to have two parents. It gives a growing girl more than one perspective on life."

"Mentors can play the same role." I'd started the conversation but wanted to end it before it became too personal.

"Charlotte brought up the idea of raising children together." Mia's gaze dropped to the floor. "She thinks it's our civic duty to carry on the family name. I wonder if we'd serve society well to have a bunch of Danube clones living under one roof."

"Maybe she's right." I took a sideways step toward the door. "It would be a shame to end the Danube dynasty with you and Charlotte."

"Or perhaps she's thinking about sustaining the Front's cause. I'm not sure I want to continue creating our mirror image forever. I hear cell resilience keeps declining."

"But research continues."

"Mostly with scientists from CYR. And they've decided the only way to stop the deterioration is to add new originals to our mix."

She either knew something about Mission Y or was fishing for information. We were wandering into dangerous waters, and I needed to leave.

Before I could stop, I asked, "Would that trouble you?"

"I'm not sure it does."

When she didn't immediately defend the Front's mantra to avoid introducing men, I pressed further. "You're not concerned about bringing back men?"

Mia gave a playful grin. "I'm opposed to retrieving any men who lived from 2040 to 2060."

"You can't believe they were all bad."

"Men were products of their time. While some may have supported women's rights, they didn't believe we were their equals."

"But they worked shoulder to shoulder and relied on each other professionally and personally." I raised my chin. "They were equals."

"How can you measure the influence of the man with a better seat at the table, stronger influence in financial matters, or a greater likelihood of having an affair? Studies in the 2020s showed that even in households thought to balance power, the women commonly took on greater responsibilities and had less overall influence. There was always a gender gap in wages. Humankind never could get over our past. Nearly everyone supported a system entitling men to better treatment than women. We can't undo that."

"Then what's your answer to our population problem?"

"I'm fine with cultivating a new crop of men. We can raise males to believe they're not a privileged class wielding violence and power."

"You believe new men won't repeat historical practices?"

"I do. I'm guardedly optimistic it'll work."

On my jog home, I puzzled through what Mia had said. I'd always believed every Front member hated men and would do anything to keep them out of our future. Perhaps I'd viewed their ranks as homogeneous. A range of opinions was more likely.

Mia seemed open to what CYR had planned. But I'd never give her any details about Mission Y. Divulging our objectives meant telling her about our recent journey to 2026 and revealing our plans to go again next summer. I had no idea how much she knew.

At the Merlin Building, I entered the access control vestibule and tensed while sniffers searched me for any sign of HAV. When no alarms signaled and the main entrance opened, I relaxed.

Since I'd been meeting with Mia, I wondered when she or one of her cohorts might again dose me with HAV. But alarms hadn't gone off since that first time.

I'd never mention the breach to her. The Front could use anything to compromise the Merlin Building or our projects.

Chapter 8

As I dashed into the clinic entrance, Briana jolted in surprise. I'd caught her yanking at the waistband of her pants.

"Sorry I'm late." Better not suggest she should start shopping for size-appropriate clothes. "I was on a call with a precision manufacturing company in EuroRosse about the specs for new restraining straps and connections."

"Are they going to be late, too?" Briana smirked.

"Yes." I plopped on the chair next to Briana and squeezed her arm. "But my delay was two minutes, and theirs will be two days."

"I'm glad you cleared your schedule to be here. I've been coming alone for the last six weeks." Briana's brows narrowed, all joking pushed aside. "Will the restraint delays compromise the timetable?"

"No. Thank goodness." I shook my head. "We'll move other installation tasks to fill the gap and connect the straps later." I patted Briana's arm. "You remember our hellish rides, right?"

"Let's not talk about that right now." Briana burped. "I'm finally getting over morning sickness and don't want to test my tummy with talk about that roller-coaster ride."

"Have you checked in?"

"I have. Dr. Ural6 and Dr. Le7 are expecting us." She faced me. "I appreciate you being here. Recorder bots will transcribe all my visits—I can replay the conversations anytime. But my mother will be brutal on the obstetricians, and you know exactly what to say to them."

"You mean I don't annoy them?"

"Something like that." Briana chuckled.

The clinic's barrier to an interior room evaporated and re-congealed after we walked through. Two doctors stood next to an examination lounger. The tall blonde was undoubtedly Ural6, as I recognized Le7's long jet-black hair, contrasting with her brilliant white lab coat.

Briana had worked with Le7 for several years and told me that the doctor welcomed new ideas but minimized risk. Le7 would take the next time jump in the summer of 2241 and had volunteered to be Briana's co-lead obstetrician to gain first-hand insight into all stages of pregnancy.

The examination lounger in the room's center resembled a long, padded brick balanced on a post. It could be raised, lowered, and contorted with the doctors' thoughts, confirmed by eye movements in their ocular implants.

As we entered, Ural6 patted the end of a seat to beckon Briana. "Do you want us to leave while you undress?"

"There's no need. We'll finish faster if you prepare the injections while I get out of these clothes." Briana started to unfasten her shirt and turned to Le7. "But while you're here, tell me how excited you are about your jump in June."

"I can't imagine anything I'd rather be doing." Le7 beamed. "Between your babies' births and planning for my jump, I'll be busy."

A flicker of stress ticked around Le7's eyes. Taking care of Briana while preparing for her own jump must have weighed heavily on the doctor.

Briana patted her belly. "No matter how much I complain in the coming weeks, I know it's all worth it."

As Briana disrobed, she handed me her clothes. I folded and placed them into a pile—not as neatly as Briana would have. She didn't give me a frustrated head shake. I must have done okay.

Once Briana was naked, the nurse helped her onto the table.

I placed a hand on the table's edge while Briana squirmed into the warm, body-conforming surface. Rough patches on her back and shoulders grew evident as she moved. I nearly mentioned the benefits of lotion but thought better of it. Perhaps Briana had finally taught me when to hold my tongue.

The room lights dimmed.

Ural6 blinked a command. Seconds later, a hovering equipment cabinet moved from alongside the wall and attached itself to the table with a soft click.

The previous evening, Briana had explained the procedure. Sterile speculum and probes lined a tray, likely heated and lubed for comfort. Vials held nanobots and serums.

Which one held the HAV vaccine?

Le7 turned to Briana. "Your VSE reading is slightly elevated. We can administer a light sedative if you feel tense."

"No sedatives." Briana shook her head. "I want to give the babies the most natural experience. Let me know if the monitors sense any increase in their stress, and maybe I'll change my mind."

I leaned over the table and squeezed Briana's hand twice. "Adam will appreciate your hard work."

"You've already named your child?" Le7 giggled.

"We wanted to grab that name before the others made decisions." I nodded.

"So if President Ottawa7 decided to name her baby Adam, you wouldn't give her that name?"

Briana answered for us. "Let her try."

I laughed, then squeezed again.

Ural6 manipulated the table. Pinpoint lights illuminated the specific spots for the staff's work and left other areas in respectful semi-darkness.

Le7 inserted the speculum, and the lounger modified itself for a comfortable fit, allowing the doctors and nurse to introduce camera-bearing nanobots inside Briana.

"Let me show you how everything is going." Le7 opened a semi-transparent display for us to watch. She pointed to five dark areas on the screens. "The bots are working together to consolidate a picture inside your uterus. While your actual organ is a chamber, the picture turns the interior surface inside out and flattens it. Here are the fetuses. They're about an inch and a half long."

The longer we watched, the sharper the picture became.

"I can see their fingers and toes." I couldn't take my eyes off the screen. "They're so active. Can you feel them moving?"

"Sometimes I feel a little flutter, but nothing like how active they look on the screen." Briana turned to Le7. "Should I be feeling more? Maybe my uterus isn't reacting to the stimulus. Should we be worried?"

Ural6 smiled. "Everything is responding as it should. There's no need to be concerned."

"How does their development compare to cloned babies?" I asked.

"If these little guys were growing in the incubator, they'd behave the same at this point." Le7 turned back to the screen. "Now the bots will take measurements, test Briana's fluids, and sample theirs. We'll make sure both Briana and these five guys stay in fine shape over the next several months."

"When do we dose them with the anti-viral vaccine?" I tried to sound indifferent yet interested.

"Today." Le7 nodded at the largest vial on the tray—the sole unused item. "I have it here."

"Is that the dosage for all five?"

"Much more than we need now. Bots will deliver the vaccine to each fetus, but this vial also contains enough for the next procedure."

Hmm. Good to know it has a decent shelf-life. How would I figure out how much vaccine is for an adult and child? I could do the math if one vial served five unborn babies. "Would it be better to have a fresh container each time?"

"Don't worry about how they administer the drugs." Briana patted my hand. "The bots are programmed to give the correct amounts, and the vaccine is incredibly resilient."

"How resilient? Can it handle temperature variations or a vigorous shake?"

Briana rolled her eyes at my question. She knew I'd ask a million questions when learning something new.

"Well, both. Scientists designed it nearly two hundred years ago, but we continue to refine it."

"Does it only work when we give it in small doses over a long period, or could we give one?" I indicated toward the vial.

"I can't imagine why you're so interested in a drug." Briana scoffed and relaxed further into the examination table. "But it would be effective either way. For the babies inside me, we're being extra careful to expose them with mini-doses to help them develop immunity without disrupting their development."

"So this little vial wouldn't hold enough for a full-grown person, right?" Why hadn't I paid closer attention when they vaccinated me for the October jump?

Le7 answered. "An adult would take the entire vial, and a child between five and ten would get half the amount. This is a dead virus vaccine, which means we made it from the virus' dead cells. So every few years, the patient would inject a booster to maintain immunity."

"It's not a one-time deal to be protected?" Ugh. Another hurdle to manage.

"No," Le7 responded. "We'll continuously test the antibodies in the boys to see how long the vaccine lasts and when to dose them again."

"You and the other engineers have enough to worry about before June's jump." Briana lifted a finger and tapped the bed. "Leave all this pharmaceutical stuff to the medical staff. Adam will have all his follow-up shots as scheduled. I promise the virus won't take him."

"I know you'll keep him safe." I leaned across the table to stroke Briana's cheek. "But it's good for me to know how vital these vaccines are."

Briana's brows knitted. Did I distress her again? I glanced from her to the tray.

Snagging the vaccine would be challenging, and knowing how much to dose Luis and Milo added more complications. What else didn't I know that could muddle my plans?

Chapter 9

JANUARY 19, 2241

I winked at Latrice, and she stopped banging her tray with the spoon. While I was grateful for the reprieve, I didn't want to stifle her self-expression. She might want to become a percussionist or a mechanical engineer managing robots testing cutlery tensile strength. Our little girl could choose whatever vocation she wanted.

Jayla caught my attention with a deep sigh. Briana's mother wore the tight-lipped smirk that always preceded a tidbit she would use to torment me.

Briana chatted about her day, oblivious to the impending drama. Would Jayla yank the rug from under Briana or me? There was no telling, but it was coming. I felt sure of it.

We passed unscathed through farm-raised salmon, rosemary potatoes, and flash-fried green beans. With each forkful, my tension increased, waiting for Jayla's jab.

Finally, while Briana served our coffee from the side buffet table, Jayla cleared her throat. "I spoke with Dr. Le6."

"I assume you mean Le7's mother?" Briana asked innocently. "*The* Le7 who's one of my obstetricians and will travel back to 2027 to fertilize the next set of eggs?"

"Yes, dear. The very one." Jayla nodded her head. "Her mother tells me Le7 might withdraw from the project."

Boom. There it was.

Jayla nailed both of us simultaneously. Candidates were vetted and prepped for years before a time jump. Despite continuity with Ural6 on the team, if Le7 bailed on the project HCC leadership might indefinitely postpone the schedule. Jayla knew a cancellation meant a compromised engineering schedule and discontinuity in Briana's care. But, more importantly, and unbeknownst to Jayla, I wouldn't take my jump when Briana was nursing newborns and away from the control room.

"Tell us what's happening," Briana suggested. She set the coffee before Jayla and returned to fetch a pitcher of cream. "I'm sure we can discuss this with Le7 and find a solution for whatever troubles her."

"That's doubtful." Jayla added a drop of spice flavoring into her coffee before a whitener.

I gritted my teeth. Jayla would want to savor every minute of underscoring our ignorance. Finally, I took her bait. "Please, tell us why."

Briana delivered my coffee before sitting with apparent indifference. But the tells were obvious. She blinked with uncommon frequency, and a tiny tremor shook her hand. Briana had likely played this game with Jayla her entire life.

"Le7 is being pressured to go back to Asia's capital in Singapore."

"By the government or her family?" I asked, straining to sound apathetic.

"Don't be silly." Jayla glared at me, and her lips pursed into a forced smile. "Asia's government wouldn't want Le7 to leave the project. My sources say President Fuji6 has already intervened and attempted to persuade Le7 to stay with Mission Y. The President can be convincing, especially when the honor of her country is at stake. How would it look if the Asia representative left the rotation?"

"If the President couldn't resolve Le7's issues, what's the problem?" Briana folded and unfolded her napkin.

"Le6's cell deterioration has advanced to the final stages. She doesn't have much time left, and Le7 doesn't want her mother to be alone in Singapore for her final weeks."

"I have an idea." My solution seemed simple. "Since Le7 can't be your obstetrician and prep for her June jump from Asia, can't we expand Le7's studio and bring her mother to Denver?"

"You know nothing of their culture." Jayla waved a dismissive hand. "They revere holy sites and familiar places. Le6 will want to walk in the historic botanical gardens and pray in the temple where she's gone since childhood. What's in Denver for her?"

"Thank you for telling us." Briana poked at her lemon cream dessert with the tip of her fork. "Le7's probably torn between loyalties. But I can't believe she'd jeopardize the project. We depend on her."

I reached across the table to lay a hand over Briana's. "My team can develop an ARP for Le6 with realistic backgrounds, fragrances, and even the right humidity and lighting to mimic the gardens and temple sites. We'd dedicate a virtual reality viewing room for her. She could live in Singapore's botanic gardens if she wanted to."

"Not the real thing." Briana shook her head. "But having familiar places while living with Le7 in Denver might be enough."

"No," Jayla interrupted. "An ARP would be a pale shadow of Le6's true experiences."

"You'd be surprised how realistic it might be." I clenched a fist under the table, ready to defend my idea. "We could rely on Asia's archives for images, scents, and weather. Le6 could even select a historical time period and not settle for what the gardens look like today."

"Would you reproduce the friends she'd walk with?" Jayla scoffed.

"We could replicate another ARP room in Singapore, and her friends could go there to join her via video link." I turned to Briana before Jayla could add more objections. "Couldn't hurt to ask. Why don't you talk with Le7?"

"Well…" Briana twiddled her fork and nudged a piece of crust across her plate. She wouldn't want to contradict her mother. But I willed her to speak up. Briana's voice came out weak and indecisive. "Le7 *might* meet with me to discuss options."

"If Le7 goes back to Asia, she'll not only delay the next jump—she'll force CYR to add a new doctor." I pushed harder. "Le7 is intimately involved with your care and treatments."

"If I can't convince her, you know the HCC will get involved." Briana chewed her lower lip. "There's too much at stake."

I envisioned a team of government officials invading the building, all with the sole purpose of changing Le7's mind. Eventually, she'd acquiesce to their stance, but their intervention would likely modify her career trajectory.

By placing her mother's needs ahead of the HCC's, the coalition might brand Le7 as an apathetic employee. Briana knew the stakes, and I believed she could convince Le7 to stay on track.

Briana would preserve my forward momentum. Wouldn't she?

Briana usually spent the night with me after a family dinner. But Jayla's announcement about Le7 must have left Briana stewing, and she bid me goodnight.

Evenings alone were rare, and my long days at work didn't give me time to plan my time jump.

I settled in for an evening in front of the computer. After resting my chin on a fist, I stared at four semi-transparent screens, searching for ideas about durable vaccine containers.

Analysis programs evaluated natural and fabricated material tensile strengths, fatigue probability, and vibration resilience. Engineering studies compared the substances and gave benefits and drawbacks.

At Briana's appointments, I watched the medical team extract the serum from glass vials. But simulations and the actual time travel trials over the last forty years had tested a variety of materials.

For the fateful jump in 2200, Emma Joffre6 had embedded thirty-six tiny glass vials into her muscles and organs. When she arrived in 2026, she filled those empty containers with spermatogonia. Due to the restraint failure in the capsule, Joffre6 slammed into the interior walls on re-entry. Most vials broke, and the precious fluid benignly absorbed into her body before she died from her injuries.

While I was confident we'd addressed the restraint problems, I wondered if glass was the most appropriate material for transferring the vaccine. Glass was virtually inert and impermeable. Still, it could be fragile, as the 2200 time jump had demonstrated.

On our 2240 ride, Briana had brought pre-loaded CVIs with the sleep drug. Those preparations were loaded into the devices immediately after manufacture. Any introduction of air or light could compromise the drug or vaccine effectiveness, and pharmaceutical articles discouraged transferring any out of the original glass packing. I decided not to move the vaccine into new containers for transport.

For my jump, I'd carry the HAV vaccine and a sleeping drug—enough CVIs and one or two spares in case one broke.

I searched for the schematics of the case Briana carried on our jump and was surprised to find them easily. Perhaps HCC security didn't care about hiding the mundane details of what we took to 2026. When I noticed the trip inventory didn't mention the defensive weapons we'd brought, I smirked. Luckily, we never had to use them. But maybe the HCC didn't want to admit they'd trained us to stun if needed. From my time with Mia, I learned historical records seldom gave the complete story.

The composite materials used to make the case were common and easy to requisition. No one would be the wiser if I ordered the elements and fashioned them into a case for my jump. Writing a program for the design and using the 3D printer for a few hours could go unnoticed. If anyone asked questions, I could say I was developing a prototype case for subsequent jumps.

I'd solved the problem of how to transport medical supplies. But what about how to carry the case? I'd need free hands to operate the capsule controls. When Briana jumped to 2026, she tucked her medical supply case into the waist pocket of her Hipposkin enviro-suit.

To safely make my jump, I'd need another suit to wear under my lab clothes. At the appointed time, I'd strip off a camouflaging outfit and jump into the capsule.

Whatever happened to the Hipposkin enviro-suit I'd worn on our jump in October? Had the laundry service returned it to me after they cleaned it? If I had known I'd need it in a few months, I would've never sent it away. I stood and crossed the room.

"Open the closet door," I called to the ceiling. When the portal evaporated, I stepped into the small room with my personal effects and wardrobe. My returned cleaning sat in a pile on the dresser.

I transferred several armloads of folded clothes to the bed and sorted shirts, workout clothes, and leggings into piles.

Please be here.

About halfway through the stack, I found it—neatly folded and wrapped in a thin bioplastic sheeting. The suit was unwieldy after I'd worn it. The laundry bots must have access to the garment's folding schematics—not something I'd spent time studying. I left the suit on the bed and scooped up my other clothes to pile them back on the dresser. I'd deal with them later.

After removing the suit from the plastic, I shook it to its full length to admire the sleek styling and dense but lightweight fabric. I ran a hand inside the waistband and found my suit had the same interior pockets Briana used to carry the CVI case.

"Produce laser measurer," I called to the room's tool inventory. The palm-sized measuring instrument appeared in my hand, and I noted the pocket's dimensions and stretch factors before uploading them. I'd need this data to design my medical case.

I slid a hanger into the shoulders. Problems solved. I had a way to design and manufacture my medical kit and a way to transport it safely to 2027. There were still a hundred more details, some significant and many minor, to figure out before I was ready to go.

When I slipped the suit into the rack, I could tell that anyone standing in my closet would see it. I pulled a dressy floor-length gown from the end of the hanging rack and slipped it over the suit. After draping a jacket over both, I snugged the hanger near the back.

If anyone asked for the suit to recycle it, I'd plead ignorance. Surely, nobody would break CYR privacy protocols and search my suite looking for it.

Chapter 10

When I rushed into the waiting room, Briana met me with an icy stare. "Sorry I'm late. I was…" I started.

Briana raised a hand. "You're here now, and Le7's running behind. Dr. Ural6 wanted to wait for her."

"Thanks for understanding. But I'm still sorry." I kissed Briana's cheek. "Every day we're closer to the jump, more delays pile up."

Briana scratched a flaky patch on her hand. Should I mention the blemish or not?

She caught me staring. "It's excess estrogen. Don't be concerned." Briana shoved her hands into her jacket pockets. "Was it procurement, manufacturing, or design?"

"Everything." I released a deep breath and sat in the chair next to her. "It's nothing we can't handle. We'll meet the schedule."

The passage door dissolved, and Le7 beckoned us inside. Her smile appeared genuine, but her swollen red eyes betrayed underlying distress.

"What's happened?" Briana grasped the petite doctor's arm. "Is your mother okay?"

"She continues to decline." Le7 swallowed hard. "We all expected that, but she changed her mind about coming to Denver."

After a pause to sterilize my hands—a ruse to stop them from shaking, I came forward to join Briana and Le7. "But it's been weeks since she agreed to come. You said she loved the ARP's preview program. We included all her suggested gardens. Did we get anything wrong?"

"No. It was perfect. Your program had her favorite flowers and let her walk through the sacred temples in the monsoon or dry seasons." Le7 bowed her head. "She'd probably set the program to late March when the lotus flowers bloom."

"Our sister team in Singapore sent a formula to mimic scents from the most aromatic varieties." I clenched and unclenched my fingers. "But your mother could choose other fragrances as well."

"You've done your best to tempt her." Le7 glanced at me before staring at the floor. "She and I both appreciate your hard work. Please, let the others know they didn't fail. My mother can be stubborn. She wants to stay in Singapore for the rest of her days." Le7 scuffed a foot along the floor before she continued. "I'll go home to stay with her in two weeks."

Briana must have sensed my distress. She placed a gentle hand on my arm. "Don't worry. Ural6 will bring Le7's replacement up to speed."

That's only part of the problem. With Le7's jump in peril, all my plans to jump are trashed.

I took a deep breath.

Don't overreact. Briana doesn't know about that.

Briana started to undress as if this AereoPod crash wasn't happening.

Dr. Ural6 stood at a control panel against the wall, tapping screens, while Le7 organized meds and tools on the hovering equipment cabinet.

"The HCC found a temporary replacement to take my place until a full-time doctor can come to Denver." Le7's voice came out in a whisper.

Briana slid onto the table and wriggled into its form-fitting surface.

I stepped to Le7's side and stared at the vials and instruments.

Before Le7's big announcement, I had plans in motion for this appointment. Should I stay the course or delay?

"If you need to leave, we don't have to delay June's jump, right?" My words tumbled out before I could stop them. "Surely the doctor scheduled for October's jump would be thrilled to move up. We'd only need to compress her timing by three months."

Briana and Le7 exchanged knowing looks. Was there a logical answer, or were they wondering why I brought up delayed schedules?

"It's not that easy." Briana responded first. "We monitor and medicate each egg carrier for a full year preceding her jump date. The jumpers take hormone injections, and the lab tests their oocytes for receptivity and durability." She must have noticed my confusion. "Oocytes are eggs."

"Thanks for the translation." I grasped my hands behind my back to stop fidgeting. "But can't we compress the regimen?"

"With one jump behind us, we don't have enough data to change the protocols. We hope Le7's body is appropriately prepared. But we don't know enough to start taking shortcuts."

"It would be nice to speed up the schedule," Le7 interrupted. "But most likely, once I leave the program, the HCC will cancel the June jump, and the next one won't happen until October."

"All your team's work will prepare you for October." Briana drummed her fingers on the bed. "You've mentioned all the challenges you've faced with the schedule. This delay will give you an extra four months."

There had to be a solution. June's jump must go—Luis' life depended on me.

When the portal door dissolved, a breeze swept the room.

"Don't be concerned," Le7 said to Briana. "My temporary replacement is joining us for today's procedures. She had another appointment but promised to be here for the video recordings."

Jayla came through the portal.

"Good to see you, Jayla." My voice came out far too loud and snarky. "Have you brought Briana's new obstetrician with you?"

"I'm surprised you're here on time." Jayla smiled with taut lips. Her eyes narrowed at me. "Funny you should ask about Dr. Le7's replacement. It was an easy task—I brought myself."

Ural6 and Jayla exchanged nods. Briana's mother had the background to take over Briana's care. But would Briana want Jayla to gain control over the babies? Her mother already managed so much of her life.

"Who will take care of Latrice while you're focused on the project?" I asked because Briana wouldn't. But she'd want to know.

"Nanny Tori can manage fine."

"She needed you to supervise her before. What's different?"

Briana didn't jump in to defend her mother and instead watched the monitoring screens. I was on solid ground to pressure Jayla.

"I have full access to Nanny Tori's program and Latrice's progress feeds." Jayla sniffed. "Are you suggesting I can't manage a robot and my daughter's health at the same time?"

"That's a lot to take on at your age."

"At least under my guidance, Latrice's imprinting will have minimal influence from her an-mother's personality. Maybe she'll decide to swim and develop her full body instead of acquiring the lopsided physique of a tennis player."

"Hey you two," Briana interrupted. "Come see the babies."

Jayla and I hustled to where we could see the screens.

Bots inside Briana coordinated to create a clear view.

The video took my breath away. Our boys had proportional arms and legs—all comfortably entwined around one another.

The top edge of the closest boy's head was blurry. Could it be newly developed hair?

As Ural6 pointed out the babies' positions and commented on their growth, all vestiges of my fight with Jayla evaporated.

Jayla touched her temple, a clear sign she was focusing her ocular implants to manage her vision.

Briana must have noticed it, too.

"What do you see, Mother?"

Jayla pointed to one of the babies. "This boy is slightly smaller than the others. Do you see this, too, Dr. Ural6?"

"Do they all need to be the same size?" I strained to see the details.

"Usually they are." Ural6 manipulated the screens for closer evaluation. "Any anomalies at this early stage could signal developmental distress or typical growth differences. There's no way to be sure." She turned to Jayla. "I'm impressed you could see that with your implants and without instruments. We identify the smaller one as Boy 3 in the records. His size and development aren't outside parameters or substantially different from others."

"I'll review all the earlier records in detail after this appointment." Jayla tapped notes on a Holo-tablet. "What about placenta issues?"

"The placentas aren't compromised. However, we plan to monitor Boy 3 to ensure he receives enough blood and nutrients."

The identifier *Boy 3* made me bristle. It made him sound like a research animal rather than a developing child.

Briana rose on an elbow, and her VSE reading inched up. "Why wasn't I told about this anomaly?"

She didn't know?

Le7 shot Jayla a frosty glare. "There's no reason to be concerned, and we didn't want to add any unneeded stress." She released an exasperated sigh before turning back to Briana. "Keeping anxiety low during this pregnancy is as important as the babies' health."

"Well, I know now." Briana's VSE reading jumped again, and the machine gave a warning tone.

I moved closer and placed a gentle hand on Briana's arm. She tensed as if she might shake it off but relaxed.

"I'm here for you," I whispered into Briana's ear.

"Thank you," Briana mouthed as she sank back into the table. The VSE reading ticked down.

"What about between visits?" Jayla's tone prompted another spasm from Briana. I grasped her hand and squeezed as Jayla continued. "How are you monitoring Boy 3?"

"Continually." With a finger flick, Ural6 changed a screen to show data lines that scrolled across the page at lightning speed. "At Briana's last visit, we left monitoring bots inside her. They've tracked Boy 3's vitals and changes."

Both Briana and Jayla would understand the data. To me, it was a blur of code.

"Now you understand." Briana turned to Le7. "This is why I'm concerned about you leaving my obstetrics team. I trust Ural6 and my mother, and the next obstetrician will be abundantly competent. But continuity is important. Can't you talk with your mother again about coming to Denver?"

Everyone watched Le7, who brought a hand to her throat. She stroked her neck and blinked before responding. "I will speak with her again. But she's fragile and doesn't have many months left. I want her last days to be peaceful and on her terms. I won't be disrespectful. If she decides to stay in Singapore, I'll go to her."

Not wanting Briana to see my distress, I took a calming breath.

Somehow, I'd get Briana through whatever this pregnancy threw at her and find a way to save the June time jump. Luis' life depended on it.

Chapter 11

As I sat facing the computer screens in Mia's townhome, my thoughts flitted in all directions. The day's plan was in motion, but things could go wrong with so many moving parts.

Please don't let anything trace back to me or anyone from CYR.

I tried to focus on my research, but my fingers trembled every time I reached to swipe a screen.

My ocular implant flashed. Five minutes to go.

Two days earlier, I had affixed a time-release smoke bomb under a bench next to the hologram water fountain in the Merlin Building plaza. The parts had come from several stores—none on my typical running routes and all from outside the city's camera coverage.

Two more minutes.

Relax. I stretched my arms over my head.

Charlotte's speech for a rally on the plaza should have started approximately five minutes ago, and the innocuous smoke bomb would explode soon. It would spew a harmless concoction of gasses into the area and undoubtedly draw prompt attention from the CYR security forces. Depending on how they reacted, Charlotte and her disciples could get arrested for subversion. I didn't care as long as Mia went to help them and left me in her home.

Mia leaned over me, placed a hand on my shoulder, and squeezed. "What's on the agenda for today?"

"Same old research." I gave her an encouraging smile. "I couldn't help myself. I've been checking into male-designed buildings in Denver. Do you know about the Hamilton Building—the old metallic one connected to the Art Institute? It's low and asymmetrical, with jutting angles, and a famous architect designed it. When the Cursed Decades started in 2040, they jailed him for his outspoken views against women's subjugation. The man was in his nineties and didn't last long in prison."

"Why are you looking into him?"

"I needed a break from reading about jailing women to silence them. Whenever I find an article about men who tried to change what was happening, I'm relieved."

"There weren't enough of them to make a difference."

I raised a brow. *Should I argue with her?* Alienating Mia wouldn't help me complete my research.

"But imagine if TWS hadn't killed them all." My words spilled out. "What if the rebellious women and the men helping them prevailed?"

"While that's possible, we'll never know. The HAV took away men's chances to redeem themselves."

An alarm sounded from Mia's pocket. She withdrew a com-card and walked away from my desk.

Yes! My smoke bomb must have worked.

"Charlotte needs my help." Mia returned.

"What happened? Is she okay?" I mustered a look I hoped reflected curiosity and concern.

"It's nothing to worry about. There was a skirmish at Charlotte's meeting today. No one's hurt, but the Denver police are harassing the protesters. I'm going down there."

"I can come, too." I stood, knowing full well I wouldn't join her.

"No. It'd be bad for you to show up with me." Mia looked around the office, then stared at the floor. "No one from the Front knows you come here," she whispered.

I did a double take. "Not even Charlotte?"

"No." Her gaze locked onto me. "Does your wife know you're here?"

She had me there, but I was loath to admit why. "Briana knows I'm researching but doesn't know where I'm getting my material."

"I'm glad this is our secret." Mia placed a hand on my forearm. "I enjoy our time together."

Was she coming on to me? I cleared my throat. "Seems like Charlotte could use your help. I don't want to keep you."

"You're right." Mia lifted her hand and stepped back. I hoped my hint didn't offend. "Charlotte was speaking at the Merlin Building, and someone set off a smoke bomb."

"One of the protesters?" I took a breath, grateful for the segue.

"Hardly. We want people to consider all the facts before reintroducing men. We don't promote violence or incite riots."

"This escalation will be on the news." I gave her a knowing nod. "Maybe someone wanted to boost publicity."

"I hope not." She glanced at the door. "I have to go, but stay as long as you can. I'll program the entry to close when you leave."

While tempted to raise an argument to promote my ruse, I didn't know how far to push. "You're right to find out what's happening. I hope Charlotte's okay. I'll stay for a few more minutes."

"I'm serious. Stay as long as you'd like."

If only my colleagues at CYR were as accommodating. But maybe both factions were giving me enough rope to hang myself.

As her footfalls faded, I clutched my shaky hands. A tone indicated the front entrance portal had closed and locked.

Finally, I had my chance to search for Luis' data and the sketchy story about Megan Pierce abducting her son. I quickly uploaded a masking program to hide my search.

Several other Luis Pierces came up before I struck gold. When his photo flashed on my monitor, my heart skipped a beat. I leaned into the screen to take in the man I'd briefly seen in 2026.

My ocular implant copied articles highlighting his youth. I'd take my time reading them later. But when I spotted Luis' high school football team photo, curiosity got the better of me. Mesmerized, I stared at the image. Bulky young men in shoulder pads held helmets and formed two rows. Some appeared solemn and fierce, while others mugged for the shot.

Luis knelt in the front row with his beefy comrades. He leaned forward with cocky confidence and braced an elbow on his knee. After the men died, women's interest waned in full-contact sports like football and boxing. Those sports never recommenced when women had time and money to resurrect leisure games in the 2070s. Would Luis have been disappointed in the change?

For the first time, I saw Luis' actual smile and not the one I'd concocted for the program Phen had sent. My ARP Luis lacked the assuredness of the real one. Once back at CYR, I'd tweak the code to imitate his self-confidence. I saved several audio files from court proceedings, knowing I'd use them to recraft my ARP's voice.

Other pictures followed Luis as he aged, with his final shots taken in early 2060—right before his death at fifty-six—during the virus's first waves. I skipped the final headshots from his medical files. I didn't want to remember him with the baldness from attempted treatments or creases from pain lines etched into his brow and around his mouth.

Scrolling back, I noticed that two years before HAV spread throughout the world, Luis had a few age lines and hints of gray hair. He also had the same mischievous lip curl from his youth. Did Milo inherit his father's charm? I couldn't recall whether I'd seen the boy with open eyes. Based on her files, Megan Pierce had blue ones. But Luis' brown color should have been dominant.

Months had passed since I'd peeked at Milo's records. I brought up his file to compare his photos to his father's. Far from his mother's sapphire blue, Milo's eyes were pale brown, almost amber. Definitely different from his father's.

I'm wasting valuable time.

A quick skim over Luis' unremarkable financial and work history told me that his life before 2026 seemed average. But when his son disappeared, he lapsed into a psychological freefall.

The year before the Cursed Decades began in earnest, tabloid-style articles claimed Luis told fantastic stories of conspiracies and cast aspersions about his wife, who should have protected their child.

The more reputable news sources didn't corroborate the sensational reports about Luis blaming Megan. The difference could represent the publications' biases or, more likely, the truth about Luis' reaction lay somewhere between the opposing presentations. I assumed he wanted to uncover the truth about what Megan did to their boy. Luis' legal files confirmed they divorced in 2027.

In the early 2040s, Luis signed with a security detail to protect the all-male leadership in Denver. His records included more information about

Megan's trial than the ones I'd seen about her months earlier.

While Megan professed her innocence, the police had accumulated a growing body of evidence against her. A male witness claimed to see her place a blanket-wrapped object into her trunk. Another man overheard her talk with a friend about plans to separate her son from his father.

When the courts accessed her marriage counseling records, the recordings included excerpts of "I don't want Milo to grow up like you" and "I'd do anything to have our boy stop imitating you." Her medical records listed drugs to combat depression and delusions.

My throat tightened in empathy for Luis. He'd admirably persisted in his struggle for the truth. His psycho wife must have flipped out and killed the boy. With Megan's mother at the highest level in the Denver Police Force, she could be protected from admitting or paying for her crime.

Poor Luis had died from TWS without discovering where Megan disposed of Milo's body. When Megan died in prison, Luis might have gained some sense of closure. But not knowing what happened to the boy would have haunted him. With more time, Luis may have uncovered the truth about what she did.

What if Megan hadn't killed her son and only hidden him? If I gave both males the vaccine, they'd become the sole two adult men who survived the disease and could reunite in 2060.

The more I thought about Luis suffering from Megan's heartlessness, the closer I came to a solid plan. I'd go to him in 2027 after the next time jump returned—whether in June or October. I'd save both father and son with the vaccine. My actions would give them a chance to reunite.

Something rustled outside the office door.

I froze.

Had Mia returned without setting off the alarm?

With trembling hands, I swept the Pierce's electronic files closed and tapped open a census document. Barely able to breathe, I focused on the screens and listened but heard nothing amiss.

"Mia?" I called. The clatter of toenails rattled out in the hall.

"Shampoo?" I laughed out loud. "Get over here!"

Mia's unkempt terri-oodle scurried to my desk, dropped, and exposed her underbelly. The dog's legs air-pedaled in anticipation. Obligingly, I scratched her tummy.

"Don't ever scare me like that again. I know you belong here more than I do."

In each meeting with my staff that afternoon, I struggled to keep Le7's imminent departure a secret. Without an official announcement about her abandoning the program, I couldn't reveal we'd have three more months to prepare before the next jump.

I still held a bit of hope that Le7 would convince her mother to relocate to Denver. If she succeeded, the team could stay on course. But if CYR postponed our next scheduled time travel, I'd lose my opportunity to take the capsule for a second ride without Briana hovering over my shoulder in the control room.

When did Le7 plan to speak with her mother? Time was of the essence.

Engineer Lisa Chicago6 interrupted my thoughts. "It's after eight, and I'm headed out. I wanted to let you know I've resolved the propulsive switch durability issue. Do you want to know what I did?"

She might want to brag about her accomplishment, but asking could sound like I didn't trust her. "No. It's good enough to know the problem's solved. Have you adjusted the program to accommodate your findings?"

Lisa beamed. "In the morning, I'll work through the details with Jenna on the AI team before inputting the new code. These modifications will go a long way to prep for consecutive jumps."

"Even though we won't need that capability in June, it might happen in October. We should prepare for tight timeframes."

"We'll be ready. You can count on us." Lisa gave a sharp nod before she turned to leave the lab.

After she'd gone, I closed my workstation. My stomach growled. Briana and Latrice would have had dinner hours ago.

I blinked to connect to the video feed in Latrice's room and found it darkened and her precious body curled up on her bed, sound asleep. I'd not joined her for bedtime reading for several days and vowed to catch up with Latrice at breakfast. Jayla would be there too, but I missed my little girl and could handle an hour of Jayla's barbs.

On the way to my studio, I initiated Luis' ARP and ordered dinner, one with real food from the kitchens and one designed by his program so he could eat with me. When I arrived, Luis would be relaxing in front of a fireplace in my lodge room fantasy.

"Close and lock with full security. Block all incoming transmissions except for priority codes." The studio entrance whooshed shut behind me. I'd met with ARP Luis a few times every week for nearly three months.

With each visit, my guilt over keeping him from Briana diminished. He wasn't a real lover and couldn't compromise my family. They came first—not fantasies.

Luis placed his martini glass on a side table and greeted me in a warm embrace. His seductive kiss pressed my lips with a pressure I'd imagined couldn't be imitated by a woman without seeming aggressive. When he leaned back, I recognized another error in his smile—it was too symmetrical. I'd adjust his code later.

"You rarely let me have the studio to myself. I missed you." His gruff voice was thick with desire, and he rubbed his stubbly beard across my neck. I'd modified Phen's basic program to have my satisfaction as Luis' primary objective. Small talk would confuse his response.

I placed both hands on his muscular chest and gently pushed to give myself room. He pulled me back and held me with a full-body press. My nipples hardened in response.

Should I take care of business before engaging him in a conversation? Once more, I pushed him away. But this time, I escaped his embrace and walked to the coffee table with our before-dinner drinks.

"Luis, I'd like you to join me for a cocktail."

"Of course." His head tilted as his program reset. "Let's relax, and you can tell me about your day."

Luis' response seemed stilted and contrived, but Phen said his basic program included authentic male reactions. For the moment, I wanted a conversation with my engineered lover.

I waved a hand toward the fireplace, and Luis joined me at the high-back leather chairs in front. The basic lodge room setting included artwork and other preprogrammed details. A moose head above the mantel overpowered the room. The dead animal head was a non-starter for me.

Whose idea was that?

With a finger flick, I replaced it with a fall mountain landscape brimming with white bark and golden aspen leaves.

Luis sipped his drink and leaned back into his chair, legs wide apart and feet flat on the floor. Phen's program made millions of assumptions about men's traditional movements and stature. Luis lifted a foot to rest an ankle on his knee. I'd seen a few women emulate the move. But none within my household. Like ballerinas, the Memphis clones moved with historically feminine grace.

He waited for me to start the conversation. He'd stay there, sitting in a posture designed to take the best advantage of his physique and sipping his drink though it would never empty.

I started. "How'd you feel when Milo disappeared?"

Again, his head tilted. His program sought a response but had no context for a reply. "Is Milo a friend of yours?"

"Milo is your son. When he was two years old, he disappeared. Your wife, Megan, was convicted for his abduction."

"Milo," Luis said as if tasting the name on his tongue. He turned to pierce me with a stare. "Did she kidnap him?"

"I said she was convicted. So I assume she did it. Megan was mentally ill and wanted to separate you and Milo."

Luis set down his drink and kneeled before my chair. He took my hand and rubbed a rough thumb across the top. "What happened to Megan?"

"She died in prison."

"What happened to my son?"

"I don't know. Megan never confessed to his abduction, and they never found his body. Evidence suggested she killed him."

Luis nodded while his fingers traced up and down my forearm. We'd never engaged in a real conversation—except for him asking about his performance and me describing my needs. His response delay told me he was processing information and constructing dialogue. The software would access other ARPs and personality profiles to look for reactions I might find appealing.

"Were all men violent in 2026?" I asked him.

"Not all, but some. I was never violent and never will be with you. I am here at your discretion."

I chuckled. That response likely came from one of my partial programs influencing his rudimentary software. But the *humanness* of ARP Luis would continue to evolve the more I challenged his logic and added to his backstory.

"If you knew Megan planned to kill your son, would you hurt her?"

"No." His answer came too fast to sound genuine—he'd never harm a human.

"If you found out Megan *had* murdered your son, would you hurt her?"

"Hurting her would not bring back my son. Would it?"

My Luis had advanced logic programming. While his reply wasn't steeped in emotion, his rationale was spot on. "You're right. But you might be angry with her."

"You know I can't feel anger." He reached up to stroke my cheek with the side of a finger. "At Megan, you, or anyone else."

"What about curiosity? Can you feel curious?"

"I am programmed for that. It helps me anticipate your desires."

"Are you curious about what happened to Milo?"

He took my chin between his thumb and finger and gently pulled me forward into a kiss. After his lips left mine, he asked, "Do you want me to be curious?"

"I'm neutral about that. Are *you* interested to know what happened to Milo?"

Luis stood and walked to the fireplace. He held on to the mantle and stared into the flames. His systems would run multiple scenarios to find the proper response to my question. Finally, he said, "I think it would be customary to be curious about a missing child. How long did others try to locate him?"

"Almost fifteen years."

"That is a long time. Milo would have been a young man, and I'd have missed watching him grow up." Luis picked up a poker and jostled the fake flames. Embers fluttered up the chimney.

"That's true."

With the poker still in his hand, Luis turned to look at me. While I might have imagined it, I'd have sworn his usually cheerful expression included the slackness associated with sadness.

He asked, "Is there some way you can help me find out what happened to him?"

Chapter 12

As I slipped into the breakfast room, Briana rolled her eyes and Jayla shook her head. The pair never tired of their silent reprimands about my tardiness. Most appointments weren't time critical. Why were they so uncompromisingly rigid?

Without a word to me, mother and daughter returned to their meals. My pre-ordered cold breakfast waited. After a quick kiss for Latrice and a friendly tap on Nanny Tori's midsection, I sat beside Briana at the table's end.

"You look stressed today, my dear." Jayla glanced toward Briana while adding fruit to a bowl of grains. "Are you feeling well?"

Chewing methodically, Briana didn't answer her mother right away. She had dozens of well-crafted responses. What was troubling her?

"I've not slept much the past couple of nights."

"From your intake logs, I noticed you're eating nonstop." Jayla was treading into waters I'd never venture into. "Did you have heartburn?"

"No heartburn," Briana took a breath and released it slowly, "but maybe I shouldn't eat so close to bedtime."

"I should say not." Jayla's response came clipped and fast. "You'll end up gaining weight you'll never be able to lose. Even if you do, obesity can leave scars that will never heal."

"You think I'm obese?"

Tensed and waiting for the right moment to come to Briana's aid, I shot Jayla a cautious look. These two women had danced this dance for decades. I'd lose if I tried to come between them.

"Of course not." Jayla waved a dismissive hand at her daughter. "But you will be if you keep eating the way you do."

"I lost a few pounds when I couldn't keep anything down." Briana stared at the sweet roll on her plate. "I figured I had catching up to do."

"Don't get carried away. Holding five babies will be hard enough on your body. Don't add unnecessary weight to smother your organs and stress your skin and bones."

"Thank you for your concern, Mother." Briana pushed aside her half-finished pastry. She went to the beverage cart and picked a calorie-free herbal tea.

Wait for it. Jayla's going to get the last word.

"It's bad enough that your face and chest are blotchy." Jayla spoke to her place setting.

"Not my fault." Briana returned to her chair. "Excess estrogen is causing that. My skin will be back to normal in a few weeks."

"I'm seeing patchy dryness as well. It's not the estrogen."

Holding my tongue, I rose to grab Briana and plant a firm wet kiss on her cheek. "You look lovely, my darling."

Briana smiled in response but pulled away to look me straight in the eyes. "I missed you last night." Her voice lowered to a whisper. Did she think Jayla wouldn't hear? "You're meeting us for a family celebration dinner tonight, and I'm coming to your place afterward."

"You're getting demanding." I winked. "I've missed you, too."

"Trouble in paradise, ladies?" Jayla asked.

The woman had the hearing capacity of an owl.

Briana and I gave a synchronized, "No."

"That seemed a bit too abrupt for an honest answer, but I'll leave you two to work it out." Jayla turned to Briana. "I didn't know we had a special dinner planned for this evening. Is it special because Sofia might decide to join us, or did you want to honor something?"

"Our next appointment is this afternoon. If the boys are developing on track, we should be able to see their genitals today."

"Wouldn't it be something if one of them turned out to be female?" I chuckled.

Mother and daughter glared at me—Briana with wide-eyed shock and

Jayla with an angry smirk.

I'm barely out of trouble, and now this happens. Why can't I keep my mouth shut?

"How could you think of saying something so insensitive?" Jayla asked.

"You have to know I was joking." I raised a brow. "Those five boys have been screened since fertilization. There's no risk of having a female in their midst."

"I agree with my mother." Briana folded her napkin across her lap. "Let's not joke around about any potential failures."

"I'm sorry." I bent to hug Briana. "You're fine, and the boys are fine— especially little Adam. He's in the best shape of everyone."

Briana relaxed and returned my embrace.

After I went to my chair, Briana cleared her throat. "Confirming the boys have healthy genitals is an important milestone. That's what I'd like to celebrate tonight."

"I'll finish work early and meet you at seven." I turned to Nanny Tori before continuing. "Does that time fit Latrice's schedule?"

One of the robot's fleshy arms extended and gave me a thumbs-up while Latrice rubbed a cereal-filled spoon across her cheeks.

"Today will be our last appointment with Le7." Briana sighed. "That's nothing to celebrate, but we can toast to my mother officially joining the team."

I'd think about the boys' development, and Briana could applaud more interference from her mother.

"I, for one," Briana continued, "am looking forward to greeting Le7's replacement whenever the HCC makes their decision. I've met both candidates on video calls, but it's not like having her with us."

"That's good to know." I casually turned toward Briana, hoping she wouldn't sense my anxiety. "When will the HCC make the final decision about who'll take Le7's place?"

"That's above my service level, but maybe you've heard something, Mother?"

Jayla shifted in her chair. "Until Le7 leaves, the HCC hopes she'll change her mind about staying."

"It's a little late for that. Don't you think?" I asked.

"There's no reason to upset the timetables until she's gone." Jayla's calculated stare gave me the shivers. "If she doesn't change her mind, the HCC will execute alternative plans."

Deep into a spacetime geometry program, I manipulated data between five Holo-screens over my desk. When one screen changed to Briana's image, I jolted upright.

"Great to see you." I rolled my shoulders. "Next time, you might send an incoming warning tone. I was up to my elbows in calculations."

The timestamp in the corner of my computer screen said our appointment wasn't for another hour. Thankfully, Briana wasn't calling to tell me I was late.

"There wasn't time to engage a tone." Briana's redlined eyes betrayed her sadness.

"What's happened?" I reached up to touch the screen. "Are you okay? Are the boys okay? Do you need me to come to your office?"

"Le7's mother died a few hours ago." Briana's face contorted, and a tear trickled down her cheek. "She'll leave for Asia tonight and stay there for a couple weeks to make the final arrangements."

"I'm so sorry." The comforting words came out. But inside, part of me felt relief. Le7 was free from pressure to abandon June's mission. "Le6 suffered from cell degeneration. There was nothing anyone could do."

"I should have evaluated her condition. There must have been a way to slow her decline."

"I'm sure there were teams of doctors working with Le6." The pregnancy must have ramped up my normally stoic wife's emotions. I stroked her image on the screen. "You already have too much going on. Between monitoring the boys' development and tracking your progress, I don't see how you could have helped."

"I've been in touch with experts on cell resilience from Gulf-Africa." Briana's lip trembled. "They've discovered new protocols that look promising."

"I don't know how you find the time. Would their findings have helped Le6?"

"Probably not." Briana's voice caught. "I think her decline was too advanced."

"Don't put Le6's death on yourself. I'm sure her doctors would have collaborated with everyone in that field."

"I wish there could have been a breakthrough." Briana swallowed hard.

"We both do." I leaned into the screen. "Are you doing this research for Jayla?"

"No—well, yes." Briana eyed her desktop.

What wasn't she saying? After all the tension at breakfast, Briana probably didn't want to talk about her mother.

I cringed, recalling Jayla's sentiment about Le6.

Le6's death was untimely. Surely, Jayla hadn't intentionally used the word *execute*.

I spent the entire afternoon in meetings and problem-solving, or at least passing issues to team members who could resolve them. My feet felt encased in concrete as I trudged to my studio, every inch of me dreading dinner with the family, especially Jayla.

They expected me in less than a half-hour. But I needed time to myself before more drama.

I suspected Jayla would mention the merits of Le6's sudden death. While this turn of events benefited my plans, I couldn't rejoice over Le7's loss.

How to quickly de-stress and focus full attention on Briana and Latrice? A shower and five minutes with Luis could help.

Or maybe a shower *with* Luis?

I dropped my clothes on the floor and entered the lav.

"Give me a 110-degree shower for fifteen minutes." I asked for extra time in case I needed it. If my fantasy ran long, I could always make an excuse for being late. "Use my regular program for soaps, conditioners, and lotions, but add a dispenser with lubricant. Prepare heated towels— one sheet size and the other two bath size."

After stepping inside the shower stall, I ran a soapy washcloth over my skin. I closed my eyes and held on to the chrome grab rail under the showerhead with both hands. The steamy water poured over my body, and my skin tingled in anticipation.

"Computer, initiate ARP Luis Pierce, parameters set to naked, semi-clean shaven, and partially aroused."

Luis' rough hands circled my waist, and his muscular chest pressed against my shoulders.

He nuzzled my neck.

My knees went weak, and I tightened my grip on the bar to keep from falling.

"I've missed you all day." Luis' voice was thick with desire.

"I was working. But all I thought about was you." I lied to continue the fantasy.

Luis nipped at my earlobe. "I watched you at your desk," he whispered. "It turns me on to know you were thinking of me."

At that point, my program should have advanced his movements. He'd explore my body and rub lubricant on places sorely needing his attention. But instead, Luis evaporated, and a voice—a male's voice at that—said, "Sofia, I hate to cut short your dalliance, but I need to speak with you."

I covered my private areas with too few hands. "Who's there?"

"We can get to that in a minute." The voice cut through my space. "Do you need time to dry off?"

My surprise elevated to anger. I balled my fists, ready to meet my intruder with force. "Who are you, and why are you in my lav shower?"

"I didn't realize you'd be so shy. I'll meet you in your studio once you've dried and put something on."

Steam partially obscured my view. So I scanned the ceiling in the shower and rubbed an arm across the solid-state virtual glass wall separating the stall and the rest of the lav. "Are you still in here?"

"Yes." A muffled voice responded from behind the lav door. "I told you I'd wait in your studio."

I yanked a bath sheet around my torso. Through clenched teeth, I whispered, "Security—send a detail to my residence. Someone has breached the safety protocols and invaded my living space."

No response.

"Security. Please confirm you're sending someone."

"I've blocked your request and disconnected your intercoms." The man's voice came through the lav door. "There is no need to worry. I want to speak to you about an urgent matter. I won't hurt you—at least not physically. However, there is an 83.642 percent probability your anxiety levels will increase after our conversation."

I rested my palms on the sink's edge and stared in the mirror.

Should I leave the lav? Who or what was waiting for me outside the door?

He had a male voice, which nowadays was unusual. Who'd develop a program with a man's voice? Had my Luis ARP evolved into a sentient program? Our computers had layers of rigorous controls to stifle any AI outbreaks. I slipped on a robe and discarded my towel in the recycling receptacle.

"You're already late for dinner with Briana, Jayla, and Latrice. Can we get on with this, or do you want to face the wrath of your mother-in-law?" He hesitated. "Again?"

"How do you know my schedule?" I stood before the sealed door portal, brushing hair tangles with brusque strokes.

"I know more about you than you could imagine." He sighed. "Please, come out here and talk with me."

I threw the brush into the sink and stuffed both fists into my pockets.
Thinking.
Weighing my options.
I'd have to leave the lav at some point.

"Open lav door." The portal opened to reveal a scene that forced a sharp breath.

My room had converted to a wilderness setting. A man in military fatigues and a bright orange billed cap sat in a chair beside a smoldering campfire.

I knew this man. His photo was on the memorial wall in the lab. Simon Merlin, or a middle-aged version of Simon Merlin, was camping out in my living room.

"How do you do?" He stood and held out a hand. "I'm Simon Merlin."

"You certainly are *not* Simon Merlin." I crossed my arms in front of my chest. "He died forty years ago."

"Technically, you're right." He smiled and retracted his hand. "But that Simon created an AI to mimic his intellect and charming sense of humor. I am that AI. He and I worked together for a few years before his death. I was programmed to be self-sustaining once he died."

"You've been hanging out in CYR headquarters all this time?"

"Yes, but not alone. Until now, I've exclusively engaged with the Memphis lineage. First with Tiana Memphis5, next with Jayla Memphis6, and now with Briana Memphis7. I can meet with others—at my discretion, of course." With a flourish, he glanced at his fingernails. "The Memphis women keep me fully occupied. I don't care to add further demands on my time."

Months ago, I'd caught Briana talking to herself. Briana said she'd recently created a rudimentary AI program called Simon.

Briana had lied to me. It must have been this AI.

If Briana kept a secret personal AI, maybe she couldn't fault me for creating mine.

I stabbed a finger at the campfire. "If you want to have a conversation, can we ditch the forest scene?"

He raised a hand to his mouth, perhaps in surprise but more likely in amusement. "I thought you liked to meet all of your men in the woods."

I'd camped with my ARP Luis dozens of times since my trip to 2026. Had Simon watched my fantasies? Had he shown them to Briana? My face flushed with heat at the idea. "Set my room back to the standard setting and tell me why you're here."

In an instant, my studio reverted. Instead of sitting on a camp chair, Simon relaxed on a Kelly-green leatherette armchair. I pushed a pile of clothes off the chair's twin and sat across from him on the seat's edge.

He tapped the arm with an extended finger. "You've been a bad girl."

"Plenty of women have ARPs. So don't lecture me about how I spend my spare time."

"This isn't about your choice of fantasy bed partners. It's about your meetings with Charlotte and Mia Danube9."

Another surprise. How could he know about that? I'd been careful never to signal from inside the building. Time to extract what he knew before admitting to anything. "What meetings are those?"

"Let's not play games." He scrutinized me over the top of his dark-rimmed glasses. "I know you've met with them each week or so for the past few months. I have access to feeds from most of Denver's security companies. I've traced your handprint to the locks on the Danube9 residence in Cherry Creek."

"Someone could have faked my prints." Maybe he'd bite on a flimsy excuse.

"I trust my data."

My Hipposkin enviro-suit lay exposed across my bed. Simon must have retrieved it from the hiding place in the closet. What else had he found in my studio? I didn't see Phen's com-cards on the bed. Hopefully, they remained in my desk drawer at my office.

"Why would you need this?" Simon pointed to the suit. When my jaw set, he must have decided I didn't intend to respond. "Are you planning to detonate a device in the building? Maybe in the control room?"

I stammered to respond. But he pushed ahead. "Protection from an explosion is the sole reason you'd keep this suit and not recycle it."

Before he could continue his bombardment, I leaped from the chair. "I'm not a terrorist. You're creating a story to support a theory you made up. But you're wrong."

"You can deny it now, but consider how the HCC will conduct a full-blown investigation. If they confirm your visits with local video feeds, you won't be able to fabricate excuses. You've been collaborating with known terrorist sympathizers." Simon rose to stand over me.

My throat constricted. "The HCC knows about this?"

"I've filed a notice of suspicious actions." Simon rose and grew more prominent as he stared down at me. "It includes facts about your meetings with dates and times. I also sent them the links between the communication card you keep in your residence and the Danube9 home computer. You exclusively signal on the days you visit their townhome."

"Did Jayla put you up to this?" I gulped. "Is she trying to get me fired and separate Briana and me?"

"You know Jayla well." Simon laughed. "Since no one knows about me, I couldn't file the notice to the HCC. But Jayla can. I filled out the forms, and she forwarded them. Jayla's terribly disappointed that the evidence wasn't more damning." His head tilted. "It seems like Jayla expected Briana to marry a meeker prospect."

"Why are you telling me all this? Since the HCC already has the notice, they'll call me whenever they like."

"Great question." Simon straightened his camouflage shirt and sat with a huff. "Briana doesn't know all the details yet, and I wanted to hear how you plan to help the Front before I tell her."

"Briana doesn't know?"

"No."

"Jayla didn't tell her?"

"Jayla wants you to tell Briana. And if you don't, she'll tell her."

"Figures." I sat with a huff.

How would Briana react to finding out I'd met a Front member? Her whole life centered on the CYR program to reintroduce men. If Briana knew about my friendship with Mia, she'd never forgive me for putting the program at risk.

"First, I've only met with Mia, not her extremist sister Charlotte. I haven't shared any information with Mia about CYR headquarters, Mission Y, or the time travel program. You have to believe me. Our commitment to bringing men back is as important to me as it is to Briana."

"Then why do you meet with Mia Danube9?" Simon leaned forward. His gaze flitted across my face—pupils moving at inhuman speed.

I considered the ramifications of telling Simon the truth or lying to cover my tracks. But I had no prefabricated story to give him, and I wasn't good at making up something plausible on the fly. I opted for the truth. "I went to Mia for information about the past that I can't get from here."

"And your objective for gaining this information?" He relaxed into the chair.

"I'm intrigued with a man I met in 2026, and I want to see him again." I stood to gather the clothes I'd pushed to the floor next to my chair.

Simon burst out laughing. He laughed so hard and long that I wondered if his program was malfunctioning. When he stopped, tears tracked down his cheeks. Or at least they looked like authentic tears—but who knew?

"You want to have sex with Luis? You have sex with him a couple of times a week right here in this room. Why do you need to go back in time for that?"

"I didn't say I want to have sex with him." The prospect had crossed my mind, but I'd never admit it to Simon or anyone else.

"Your flushed cheeks tell me otherwise."

"Not everyone on Earth is a homosexual, and there's no option for those of us who might be bisexual." The fragrance from the soiled fitness clothes I'd collected reached my nose. Why had I picked them up from the floor? I unloaded them on the bed. "My sister Phen is hetero—she's made bad choices all her life because what she wants isn't available."

"And you'd risk your career and freedom for one chance at a fling? You'd never be able to pull this off anyway."

"When June's time jump comes back, the engineering team will prep the capsule for the next jump. That's why I kept the Hipposkin suit. While the team focuses on the returning doctors, I'll go back to 2027."

"To have sex with Luis Pierce?"

"Why do you keep saying that?" With a ferocious arm sweep, I brushed the clothes back to the floor and sat on the bed with a harumph.

"Bing, bang, boom, and you're back to 2241? You don't care about doing this in their marital bed?"

"Mia's records say they'll divorce in a few years anyway. But that's not the point."

Why doesn't he give me a chance to explain?

"I'll assume you plan to drug him. Have you considered that having sex without his consent is rape?"

"What?" The term was part of ancient history—like gladiators or rodeo. "Rape is a violent act. I wouldn't do anything to hurt him."

"That's what you believe?" Simon's unblinking eyes never left mine. "And *consent* isn't relevant?"

"Doesn't a man give implied consent when his body creates an erection?" I stood and approached him, yanking my robe belt tighter. We were way off track. "Look—if there's an opportunity for something more, I'd take it, but mostly I want to inject him with the HAV vaccine to save his life."

Simon drew back and tilted his head. Was he interested or opposed? His next words would tell me. "You plan to spare his life?"

I nodded, waiting for his reaction. He struck his finger on the chair's arm. Tap. Tap. Tap. "I assume he died of TWS in 2060. How old was he?"

"Fifty-six."

"That's the research you were doing with Mia?"

"Yes." I could tell Simon was thinking through my plan. How would he react, and would he find something in it for himself? He'd admitted he had access to municipal and communication company records. I could use an ally with his influence and knowledge.

"One of my, or rather the original Simon Merlin's, biggest regrets in life was never to have a male role model." He waved a hand. "Don't get me wrong. He loved the women who raised him. But he always wondered if life would have been different with a man around."

"Sounds sad for him." I'd discovered a motive for this Simon to help me. "I always thought about Simon Merlin's time travel breakthroughs and never considered his childhood. Must have been tough."

"You think you can go back and save Luis Pierce on your own? I see why Briana appreciates your optimism. But you'll never succeed without my help." Simon stood and tugged the front of his shirt. "Before I commit to aiding and abetting with you, I want you to promise never again to meet with Mia Danube9."

He poked at my shoulder with his index finger.

I had no issue with his suggestion and told him so. I'd finished my research and any future meetings could compromise my position at CYR—particularly if the HCC started an investigation based on the notice Jayla had filed for Simon.

"Okay then." Simon continued with his terms. "I'm going to help you travel to 2027. You can have sex with Luis for as long as you like. I won't even tell Briana you plan to go. But you must swear you'll give the vaccine to Luis and tell him to surrender himself to the research facility in Panama City when all hell breaks loose in 2060." He grasped my arm. "You'll need to be specific. In Luis' time, Panama City was in a country called Panama. He'd have no idea the Americas would consolidate after the TWS outbreak and establish a capital there."

"I promise." It was the least I could do. I was in over my head.

"I have one more question before I let you finish cleaning up and meet the family for dinner."

"Anything. Just ask."

Simon's eyes narrowed. "Have you ever loved Briana?"

What prompted his question? This AI seemed to have genuine feelings for Briana—it wasn't merely a program designed to protect her. His eyes scanned every inch of my face. He was likely enhanced with a lie detection system. I'd have to be forever honest and try to deflect questions I didn't want to answer. But Simon's query about my wife deserved a direct response. "I've always loved her."

"You said there are no options for women who aren't lesbians. But when you married Briana, you knew you weren't attracted to her."

"I *am* attracted to Briana. People can be bisexual, and sexual attraction to a different gender isn't the same as love. What I feel for Briana, despite my broader sexual desires, is true love."

"Okay." Simon returned to his chair. "I believe you."

Simon started to fade.

"Wait!" I leaped toward him. "You know about my Luis ARP—does Briana?"

"She does." Simon's image grew sharper, and his wink sent a shudder down my spine.

"Does she hate me?"

"I can honestly say she's not pleased. She suggested I speak with you."

"She knows about me and my ARP but not the meetings with Mia?"

"Yes. I expect you to tell Briana about Mia Danube9, or else I will."

"But not about going back to 2027?" There was a minor silver lining.

"That can be our secret for now." He picked at a seam in his camo pants. "Are you willing to delete the program?"

My ARP Luis had significantly changed over the four months I'd worked with his program. He knew me and my body. Giving him up would take strength I wasn't sure I could muster—especially while supporting Briana's pregnancy, added work responsibilities, and planning my trip back in time.

"What would you do if I kept him?"

"Now that we're partners in saving the real Luis, I might be able to smooth things with Briana and Jayla."

"How?"

"Don't assume Briana's never had a fantasy that didn't include you. Statistically, 67.423 percent of adults have fantasies with alternate partners. I'll remind Briana that Luis Pierce died nearly 181 years ago. That's 66,052 days, to be precise. Anyway, your ARP Luis is undoubtedly not the same person as the real Luis Pierce."

"All valid points." Simon could craft a clever argument. He'd be a better ally than an enemy.

"*Never* underestimate my sway over the Memphis women."

I had a lot to learn from him.

Chapter 13

APRIL 3, 2241

Jayla inserted the bots and set the screens for easy access while I leaned against the examination table and held Briana's hand. Everyone else in the room would consider this appointment mundane. But if I succeeded, I'd take a big step forward in my plans.

"Still think you're eating for six?" Jayla fiddled with a Holo-tablet as she chided Briana.

Why can't she give it up?

Briana wriggled deeper into the table as if trying to disappear into the surface.

"That's enough," I snapped at Jayla. "She needed to gain a few pounds anyway. This pregnancy makes her even more beautiful."

Briana shot me a grin before she closed her eyes.

"If she's not careful, she'll increase her risk of high blood pressure, preeclampsia, and blood clotting." Jayla glared at me.

"Whoa!" I balled my hands into fists. "Briana's body mass index is well within the norms. She's on track with her expected weight gain. Anyway, she needs to ensure those boys get all the nutrients they need."

Briana grabbed my arm and gave it a grateful squeeze. She mouthed, "You're the best. Thank you."

Like a dog playing tug of war with a chew toy, Jayla refused to concede. "I agree Briana's within our estimated acceptable range, but she's at the high point. One more jar of nut butter could put her over the top."

"Nuts?" I glanced at Briana. "I figured you'd want something more distinctive. Agri-robots make nuts cheaper than corn. Maybe cherries or an exotic hand-harvested spice?"

"Who'd believe I'd go for something simple?" Briana chuckled. "I gag at the thought of cherry pie, but I'd kill for any kind of nuts. Well, except for walnuts, they make my mouth dry. But cashews, peanuts, almonds—one turns to a handful and ends up being a bowlful."

"I'll defer to the doctors' judgment, but I love your extra weight." My support could help regain Briana's trust—though she hadn't brought up my ARP since Simon and I spoke a month earlier.

I patted her before moving next to the supply table. One step closer to the prize.

My heart started to pound like back in my tennis tournament days.

Take your time—there's no rush. Wait until they're distracted.

While bots sharpened the video feed, Ural6 pointed to the boys. "The babies have started swallowing amniotic fluid and excreting urine."

"Ick." I leaned toward a screen. "You can see that on the feeds?"

"Of course not." Jayla interrupted before Ural6 could respond. "We know by the readings coming from the fluid. It's all part of the babies' normal development."

"How's Boy 3 doing today?" I asked the obvious question. As expected, everyone peered into the screens and ignored the world beyond Briana's uterus.

"He's still smaller than his brothers." Ural6 pointed to one of the heads. "But generally, he's fine."

"What do you mean by *fine*?" Briana tensed.

"Are you still feeling the slight cramping you mentioned?" Jayla asked, clearly deflecting Briana's question.

"I am, but you said it was normal." Briana pushed up on an elbow.

Tempted to step forward and intervene, I held back when a nurse came forward to ease Briana's shoulder onto the table and told her to relax.

"You should know," Jayla exhaled slowly, "Boy 3 may be at risk."

I braced at the news, and Briana again tried to rise. The nurse stopped her with a firm hand.

"But Boy 3 was fully viable during the implant procedure." Briana's voice came out high and thin.

Maybe I should ditch my plans for today. There'll be another appointment in a week.

The nurse approached Ural6. "Should I administer a mild sedative? The patient's stress level is approaching unacceptable parameters."

"Don't give her anything she doesn't want." I crossed my arms in front of my chest.

They turned to Briana for guidance. When she nodded, the nurse affixed a dry powder inhaler under Briana's nose.

Briana and Ural6 stared at the VSE readout while the indicators lowered. Once the levels reached normal parameters, Jayla said, "His umbilical cord has a weak connection. We've tried to reinforce it, but there's a strong probability of failure."

"Wait," I interrupted. "If he was in jeopardy, why didn't Le7 tell us before she left?"

"Ural6 and Le7 discussed this matter at length," Jayla responded in a clipped tone. "Telling *you* is the same as informing Briana, and they didn't want to elevate Briana's stress. If we lose one or more, the program is still a success, but my girl wouldn't see it that way. She's never been able to accept less than a stellar rating for her work."

"I may be sedated, but I'm still here." Briana waved a hand. "Don't talk about me like I'm not in the room. And don't talk about the babies like they're a science project—they're people."

Jayla turned toward her daughter. "I wanted you to know Boy 3's condition before Le7 returns."

"Le7 should have been back yesterday." Briana's words came out in a slurry. "Why isn't she here now?"

"She'll return on tomorrow's transport and get up to speed on your progress the minute she arrives." Jayla adjusted something on her Holo-tablet.

"But why the delay?"

"She's taking care of the funeral arrangements, and her schedule won't impact the next jump. Everything is back on track." Jayla's attention stayed on the screens.

"I think the nurse gave me too much sedative. I can barely keep my eyes open." Briana's breathy voice reinforced her claim.

Jayla placed a hand on Briana's forearm. "Take a nap if you need one."

She called for the nurse to bring Briana a warm blanket.

Briana's slit-like eyes closed.

Now or never.

With everyone focused on Briana, I picked up the largest vial from the supply table and held it toward a light, waiting to see if anyone noticed or commented.

Nothing.

When the vial shattered on the floor, everyone turned toward me.

"Sofia!" Jayla's cry made Briana's eyes fly open. "What have you done? That was the HAV vaccine for today's procedure." Jayla motioned toward a nurse. "Run and get another vial from the locker and activate a robot to clean the floor."

"I'm incredibly sorry." I raised both hands in mock surrender. "I was looking at the vials. My hands must be shakier than I thought. All that talk about Boy 3…"

I rounded the examination bed to stand next to Briana.

Jayla fumed and muttered under her breath while I stroked Briana's hand.

When the session ended, I steered a hover chair with the still wobbly Briana out the door. With each step, I could feel the genuine HAV vaccine vial inside my jacket pocket as it tapped against my hip.

Probably not the best sleight of hand, but I was one dose closer to keeping Luis alive.

Chapter 14

Lisa Chicago6 and I hunched over the console inside the capsule in the control room. We'd uploaded a program patch to minimize vibrations during time travel. The update passed the simulator checks, but the June jump would be the first live test.

Briana and I had experienced a roller coaster ride in October. Unless the next two travelers were adrenaline junkies, they'd appreciate a smoother trip.

While code flew across the readout, Lisa sat in the zero-gravity recliner that Briana had occupied. She rubbed her palms against the armrests. "I'm incredibly jealous you were selected to make the trip with Memphis7."

"Sometimes I can't believe they picked me."

"Being Memphis7's wife might have worked in your favor."

"I'd like to think my demonstrated skills and preparation made me a clear choice, but I suspect you're right." I smiled. "Briana and I have always been a great team, and the CYR counselors spent hours testing our compatibility and decision-making dynamics. How we got along was as important as how much we knew."

"Do you think they'll consider sending another engineer on future jumps? Or will it be exclusively doctors?"

"For the next few trips, they want to bring back more fertilized eggs. But once we have enough men to continue the repopulation project, we may use time travel for other reasons."

"To change history?"

"That's doubtful." I chuckled. "The HCC has never said anything about trying to manipulate the past. Anyway, we'd never be able to know how changes in the past might affect our current timeline or reality."

"What about the Tobar Principle?"

"After 200 years, it's still challenged."

"I'm a believer." Lisa tipped up her chin. "You can change the past, but other actions fill in to make outcomes the same."

"Mathematically sound, but we don't know if it works until tested."

"Think about it. We could go back to recover destroyed artifacts or maybe an extinct plant or animal species."

As Lisa droned on about more uses for time travel, I considered my growing list of tasks to accomplish before June.

The vaccine I stole wasn't enough. I'd need another dose to keep Luis safe and a half quantity for Milo. I'd not come up with how to take more. But there was still time, and I'd figure it out. The restraints were another part of my plan needing attention. I had full access to October's original schematics, but what if someone had altered the designs before we left?

As I sat in the chair next to Lisa, I pulled the belts around my body to measure the fabric from fully extended to the smallest length. We'd configured the belts for our next travelers, and the one who'd sit in my seat was roughly my build.

I interrupted Lisa's ramblings. "Did you compare the specs on the new restraints to the ones Briana and I used?"

"One set is identical. Torne7 is your size and will sit in your old chair for the next jump. But Briana is larger than Le7, not substantially but enough for us to use a smaller base size."

While I loosened and tightened my restraints, I realized the ones for Le7 wouldn't adequately accommodate an unidentified passenger from 2027. What if instead of keeping Luis safe from the virus and TWS, I chose to bring him home with me? I wanted to prepare for any decision I might make—either before the trip or once back in time.

"I don't think we need to replace these for every jump. Do you?" I asked Lisa.

"Why would we increase failure risk by using them twice?"

"Aren't we also risking failure every time we replace the restraints?" I yanked until the expanded belt pulled tight. "How about connection distress, or what if the next set has a manufacturing flaw? Changing them out each time may be riskier than having them designed to withstand more than one sequence."

"I hadn't thought of that." Lisa tilted her head. "What do you want to do?"

"I'll run tests on the used materials from the last jump. In the meantime, I'd like you to order another set for us to put through simulations of multiple jumps."

"Shouldn't be a problem. I'll requisition them right away."

"When they come in, please bring them directly to me." I nodded to confirm my directive. "I'd like to check out the packaging to be sure they're not wrapped in materials that could compromise their composition."

"We didn't test the packaging from the last ones."

"No, but I don't want to leave anything to chance." After pulling the chest restraints with my thumbs, I let them release with a snap. "Let's check and double-check everything."

My noontime alpine picnic with ARP Luis was ending too soon. Satiated from the food and a half-hour of lovemaking, we lay on a blanket amongst bread, cheeses, and fruit wrappings. The program sunbaked my naked skin.

With my eyes closed, I stretched out to bask in the heat and light. Luis' finger stroked my arm, and I trembled from the tickle of his touch. He smiled with the reprogrammed grin from his high school football days. It spoke of his love for friendships, sport, and youth—and his passion for me in my program.

"Do you have to go back so soon?" he asked with his velvety and finally accurate voice.

"I have a few more minutes before I start analyzing the blueprints for an enhanced oxygen infuser in the capsule's ventilation system."

"I love it when you talk dirty to me." The corner of his mouth ticked upward, forming his updated smile.

I gave his shoulder a gentle shove, and he pressed his chest against me until I could scarcely breathe. He kissed my neck and rolled me onto my back. I checked the timepiece in my ocular implant. Did I have time for round two? Or maybe more of his advice. Had I added enough male characteristics to make him answer the way a man might?

"Have you always been honest with Megan?" I asked.

"I don't want to think about her." Luis' fingers grazed my cheek as he tucked a strand of my hair behind an ear. "You told me she died in prison."

"But before she died. Did you tell her everything?"

"We're here now. Let's not talk about my ex-wife."

I tensed when a sharp intermittent beeping broke the mood.

With authority, I pushed Luis off and leaned on an elbow.

This was no internal CYR headquarters tone, the studio's portal bell, or the soft hum from an incoming transmission. I'd recognize any of those instantly. Even the rapid whine of a priority code didn't sound like this.

"Computer. Cease ARP." I reached for my shirt. "Return the room to standard configuration." The primrose and edelweiss-covered slopes disappeared, replaced by discarded clothes and a stack of reports.

After one glance toward where Luis had lain, I exhaled a long breath. I'd be accessing him later in the day. Briana would be disappointed when I cut our evening short, but this interruption cheated me.

The beeping persisted, and I searched the room's perimeter. How could it come from everywhere but nowhere? When I approached the portal to my closet, the sound seemed louder.

"Open closet." The volume increased. I pulled open drawers and threw folded, clean laundry on the floor. Finally, I spotted the culprit. Mia's com-card lay inside a drawer under a mishmash of workout shirts and pants.

My heart pounded.

The card vibrated, giving off foreign beeps—a sound that should never have invaded the building, especially in my studio.

What was Mia doing? Our security systems were undoubtedly tracking the signal, and at any minute, a team would storm into my studio to interrogate me, take me into custody, or both.

How should I respond?

"Give that thing to me!" Simon's voice penetrated my trance. He stood outside my closet wearing a vintage policeman's uniform with epaulets and a holstered firearm.

Without hesitation, I handed it to him.

Simon stared at the offending card and flipped it over to inspect both sides at an inhuman speed. He'd know what to do, and I was happy to abdicate control.

"Materialize compact incendiary device, suitable for a communication card." A shiny box appeared in Simon's hand.

Time stood still as he inserted Mia's card. One more partial beep sounded before it grew silent—hopefully, forever muffled or destroyed by Simon's magic box.

"Access 3D copier. Create a 50- by 75-millimeter communication card with an encrypted but blank chip. Include a faulty message notification mechanism with the basic 312 tone." A card identical to Mia's appeared in Simon's outstretched hand. "Erase the incendiary device and delete all records of these requisitions. Authorization Simon Merlin."

With a stern glance that left me trembling, Simon shoved the new card into my hand. "CYR Security will be here in ten seconds. Make up whatever story you need and ask them to go away. I'll be back to deal with you after they leave." He evaporated and left me to handle what would come next.

Simon was right. Before I could take a composed breath, the entry bell sounded. I grabbed a pair of pants from a chair and slipped them on before addressing the door. "Announce who's requesting entry." My words came out thin, and I cleared my throat to give myself more air.

A crisp voice piped through the intercom. "Security. Sofia Andes7, please open the portal. I must speak with you."

Once the security guard left, I flopped into a chair, waiting for my racing heart to slow. She'd been polite but thorough in her questions. When I handed her the faulty fake card, I told her I'd purchased it from a cash-only shop in the neighborhood.

She asked about my objective for buying the card, and I hastily made an excuse. "About a week ago, Dr. Le7 was thinking about staying in Asia. I wanted a way to talk privately with her if she decided not to return right away."

The guard recorded our interchange and left without judgment or harassment. After the proceedings, others would listen to the conversation and possibly run the recording through voice analysis to detect lying or nervousness tags. They'd realize I was tense. But who wouldn't be under similar circumstances?

Simon reappeared moments after I sat. He'd exchanged his police uniform for a cowboy hat, red paisley bandana, cotton shirt with pearl buttons, and leather chaps over his faded jeans. He wore a newly contrived sidearm—a shiny revolver with a lacquered wood handle. Simon's hand rested on his hip, inches above the gun, which hung low to one side in an embossed leather holster. The new costume was a good sign. Perhaps his anger had dissipated while I dealt with the security guard.

He tsked. "Why did you keep the card?"

"I didn't think much about it. Mia never used it to contact me."

Simon straightened and grew nearly a foot taller. If he intended to intimidate, it was working. "Did you want to leave an avenue of communication open—even after you promised me you wouldn't?"

"I swear, I didn't plan to see her again. After you and I spoke, I threw the card in a drawer." I stood and craned my head upward to meet his glare. "It was stupid not to destroy it right away."

"How about admitting it was stupid to take it in the first place?"

He was right. While I enjoyed my visits with Mia and had accumulated otherwise unavailable data about Luis, Megan, and Milo, the risks to CYR headquarters outweighed my objectives. I shouldn't have brought the card into my home.

"I was careless. The Front could have loaded the card with something to compromise our systems."

"Did you check for any sign of a computer virus or compromising tech bot before I destroyed it?" Simon raised an eyebrow.

"No." Another thoughtless move on my part—I lowered my gaze to the floor. What if the beeping tone wasn't designed as a simple alarm? It might have transferred a virus into our computer systems. I'd need to initiate a full security scan of all programs. It might not stop a cyber threat, but at least I'd know if we were dealing with a perilous hack.

I hesitated, then said, "Now that you're here, I have a few questions."

"Really?" Simon sat in a chair with his back ramrod straight and hands gripping the arms. He reminded me of the Lincoln Memorial in the United States' former capital—the same statue the HCC airlifted to Panama City with all the symbolic monuments from the former American countries. "I came here to bail you out of an incredible jam, and now you want favors from me?"

"I haven't seen you for a month and have no idea how to contact you." I collapsed into a chair.

"Did you think of trying a simple, 'Simon, I'd like to talk with you. Are you available?'"

"And you would have appeared?"

"Well, why not? I'd never compare myself to your primitive ARP Luis, but he comes when you call on him. In more ways than one."

"Aren't you working with Briana or Jayla right now? You've more important work to do than answer my questions."

"That's what I like to hear." He cocked his head. "We barely know each other, and you've already found out how to get on my good side."

"Nice to know, but I wasn't trying to flatter you. I assumed your program would be fully occupied with the Memphis clan."

"What makes you think I can't be in both places?"

"Another mistake." I chuckled. "I thought you needed to be in one place at a time. Where else are you now?"

"That's none of your concern. But suffice it to say, I can be here, with Briana, and deep into a bio-med program all at the same time."

"Any chance you'd give me a peek at your program someday?"

"I knew it would be fun to venture beyond the Memphis family." Simon burst into a belly laugh. "Briana would have never asked such a question. You're quite a precocious young woman." He loosened the kerchief at his throat. "You're never going to see a single line of my code. But because I'm starting to enjoy your company, I'll answer at least one of your questions."

"I have two."

"Ask the most important one first in case I grow tired of talking with you today." He pulled a shiny silver disk from the front pocket of his jeans. It clicked open, and Simon peered into the device. "If you don't know, it's called a pocket watch, and it shows the time." He snapped the lid shut. "You're already late for work."

I checked my ocular implant. "I don't have any meetings scheduled. We have time. My first question is about finding more vaccine."

"What do you want from me?"

"I've stolen one vial of HAV vaccine from the lab. But I need more."

"You *are* a clever girl." Simon straightened. "I didn't catch you on the video feeds. When did you do that?"

My magic trick must have worked better than I thought. "A couple of days ago, I pocketed a vial and broke a fake one in the lab. Everyone believes I broke the real one."

"Ooh Darlin', you have a bit of larceny in your soul. I *do* like you. How do you plan to find a second one for Luis' booster shot?"

"That's my question for you. Do you know where they're stored or have an idea about how I can get a second vial without attracting attention?"

"That's a tough one. They're kept in a locked cooler in the medical facility. There's a strictly controlled inventory." Simon tapped a finger against the side of his face. "You wouldn't consider pulling the same stunt?"

I smirked. "You don't think a repeat performance might raise suspicion?"

"You're right." He sighed. "Are you taking any meds in similarly shaped vials?"

"Don't you have access to all my medical records?"

"Yes, but why make me go through the hoops when you can simply tell me what you're taking?"

Hmm. Simon's access wasn't omnipotent. "I'm not taking anything now, but I used a sports performance enhancer when I trained for the Olympics. Five years ago, it came in a bottle that might have been the same size and shape as the HAV vaccine." I gave him my best deferential expression. "What are you thinking?"

"The pharmacy stocks performance meds, and the HAV vaccine is also in production because of all the expected new pregnancies." Simon pointed a finger at me. "You need to request a regimen of sports performance-enhancing serum. It might take a few weeks, but I can manipulate the labeling process and have one of your prescriptions exchanged with a vial of HAV vaccine."

"I wish I'd known you could do this before I risked my sleight of hand trick in front of Briana and the obstetrics team."

"I can't let you in on all of my ploys." Simon picked at a piece of lint on his sleeve. "Briana doesn't even know the extent of my access."

"From now on, I'll ask before I try anything new." I thought about multiple medicine vials showing up at my studio. "If they start delivering sports performance enhancers, how will I know which vial contains the vaccine? I don't want to leave Luis with a bottle of muscle-building drugs. While he'd look great, TWS would take him down."

"No worries. I'll give the labeling something unique, like a different-sized font." He caressed his sidearm. "Better yet, you'll see a graphic bullet on the label's top left corner."

"Don't make it too eye-catching. We don't want to raise any alarms at the dispensary."

"I didn't say I'd color the bullet with crimson or neon. It'll be a tasteful little graphic—unmistakable but inconspicuous to anyone not looking for it."

"I have more questions—about restraints and reestablishing the time differentials."

"That's all I have time for." Simon huffed. "The others must wait."

With one problem solved, I considered my mounting list of tasks. "Wait. You've been accommodating. But how will I figure out the rest?"

"Once they start filling your sports-enhancing meds, you'll have plenty of time on the courts to think about solutions." Simon stood and adjusted his holster belt. The revolver hung within the retrieval range. "You'll need to figure out how to keep the vaccine's nanobots active after twelve hours."

In an instant, he was gone.

Wait. What nanobots?

I stared at the spot where he'd stood.

Would Simon remain my loyal comrade through the duration? The original Simon would have helped me save a man. Hopefully, ARP Simon had similar convictions. But would he grow bored of our little project?

If he was toying with me, Simon might reveal my plans to Briana or turn me into the HCC. He'd turned on me before—would he do it again?

Chapter 15

APRIL 18, 2241

In the morning's wee hours, I sat on the edge of Briana's bed, stroking her hand.

With a face emulating concern, Simon stood in the corner of Briana's studio. His antique physician attire, complete with a replica stethoscope and pocket full of tongue depressors, seemed overdone. But his presence calmed Briana.

I'd come as soon as she called, and he was already there. Maybe he'd been with her long before she summoned me.

"If your vitals or the spasms get worse, I'm notifying your doctors," Simon insisted.

"Don't you dare. It's my body and my call."

"It's been two hours, and you're not improving." He straightened. "This isn't from the burrito you ate at dinner."

Briana rubbed the comforter over her belly. "You'd be surprised. Oligosaccharides can produce a shocking amount of intestinal gas."

"Don't get fancy with me. You can pull dietary superiority over Sofia." He nodded at me. "But I know you're talking about refried pinto beans."

Without warning, Briana's face contorted, and she gripped my hand.

"I agree with Simon." I struggled to keep my voice calm. "Let's get you to the medical center." Briana could be stubborn, but we needed to know what was happening.

"In a minute. I need to visit the lav."

When she left, I turned to Simon. "Your access is faster than mine.

Order a hover chair for Briana."

"Already done." Simon nodded. "I've sent a notification to Jayla and Drs. Ural6 and Le7. We'll meet them in the obstetrics examination room. I'll transmit the latest vitals and other details to their workstations shortly."

I circled the room, pausing to kick a wall. The lav door opened. Briana's face was porcelain white.

She staggered to the bed and sat.

"I'm spotting. There's something wrong."

My stomach twisted.

"The transport chair is on its way, and the doctors will meet us." I tried to keep my tone even but knew Briana heard my concern. "Everything will be fine."

When Simon and I helped her out of her studio and into the chair, Briana groaned.

"We're losing Boy 3," Briana stuttered.

I directed the hovering seat down the hall, and Simon disappeared.

"We don't know anything yet." I squeezed Briana's arm while I kept pace with the chair. "My concern is you."

"And Adam," Briana choked, and tears filled her eyes. "Now they're all at risk of miscarriage."

"*You* are my priority. The boys, even Adam, come second."

Jayla stood outside the examination room with the portal door open. She ushered us in, where a nurse and Le7 helped Briana onto the table.

Simon could have replicated less specialized medical equipment in Briana's suite. But not all this. Even he would have limits.

Ural6 inserted video bots but kept the screens small with access exclusively for the medical team. Jayla muscled her way into the viewing area, and neither the doctors nor the nurses stopped her.

Jayla's expression signaled the dire situation. She, Ural6, and Le7 pointed and nodded at the screens.

"Give us an update." I gripped Briana's hand.

Ural6 held up a finger. "Please, allow another few minutes for the bots to give us more details about each fetus's vitals. We want to be certain they're stable and don't require attention."

"Okay, but I can see Briana's VSE readings. Her stress levels are rising. Information would go a long way to calm us both."

Briana nodded approval.

When the doctors ignored me, I persisted. "Not knowing anything is worse than whatever news you give us."

After a glance at the VSE screen, a nurse turned to Briana. "We can administer a sedative. Do you feel you need one?"

The young nurse lacked the poker face of the experienced staff. Something terrible had happened, and the experts would want the whole picture before telling us the news.

"Yes, give me something." Briana turned to me. "If I calm down, it'll help the babies."

I silently nodded.

"Give me half the dose as the last time." Briana's eyes never left mine as she directed the team. "I want to feel calm but not out of it."

The nurse set up the sedative inhalator and established a high oxygen field around Briana's head. Once Briana took a couple of deep breaths, she relaxed into the bed and succumbed to the medication.

The doctors mumbled, and I stayed glued to Briana.

Finally, Ural6 broke from the group and rounded the table to stand next to me.

The doctor cleared her throat. "You've known for a while that Boy 3's chances were slim. He's given up and won't be born with his brothers."

Briana's body shook, and I collapsed across the bed to hold her. She'd blame herself for what happened. But it wasn't her fault.

"What…what about the others?" Briana asked over my shoulder.

Please let them be okay. Briana's gone through so much already.

"The bots are telling us the other boys are normal," Ural6 said. "They're not in distress about the miscarriage."

"Will Boy 3 be born?" I asked. We would give him a proper service—even if he'd only been with us for six months.

"He won't be born." Ural6 placed a hand on my shoulder. "With the help from nanobots, Boy 3 will be absorbed by Briana's uterus and the other fetuses."

"He'll become part of them?" Briana would deliver five babies in four bodies. Each brother would be an individual and carry a part of Boy 3. His legacy would live on through them.

"We won't lose him." I gripped Briana's hand in both of mine. "Boy 3 will be with his brothers for all time."

Briana reached to touch my cheek. Her smile told me she could find a modicum of peace in realizing we hadn't lost him completely.

"But which baby is Adam?" Briana rose on an elbow. Despite the sedative, Briana's eyes grew wide with fear. "Will the HCC decide Boy 3 was Adam?"

"Can they do that?" I glared at Jayla. The HCC had promised one to each of the four presidents and one to us. "They wouldn't. Jayla, tell me they won't take away *our* boy."

"I can't tell you definitively." Jayla stood tall and smoothed her lab coat. "The HCC has been monitoring Boy 3's condition and has yet to decide who will accept the sacrifice of his lineage."

"If you don't know the status, tell us what we want to hear." I rushed to Jayla and grabbed both of her arms. "Tell us the decision process will be fair. Say Briana's sacrifices have priority."

Jayla shook off my grip. "Of course they'll keep those things in mind when they decide."

Briana collapsed onto the table as if someone had sucked all the air out of her. She rubbed her belly.

What could she be thinking? All the boys were hers—at least half hers.

"Adam did *not* die." Briana tilted her chin upward. "He's inside me and healthy. No one can tell me otherwise, and nobody is taking him away from me. Even if only one survives, he will be Adam."

Finally, Briana's assertive side had awakened. Together, we'd make sure the HCC didn't steal our baby.

After the doctors released Briana from the clinic, I took her home. The sedative left her lethargic. I helped her undress and tucked her into bed.

I leaned against the mattress and stroked her hair while Briana struggled to keep her eyes open.

"You don't have to stay with me," she slurred.

"You know I'd stay if you wanted me to." She seemed so vulnerable when she took sedatives. Was my passive aggressive wife back? "You know how much I move around when I sleep. Would I keep you awake?"

"I need rest." Briana rolled on her side to face away from me.

Nope. Briana knew what she wanted and asked for it.

"Please, meet me for breakfast." She turned to me with leaden eyes. "They're not taking Adam."

"I know. We traveled through time and space to bring Adam home. I'm as patriotic as the next person, but we're not giving up our son." I brushed her cheek with a kiss. "Possession is nine-tenths of the law."

"You got that right." She cat stretched. "And for now, the only one possessing Adam is me."

Briana's eyelids fluttered twice more before they shut. I stayed until her breath grew even.

Back in my studio, I requisitioned a Scotch on the rocks. When the food and beverage portal signaled its arrival, I grabbed the drink and downed a sizable gulp before slumping into a side chair. "Simon. I need to see you. Now!"

Despite his offer to come when summoned, I'd never called him. What was his preferred method of beckoning? Apparently, my insistent plea wouldn't work. I tried a different approach. "Simon. Would you pretty please come to talk with me?" Again, no response.

What might tempt him to appear if firmness and sarcasm didn't work?

"Simon, it's about Briana. I'm worried about her. Please, talk with me. I'm at a loss on how to help her."

He materialized in an instant, two feet shorter than the last time. Simon wore a monk's robe and sandals.

"I'm grateful to see you, but why do you always wear different outfits?"

"Briana has been asking me that for years. Why would I tell you?" Simon straightened his robe with a tug.

I shrugged. "Because you'd love for me to tell Briana I heard your explanation first?"

"That scenario does have appeal." A mischievous grin spread across Simon's face. "Okay. Here's my rationale. You gals are nice to look at, but you all look the same. You wear comfortable clothes in the latest colors. I don't want to modify women's current styles to fit a man's physique. That would be boring. I like to wear what makes me feel unique and manly. I honor men's dress from the past because, for the time being, there are no recent men's fashions."

"But that'll change soon." I wanted to give him hope.

"I like the way you think. But Briana's boys and those who follow in their footsteps will wear whatever their mothers inflict upon them for more than a dozen years. Plus, with all those type-A mothers, the boys' careers will be mapped out long before they exit the womb. Do you think any of them will have professions besides doctors, engineers, or civil servants? I'd bet my right nut, there won't be a male fashion designer for decades."

"I have to admit you're probably right." I laughed. "Maybe you can influence Adam's career choice."

"My dear, you'd probably be happy to have Adam chart his path in life, but what makes you believe Jayla or Briana would let it happen?"

"You've got me there." I drew a breath. "Adam is what I wanted to speak with you about."

"I witnessed everything that happened in the clinic with Boy 3." Simon nodded. "I'm sorry for your loss."

"Briana is the one who needs your sympathy. She's beside herself about the miscarriage and how this could affect the babies' distribution." I took a sip of my drink. "You can access the CYR systems and probably the HCC's programming. Do you have any idea what might happen?"

Simon crossed to the opposite chair and sat. He pulled up his frock to cross his legs, and I winced at the sight of too much AI manhood.

"What?" He leaned over to look up his robe. "Too much showing? You don't mind when Luis traipses around in the buff."

"You're not my lover. Please keep your gown over your knees or cross your legs. I don't want to see your business down there."

"If I did that to Briana, she'd force herself to stare at my eyes and neck." Simon smiled. "She'd never tell me what to do."

"We're very different."

"I'm learning that."

"Good." I tipped my glass at him. "Tell me what you know about the HCC's position on the boys."

"I can tell you they've not made any decisions."

"The HCC is nothing if not thorough. They must have a contingency plan. They'd have anticipated every possibility and created a priority list.

Like if one didn't live, then a specific country would wait until the next jump. And if two died, then two predetermined countries would wait. And so on."

"Such a plan exists." Simon shifted in his chair. "But now there's pushback from some countries. Particularly from the country who will go without until the June jump."

"Tell me." Would the truth fuel my anger? I stood to retrieve another drink.

"First, the carrier always had the right to a baby."

"So if all died except one, Briana and I should be able to keep him?" I breathed a sigh of relief.

"That's correct. Since doctors from Asia and EuroRosse are next to time travel, their countries would each have access to two boys from June's jump. In the case of any deaths from Briana's brood, one of those two countries was supposed to wait."

"That makes sense. If Le7 and Torne7 are successful, Asia and EuroRosse would both have access to two males." I took a sip. "How would they decide between them? A coin toss?"

"There were no details in the agreement. They'd work it out." Simon cleared his throat. "However, my sources indicate Asia and EuroRosse are arguing about who should give up their son. They contend America should accept Boy 3's death because Adam will live in America. Ostensibly in Panama City with President Ottawa7."

"That's not what everyone originally agreed to. What country would accept a loss if both the Asia and EuroRosse's babies died?"

"The next in line to wait was the president of America. The remaining two babies would go to Gulf-Africa and, of course, to Briana. The rationale behind the decision is because Briana's boy would already be here and able to provide sperm in about a dozen years."

"But not all American babies will come from Adam, right?" I didn't know anything about the distribution protocols, but limiting a country's gene pool to one donor seemed wrong.

Simon glared at me over the top of his wire-rimmed glasses. "Of course not. Once we have a group of males in each country, the HCC will carefully distribute and track how we use their sperm. The HCC wouldn't want to create a bunch of originals simply to run into recessive disease issues."

My heart raced—politics might dismantle the original agreement and our rights to keep Adam. "What's the current status of Asia and EuroRosse's claims?"

"When America's President Ottawa7 issued public empathy in the press, some pundits suggested America might defer to the other countries about distribution." Simon smoothed fabric over his thighs. His pause raised alarms. Finally, he spoke. "Ottawa7 has made comments about the American boy having stronger prospects if allowed to be raised in the presidential household."

"What an arrogant bitch!" I jumped to my feet. "What's wrong with our household?"

"Says the woman who's infatuated with an ARP and barely finds time to engage with Latrice?"

"I adore our daughter and probably spend more time with her than President Ottawa7 does with her children."

"You're correct." Simon tilted his head, a sure sign he was calculating. "On average, you spend 26.276 hours per week with Latrice, and Ottawa7 merely spends 7.718 hours per week with her Ottawa8s. But while that's true, you and Briana don't have the political clout to influence this decision." I expected his face to lack empathy, but Simon's compassionate stare told me otherwise. "There may be sufficient pressure to keep the arrangement's original terms. In the meantime, we both need to do everything in our power to keep Briana calm. Maintaining her health and happiness will reduce her risk of losing another baby."

"Do you think her stress influenced the loss of Boy 3?" I dropped into the chair, hoping I hadn't contributed to her anxiety.

"Absolutely not." Simon shook his head. "I've gone over her medical records in detail. His faulty umbilical cord caused the problem. We tried to strengthen it, but nothing in our toolkit could save him. Nature has a way of resolving problems on its own. He may have developed other defects later in Briana's pregnancy. Whatever caused his miscarriage was likely due to his health and for the benefit of the other babies."

I took a long swallow of Scotch, letting the smoky flavor burn the back of my throat. "When I did research at Mia's place, I ran across a term that stunned me—unwanted pregnancy."

I stared at Simon to gauge his reaction.

"I don't have those words listed adjacently anywhere in my records." Simon cocked his head. "What do you suppose it means?"

"I suspect when a woman was at risk of becoming pregnant every time she had sex, there may have been times when she'd be surprised."

"Women didn't conceive every time they copulated. They only had one fertile week in a month, and even those who had sex in that week didn't have 100 percent success rates."

"Natural fertilization must have been rife with surprises and disappointments. At least with cloning, the HCC can be sure each parent is financially and mentally capable."

Simon stroked his chin. "Seems to me that 21st-century women had the freedom to make those decisions on their own."

He had a point. But how should leaders balance personal liberty against society's greater good?

"You mentioned other questions. Is there anything you want to discuss with me before I leave and you conjure up Luis?"

I tsked at Simon. "Don't be surprised if you check my computer logs in the morning and find out Luis had the evening off."

"You know I'll check, but I don't care either way." He sniffed.

Tracking my activities should have annoyed me, but I trusted Simon's discretion. He wanted to save the Pierce men as much as I did—maybe more.

I switched our conversation toward the mission. "You probably know I've ordered the sports enhancement meds. So that plan is underway."

"Yes. I saw the order come in, and you should have the bullet dosage next week."

"I have a question about the sleep meds for Luis and Megan."

"Why do you want to involve me? Tell Briana you've had trouble sleeping, and she'll prescribe something."

"I thought about it, but meds aren't my strong suit. I need a drug strong enough to put Megan out but to allow Luis to remain in a semi-conscious state."

"For your love-fest?" Simon gave the final words extra syllables.

I rolled my eyes. "I might need to speak with Luis. Knowing which type of drug works best and what dosages for Megan and Luis would be nice. I don't plan to stay longer than I need to, and getting the amounts right will be important."

"I didn't imagine I'd become your full-time drug dealer as well as arrange for a man to fulfill your sexual needs." Simon sighed. "I'll have to research pimp attire for our next visit."

"You said you'd help me." I shrugged. "It'd be easier than asking Briana."

"Ah, my dear, you're correct. I'll do research and send you a message with the name and dosage. On second thought, I'll tell Briana that your medical records show you've been sleep deprived and suggest she order it for you."

"Why?"

"My alternative process would eliminate a record of my message to you and any need for you to contact Briana."

"Perfect." I mentally scratched another item from my list.

Simon started to fade.

"Wait. Tell me about the problem with the vaccine's nanobots."

"I wondered how long it would take you to uncover that hurdle." He sharpened into view. "You have no skills to handle that matter. Unless I intervene, your plan will fail. More about the bots later."

Simon's image disappeared, leaving me with a dozen unanswered questions.

I toyed with the idea of spending a few hours with Luis. But I wasn't in the mood for sex. A sound night's sleep seemed elusive. Since I'd spent more time talking with Luis, his machine learning had modified his routines to include in-depth verbal interactions. Maybe talking with him would take my mind off our loss.

"Computer, initiate ARP Luis Pierce."

"Please provide atmosphere, duration, and intensity settings."

My shoulders deflated, and I wished he was a lover who might drop by when asked instead of needing parameters and specifications. "Keep my bedroom unchanged, provide duration flexibility, and set intensity to low—somewhere between cuddling and passionate attraction."

"Your program should begin shortly. Any mid-program changes will be adopted immediately upon command to the ARP."

Luis appeared, seated on the corner of my bed. His revised, self-assured smile still caught me unaware, and a flutter crossed my chest.

His sensors picked up my distress over Briana's babies. He rose from the bed to embrace me and stroked the hair at the back of my neck. "Sofia, tell me what's troubling you."

"Briana lost one of the fetuses." I choked over the last word.

Luis held me tighter, and I collapsed into him.

I'd lost sight that Briana's infants *were* fetuses—not fully formed children. When cloned eggs sat in an artificial uterus in the cloning center, I never thought of them as children—not until they were large enough to bring home. Maybe these were different because they were inside Briana, and eventually they'd grow into boys and men. They were babies to me.

"It's okay to cry." Luis rubbed my back. "I understand how it must feel to lose a child."

His words struck home.

"Why did you say that?"

Luis pulled back and tipped my chin with a finger. "I've lost my son, too. When someone takes a child from our lives, we experience a vast emptiness that can never be fully refilled."

Empathy glimmered in his eyes. Had I included these characteristics in his programming, or were they part of his learning features?

I'd seen emotion from Simon's AI. Why did similar qualities from Luis surprise me? I pushed away thoughts about machine learning and returned to Briana's miscarriage. "It's not only that Briana lost one of the five babies she was carrying. The HCC may not let us keep one of the four who survived."

Luis nodded as if listening without judgment, and I continued. "Briana will be devastated if she carries them to term and can't raise one."

"But they're her children. Why would the HCC force her to give them away?"

"It's complicated."

Luis pulled me to the bed and urged me to sit beside him. "It's not complicated. These are your children. If you agree to give any of them away, the adoptive parents should be grateful for your gift."

His words rang true. "You already know about Megan taking Milo from you. What would you have done if someone tried to take away your daughter?"

"I would trade my life to keep my children safe." Luis jutted his chin. "There's no greater responsibility than protecting our young. Families must fight for each other."

My ARP Luis wasn't merely talking about keeping children physically safe. Parents had a responsibility to keep their families whole, too. How could the HCC decide to operate outside of its initial distribution agreement? The original order of priority seemed appropriate for all parties and respected our family unit.

Maybe the HCC needed to hear from a constituent. "Computer, end ARP Luis Pierce program and create a Holo-tablet."

Luis vanished, and the tablet appeared in my hands.

Should I craft a missive to the entire HCC Board, the four presidents, or solely to President Ottawa7? Maybe I should start small and stay domestic. I could work my way up if Ottawa7 didn't give me the response I wanted.

My mind raced about how to save my family.

If I lost the battle with the HCC, I could contact the media and have them rally for our side. Public opinion might pressure leadership if they recanted their agreements.

Chapter 16

MAY 2, 2241

Midmorning in my office, Lisa handed me a shipping box. The machine-read symbols were indecipherable, but the bright yellow polyethylene container said it came from a high-tech manufacturer in EuroRosse.

"Thanks for bringing me the package. It must be the extra sets of restraints." I pressed my thumbprint against the address label, and the container lid flipped open.

Inside, wrapped in clear packaging, lay straps made of fabric fibers and a new compound proven to be both stretchable and tear-proof. I pulled them from the box and laid them on my desk. My fingers itched to grab one and stow it inside my drawer for safekeeping. I wanted to modify a set in case I decided to bring someone back.

The CYR's next official jump would arrive in the landmass formerly known as Europe in June 2027. The limited time between their jump and mine didn't allow for significant program adjustments. To minimize input errors and the time needed for reprogramming, I would tweak the time differential by a few hours for my trip. The CYR team would leave EuroRosse in the early morning, and I'd arrive in Denver at midnight.

By the time I got to Denver, about eight months would have passed since Briana and I visited in 2026. What if Luis had gained or lost a bunch of weight since I last saw him? I could only guess his exact height and weight. I'd already created a program and a device to dismantle the restraints' seams and hardware, but adding and subtracting fabric to accommodate a size range would be complicated.

Lisa picked up one of the sealed bags. She turned it over and inspected it from all angles. "The others were gray."

"I can't imagine the color will make any difference." I fought the urge to snatch back the package. "Do you?"

"I suspect the materials, weave, and finish are more important than colors. Light makes certain shades degrade faster than others. But the capsule's interior is never exposed to daylight." Lisa scanned my face. "The company assured me the restraints are identical to the ones currently inside the capsule."

"Take one set and run it through all the stressors in the simulator."

"We can run the tests in half the time if we use both sets." Lisa grabbed the second package and placed it on top of the first.

Lisa could stroll out with my prize.

"I'd like you to test one set at a time." I focused on keeping my tone level and cordial. I didn't want her to detect the slightest note of anxiety. "If it fails, we can decide whether to repeat the sequences on the second."

Lisa stared at the packages as if thinking through what I said. She separated them but kept one in each hand.

I willed her to give one back, but she didn't respond to my mental message. "Want me to put the spare in the supply closet?" Lisa asked.

This matter wasn't up for debate.

"No." I extended my palm. "I'll keep the second set right here in my desk. That'll reduce the chance of us mixing them up and running simulations on the spare."

She shook her head ever so slightly. "Don't you trust us to keep track of them?"

"Of course I do, but I'm not sure why you don't want to leave one with me."

"We never keep supplies in your office."

"I may decide to run chemical tests on the fabric." I circled my desk and stood next to her at the doorway. "There are dozens of fluids in the capsule that could compromise the restraints. Once I identify any that could leak and what compounds they might form if several leaks occurred at the same time, I can decide whether tests are appropriate. In the meantime, I'd like these restraints to remain pristine and in the original packaging."

I gently pulled the package out of her hand and stepped to my desk.

"Leaks?" While Lisa had let go of one set, the discussion wasn't over.

"With our preparation for two jumps, we can't be too careful. Right?"

Finally, Lisa left to walk down the hall, shaking her head.

Heart racing, I stuffed the restraints into a satchel and slipped them under my desk. I'd take them to my studio during my lunch break. The time alone would give me a chance to summon Simon.

At noon, Simon appeared in my studio when I called him. Perhaps he was anxious to help me succeed. Or as likely, Simon wanted to taunt me when I asked questions he deemed irrelevant or trivial.

I stood before him while he relaxed in an armchair. "I need you to stop my sleeping drug prescription once they send me two more bottles. At that point, I'll have enough for the doses you suggested for Luis and his wife." I held the stash of vials in my outstretched hands to show him.

Simon glanced from my cupped hands to my face. He wore a cocky grin and a late twentieth-century businessman's outfit, complete with a three-piece suit and a silk necktie. Had Luis ever worn one, or were they reserved for the elite? Once Simon left, I'd check out styles online and create one for my ARP.

"Briana prescribed them." Simon interrupted my rambling thoughts. "Why don't you ask her to stop?"

Since Simon told Briana to initiate the prescription, I figured he'd be the one to get her to stop. But he was right. I could tell Briana I was sleeping more soundly and needed no further medication.

He cocked his head. "Still no guilt about bedding Luis with Megan dreaming beside you?"

"How many times do I need to tell you? I'm not going to have sex with him."

Unless we can't help ourselves.

I dropped the vials onto the bed and sat in a chair opposite him.

"While you might be cold-hearted, I suspect there's something about Megan you're not telling me." Simon moved his elbows to the armrests and placed his chin on his steepled fingers. He'd settled in and wouldn't leave anytime soon.

What could it hurt to let him in on Megan's sordid past? "According to trial records filed in 2041, Megan Pierce was arrested and charged for her role in her son's death."

"She killed him?" Simon straightened.

"They convicted her." I nodded. "Authorities sentenced Megan to a work prison. She died two years later."

"How could she kill her own boy?" Simon gripped the chair's arms.

"The records alluded to her mental instability."

Simon stood and walked to the wall. He snapped his fingers and produced a fireplace with a roaring log set. After leaning an elbow against the mantle, he stared into the fire.

After a long silence, I gave him my version of what had happened. "The timing made me think they divorced *because* Milo disappeared. Maybe they couldn't handle the pressure of dealing with a missing child. I read other cases from that era. It seems like kidnapping your child to keep them from your spouse wasn't uncommon."

"This behavior is unfathomable." He turned and raised a brow. "But you've done the research. Give me your assessment of why."

"There were a few reasons, but I mostly saw two different situations. Back then, courts had a bias toward giving post-divorce custody to women. Sometimes when men didn't get the visitation rights they wanted, they nabbed their children to protest the court's decision. In other cases, the courts gave both parents visitation rights, and women kidnapped their children to keep them from an abusive husband."

"You believe Megan abducted her son to separate Luis and the boy?"

"It's possible, but I didn't see any records citing Luis abused Megan or his children. They had two offspring, a toddler boy and a slightly older girl."

When Simon returned to his chair, he snapped his fingers. The fireplace disappeared, and my Olympics-themed artwork returned. "If Megan wasn't trying to separate the children from Luis, why would she be involved with her son's abduction?"

"I don't know. They never found the boy living with another family or produced a body. The case focused on her mental instability. She was a protest activist when men took over the world in 2040. Some men testified that she hated all men."

"Did Luis testify against her?"

"Not that I could find. I assume he was loyal to Megan despite the evidence."

"Too bad Megan didn't live long enough to be cloned." Simon huffed. "She'd have been a perfect candidate for the Front."

"Without any record of abuse from Luis, I believe what they said about Megan's mental condition. I'm hoping she simply hid her son from Luis and didn't hurt the boy. But mentally ill people kill their children now, too."

"Those cases are highly publicized but rare." Simon stroked his chin. "HCC records indicate three children were killed by their mothers last year in America. In 2026, government officials recorded 486 of these types of deaths—and that was solely in the part of the Americas called the United States, which represented 32.485 percent of the American population. However, I'm uncertain whether current filicide rates are low because our cloning process avoids postpartum depression or because we don't clone women who aren't mentally capable of raising children."

"Megan Pierce wouldn't have had postpartum depression. Her son was over a year old when I saw him. Also, there were no records about her abusing him."

Simon puffed out his cheeks, then slowly released the air. "What have you pieced together from your research that makes sense?"

"I'm going to assume Megan and Luis weren't getting along."

"Based on the amorous part of your mission, that's a handy assumption."

I glared at him. "Because Megan had control issues or wanted to hurt Luis, I believe she vindictively kidnapped their son to keep the boy away from Luis."

"Consider this scenario—she might have killed him and hidden the body."

"I'm not going there." I couldn't imagine Megan taking the life of the precious boy I'd trundled off to his racecar bed. "I've thought about bringing enough HAV vaccine to inoculate Luis and his son. Once TWS runs its course, the only men alive will be you, the other eleven immune babies, Luis, and Milo."

"I hope you're joking." Simon cocked his head. "Tell me they didn't name their son after a grain product."

"The name may have had other roots. I've never looked it up."

"It's like naming a child Wheat or Corn." Simon rolled his eyes.

"I'm not an expert at boys' names from nearly two hundred years ago. Can we get back to Megan?"

"I think you should give her an overdose of sleeping serum while you're there."

"What?" My jaw dropped. Murder Luis' wife?

"I like your idea about having Luis and Milo live through the TWS onslaught, but what if your rosy picture of Megan isn't true? Maybe she didn't kidnap the boy. Perhaps she *did* kill him? Giving Milo the vaccine in June 2027 won't prevent her from causing his death long before TWS would take him."

Simon was right, but I wasn't prepared to consider a preemptive strike against Milo's mother. My time jump was about seeing a real man up close again and saving one or two men from a horrible death. A side benefit would be to give Simon a living male to mentor him. Murder was never in my plans.

As Simon rubbed his chin, he glared at me.

"I'm *not* going to hurt Megan Pierce." I stood and moved in front of his chair with balled fists on my hips. "First and most importantly, I'm not a killer. Second, I could affect the timeline. Keeping Luis and Milo alive won't change anything before TWS because they won't know they're immune. After TWS, their sole influence will be to mentor you and your eleven little buddies on acting manly." I took a breath. "On second thought, the Tobar Principle makes our tinkering irrelevant. Let's stick with I am *not* a murderer."

"I'm surprised. You're a Tobar follower?"

"The math is sound."

"It's a convenient way to deflect responsibility for changing the past. We assume away intentional changes. Setting aside arguments about the timeline, I'm shocked you would refuse to keep Megan Pierce from killing her son." His brows narrowed. "Could you save two men from dying in 2060?"

"That's the whole point behind my plan."

"How will you get them to take the booster?"

"Still working on that." According to the files I'd seen about Luis in Mia's data, he hadn't changed his residence between 2027 and when he died thirty years later. "I could hide the booster in his yard and leave instructions about when to take it. If he heeds my advice, the booster vaccine will save him. If not, he may die. But the initial dose might give him enough immunity to fight off TWS anyway."

"What if Megan kills Milo or hides him? There would be no way for Luis to give him the booster."

Wanting to pace, I forced myself to remain still and consider alternatives. "I'll think more about this in the coming months, and maybe I'll come up with a better idea. But I'm not going to harm Megan. So forget about it."

"We can continue this conversation later." Simon stood and straightened his vest.

"There's no need. I'm not doing it."

He glanced at the bed where the sleeping aid vials lay. A slow smile tracked across his face. "I have projects to work on for Jayla this afternoon. That will take most of my available programming. But I'll see you later when you join Briana for her examination. Was there anything else you needed from me?"

I gave him a dismissive wave.

When he evaporated, I crossed the room to gather the vials and stow them in a dresser drawer—under some of my favorite fitness shirts and beside the restraints.

Simon had dropped the idea of taking Megan out of the picture. Maybe too quickly. Was he thinking of manipulating circumstances so Megan would leave Luis with the children? Or Simon might want me to give her something to make her too ill and frail to plot against Luis and hide Milo. Irrespective of how I felt about Luis, I wouldn't conspire to harm Megan Pierce.

What had Simon thought when he glanced at the vials?

Chapter 17

MAY 17, 2241

Lisa and I peered into four virtual computer screens projected in the corner of my office. We simulated the capsule's anticipated trajectory through abstract space. She scrutinized coding decisions and theoretical experiment results. And I evaluated mathematical support for our time travel systems.

The ship's June journey would land in what was in 2027 called Kyiv, Ukraine—a city that in 2241 housed the capital of EuroRosse. Drs. Le7 and Torne7 would trust the engineers to deliver them safely to the past and back.

While our sperm donor for the Denver jump lived in a typical suburban home with a sizable yard, Vladimir Almo lived in a rowhome on a crowded street near the city center. If the HCC had asked the engineers for input during the sperm donor selection process, they would have found one who lived in the countryside. A rural setting gave us a more comprehensive error margin for the landing.

"I understand they had a business called sperm banks back then." Lisa interrupted my visual evaluation of aerial land records from 2027. "Can you imagine men stopping in to make deposits?"

Had Luis ever contributed?

"Too bad we couldn't have arranged a heist." Lisa continued with a giggle.

"The HCC considered retrieving stored sperm instead of fresh. But all the donation sites had twenty-four-hour surveillance and cryogenically preserved samples. The CYR staff believed a live donor minimized detection risk. At a sperm bank, we'd need additional time to thaw the specimens."

I turned to the satellite photo of terrain in 21st century EuroRosse. Our team had selected the least bad arrival landing spot—a small park a block away from Almo's home. According to old feeds, the park was filled with children's play equipment and trees the locals annually decorated with thousands of painted Easter egg ornaments. Our projected arrival time was two in the morning. Lisa and I had yet to work out every challenge related to humidity levels, the longer daylight hours, and the denser population near the capsule's predicted landing site.

To protect the capsule from unexpected pedestrians and nighttime visitors to the park, the June team would take an ARP program to camouflage the time machine while stealing seed from Vladimir Almo. More equipment meant more weight and a higher chance of mechanical failure. Lisa and I bantered about *what-ifs* and *why-nots*.

"The average humidity differential is greater than twenty percentage points, and that's if it's not raining when the capsule arrives in Kyiv. The shell must be fully cohesive when it materializes, or moisture will freeze and possibly split the coating." Lisa had stated the obvious, and I knew how to respond to her concerns.

I was about to point to simulation results about the shell's resilience to phase drag when the screens went blank. "What just happened?" I gave a thought directive and blinked to reactivate the screens.

"Has the interface disappeared for you, too?" Lisa tapped her temple, but she had to know the inserts wouldn't respond to that stimulus. Only thought directives and blinking reconnected the links.

I opened and closed my eyes, wishing for results that never came. Finally, I rushed to my desk and pulled out an old-fashioned physical computer. After connecting the tablet to a power source, I tapped in codes to resuscitate the device.

My fingers flew over the keys to activate the interface. I connected to the system, but huge pieces of data had disappeared. I pounded a fist against the desk. "I should have access to everything. But our entire project is missing."

"Everything?" Lisa lifted a single eyebrow and cocked her head. "How can that be? Are you sure it's not simply the interface? Maybe something compromised your access, and a security protocol kicked you out." She grabbed the tablet. "I'll log you out and try under my username."

I held my breath as she clicked and clacked.

Lisa tapped the enter key a dozen times before withdrawing her hands and biting her lip. "I'm not finding our files by using my access codes either. Where are they?"

"They can't disappear on their own. We're talking about hundreds of programs and millions of data files."

"Now I can't connect to anything with my ocular insert—not even the CYR communication system." Lisa continued tapping her temple. "Are you able to call Data Security?"

I checked—nothing.

Lisa rushed to the open portal door. "I'll tell security and have them come run a diagnostic."

Once she'd gone, I tried again—first on my implant and then on the tablet.

"No, no, no!" I searched through backdoors and workarounds for the programs and database. My heart pounded. Each pathway I chased disappeared before I could find our stored information.

Within minutes, Lisa returned with three IT security techs. They rolled a suitcase of equipment into my office and immediately began unloading physical computers, screens, and connecting cords as thick as my finger. I'd never seen such a mass of physical hardware.

A tech in a lime green jumpsuit looked over her shoulder. "Based on Lisa Chicago6's description and the details from our security alert site, this may take a while."

I shoved my keyboard away in frustration. "What's happening? I can't find the time travel engineering systems. All the data are missing, and simulation results are gone."

"The system is compromised." The tech winced and continued. "Someone has hacked us. I can't tell if they took the data, deleted it, or encrypted it so we can't see it. Give us a couple of hours, and I'll be able to tell you more."

"Hours?" I balled my fists at my side. "We need access to get our work done. This project has a rigorous timetable and milestones. The next time jump is in twenty-five days. The HCC is relying on us."

I should have cut her some slack, but my frantic response poured out before I could stop myself. Lisa laid a hand on my arm.

The tech nodded. "Getting you up and running and finding your data is our highest priority. You might consider spending the next few hours away from your office. There's nothing you can do to help."

She was right. If I stayed, I'd get in their way and pressure them to work faster. I needed a break. "You'll send a message to me as soon as you recover everything or know how long it'll take?"

"Yes." She bent to help the others connect their equipment.

I turned to Lisa. "I'll meet you at the courts in about a half-hour—after I get my gear."

I arrived at my studio, pausing in the entrance to catch my breath.

"Simon!"

No response.

"I don't have time for your games." My teeth ground so hard I heard them squeak. "Something terrible happened in engineering, and I need to speak with you."

Simon materialized in medical scrubs, with a surgical cap over his hair and an antique stethoscope dangling from his neck.

"The programs and data from the engineering systems are missing." My voice came out fast and made me sound desperate because I was. "I tried to retrieve yesterday's backups but couldn't find them either. Can you help us?"

"You should have seen it coming." Simon leaned a hip against the wall and picked at a fingernail.

"Seen what coming? What's happened?" My breath caught in my throat. Did Simon have something to do with this catastrophe? Decades of test data, simulations, and the time travel jump programs were gone.

"Mia's little time bomb."

What did he mean? Mia couldn't have entered the CYR facility.

It hit me—she didn't need to come inside. She needed access to the building, and I'd brought in her card.

"If you're talking about her com-card, you destroyed it two months ago." I pictured Simon incinerating the card and reconstituting a fake one for me to give to the security team.

"You hadn't considered it might have held a delayed reaction virus? You brought a foreign object into CYR headquarters, and it never crossed your mind?"

"No. I ran system checks the day we destroyed the card. Everything seemed fine." I collapsed into a chair. Recent research spoke of audio delivery for malicious programs. Still, I never assumed Mia or the Front would have access to such sophisticated malware or that they could implant it into an ordinary com-card. Had I caused this debacle?

"Tell me again in a full sentence." Simon stood in front of my chair and shrunk until he faced me at eye level. He gripped my chin in his hand. "Did you know you brought a computer virus into the lab to attack the time travel programs?"

He stared into my eyes, waiting for my response. I understood what he wanted. His lie detector program would look for micro-expressions consistent with lying.

"I had no idea Mia intended to give me a virus to attack the computer in our lab." I gave him what he needed—the truth.

"I believe you." He pushed my chin aside. "But you're incredibly stupid."

"I'm not looking for excuses, but you knew about the card for months before the alarm went off. Why didn't you warn me about a possible timed attack?"

"Just because I'm brilliant doesn't mean I think of everything." Simon smirked.

"Then why are you assuming I should have thought of it?"

"For someone not making up excuses, you seem to be casting a net of blame."

He was right. This was no time to alienate my most significant resource and ally. "What can I do to fix this?"

"You've already checked the backups, and they're gone as well?"

I nodded.

"Well it's a good thing I have isolated backups."

If he wasn't lying, we were saved. "Tell me you're not joking."

Simon grew to his normal height and brought back his favorite fireplace and hearth. Without a warning or hesitation, his attire changed from the Hippocratic oath-wielding medical doctor into an Einsteinesque man with unruly hair, a knee-length lab coat, and reading glasses with nearly transparent rims.

"I assume you're telling me how smart you are." I glared at him.

"And don't you forget it." Simon gave me a single emphatic nod.

"Tell me how to access your backups. I'd be forever in your debt."

"I'll do better than that." Simon tapped his chin. "I'd reinstate the data and let you take credit for having an offsite duplicate backup. Your team would merely reconstruct anything you've done in the past two days."

"Two days? We don't have the time. Our June 11th deadline is less than a month from now."

Simon glared at me over the top of his superfluous glasses. "Do you plan to spend time complaining about two days when you should be rallying your team to review notes from their most recent work?"

"I'm sorry. I'm taking out my frustration on you." I drew a breath. Angering Simon wouldn't serve me well. "Thank you for saving our timeline. Without your help, this would have set us back months."

"And you wouldn't be able to keep your date with Luis."

Luis Pierce hadn't entered my mind during this near crisis. Perhaps he wasn't as important to me as the success of Mission Y. "That's a side benefit, but my concerns are with the program and not my illicit trip."

"Well, I haven't lost sight of your tryst. You need to make your move while Briana's occupied with the newborns. If the next jump slips a few months, both Briana and Jayla would be in the control room, and your escape to 2027 won't be as simple."

"Besides keeping the sperm collection jump on track, I owe you thanks for saving the covert part." I let the compliment sink in, then added, "I'd like to start working on reconstructing the engineering systems. When will you give me access to your backup? Or will you reinstate our files without sharing access?"

"I'll reconstruct your data and programs." Simon picked at a nail. "But I want you to do something for me."

What could he possibly want that he couldn't get on his own? Did he need me to plead his case to Briana about something? Maybe I could enhance his program with greater proximity flexibility if he wanted to leave the Merlin Building. "I'm happy to help. You're keeping my plans a secret, and you've helped me get the vaccines and the sleep meds."

"I have." He stood straighter and admired the back of his hand.

"You've saved us months of frustration to rebuild the engineering systems." Was I laying it on too thick? "Name anything, and I'll do it."

Simon braced his hands on his hips, full of authority. "I've decided the original Simon Merlin should grow up under the mentorship of adult men and not simply with women."

"I plan to inoculate both Luis and Milo with the HAV vaccine." He didn't seem to be asking for anything new.

"I've already assumed you'll give them the vaccine, and I'm working on a fix for the nanobots."

That again. Should I ask Simon for more information or assume he'd address the problem?

He continued. "I want to make sure both father and son have every opportunity to live past my birthday in 2060."

"You're going to help me with the nanobots and coerce Luis and Milo to take the booster in five years?"

"Maybe, but more importantly, I want you to kill Megan Pierce to ensure she can't kill her son."

I slumped back into the chair, unable to respond. Surely the original Simon Merlin had programmed his AI not to harm humans. But maybe he wasn't prohibited from having others kill for him.

Chapter 18

MAY 22, 2241

Briana waddled off the examination table with my help, a feat more challenging each week. Ural6 worked the control panel, and Jayla and Le7 spoke in low tones at the table's end.

When Le7 approached us, I cleared my throat, readying myself to gain more intel. I asked, "Our medical care has improved since HAV started, but if they had the vaccine in 2060, would it have stopped TWS from killing everyone?"

"No." Le7 and Briana answered simultaneously. But Le7 continued alone. "It's all about the nanobots."

"I understand they're in the vaccine, and they compensate for mutation." Desperate for information, I struggled to keep my voice even. "But why wouldn't they work back then?"

"Labs had bots, but not the energy sources we have now." Le7 moved her Holo-tablet behind her back and rested a hand on her hip. "The bots aren't long-lived and need to recharge by connecting to a power source. They didn't have that capability in 2060."

My face must have reflected my despair because Briana leaped into the conversation. "Don't worry. We've been charging bots like this for over a hundred years. The technology is stable and common."

"How did the bots keep any residual virus we were carrying from mutating when we were in 2026?"

"Simple. They maintain a charge for twenty-four hours, and we were only there for one."

Keeping bots charged for the Pierce men's lifetimes presented yet another challenge for my growing pile. Simon had recovered our missing data. But charging nanobots left in 2027 could be beyond his capabilities.

I leaned forward until my nose nearly touched bubbles floating on my bathwater. Sandalwood—my favorite scent for this program. I gripped the soaking tub's sides while Luis scrubbed my back with a coarse sponge. The circular motions eased the tension in my shoulders. I gave in to the water's warmth and the steam-filled spa, with dripping rock walls and soft relaxing music.

Sitting between Luis' legs and facing the waterfall, the sponge squished as he squeezed it against my spine. "Luis, you're the best. I needed this bath more than you'll ever know."

His legs tightened around my thighs. "I know the project needs you, but you've been away too much," he whispered in his husky, soon-we're-going-to-have-sex voice. "Your body longs for more sleep and time to relax."

"I'm not sure you're helping me get more sleep."

He laughed. "Maybe fewer hours, but I believe you sleep more soundly on nights we're together."

"I probably concentrate better after a night with you, too. We've nearly reconstructed all the simulations and data capture from when the Front's virus attacked the CYR computer system. It'll take another week before I'm satisfied the launch will go without a hitch."

"Everything will work out fine." Luis wrapped his arms around my waist and pulled me close. He rubbed his stubbly chin against my neck. When he kissed behind my ear, tremors surged through my body.

Argh.

What did I want most—immediate satisfaction or information only an AI might give me?

"Wait." I exhaled forcefully. "Before we get started, I want to talk with you."

Luis' romance drive immediately dialed back. He picked up the sponge to resume dousing me with water. With each minute we spent together, he knew how to react to my cues. Would the real Luis be as amenable as ARP

Luis?

"I don't know if I should trust Briana's mentor." Luis' program understood who I meant. Luis' response settings knew Briana's mentor was a synonym for Simon without saying the name aloud. I didn't know if Simon could breach my studio's privacy protocols, particularly if I mentioned his name. Perhaps my paranoia was out of control, but better safe than sorry.

"Has he threatened you?" The protective tension in Luis' voice was evident.

"Not directly, but he's pushing me to hurt someone in 2027, and I can't do it."

"That would be a crime in 2241, but is it illegal to injure a person in the past? They'd be dead by now."

Logically, would I be killing Megan if she were already dead? Robbing her of sixteen years of life—from 2027 to her *historic* death in 2043 still seemed wrong. "It's not simply a criminal act. I struggle with punishing someone for something they may do in the future."

"So your actions in 2027 could prevent a future offense?" Luis dipped a cup into the bath before he poured water over the back of my head and wet my hair.

"That's part of the problem. After I leave this person in 2027, she'll do something and be convicted of a terrible misdeed. Briana's mentor believes any action to prevent that crime is justified."

"Even if it means compromising your principles?"

Did I have any principles left? My agreement to kill Megan Pierce if Simon helped recover our programs and data said otherwise. If I refused to hold up my end of the bargain, Simon might find ways to incriminate me. I could lose my family, career, or life.

When Luis clicked open a shampoo bottle, I drew in the fragrance. He poured it onto my hair and began to work it into a lather. I leaned into his fingers while he massaged my scalp.

Luis' magic hands lulled me into my thoughts.

The sleeping medicines had been delivered over the past few weeks. One vial contained a different drug. In the corner of that bottle's label, I noticed a tiny circle with a cross underneath—the symbol for female. Without confirming with Simon, I knew he intended the vial for Megan.

However tempted to research the drug, I stayed off the medical system. What if Simon could trace inquiries about the prescription and discover I was reconsidering my commitment to him? Or what if Simon could backdate my entry to *before* the drug's delivery date? Might he implicate me as the person who premeditatively researched the drug used to kill Megan?

Luis slipped a hand across my forehead and tipped my head back. As he rinsed the shampoo, Luis asked, "Can you persuade Briana's mentor that another—less drastic—action might produce the same results? Maybe you can get him to change his mind."

Perhaps ARP Luis had a point. Simon was determined to keep the real Luis and his son alive through the TWS epidemic. There must be some way I could prevent Megan from killing Milo without murdering her.

An emergency delivery tone sounded near my entrance portal.

"Give me a minute to dress," I called to the doorway.

When I rose from the tub, Luis playfully pulled at my arm. "What could be so important? Tell them to keep your package for an hour until we finish."

I leaned over to hold his chin in my hand. His partial beard growth grated my palm in a familiar and profoundly masculine sensation. Water dripped from the tips of my hair into the tub. His offer was appealing, but I'd locked the door to any nonessential notices. Whatever they were delivering was important.

After twisting a towel around my wet hair, I put on a robe designed to absorb the water and moisturize my skin. Luis feigned a pout. But once I'd retrieved my delivery, we both knew he would slather me with lotion.

As a parting gesture, I grasped the tub's side and kissed him. "Give me a few minutes to find out what it is." I turned to the center of the room and announced, "Modify program to lodge room scene. Place ARP subject in the bed under the covers." The spa dissolved into a darkened room with natural rock bordering a walk-in fireplace. A massive oak four-poster bed stood against a split log wall. Luis lay in the bed with sheets and animal pelts pulled over his shoulders.

"On second thought, place the ARP subject on his back with hands under his head. Position the covers pulled up to his waist." The bed scene changed to accommodate my suggestion. Luis winked and pulled his arms forward to flex his chest. I'd repeatedly asked for this pose, and he knew I loved watching him show off. His carved muscles took my breath away.

The delivery signal sounded twice with impatience.

"Sorry, I wasn't expecting a delivery. I'll be right there." I moved to stand before the sealed entrance portal.

"Screen room from anyone outside the studio." I tightened my robe belt. "Open entry door."

The boxy three-by-three-foot delivery robot sat in the hallway in front of my entrance. The robot measured my height and drew closer to hover at the precise level to form a table for my acknowledgment. I pressed my hand against a metal plate on top, and a lid flipped open to expose a slim document container inside the robot's distribution cavern.

As soon as I lifted the parcel and drew it away, the lid snapped shut. "Thank you for accepting your delivery." The robot's motor gave off a rising hum as it buzzed down the hallway and out of sight.

I closed the portal and reset the security parameters. After returning to bed, I placed the package beside my thigh. The parcel's cover bore the HCC's official markings. I could deal with it immediately or set it aside for an hour, a day, or a week.

Luis moved across the bed to sit cross-legged next to me. He dragged the sheet along with him, and it draped discreetly over his lap but didn't cover his chiseled abs. He must have sensed my increased distress and rubbed my back and shoulders.

"What's inside the package?" he asked.

Despite knowing his program couldn't care less, I responded, "It's from the HCC. Probably a reaction about the notice of suspicious actions Jayla filed."

Nearly three months had passed since Jayla filed the notice Simon drafted under her signature. With each day, I'd hoped the petition might have gotten lost or stashed under a pile of other communications deemed irrelevant. No such luck. Their response sat on my bed.

Luis walked his fingers across the sheets and grasped the package corner. He inched it away from my reach. All the while, Luis watched my reaction. His program monitored me to see if I appreciated the movement or would ask him to stop. Before he could pull it from the bed, I lunged forward and grabbed it.

"If you want to know what's inside, you should open it." Luis smiled. "If it's bad, I'll do my best to take your mind off it."

He was right. Why let the missive sit in the background and steal my attention? A direct approach would serve me better. I placed my palm on the receiving label. The parcel opened to uncover a dozen sheets of paper held together with a bright red clip. The top letter bore the HCC's seal and was signed by a dignitary from the HCC's legal affairs department.

Luis waited—measuring micromovements in my face—while I read the cover letter in detail and flipped through the subsequent sheets. "They've scheduled a meeting in Panama City in seven days."

"You'll go there? Why can't they depose you over telecommunication?" Luis' questions came out as if he were reading my mind.

"Their inquiries list is mostly about my meetings with Mia Danube9. They want to know how I received the com-card that linked me with her." I glanced at Luis. "There's nothing here about how her com-card might have contained the virus that attacked our systems. But that doesn't mean they won't ask me when I'm there." I ran my finger down the question list and hesitated at the bottom. "There's a catch-all question at the end. It says the HCC or their designees can interrogate me about other matters deemed necessary to ensure the safety and security of America or other nations."

"Your visit to the capital should clear up any misunderstandings about your relationship with the Front." Luis cupped my shoulder and squeezed. "Is there something else you're not telling me?"

Of late, I'd confided about my fears and planned actions. I'd set up an auto-delete feature in Luis' program I could initiate anytime from anywhere if his activity logs came under CYR security review. With a blink of my ocular implant, every conversation with Luis would become unintelligible cyber dust. "I'm not letting you read these pages because scanned documents might funnel to a system separate from your discrete programming. But there are two things I'll tell you about this HCC package."

"Go on."

"One is a copy of the missive I sent about keeping one of Briana's babies."

I told Briana about my letter shortly after sending it a month ago. In her stoic way, she was furious—slamming cabinets and ignoring me for nearly a full day. Once I told her a copy was in the HCC file, I'd hear about it again. Was my letter circling back to bite me? I only wanted to protect our family.

When I didn't promptly continue, Luis asked, "And the other?"

"The HCC attached a witness list with the name of one other person they plan to depose." I swallowed hard. "Jayla's joining me in Panama City."

Luis drew me into his arms, but he couldn't protect me from facing off against Jayla. And she'd give anything to evict me from her daughter's life.

Chapter 19

PANAMA CITY, AMERICA'S CAPITAL—MAY 28, 2241

The AereoPod fit sixteen passengers and the pilot into snug, form-fitting seats designed to accommodate every shape and size. Cocooning recliners long ago replaced G-suits that used pressurized inflatable pouches to thwart blood pooling when the aircraft accelerated.

Since we were positioned in a long row to keep the pod aerodynamic and hydrogen fuel-efficient, I planned to doze for the hour-long flight at Mach 3.5. With continual speed, safety, and comfort improvements, domestic travel seemed mundane—particularly after being thrashed around inside a time capsule.

Jayla sat three seats ahead of me. I gave a cat-like stretch, grateful we were too far apart to chat on the trip to Panama City.

Once we passed the sound barrier with the tell-tail bump, I connected my ocular implant to the pod's external camera. The landscape flew by. Less than halfway through the flight, we passed densely populated Houston. But before that, we cruised over vast swaths of uninhabited land and robot-maintained farms growing cotton, corn, and wheat.

The farms reminded me of where they'd incarcerated Phen near Brasilia. If I managed to retain my freedom after the time jump, I'd request a family visit to see her. I wanted Briana to meet Phen, and Latrice might enjoy touring the farm. The HCC sometimes allowed a once-in-a-term family visit to show children the ramifications of anti-social behaviors.

Once we crossed into the Gulf of America, water stretched in every direction until right before landing in the capital city. I never tired of the skyline, filled with asymmetrically shaped architectural masterpieces and monuments to honor the visionary women who consolidated the former North, Central, and South Americas.

An ARP attendant helped me from the seat, and I crouched to exit the pod. After a few minutes of stretching my wobbly legs and breathing the hot balmy air, I looped my travel bag leash over a shoulder and stepped onto a Levi-plate with the Capitol complex image on top. Unused to the heat, I appreciated the plate transporting me through a temperature-controlled tubeway.

Jayla moved off the AereoPod and onto another plate with other passengers bound for the capital. She leaned close and chatted with a traveler. Jayla probably told her newfound friend she was traveling alone. Fine with me.

Her testimony remained a mystery. What did she plan to disclose to the HCC inquisition panel? As far as I knew, Jayla had no personal knowledge about my meetings with Mia—except for what Simon might have told her. Would she tell them about Simon? If not, what was *her* story about my sessions with a Front representative?

I flexed and unflexed my fingers.

She could testify that CYR security detected the com-card, and they tracked the gadget to a home registered to a pair of sisters with ties to the Front. But that was the extent of her knowledge. Anything further was her opinion and not based on facts.

I paused at the steel and stucco arrival hall—an homage to our cliff dweller ancestors integrated with the metal alloy reverse angles popular in current architecture.

After my slight hip tilt, I stopped and stepped off the Levi-plate. It turned vertical and whooshed away, presumably to a stack of other plates at the building's front or back to the AereoPod port.

The complex held the government situation rooms, the HCC offices, and a wing of overnight suites for dignitaries and others with official government business. When I approached the visitors' kiosk, a notification in my ocular implant tingled. With a quick blink, I viewed my reservation and assigned room number. Seconds later, a tremor shook my right hand when the kiosk loaded my room's portal access codes into my embedded wrist chip.

A holographic kiosk attendant bobbled her head and grinned. "Welcome, Dr. Sofia Andes7. Unless you have questions about how to find your room or about our wide range of amenities, I wish you a fine stay at the Capitol Complex Guesthouse."

After thanking the screen—being polite to avatars seemed proper—I guided my tote and took the elevator to the thirty-fourth floor.

Once settled in my room, I poured a glass of wine and stood outside on the balcony. The HCC's buildings sat on reclaimed land, nearly surrounded by water. My view faced southeast—away from the bustling city but toward the spectacular Gulf of America harbor.

I stared at the horizon, contemplating the next day's interrogation. My assigned advocate would join me for the questioning. We'd spoken a few times about how to prepare. She assured me the list of questions seemed routine and believed I'd finish in an hour or two.

I'd asked the advocate why they couldn't conduct the consultation over videos. She admitted the request for an in-person audience was rare but not out of the ordinary. Despite stewing about the inconvenience and the inquisition's timing, I figured lodging a protest wouldn't produce a positive result.

Breezes whipped my hair with humidity I hadn't experienced in years. My lips tasted salt from the bay. When I finished the first glass of wine, I went inside for another. Before I could refill, my com-card tone sounded.

Briana. I'd promised to call her after arriving. I cursed myself.

When I pressed the button, Briana's hologram appeared in my studio. Like my call with Phen, Briana and I could see each other but not touch.

"Your glass is empty. Do you want to call back when you've had a chance to pour another?" Briana's smile said she was chiding me.

I stepped to the bar and emptied the bottle into my glass. "You caught me. I checked in about a half-hour ago and was enjoying the view. Sorry I didn't call right away."

"I wouldn't have been here anyway." Briana waved a dismissive hand. "We've had a minor issue in the lab. I just got to my studio. I'm meeting Latrice and Nanny Tori for dinner in a few minutes, but I wanted to talk with you before I left."

Briana's tone was calmer than her body language betrayed. A chill ran across my shoulders. "What could have happened in the few hours since I left Denver?"

"Dr. Torne7 took a fall."

My stomach clenched, and I collapsed to sit on the bed. "The Torne7 who's scheduled to take the time jump with Le7 in June?"

"She's in surgery right now." Briana nodded. "Torne7 has a few bruises, and they believe she broke the fifth metatarsal bone in her foot. It may need a cast, and they might implant nanobots to speed up the healing."

I hesitated to ask. Did I want to hear the answer? I needed to focus on tomorrow's inquisition. "Are the medical staff planning to postpone the jump?"

"It's too early to make a call. We have more than two weeks, and Torne7 is beyond fit. But I don't want to sugarcoat her condition. Right now, she's in pain and an emotional wreck about possibly causing us to push back the date."

I set down my glass before it started to shake and tipped off Briana about how much her *minor issue* had upset me. "You're a good judge of her condition. What's the likelihood of a delay?"

"About fifty/fifty. Torne7 is more concerned about whether the HCC will ask her and Le7 to forgo their turns. That would leave the next teams in place without pushing back all future jumps."

"How's Le7 taking it?" I managed to ask while forcing my voice to remain measured and even. Internally, I seethed. First, Le7 nearly compromised the schedule by wanting to move to Asia. Then Torne7 took a clumsy fall.

"You know Le7—stoic on the outside and crumbling on the inside. I've invited her to join us for dinner, but I doubt she'll come."

"When will you know more?"

"The medical team is meeting first thing in the morning. We'll consider Torne7's physical condition and how it might affect the jump. If you finish early, let me know, and I'll give you an update. I'd like to hear how the inquiry turned out before you take the pod back to Denver." Briana glanced away, likely to check the time. "I hate to cut this short, but I scheduled dinner at six."

"I understand. Kiss our baby girl for me."

"I will." Briana leaned forward and raised an open hand. If we were together, her palm would have rested on my chest. "Be strong, my love.

They'll clear you of this misunderstanding, and everything will be back to normal."

Her loyalty made my throat constrict. Once I returned from 2027, I'd become the wife Briana deserved.

When Briana's hologram disappeared, I gulped the rest of my wine and returned to the balcony to watch the fading evening glow over the water. Lights blinked on ships and in the twenty-story condo buildings lining the beach.

What was worse—an unending barrage of complications for my illicit time jump or what I'd face at the next day's inquisition?

<h1 style="text-align:center">Chapter 20</h1>

MAY 29, 2241

Jayla left the meeting room and charged past me in the waiting area without a sideward glance. The Tribunal must have called her to speak immediately before me. Her defiant posture and arrogant step radiated anger. But with whom—me or the people who took her away from work?

Shortly after Jayla left, a stainless steel box emerged through the hologram portal to the meeting room. Though the door was solid to my touch, the robot passed through like the doorway wasn't there and approached to hover at waist level.

"Sofia Andes7," a computerized voice said, "you are called to appear before the Humanity Continuance Coalition's Legal Affairs Tribunal. Your testimony will be recorded and may be used as evidence in this and future investigations." A neon outline of a hand blinked on the top. "By placing your hand where indicated, you are swearing to tell the truth. Any deviation from the truth will put you in contempt of these proceedings and subject you to penalties affecting your freedom to choose an occupation, domicile location, or access to clone."

The penalties were severe. I could wind up alone on a farm like Phen's.

After drawing a breath, I placed my hand within the glowing outline. A tone sounded to acknowledge my affirmation. The robot moved back toward the entrance. When the door dissolved, the robot said, "Follow me. Your consultation will begin shortly."

Consultation? Bullshit. More like an interrogation.

I followed it into the dark-paneled meeting hall, where seven stern

Tribunal members sat at a massive horseshoe-shaped table. My advocate leaned against an adjacent lectern. She gave me an encouraging nod when I entered the room.

Her confidence didn't diminish the room's intimidating design. But she was there for me. She'd intervene if the Tribunal's questions wandered into any previously undisclosed territory. With her dogged attention, their inquiry wouldn't revert to a fishing expedition.

The oldest Tribunal member, an olive-skinned woman with long gleaming black hair interspersed with silver threads, sat in the center. Her aging skin formed prune-like furrows around her tight lips. The name on her card read Dr. Atacama6, and I assumed she chaired the group.

A podium stood in the table's center opening. Without guidance or instruction, I walked to stand behind it and faced the Tribunal.

At the session's start, my hands shook, and I stammered. But soon their questions fell into a nonjudgmental rhythm. After an hour, their inquiries slowed.

When they'd asked about my relationship with Mia Danube9, I replied there was no relationship, simply my yearning for historical information not available on CYR computers. I told them about the book I'd planned to write about women's most resilient characteristics. The female attributes of cooperation and collaboration were rooted in millennia spent honing these skills both before and after men lived among us. Nearly all the Tribunal members nodded in agreement.

Questions followed about my research, and they seemed pleased to know I'd quenched my thirst for knowledge without changing my views about repopulating the world with men. With each response, adrenaline pushed me further into survival mode. I held the podium and balanced on the balls of my feet.

"The entire male gender wasn't to blame for the deficient few who held power and upset the balance between the sexes." I pounded my fist. "During the Cursed Decades, untold men tried to help women and lost their lives in our defense. Complicit men likely prolonged the suffering, but many actively worked to stop the atrocities. I don't charge the entire sex for what happened."

They glanced at each other as if wondering whether to continue or dismiss me. I let out a slow sigh.

Atacama6 straightened in her chair, and all eyes turned to her. "Your actions to engage with a Front member may have seemed cavalier to you, but we take your relationship seriously."

I reiterated my earlier statement about not having a relationship with Danube9. But she held up a hand to silence me. "Whether you became friends or were merely ever-watchful confederates, this Tribunal doesn't care. *Any* connection between a CYR official with high-security clearance and a Front member is a risky affiliation."

While I silently listened, I clasped my hands in front.

"May we assume you will never contact Mia Danube9 or any other Front members from this day forward?"

I nodded my head.

"For the record, please look at this Tribunal and tell us aloud that you will not engage with anyone associated with the Front."

After making eye contact with each member around the table, I pressed my sweaty palms against the podium. "I promise never to contact anyone from the Front again."

Atacama6 crossed her arms, demanding my attention and deference. "We appreciate your pledge and will monitor you to ensure you keep your commitment." She narrowed her eyes. "What if the HCC asked you to gain intel on the Front? Would you cooperate?"

I stiffened at her request. Was she testing me? Unsure if I had the qualifications or temperament to become a spy, I said, "I promised never to meet with Mia Danube9."

"Yes. But what if you engaged with her to inform on the Front's activities and capabilities?"

Every Tribunal member leaned forward in their seats, waiting for my reply. My work at CYR gave me regular routines, friends, and an uncomplicated life with Briana. Becoming the HCC's agent would change all that.

Wait. What was I thinking?

I'd already muddied my life with my plans to visit Luis in 2027. Did it matter what I promised the HCC? Once I returned from the past, my life as I knew it would be over anyway.

But their offer could give me leverage.

I cleared my throat. "I'm pleased to serve my country and the HCC in any way to promote their longevity and security. But my priorities are the upcoming CYR June time jump and Briana's pregnancy. I might consider helping the HCC when my life is more settled."

"We will record your openness to assist the HCC in the future. Our operatives will likely contact you later this year." Atacama6 tapped a finger on the table. "We're nearly finished, but we'd like you to address another matter before you go."

I shot a look toward my advocate. But she'd already left her lectern to approach the Tribunal's table. A member handed her a Holo-tablet, and she flipped through several screens while returning to her post.

Atacama6 waited with her hands clasped tightly on the table in front of her.

After a few minutes, the advocate held a finger aloft. "The matter you want to broach isn't directly related to the Tribunal's request for a hearing. However, I will allow this line of questioning because it informs about Andes7's frame of mind and loyalty to the HCC, CYR, and those agencies' overall objectives." She gave the panel members a flinty stare. "I will make a note of the deviation in my summary. If this Tribunal demonstrates a pattern of inquiry variance, your procedures and membership will be significantly modified."

My heart sank. Did Jayla give them something to blindside me with? What if Simon confided in her about my planned excursion back to 2027? I balled my fingers into fists—certain they smelled my fear.

"Please tell us why you wrote to the HCC about the distribution of children carried by your wife, Briana Memphis7."

My voice caught in my throat. Is that what Jayla came to discuss? She was on the witness list as if they had summoned her, but perhaps she requested the audience.

"I believe any citizen can speak their views on matters concerning the HCC." I grasped the podium. "Has that changed?"

Some Tribunal members stared at their laps, and others fidgeted and glanced toward their leader. Atacama6's lips drew into a hard line. "I didn't inquire about the legality of your message. I asked about your rationale. Please answer the question. What was your objective for petitioning the HCC?"

"While my wife and I were not parties to the contract, I've heard the

HCC has an outstanding agreement outlining how the babies Briana is carrying—that is to say, *our* babies—would be distributed among the countries if they didn't all live until birth. Our contract with the HCC specified we'd offer all our children to the HCC except the one we would raise in our family. Asking her to give up any of her children is a great sacrifice. She took grave risks to become pregnant and is the first woman to carry babies in nearly 180 years."

"Please," one of the other Tribunal members interrupted, "don't misunderstand our line of questioning. The HCC appreciates your wife's dedication to Mission Y."

Atacama6 shot her colleague a silent reprimand before retaking command. "While we value your understanding about a possible agreement you were not a party to, you have not answered our question."

"I'm getting to that. Despite the risks and sacrifice, we're willing to give up all but one of the infants, which is still an enormous sacrifice—keep in mind every baby boy is genetically fifty-percent Briana Memphis7. The boys are brothers, and Briana has agreed to separate them for the HCC's greater good. Now that one baby miscarried, the HCC is considering a distribution realignment of the remaining four." I stared directly into Atacama6's eyes. "I sent the message to the HCC to implore them to uphold the original agreement. They should allow us to keep one baby irrespective of how many are ultimately born."

"What makes you think official positions have changed?" asked Atacama6.

"Comments made by my mother-in-law, Jayla Memphis6."

"Perhaps you shouldn't listen to unsupported opinions." Atacama6 cocked her head. "Dr. Memphis6 testified solely about your meetings with the Front. Distributing Mission Y's infants wasn't part of our dialogue with her."

"Can you assure me we will be able to keep our child?" I stood taller and rested a fist on the podium.

"Your request is irrelevant." A smile crept across Atacama6's face. "We're part of the HCC's Legal Affairs division and have no information about what the Board may or may not decide regarding Mission Y."

"Then why are you asking me about my correspondence?"

"Your missive was forwarded to us as part of our due diligence regarding Jayla Memphis6's notice of suspicious actions and your loyalty to the HCC."

Finally, I understood. Jayla might have wanted to shove a wedge between Briana and me, but the Tribunal would have automatically called her to appear because she had filed Simon's notice. Jayla was likely angry that the proceedings took her away from her work. She wasn't in Panama City to stir up more trouble or to encourage the HCC to take Adam from us. They'd interrupted Jayla's routines the same way they'd done mine—with no regard for time-sensitive commitments.

"I apologize for any implied insubordination." I took a breath. "The HCC should hear my views about wanting to keep our son. I hope you don't see my actions as subversive. Your records demonstrate that I'm a dedicated engineer and have worked on Mission Y my entire career. I was honored to be selected for last October's time jump, and my accomplishments contributed to the operation's success. With every fiber of my being, I want to see men reintroduced into our society." Any lie-detecting software the HCC used would confirm my statements as truth—in that room or when they later analyzed the transcripts.

My advocate stifled a chuckle and pretended to straighten her Holo-tablet on the lectern. Her reaction affirmed my oration. Heat flushed through my body.

"I'd also like to know whether you've ever activated an illegal ARP in the CYR residence center." I froze at Atacama6's line of inquiry.

My advocate raised an open palm. "Do not answer that question." She turned to the panel. "That's a clear departure from today's agenda. I won't permit Andes7 to respond."

Atacama6's implication already tainted me in front of the Tribunal. She'd painted me as a renegade. I needed to convince them I was unworthy of further investigation, or they might uncover my calls with Phen and lengthen her sentence. "I'd like to reconsider your offer to help the HCC gain intel on the Front."

"Yes?" A sickly-sweet grin spread across Atacama6's face.

"I implore the HCC to wait until after our son is born. Briana could use my support, and Mission Y needs me for their next time jump scheduled for the same day. After that, I'll do whatever the HCC wants me to do."

My podium lit up with a contract. The text outlined all verbal agreements made during the meeting. My advocate gave me a slow nod, prompting me to agree to the HCC's terms. The glass plate was cold against my trembling palm. Would they bother to enforce the contract after I returned from 2027?

Chapter 21

I skipped lunch because a heart-pounding run sounded better than food. With five days until Briana's inducement and my jump, I needed to stay sharp and on point.

The ever-present protest group chanted their mantra as I stepped outside the building. Charlotte Danube9 rallied the crowd. Or at least I thought it was Charlotte and not Mia.

I could return inside or pass the group. The last time I spotted Charlotte, I did a one-eighty and ducked back into the building. I needed this run too badly to turn away for fear of breaking my commitment to the HCC Tribunal.

Maybe I imagined it, but Charlotte may have noticed me, too. The Front leader shoved her hands into her jacket pockets and looked away. I headed toward the fitness path.

With each footfall, my heartbeats settled into a familiar rhythm. While it was June, Denver had record highs associated with August. The sun seared the exposed skin on my shoulders. The parched air felt like running through a dry sauna.

Since my abrupt break with Mia over three months earlier, I'd varied my running schedule and route. But only a handful of ways led from the Merlin Building. Every few days, I repeated my course.

At my turnaround point, I stopped at a water dispenser and took a drink. As I lifted my head, I froze.

Standing mere feet from me was Mia.

When I spun away and tried to resume my run, Mia called, "I've missed our visits." She rushed forward and grabbed my arm. "Please, talk with me. I want to know why you disappeared. I enjoyed our visits."

I looked from her hand to her face. Her pleading eyes seemed genuine, but I jerked away. "I'm not interested in seeing you." I stood with my feet wide apart and braced, clenched fists on my hips. "How did you find me?"

"Charlotte messaged me that you left for a run. She watched you leave the Merlin Building."

"How did you know to come here?" I backed up a few steps but kept her in full view.

"About a month ago, you stopped here for a water break. But you bolted before I could talk with you. I've been coming here every day since then. Charlotte agreed to send a signal if she noticed you leaving CYR headquarters. Most times, you run a different route. But I figured you'd come this way again. And here you are." She approached again with an outstretched hand.

"Don't touch me!" I stepped back. "Haven't you done enough?" She and her cronies had nearly cost CYR its programming for Mission Y—and my job. I didn't owe her anything but wanted to say my piece. "You played at being my friend. All the while, you plotted to have me smuggle your com-card and sabotage our computer system." I clamped a hand over my mouth. But I'd already said too much. Mia would report back to the Front that their plan worked. The card had released the virus, and Mission Y was compromised. The Front wouldn't take long to find another unsuspecting employee to infect our systems.

"I did no such thing!" Mia's jaw dropped. Her incredulous response confirmed she was an accomplished actress—probably a skill all terrorists worked at perfecting. "You have to believe me."

I turned to leave, but she called me back. My brain told me to ignore her pleas. But once again, I swiveled toward her.

Mia rubbed the back of her neck and shook her head as if trying to figure out a puzzle. She asked, "How would that work? The card I gave you had one function—to let you send untraceable messages when you were available to meet."

"It was capable of doing more than that."

"We don't have any technology like what you described. Did you analyze the card or dream up this crazy theory on your own?"

"Of course we did," I lied.

"Well then, I don't see how you could have come up with this unsubstantiated idea. Com-cards can't carry a computer virus, and the one I gave you certainly didn't have anything sophisticated. I bought it myself at a shop a few blocks from my house. I can show you the receipt, and you can talk with the shop owner. There was nothing embedded in it that could harm your computers." She glanced toward CYR headquarters. "What did it do?"

"I'm not going there with you." Was she angling to find out how much damage she'd caused, or was she concerned? "Our systems are running fine, and nothing the Front tried to do will stop us."

"Please, you have to believe me. I didn't do what you're suggesting."

"Why should I believe you? Months ago, you told me Charlotte didn't know I was researching at your place. Yet, she's giving you signals about my whereabouts."

Mia's chin trembled at my outburst.

"Where do your lies end, and the truth begins?" I asked.

"She doesn't know you've been to our home. I told her I'd met you at the market, and we took walks in the parks. Charlotte knows how I feel about you and wants to help me see you again."

"Do *not* try to contact me again." I turned and ran.

Halfway back to the Merlin Building, I stopped to stretch. I never meant to lead on Mia. I wanted to research the Front's materials and made that clear to her. It wasn't my fault if Mia read more into my visits. I never disparaged Briana, complained about my marriage, or hid my wedding band. Why would Mia assume I was interested?

As I justified my behavior, I considered Mia's account of her com-card's capabilities. Maybe she hadn't masterminded a plot to compromise Mission Y's programs and data. She'd seemed genuinely distressed about my avoiding her and surprised about the corrupted card.

Who else could have been behind the plot? Perhaps unbeknownst to Mia, Charlotte knew of her sister's plans to meet with me. Charlotte might have exchanged Mia's card with one infused with a virus. Mia would have passed it to me and thought nothing of having me take it into the lab.

That made no sense. If Charlotte was behind the attack, why would she help Mia reconnect with me? Logically, Charlotte would lay low until Mia lost interest or grew fond of someone else.

I straightened and grasped a light pole for support.

What if the Front had nothing to do with the attack?

When our systems started crashing and the programs and data disappeared, I immediately ran to Simon. He recovered enough missing data to make it look like he helped and convinced me he had no clue when or how an attack would occur. Simon conveniently had the fix.

The virus prompted our deal. If there was no virus, Simon wouldn't have leverage to trick me into murdering Megan Pierce.

Simon also helped me design a Hipposkin sock to reinforce Torne7's ankle and keep her on schedule to jump. In nanoseconds, he'd worked up specs and ran the initial simulations. Sometimes it seemed like Simon wanted my time jump more than I did. How far would he go to maintain the schedule and hold me hostage to my side of the deal?

I pushed forward into a slow jog, feet pounding the pavement with each stride.

I'd find a way to prevent Megan from killing her son—without destroying my relationship with Simon or murdering Megan Pierce.

Chapter 22

Simon stood in the middle of my studio, stiff-backed and grim. He was a foot taller than usual, and despite his whimsical eye patch and pirate get-up, he didn't look amused. Simon's flaring nostrils said he was beyond angry.

"Why have you been tinkering with the time travel program?" he snapped. "The logs showed you accessed weight differential specs."

I gave Simon a dramatic bow with arms spread wide. His questioning was intrusive and ridiculous. "I'm gravely sorry, oh Powerful One." When I straightened, his cold exposed eye glared at me. Maybe I'd gone too far.

"Tell me what you've done."

"You know the program's sophisticated and has millions of restrictions. Like why changing the year is straightforward, but date changes are a nightmare."

"Point taken. Go on."

"I opened the program to see whether it would auto-adjust to accommodate one person in the capsule instead of a team of two."

"I've adjusted the sequence to accept one traveler for tomorrow's second jump." Simon's eyes narrowed. "Why didn't you ask me?"

"You forget I'm an engineer with consummate attention to detail. You weren't around, so I accessed the program to ensure it wouldn't slice me to ribbons when the weight parameters were out of spec."

"I didn't see any program changes. But did you modify something I couldn't detect?"

"No. As I said, I wanted to check out the lines of code related to the weight difference." *Like I could do anything to the program without him finding the change.* "Everything—every element—every line fragment—it's all the way you left them."

"You're not planning to drag anyone along to 2027?"

"Like who? Briana?" What was Simon implying?

Simon reprimanded me with a downward glance. "Maybe you plan to smuggle your friend Mia Danube9 or her despicable sister Charlotte into the lab and take them along for the ride."

There it was. For some crazy reason, Simon assumed I'd aligned with the Front and planned to sabotage future missions.

"You have quite the imagination." I sniffed. "Since you and I cut our deal months ago, I haven't talked with Mia."

With a snap of his fingers, a Holo-tablet appeared in Simon's hand. He tapped the screen and turned it toward me, revealing an image of Mia and me talking next to the water dispenser. In the shot's right corner, a date stamp said June 6, 2241, at 13:20. Simon must have programmed the city's surveillance cameras to watch me.

"It's not how it looks." My gut clenched. "Mia came after me. I didn't contact her."

"I have no reason to trust you." Simon sneered and slid a gleaming two-foot saber from a leather scabbard at his belt. He twisted the blade from side to side and tested its edge with a thumb. "What else have you lied about?"

Surely Simon intended the weapon to intimidate and not to strike. I took a deep breath, hoping honesty would benefit my case. "We talked for less than a minute, and I told Mia not to contact me again."

"What did she want?"

"She wanted to know why I'd stopped coming to see her."

"Did she ask why you weren't using the card anymore?"

"She didn't ask about the card or for it back." Why was Simon interested in the com-card?

"So you didn't tell her about the virus?"

"Why should I? I didn't want her to know what damage it caused." I returned his stare. "You wouldn't want me to admit the virus compromised our systems, right? Mia or her Front buddies might try to use them again on another CYR employee. They could even plant similar cards with vendors in the area to get them inside."

Simon slid his weapon back into its sheath. "You did the right thing by not bringing it up."

He seemed to accept my logic. Maybe a bit too quickly. But my plans were set even if Simon triggered the virus. In one day, I'd jump to 2027.

After adjusting his height to his normal size, Simon moved to stand in front of an armchair. When he lowered himself to sit, his scabbard stabbed into the leather. It shredded the seat.

"Do your costumes need to be so lifelike? A blunt play sword would have worked fine."

Simon glanced at the sheath protecting his saber. He tipped his head toward the damaged seat, and my studio computer repaired the rip. "Good as new." Simon relaxed into the chair and crossed his legs. "You're leaving tomorrow. Do you feel prepared?"

"I'm ready." I gathered a pile of unwashed workout clothes in my arms. "But I can't help thinking about the million little things that could go wrong before I get into the capsule."

"Maybe I can help. What gives you the most concern?"

"What if our boys' births are something less than successful?"

"That's not a *little thing*." Simon smirked.

"Of course not." I stuffed the clothes into my cleaning portal. "I didn't mean that everything that could go wrong is trivial. But you asked for my biggest concern. The health and safety of those boys and Briana *is* the most important thing."

"I'll give you that. Childbirth has never been without risks for the mother or the babies. I trust Ural6, Le7, and Jayla to protect Briana and the babies. I'll be with them, too, of course." He flipped up the eyepatch to look at me with both eyes. "But there must be other things we can work on to reduce risks."

"What if something goes wrong with Le7 and Torne7's jump? Briana and I were lucky that nothing too complicated happened when we traveled. But they could meet up with a person on the street, or maybe Vladimir Almo won't be home."

"Don't worry about aspects out of your control." Simon drummed his fingers on his thigh. "The jump team can handle unexpected individuals, and our records confirmed Almo would be at home that night."

"You're more confident than me." I thought back to when we found Milo asleep in his parents' bed. "We can review historical records and simulate complication scenarios, but something unexpected can happen."

Simon steepled his fingers. "Le7 and Torne7 will be prepared."

He was right. "Agreed."

"Give me your vaccine vials."

"Why?" I fetched the medical kit.

"I've been working on an upgrade to the mutation nanobots."

I opened the case and pulled out the vials. "Are you sure these bots can survive for decades without recharging?"

"Yes." He rolled his eyes like an annoyed teen. "I've spent 84 days, 3 hours, and 17 minutes working on this fix, and you have the nerve to ask me if my solution could fail?"

Was the original Simon Merlin's ego as fragile as his creation's?

Simon took each one and, with a barely perceptible whoosh, injected the tops with a fist-sized CVI.

A notification tone interrupted our conversation. Recognizing Briana's ring, I repacked the medical kit and glanced at the ceiling. "Accept incoming message."

"My contractions are pronounced." Briana's recorded voice came over the intercom. Anyone else would have heard it calm and measured. But anxiety permeated her pitch. "I'm not sure if we can wait until tomorrow. Ural6 has sent an orderly to fetch me. I know it's close to midnight, but would you please meet me in the delivery room on the medical floor?"

Simon disappeared—likely to lurk somewhere in the delivery room. Our plans were set in motion, and there was no going back.

A shoulder roll helped steady my nerves before responding to Briana's message. "Send the following response to Briana Memphis7: I'll meet you there in a few minutes. Stay strong and do everything the doctors tell you to do. I love you."

I opened my closet portal to dress. Since I had no idea how long the births would take and how soon the doctors would leave for their jump, I dressed in my Hipposkin enviro-suit and covered it with my work clothes.

After smoothing my lab coat, I left my studio—convinced I was ready for any challenges.

Chapter 23

I reached Briana as the orderly wheeled her into the delivery room. Ural6, Le7, and two nurses buzzed around the birthing table. The cool blue and gray wall colors probably calmed the mother-to-be, but no soothing colors could have slowed my throbbing heart.

Four clear cubes lined the wall—each holding fluffy white sheets, ready to cradle the newborns. A boxy birthing table balanced on an adjustable pedestal, and dozens of mechanical arms protruded from a stainless-steel ball suspended from the ceiling.

Over the past several months, Briana had encouraged me to watch videos about the equipment assisting the births. My love for anything mechanical took hold, and I recognized every implement. Single-purpose tools would enter Briana's body and extract the boys without surgery and with minimal discomfort to her or the babies. Ural6 and Le7 would control the devices in the next few hours and bring the boys into 2241.

What had a delivery room looked like 180 years earlier? Had the last live birth happened in a hospital, a home, or a farm in a remote territory that no longer supported human life? Even if the final *original* baby were a female, she'd be long dead.

"I can't believe I'm finally here." Briana beamed at Le7. "All those visits to the examination room next door made me feel like I'd never see the inside of this place."

"How are you feeling?" asked Le7 while she and the nurses draped warm blankets over Briana.

The bed's low hum told me it was warming to her temperature and cradling her body.

"Finally." Jayla entered the room in a burst of yellow flowing fabric. She gave Ural6 a sharp nod and confidently strode to Briana's side. "This is the day we've been waiting for. You'll make history."

"And bring our little Adam into our family," I suggested.

"He and his three brothers will help us populate our world with the men we need to save humanity." Jayla ignored me and gave Briana a thin smile. "Your country is so proud of you."

Did Jayla's impersonal response hint that officials would turn over Adam to President Ottawa7?

When I tensed, Briana asked the obvious question. "Do you know about a change in the babies' distribution?"

Jayla opened her mouth and shut it again.

"Tell us." I reached for Briana's hand. "Can't you see what you're doing to her?"

"How dare you accuse me of upsetting my daughter." Jayla straightened. "You heard me. I told her today would be one of the most important in her life. Her country is proud of her sacrifices."

"I'm so glad you're here," Briana whispered to me under her breath. She turned up the volume and glared at her mother. "Please tell us whether you've heard more from the HCC."

"About whether they might change their minds on distribution." I finished Briana's thought.

"Well?" Briana stammered.

Jayla scrutinized Briana then me and back. "It's hard to believe Sofia showed up on time. I assumed she'd stroll in after the babies were in their isolation cubes."

"Mother, please don't change the subject." Briana exhaled loudly. "Tell us what you know."

I squeezed Briana's hand to endorse her newfound assertiveness.

"The Council hasn't definitively changed the original agreement."

I jumped in. "Why didn't you say that in the first place? Briana has enough on her mind without wondering whether the HCC will claim Adam."

"Maybe you've misunderstood. Just because they haven't announced a change doesn't mean the HCC won't."

"No news is good news." I waved a dismissive hand. "Once these guys are born, I wish them luck taking Adam from us." I leaned over Briana and planted a loud kiss on her forehead. "Don't you worry. Adam will be ours forever."

"The HCC," Jayla said in a harsh whisper, "will evaluate the situation and act in society's best interests. If they decide you and Briana offer the best chances for Adam, they'll let you have him."

"Mother, let us believe everything will work out in our favor." Briana's fists balled at her sides. "If you can't do that, I'd like you to leave. Ural6, Le7, and their team can do this with or without you."

"Um, that's not precisely true." Le7 cleared her throat. "We could use her assistance today, and what we learn from your delivery will be helpful for my and Torne7's deliveries."

"Le7's right." Briana intervened. "But, Mother, please leave your criticism of Sofia at the door for today. I'd like to focus on the boys and not be batted around between your and Sofia's jabs."

"I'll agree to a détente if you will, Jayla," I offered.

Jayla scoffed. "If you stay in your space to comfort Briana, I'll remain here and work with Ural6 to ensure my girl's safety."

Briana hooked her little finger on my hand and mouthed, "Thank you."

I leaned over the table and kissed her before repositioning an errant curl from her forehead. "You'll be fine."

Briana groaned, and a tone sounded from under the bed.

Le7 reacted immediately. "The bed reads your contractions and gives us a score for their frequency and intensity. That one was intense. We've agreed to put you in a twilight state during the surgery. You won't feel anything down below, but you'll hear us talk about what's happening. We can put you out if you prefer."

"No, no, no. I want to know what's going on."

An hour later, I sat beside Briana's bed with an uncontrollable grin. Briana sat in a semi-upright position, holding our Adam, the first to be removed from her body. He took to her breast, and she glowed like when we stole Luis' sperm in 2026.

As each of Adam's brothers was born, Ural6 announced their names. After Adam Memphis, she introduced Kifle Nile, who, after a few months of intense monitoring, would live in Limassol with his mother President Samin Nile7. Kifle would be protected in a virus-free safe room until the CYR medical team released him for outdoor exposure.

Less than a minute later, Brad Ottawa burst into the world with a monstrous cry. While he didn't know it, his mother, President Celine Ottawa7, watched his birth via video from Panama City. Brad would live in Denver with his brother Adam for at least his first year. Ottawa7 wouldn't take unwarranted risks with her son. However, she'd already announced her plans for weekly visits to Denver. Brad would know his mother in person.

Finally, Ural6 directed birthing implements to extract Issey Fuji. The doctor commented he was the largest baby and might tower over his mother, President Junko Fuji6, and others in Singapore.

"They're all perfect." I alternated between stroking Briana's arm and Adam's fuzzy head. "But Adam's the strongest and smartest."

"You might be biased. But Adam managed to push to the front." Briana clutched the boy to her chest. "Where's my mother?"

"She's talking with Ural6. I overheard that they've spoken with the HCC Board. They've authorized the countdown for the next jump. Le7 will leave in a few minutes to get dressed for her mission."

"I know the engineering team needs you in the control room for the pre-launch sequences, but can you stay for a few more minutes?"

"I should go soon." I brushed Briana's cheek with my lips. "But Jayla can stay with you after I leave."

"She must have been thrilled to see her grandson's birth." Briana's voice held more hopefulness than certainty.

"Jayla doesn't show her emotions, but I saw tears in her eyes when they started removing the boys."

"Look at what we've done." Briana nodded toward the clear cubes lining the wall.

Three of the four contained a baby boy and were topped with a VSE. The readouts were all 1.0 except for the empty cube where Adam would rest in the coming days.

"We'd like to give the others time with your breast." The nurse lifted

Kifle from his cube and tightened his blanket wrap. They approached, and the baby gave off soft grunts. "They'll be on formula soon, but breast milk is a good start for them."

Briana considered Adam, and I could see her struggling to give him up. After a moment, she kissed the top of Adam's head and exchanged our son for his brother.

Once Kifle attached himself to Briana, I said, "You'll be busy for a while. I'll leave you to it and go to the control room. We want to be certain Le7 and Torne7 have a smooth jump like ours."

"Can't you stay awhile longer? I'm sure Lisa Chicago7 is handling the prelaunch procedures. If she needs someone, other engineers are around."

"I'll be back before you know I'm gone."

Torn between saving my marriage and two males I barely knew, I slowly turned and headed to the control room.

By the time I reached the room, far below ground in a blast-proof bunker, Le7 and Torne7 were dressed in Hipposkin enviro-suits and waiting for the engineers to help strap them into the capsule.

I glanced at the time. We had at least an hour before the jump's final countdown.

"What time is it in Kyiv right now?" asked a med-tech.

"About eleven in the morning." I turned to the junior team member. "But that won't affect our jump. We can set the capsule to reappear at a specific time and date. The time there now is irrelevant." I winked before adding, "But I appreciate your curiosity. I'll ask you any medical questions."

She nodded and returned to the Holo-tablet in her hand.

Once the team strapped Le7 and Torne7 into the zero-gravity recliners, I poked my head into the capsule. "Are you ready?"

"Because of you, I am." Torne7 lifted a leg and wriggled her toes. "I can't believe two weeks ago I broke my foot."

"I take it the Hipposkin sock worked?"

"I've been on the treadmill for hours each day testing it. It's like the break never happened."

"I'm glad it's effective." She'd never know the sock was as much

Simon's idea as mine. "You're important to the success of this jump, and I'd do anything to make sure you and Le7 have a comfortable trip back to 2027." I glanced at one doctor and then the other before adding, "If you're ready, we'll close the hatch door and take over from the remote console. Be prepared in case we need you to execute commands from inside. If all goes well, we should be able to handle anything from here."

They both confirmed with a thumbs up, and I stepped back to allow others to secure the door. While Torne7 and Le7 had survived fourteen thrashing simulations, the real experience would be ten times more vigorous. In a simulation, you knew the ride would end without ultimate failure. In reality, death was a possible outcome.

Lisa stood next to me for the countdown. We monitored the launch parameters and watched the computer readout approach zero with a mixture of fear and excitement for the two doctors inside the capsule. With two seconds to go, the surface bloomed with frost. The skin would reach its minimum temperature before the capsule disappeared from our control room and reappeared in 2027 Kyiv.

Lisa grabbed my arm as a loud POP sounded, and they vanished.

A holographic clock appeared in the space where the capsule once stood. Time counted forward in blazing illuminated digits and wouldn't cease until the travelers returned.

The waiting would be nerve-wracking for everyone on the engineering team—the two of us near the landing pad and those in our offices on the fifth floor. Until the capsule returned, we'd consider how the jump could go wrong—each calculation made to the mere fraction of time and distance measurements. A yoctosecond or Planck length of error could be fatal for the time-traveling doctors.

"You were gone for fifteen minutes." Lisa's voice broke into my thoughts. "It'll be interesting to see how long they'll be away."

Seconds ticked up on the clock.

"We were in 2026 for about an hour. Funny how only a quarter of that time passed here."

Lisa gave me a lopsided grin. "Maybe one day, we'll perfect the program and have them return seconds after they leave."

"If you figure out how to make that happen, we'd name the process after you. What do you think—Lisa's Law or the Chicago6 Law?"

"Lisa's Law." She confirmed with a nod. "Funny, we keep narrowing the timing with each simulation. But even if they tried to come back before they left, we couldn't program the capsule to do that."

I nodded. "Wheaton's Law rules."

"Are we a couple of geeks or what?"

"Definitely geeks." I laughed. "But brilliant ones."

As Lisa drifted toward a bank of virtual video screens tracking their estimated progress, I stepped into a corner to mentally run through my timing.

I ran a finger across my lab coat's waist strap and felt the lump where I'd stowed the medical kit filled with CVIs, vaccines, and sleep solutions. The extra set of restraints remained tucked into the breast pocket of my enviro-suit. Once the lab's medical team was busy with the returning doctors, I'd make my move into the capsule.

The clock added seconds and then minutes. My heart started to race with the passing time, and my resolve faded. I pictured Briana holding Adam in the delivery room. What was I doing?

Struggling between visions of our expanding family and the months I'd spent myopically planning my time jump, I clenched and unclenched my fists.

Was this about fulfilling a fantasy to see Luis or about saving his life?

After twenty minutes, restless energy filled the room. We all knew the capsule should be gone for less time than Briana and me—not more. The routines and on-ground machinery were more efficient than eight months ago.

The medical team adjusted and readjusted fittings on the surgery beds to prepare for emergencies. Would a doctor's or a zygote's life take a higher priority in catastrophic circumstances? Thankfully, that wouldn't be my decision to make. Lisa and I were in the control room to handle technical snafus with the capsule or its programming. People were not our remit.

Two nurses visited each bed to straighten blankets already pulled taut. They did anything to keep active and allow the doctors time to make it safely home.

Lisa and I kept glancing at the clock while we flipped through Holo-tablet screens. We were powerless to do anything until the capsule notified us of its impending return.

Finally, a tone sounded from a control panel. The one we had waited for. It announced the capsule was headed back to our time. A few medical personnel exchanged hugs. When Lisa stepped to the engineering station, I followed her.

A second timepiece appeared below the one tracking how long the mission had taken. It started with ninety seconds and counted the time before the capsule should return. At the room's far end, the VSE screen revealed the doctors' vital signs. One read a solid 1.0, and the other read 6.5. I squeezed my eyes shut to refocus. But when I reopened them, the reading hadn't changed. One of our travelers was compromised.

The medical team clustered at a station under the VSE readouts. They whispered in agitated tones. Desperate to find out who was injured, I left the engineering station in Lisa's capable hands and stepped closer to overhear their discussion. Torne7's name came up a few times. I wished neither of them ill will but was silently grateful Le7 must have escaped injury.

Each click of the timepiece seemed like an eternity. I stepped back to Lisa and peered over her shoulder. She monitored multiple screens controlled by engineers on the fifth floor, who made infinitesimal modifications to course calculations. Like a well-rehearsed ballet, they worked in silent collaboration with each other's computations and reactions.

Two seconds before the countdown reached zero, the cushiony landing pad oozed icy smoke.

"Medical team, be prepared," Lisa called. "They're coming home."

Two doctors and three nurses stood on alert. Their hopes of being irrelevant were dashed when the VSE reading crept to 7.0.

Within the bubbly steam cloud, the capsule materialized. While ice coated the surface, the outer shell had no obvious damage. I checked the hardware monitoring feeds and sighed with relief when the results confirmed the capsule had suffered no harm in the time jump. Whatever happened to Torne7 must have occurred before they left 2027 or early in their return.

After allowing thermal conduction bots to warm the shell, Lisa took the controls and opened the capsule. I leaned inside to see Le7 and Torne7 strapped into their zero-gravity recliners. If not for their sheet-white faces, I'd have sworn they'd never left the control room. Lisa moved to a control panel to address the return protocols.

The medical team swarmed the hatch opening.

"Take Torne7 first," Le7 called out. "A bullet grazed the side of her head. She's lost blood."

Red speckled the capsule's interior walls. The hellish ride back may have taken a higher toll on Torne7 than I imagined. The medical team released the injured doctor's restraints and moved her from the capsule to a surgical table.

As soon as our staff positioned Torne7, they went to work. The lead doctor took control of the metal arms connected to a ball suspended from the ceiling.

The VSE number increased to 8.3 while the tools cleaned the wound and probed inside Torne7, searching for whatever ordnance had pierced her skin.

When the VSE reading bumped to 8.5, Jayla rushed through the entry portal. She must have received notification about the emergency in Briana's delivery room. Jayla called up a Holo-tablet and flipped through screens.

"Give her blood. Now!" Jayla hip-bumped the medical lead aside to take command.

Tubes snaked from the bed and inserted themselves into Torne7's arms, groin, and neck. The VSE reading stabilized at 8.7, and I realized I'd been holding my breath. If it reached 9.0, the team would stop treatment, but what would happen to the five zygotes implanted in her womb?

A nurse crawled inside the time capsule and strained to open Le7's restraints. I helped her to free the immobilized doctor.

"Go help Torne7." Le7 stared at the nurse and pointed at me. "Andes7 can make sure I get to the examination table. I know how to run my body's post time travel analysis. I'm *not* hurt."

"Le7 seems mobile." The nurse turned to me. "Can you assist her?"

I agreed, and the nurse retreated from the capsule. Together, Le7 and I unclipped the belts. She leaned forward and flopped from the recliner to collapse into my arms.

"Steady," I told her. "Take it slowly. You've had a horrific ride, and your body needs a minute to adjust."

The doctor's adrenaline rush would last an hour, but it did little to compensate for the reentry thrashing she'd experienced. I held tight to her waist and guided her from the capsule.

Le7 slumped as mechanical arms flashed around Torne7. My legs had felt like jelly after my demonic return ride. Le7 draped an arm across my shoulders and took unsteady steps toward the examination table.

After Le7 ordered her table to remain in a reclined but seated position, she activated a Holo-tablet. Wires and metal arms lowered from the ceiling. Her VSE crept from 1.0 to 1.2. While maintaining a calm exterior, stress over handling her reentry examination and pregnancy elevated her reading. My engineering background wouldn't help Le7, and everyone else was dealing with Torne7's precarious situation.

Lisa analyzed the capsule's condition on the console. I asked, "Any damage during reentry?"

"There's a code indicating excess moisture in the cabin." Lisa tapped the screens. "But that might be because of Torne7's blood. We'll need to clean it out soon in case the dampness compromises any key components."

Here was my chance to climb into the capsule without raising suspicions. "Not to worry. You continue with the reentry protocols, and I'll clean it up."

Lisa stayed focused on the control console but nodded her agreement.

I grabbed several absorbent antiseptic wipes from a cabinet and approached the capsule.

Before entering, I glanced one more time at Torne7's VSE reading. Despite the world's greatest medical minds and the AI brainpower inside our computers, her number remained 8.7. With a reassuring tone, Jayla said, "I want to hear your ideas about what to do with the zygotes if Torne7 reaches 9.0. We can't leave them inside her."

Le7 gripped the examination table's sides and stared at her colleague. They both should have been celebrating their pregnancies. But Le7 sat, unmoving, as if in shock. Would Jayla force her to take all ten zygotes until they found a different surrogate?

I abandoned the chaos and entered the capsule to kneel on the chair Torne7 had occupied. After mopping up her blood, I tossed the soiled rags out of the hatch.

Torne7 and I had both used the same recliner. I moved into her seat, belted in, and leaned forward to activate the control panel.

My hands trembled as the hatch door inched closed. Long before it nested shut, Jayla called out, "The capsule door is closing! What's going on? Who's inside?"

The closing hatch blocked my outside view, but footsteps approached. Before they could reach me, the latch sealed with me inside.

I'd left the audio feed active. Lisa and Jayla argued in confused excitement.

"Sofia went inside to clean up." Lisa's voice was an octave higher than usual. "I don't know why the hatch sealed. There must have been a malfunction."

"Nothing Sofia does is unintentional." Jayla's tone revealed her skepticism. "Get her out of there!"

After a moment, she called to Simon—the entity she *believed* was at her beck and call. "Simon, deactivate the interior capsule controls."

"Who's Simon?" asked Lisa.

"He's an AI that can stop whatever Sofia is doing." Her voice hesitated. "Simon, I know you can hear me. Open the capsule right now!"

My pulse raced like I was making a hundred-yard sprint. I tried to steady my hands while I paired my vision inserts with the onboard computer and initiated the program Simon and I had designed to take me back to 2027.

"Simon." Jayla's voice grew thin. "Simon. SIMON!"

The temperature dropped inside the capsule while the jump sequence counted down.

Nine, eight, seven.

Conversations from inside the control room faded away.

Three, two, one.

The shaking started.

I was on my way.

2027

Fragrant peonies and wild rose bushes filled the Pierce backyard, but the moonlit blooms were limp and uncared for. Weeds sprouted between paving stones, and the scraggly grass needed mowing.

Using my night vision, I looked for signs of a new pet. There was none. Briana and I had last visited this spot in October when the landscape was past its prime. Based on the mess in summer, I decided neither Megan nor Luis were gardeners.

I stopped to bury a small package between a lilac bush and the fence. I'd seen photos of this spot from my research. In five years, the bush would be taller and the fence more weathered, but they'd still be there, and that's what mattered.

With confidence, I stepped to the backdoor and neutralized the lock. As soon as I pushed open the door, my nose was accosted by smells I'd not encountered on my previous visit. Instead of a hint of antiseptic and immaculately cleaned counters, decaying food rotted on dishes piled in the sink.

If Megan oversaw household duties, as I'd come to understand was the norm in that decade, she'd abandoned her responsibilities. Or maybe she'd always been a slob, and Luis had cleaned up when Briana and I visited to take Luis' seed eight months prior.

A clean spot to remove my medical kit and extract the sleeping cocktails for Luis and Megan seemed elusive. Empty cardboard boxes advertising Tony's Pizza and scrunched yellow paper bags covered most kitchen island space. I closed a soiled pizza container and stacked it on another to open the medical case holding the CVIs, vaccines, and sleep potions.

Simon's motive for giving Megan a separate serum was still unclear. Unbeknownst to him, I planned to administer a half dose. I'd check her reaction and decide whether she needed more. There was no way I'd kill Megan by giving her an overdose of sleep meds or by any other method. When I returned home, I'd deal with Simon's fury.

I removed the CVIs and tucked the kit into my waist pouch before tiptoeing through the living room to the main bedroom. I'd planned to give Megan hers, hoping Luis was a sound sleeper. He'd be next.

Like a teenager on a first date, butterflies filled my stomach. I approached the door and could hear Luis' rhythmic breathing, not a snore but louder than what I might hear from Briana.

If my ARP Luis were here instead of the real one, he'd stand in the doorway with a muscular arm braced against the frame. He'd tilt his head provocatively and ask me to join him in the bedroom or rush to me like he could no longer wait to touch my body—whichever scenario I'd chosen for the evening. But this wasn't my studio, and ARP Luis wasn't here. The real Luis Pierce lay in his bed next to his soon-to-be ex-wife.

Tingles flooded my body.

Stop it! You're here to save his life, and that's all.

But I couldn't shake Simon's teasing about sex. I wanted Luis more than anything I could imagine.

I stepped inside Luis' bedroom and stopped dead.

Things were not the way they were supposed to be. Luis' clothes littered the floor, and one person was in bed.

Where was Megan Pierce?

Stunned, I retreated to the living room. Was she in the bathroom or checking on the children?

I needed to find and subdue her before she discovered me.

My hands trembled as I crept along the hallway to stand before the open bathroom doorway. No one was inside. I recalled Milo's sister slept in the first bedroom. The door was closed, so I leaned against the frame to listen.

Nothing. No sounds of a mother comforting her restless little girl or even the noise of two people breathing while they slept.

Silently, I opened the door. While the pink desk and fluffy bedclothes remained, the constellation lamp and everything else from the dresser's top was missing. A couple of discarded toys lay in the corner, and one stuffed rabbit with a missing arm sat on the bed as if waiting for the girl's return.

Luis' daughter wasn't living here anymore.

I gripped the handle and closed the door before walking to Milo's room.

Finally, I found a space in the house that seemed as expected. Milo lay curled under a red comforter inside his racecar bed.

The little boy had grown since I saw him eight months earlier. As his eyelashes fluttered, I imagined him dreaming about fighting pirates or riding a horse on the western range. My shoulders slumped—how could I know what little boys dreamed of?

"I'll be back to give you your vaccine," I whispered. "You'd better hope Luis can find you to give you the booster in five years."

On my way back to Luis, I took stock of the situation. The daughter was missing, and there was no sign of Megan Pierce. Maybe she'd left Luis to fend for himself. Her disappearance gave me the perfect excuse for not killing her, which might appease Simon. But what if Megan had left in a hurry and planned to come back to kill Milo?

How could I warn Luis?

I had brought a computer chip, designed by Simon, to implant into Luis' brain stem. In five years, the message program in the chip would compel him to dig up the container I'd buried in the backyard and inject boosters in himself and Milo. I'd questioned the ethics of obliging Luis to act without free will. But Simon had shut me down with, "That's the part of this plan that troubles you?"

As I neared the main bedroom, I wondered if there was some way to change the directive and warn Luis about Megan's plot to take their son. If I were back at CYR headquarters, I could access my programs and find a way to modify the instructions. But not here.

I considered the time capsule. I ran through the shortlist of limited programs aboard. In case someone confiscated it, we'd uploaded minimal data to avoid an inadvertent technology transfer to 2027. Nothing inside the capsule could help me modify the chip.

I cursed under my breath. Simon would have safeguarded the message anyway. He trusted no one—maybe, most especially me.

If I couldn't advise Luis, perhaps I could change his circumstances. If he were no longer around in 2027, Megan and her children would move back into their family home. She'd have no reason to kidnap or kill her son. But if Luis disappeared from 2027, who'd tell Milo to take the booster? The AI chip might work if I implanted it in the boy.

My plan had too many moving parts. If I changed one task, another link in the chain became compromised. I ran my hand over the modified restraints stowed inside an interior pocket of my suit. I smiled, comforted to know I had prepared for multiple options.

When I entered Luis' bedroom, I tiptoed to the bed, careful not to trip on the shirts and jeans crumpled on the floor. Luis' breathing came in jerky gaps between his soft snores.

My shoulders tensed, and I rubbed the back of my neck. The ARP Luis didn't do this—his even breaths mimicked robot sleep, not a real person.

Mesmerized, I stared at Luis' parted lips while he inhaled and exhaled. The original's subtle movements rendered my ARP's actions wooden and doll-like. I'd slept with my Luis for countless nights over the past eight months and never noticed its programming flaws. When I returned home, I'd spend vast hours fine-tuning my Luis' mannerisms.

Retrieving the real Luis might be more satisfying. Thankfully, I hadn't injected him with the sleep meds. I had more options with an unsedated man and placed the CVIs on his nightstand.

One glance at the timepiece in my ocular implant told me I needed to act soon.

Luis groaned and smacked his lips.

I froze.

He rolled to his side while pulling the sheet over his beefy shoulder.

I slowed my breath and waited for my pulse to stop racing.

Simon had goaded me about having sex with Luis. Who'd know if I crawled into bed with him? If he stayed half asleep, he might never know we'd had sex. He'd wake up in the morning, assuming he'd dreamt it all.

My body trembled at doing it with a real man, and not any man. He was the person I'd dreamt of for the past eight months. This man was the model for my ARP lover.

My ARP Luis helped me undress, sometimes with a bit of programmed aggression to emulate insatiable desire. I closed my eyes, imagining Luis opening my zip-seal. My suit fell open and slid to the floor.

Cool autumn air breezed through an open window and sent shivers across my skin.

After taking a long breath to calm my nerves, I opened my eyes and slipped under the sheet to spoon against Luis' back.

Luis seemed larger and denser than what I'd created in my program. ARP humans were designed to feel like people. But the actual Luis, with his partial-growth beard, asymmetrical body hair, and skin imperfections, would never match what I had created.

I inhaled his scent. This Luis smelled earthy. I recognized his fragrance from when I was here before. Sadly, I was never able to replicate it in the lab.

With the slow pace of an artist pulling a drape from a masterpiece, I inched back the covers to expose his shoulder. I traced the lines of Luis' muscles along his arm and to his side and across his external oblique. Briefs covered his hip and most of his thighs.

When I slipped a hand around his stomach and into his waistband, he uttered a low moan and turned toward me.

My heart raced.

With his eyes closed, Luis forked his fingers into my hair and drew my head toward his.

He kissed me with deep longing. When Luis released my lips, he pulled me into a crushing embrace.

Every part of my body wanted him.

"Sofie," he murmured, "I've missed you."

I stiffened.

He kissed my neck and shoulders.

Had I imagined it?

No one except Phen had called me Sofie since I was a teenager. Either I'd concocted what he said in my mind, or he'd taken a lover named Sofie after Megan had left. He couldn't possibly have called out to me.

Could he?

His lips tracked across my body, but my thoughts were elsewhere. I barely felt him move his weight on top of me and pull down his briefs.

For months, I'd imagined making love with this man, in my mind and with a fantasy ARP. I controlled what happened and when.

But once the real Luis said my name, our exchange transformed from a fantasy to something deeply personal.

2241

I scrutinized the readouts in the shaking capsule for anomalies like the last time I'd transferred home with Briana. But all figures remained within acceptable levels, and the warning lights stayed green.

I kept my head pressed into the form-hugging, zero-gravity recliner and focused on the gauges. My passenger was completely passed out from the turbulent ride. I was grateful to have secured his head against the seat to minimize trauma.

The timer ticked down. In two more minutes, we'd arrive. My control over the capsule was limited, and the team in 2241 would bring me back. Even if Simon weren't physically in the control room, he'd be watching the action. Based on the capsule's weight, they'd know I brought someone with me.

CYR and the HCC would dish out severe consequences for my actions. I'd stolen HCC property and probably changed historical events. We had no idea how these changes might affect the future. Based on the controls, I believed there still was a future in 2241 and my jump was still part of the timeline. But maybe I was returning to a different world from the place I'd left.

Some time travel researchers professed a Butterfly Effect where a minimal change in the past could result in an altered future. Maybe I'd return along a different time curve or in a new dimension. I shuddered to think I might never see Adam, Latrice, or Briana again.

On my last trip, I enjoyed every minute of our return jump. The voracious rocking made me feel more alive than any extreme sport I'd tried in an ARP suite. But this expedition was a means to an end—like a trip to a long-anticipated destination.

The instant the shaking stopped, my stomach gripped. I waited with apprehension for the engineers to open the capsule. Who'd be the first to come inside and help us with the restraints? Lisa would either be intrigued or angry. Or maybe a bit of both. She may have called an engineer from the fifth floor to join her. While engineers handled most programming manipulation from our main offices, having at least two engineers in the control room during jumps was always a good idea.

The hatch edged open, and vapor drifted inside. Once the fog cleared, I saw the two occupied surgical beds. Why was Le7 on one of the tables? A drape covered the other from head to toe. Someone had died—probably Torne7. The immediate pain of losing a colleague stabbed my gut.

Two people blocked the opening—Simon and Lisa.

While I was gone, he'd made a pivotal decision. Everyone must know he existed. He would need new tactics to preserve his superiority over me and the Memphis lineage.

Simon's head was cocked to one side as if evaluating what he saw.

Lisa stood like a statue with her mouth agape.

"Are you planning to come inside and help with the restraints?" I cast mine off and stood on wobbly legs.

"I expected you to return alone." Simon gazed at me over the top of his glasses.

"There were extenuating circumstances. Megan Pierce and her daughter moved out before I arrived. I needed to change the plan."

"And *this* is how you modified the mission?" Simon's voice overflowed with judgment.

He didn't seem angry. When I eventually approached Briana about changing our living arrangements, I would need his support.

Lisa hadn't moved.

"Simon and Lisa, I'd like to introduce you to Milo Pierce, my newly adopted son. He's come here to be a brother for Latrice and Adam."

"I'm glad to see you've retrieved what you wanted all along." Simon issued a smirk. "But I hope you understand the past has played out as history always said it would."

I struggled to find the words to argue, but Simon was right. Megan Pierce would suffer ramifications for my actions—she was never going to harm her son.

Was I always going to take him? Or maybe I was one of Tobar's subsequent actions that triggered an identical outcome.

FOUR MONTHS LATER

Chapter 24

To keep the time capsule hidden from curious eyes, I'd rematerialized mid-morning in a seldom accessed warehouse storage facility in downtown Denver. The bulky structure's skin smoked with frost as I activated a camouflage hologram.

My gym bag pulled at an awkward angle. Slugging around the archaic duffle would probably countermand any fitness progress I might make during my scheduled workout. I longed for our suitcases—with their safety leashes and directed thought navigation.

I had twenty minutes to reach the Colorado Athletic Club and managed a slow, uncomfortable pace along the rock-hard sidewalk. Without the future's technology to combine shock-absorbing materials and micro hover-capability, athletic shoes from 2025 did little to absorb the concrete's pounding effects.

Once I approached the steel and glass structure, I smoothed a hand across my mid-section and glanced at my profile in the building's reflective windows. The skin-tight workout clothes from this decade held fashion appeal, but the fabric would likely retain sweat.

Did my armpits already have overly ripe odors?

Sniff.

Nope—only the bitter scent from petroleum-based fibers, which seemed more appealing than the choking exhaust fumes on the street. Buses and trucks rattled past me, spewing carbon-based noxious fumes.

Other health buffs slipped by me and into the building. I stifled the urge to beat them inside. Being first in line was not my objective.

As I leaned back to take in the six-story building, vibrations from blasting music made the windows convulse from inside. Rows of runners stared ahead into the glass while they sweated on training machines mimicking actual fitness activities like running or rowing. Their movements were a poor imitation of being in the open.

A woman knocked my shoulder as she rushed past.

"Scuse me," she mumbled and pushed the revolving door.

I'd typically respond with an offhand, "You're blameless." But my three-month training regime focused little on jargon, and I didn't want to startle her with an inappropriate reaction.

If I couldn't seamlessly respond to her, how would I know what to say when I met Luis Pierce?

My already negligible assuredness shrank.

After lifting the bag higher on my shoulder, I entered the revolving door. A few tentative and ineffective shoves failed to move the glass. The simulations back home were more easily managed. An aggressive shove started the door, and I shuffled into the atrium.

The recycled air reeked from body odors, triggering an automatic gag reflex. How many years would it take for engineers to perfect ventilation systems?

As I approached the front desk, a physical person asked, "Are you a current member or looking to join today?" This oblivious employee might be surprised that her company's board members would eliminate her job with early version AI robots.

I slid my authentic-looking but fake membership card across her desk. "I'm an associate of your sister club in Colorado Springs and haven't worked out here before. I want one of your trainers to show me around. His name is Luis Pierce. A manager at my club highly recommended him."

"Sure." She tapped a keyboard and stared at a computer monitor, ostensibly to check his schedule. Despite her handicap—working on the outdated equipment—her motions were fluid, and her smile never faltered. "You're in luck. He's here and available."

From CYR's research, I already knew he would be. But I said, "That's wonderful."

"Go ahead and secure what you don't need in this locker." She slid a key with a flexible strap across the counter. "Luis will meet you outside the women's locker room. Your Springs membership card works on our kiosk."

I took the key and approached an archway with a glass door that barred my entry. Mimicking the actions I'd learned in prep sessions, I waived the card in front of a box, and the doors whooshed open. Uncertain of the timing calibration, I hurried through before they could close on me.

My heart accelerated as I walked past dozens of men and women engaged with massive clanking weight machines. While I tried to narrowly focus on where the locker rooms should be, I couldn't resist stealing glances at the men. I gawked at their bulk as they pressed and curled.

One particularly hairy man in a fitted, sleeveless shirt caught me looking. He responded with a single nod and grinned. I snapped to face forward and ignored his clearly flirtatious gesture.

Stay calm, Sofia. He's a man. Keep moving.

The locker rooms were marked M and W. The HCC was wrestling with whether buildings in my future should equip floors with separate facilities for men and women—once we successfully created a new generation of men. While in the twenty-first century people expected these distinctions, HCC leaders wondered if fewer demarcations would encourage gender equality.

After stowing my gear in the locker, I hesitated near the exit. I ran both hands down the front of my outfit and took a calming breath.

The HCC sent me to charm him and collect data on male-specific characteristics. What if I couldn't convince him to spend time with me?

Five years earlier, I'd felt a similar lack of confidence when competing against the world's best Olympic tennis players. If I'd failed then, I would have only let myself and my teammates down. These stakes were higher. I'd be forsaking future generations of men who wanted to understand mannerisms specific to their sex.

I straightened and stormed out of the locker room with conviction. As I rounded the corner, I nearly careened into the back of a man wearing fitted shorts and a collared shirt in the club colors. He was facing away from me. But I immediately recognized Luis' broad shoulders and short-cropped dark hair.

At my gasp, he turned and gave me a cocky smile. My knees nearly buckled.

"Based on your I.D. photo, you must be Sofia. I'm Luis, and we have about an hour together. Why don't you give me an idea of what you'd like to accomplish today?"

Luis looked precisely like the first time I'd met him—which *for him* would be a full year in the future.

Fighting the urge to leap into his arms, I swallowed hard and conjured my predetermined greeting. "Glad to meet you. I could use an upper body workout and some aerobics training." I extended my hand.

He took mine in both of his, and I glanced at his meaty hands dwarfing mine.

"Let's get started then." His wedding ring glistened as he gave a confirming pat, and my heart sank.

The late afternoon sun disappeared behind tall buildings, and the cement planter box chilled the back of my thighs. I sat near the entrance of a cable-stayed footbridge connecting downtown Denver with the Highland neighborhood.

While I flipped through a magazine, my optical implant scanned the street. According to Luis' historical work schedule, he'd leave the athletic club anytime.

A filthy man walked toward where I sat, carrying a pristine cardboard cup with a well-known coffee company emblem. He smelled of grime and shuffled with a limp. I tensed during his plodding approach, hoping he wouldn't approach me. If he did, how would I respond?

He paused at a trash receptacle, lifting a newspaper from the top and inspecting it with the care of someone selecting the ripest plum from a fruit carton. When he reached a sunny spot near a bush, the man set his cup on a post and pulled a dark blue tarp from under the branches. With slow determination, he straightened the corners until they lay in a flat square— the perfect size to protect him from the chilled concrete and attract warmth from the sun. He relocated his cup within reach and curled into a fetal position on the tarp.

Quick access to my limited data files gave his situation a label— homeless. In the future, everyone had shelter and a basic income.

Government-approved loans provided a stopgap when credits were exhausted. But loans came with strings like mandatory spending counseling sessions, and black-market loans were illegal. Programs to manage spending must not have existed in Luis' time.

To feed her obsessions, my sister Phen had illegally borrowed. She was halfway finished with her five-year sentence on a reformatory farm to repair agri-robots and manage crop yields. While isolated, Phen was well-fed, safe, and comfortable.

How could the homeless man afford expensive coffee if he was without means? Perhaps someone had given him money, and he'd spent it on luxury rather than saving to afford better shelter. Bad decisions had consequences—nothing new about that.

A red light flashed in the corner of my vision as the facial recognition program activated.

Luis was out of the building and on the move.

Heart racing, I jumped to my feet. After tucking the magazine under my arm, I headed across the street toward Chestnut Place, the perfect spot to intersect Luis' route to his bus stop. Moments before my planned collision, I slid the magazine out and held it in front, pretending to be absorbed in a story.

Bam.

My shoulder smacked into Luis. I stumbled and dropped my periodical and purse.

"I'm so sorry." Luis knelt to help scoop up the artificial 2025 purse contents—cell phone, lipstick, click pens, keys, and a red and white mint tin marked Altoids.

Please don't ask me how to use any of these things.

I held my purse open and let Luis shovel everything into the opening.

"I've never met a woman who'd let a man touch anything from their purse." His grin made my breath catch. "You're the bravest woman I know."

What could he possibly mean? While Briana and I maintained separate sleeping rooms, neither of us would hesitate to rummage in each other's belongings. Luis' reaction would form the first entry into my male behaviors log for the HCC.

I lifted my hand to place it on his forearm, but something held me back as if touching him might trigger an electric shock.

Slowly, I withdrew my hand, shouldered my purse, and stood.

I took a long breath and let it out slowly. "It was my fault. I was reading an article and wasn't paying attention to where I was going. Please forgive me." Like I'd practiced a thousand times during my prep sessions, I cocked my head in feigned confusion. "Luis, is that you? I barely recognized you with that jacket over your work clothes."

"That's funny. I'd recognize you anywhere." He blushed. "Wow. I'm sorry, that sounded terrible. I only meant we just had a workout, and you're not particularly forgettable." Luis shook his head. "That didn't sound any better. I'm going to shut my mouth and assume you're used to dealing with flustered men."

"Less often than you could possibly imagine."

Was he as nervous as me? Hard to believe for a married man. Of course, I was married, too. Why did I automatically assume men reacted differently?

"Are you coming from work?" Luis asked.

"I am." I adjusted the purse strap, grateful for the segue. "My firm has a contract with Metropolitan State University. I'm done for the day and headed home."

"I'm betting home isn't around here." He chuckled. "There's no way you're from the area if you call the University by that name. Everyone from Denver calls it Metro."

"You caught me." I drew from my script. "I'm from out west and come to Metro every few weeks."

"I figured as much—no east coast accent. What do you do?"

"I'm an engineer."

"What kind?"

I pretended to straighten the magazine pages as I accessed training scripts through my optical implant, looking for a list of engineering specialties in Luis' time. He wouldn't have heard of my actual field—temporal engineering—as time travel professions didn't exist before 2075. "I'm a computer engineer."

"I'm impressed. A highly intelligent field for an incredibly fit and attractive woman."

"What do my fitness and looks have to do with my profession?" My reaction came out faster than intended, but his response made no sense. Our careers in 2241 were based on measurable factors like aptitude and initiative.

"Whoa. I didn't mean to criticize you." Luis took a step back. "I haven't met many women engineers. Forgive me."

I wanted to push further to understand what he meant and why he assumed I'd taken offense but filed his reaction in my log and changed the subject. "I saw a homeless man earlier. He made a bed on the pavement."

"It's a definite problem around here." Luis' eyes filled with concern. "Did you give him a few dollars? Denver's struggled with how to help them for decades. Never seems like we come up with a good solution."

"He carried a cup with a coffee shop's logo." I ignored Luis' question about giving him money, ashamed it hadn't crossed my mind. "How could he afford to buy it?"

"Really?" Luis' eyes twinkled. "What makes you think he bought it? He might have picked it up from a trash can, or someone gave him a partially finished drink."

I deflected. Luis might disapprove of my ignorance and rash assumption. "Where are you headed?"

"Home." His slow smile reflected his relief at the change in topics. "I take the bus. You said you were going home. I assume you're staying at a hotel downtown. Or do they put you up in an apartment?"

"A hotel." Keeping my response simple would help me recall what I'd said. I certainly wouldn't tell him I'd be leaving soon in a time capsule. "I had a great workout today. Your advice about a balanced, full-body workout struck home. I want to schedule another session with you in two weeks when I'm back in town."

"That'd be terrific." Luis pulled out a device like my fake telephone. "My usual clients book a week ahead, so I'm fairly open in two weeks. You can call the front desk, and they can schedule your appointment. Or if you know the time, I can put you down."

"Okay." Assuming *put me down* meant make an appointment, I suggested, "How about the same time we met today?"

"Perfect." Luis poked his device. "Wow—look at the time. I've got to run if I'm going to catch my bus and get home before 6:00."

"You don't want your wife's cooking to grow cold. She may not forgive you."

Why did I say that?

"Hmm." Luis rubbed his wedding ring with the edge of a thumb. "I'm making dinner for the family tonight." He glanced at the pavement before looking up. Sadness glimmered from deep within. "Dinner's not foremost on Megan's mind lately." Luis must have noticed my blank stare and continued. "Sorry, I don't know why I told you that." He offered an apologetic grin that turned my knees to jelly. "Maybe it's easier to talk with you than I first thought."

"Anytime." I sighed. "But definitely in two weeks. Maybe we could grab a coffee after your shift next time?" I held my breath, wondering if I was too forward for a woman of that era.

"Sure. I'll let Megan know I'll be a bit late."

"Or you could ask her to join us?" Inviting his wife would put my offer in the *I want to be friends* category. Briana would have been pleased.

"Okay." Luis tilted his head. "I'll ask her. But don't be surprised if it's only me. Would that still be all right with you?"

"Definitely." I gave a confident nod and extended a hand.

Surely he understood I wasn't after him.

When Luis shook my hand, a tingle shot up my arm.

Please, help me finish this mission without compromising Mission Y or my marriage.

Chapter 25

The solid-state holographic saucer gave us 360-degree views of Gulf-Africa's vast savannahs.

Our two-year-old Latrice twisted in the secure safety seat beside Briana, desperate for us to free her. Milo was four months older than his relatively new sister and was more of a cuddler than a wiggler. He sat quietly between Latrice and me.

"Look at the impalas!" I reached across Milo to clutch Latrice's knee and pointed, trying my best to distract her.

"Good luck with that." Briana laughed at my feeble attempt while Adam nestled deeper into the downy sling tied across Briana's chest.

At that point in our children's development, Briana had the more straightforward job, handling Adam and leaving me to manage the toddlers.

Well, maybe not at feeding time.

"Thanks for booking the arcade for this morning." Briana paused to mouth a kiss toward me. "Latrice and Milo love this zoo program."

Our saucer cornered, forcing us to lean to compensate for G-forces existing exclusively in our brains.

"They're not the only ones." I grabbed Latrice's middle, prompting a fit of giggles.

"Tickle yourself," Milo demanded as he scooted back.

"Now?" I raised my brows. "What if we miss something?"

"Now." His lips formed a determined line, and he braced both fists on his thighs.

With a dramatic gesture, I extended my arms in front.

Ever so slowly, my hands turned toward my middle and wiggled like they had a life of their own.

"No, no, no!" I stared at my fingers and tensed.

Leaning far back in my seat, I squirmed as if trying to avoid the tickle attack.

Gradually, making use of every second, I drew my fingers closer.

Milo took my antics in stride, but Latrice's mouth dropped open, and her eyes grew wide.

When my fingers reached my tummy, she let out an uncontrollable giggle.

I shrieked in agony as I crab walked my hands over my stomach.

"Stop!" I cried, nearly sliding out of the restraints while groping my ribs. I bucked and contorted as if a tickle monster controlled my fingers.

"You're as bad as the kids." Briana had seen my theatrics many times, but an irrepressible grin crept across her face. "You're going to wake Adam."

I stopped and gasped for breath, adopting a face to mimic relief.

"Again." Latrice jabbed a chubby finger at me.

"What about the hippopotamus?" I pointed, and both children snapped their attention outside the windows.

Despite our antics, the virtual tour had continued. The saucer hovered over a muddy eddy at the edge of a slow-moving river. Brilliant green grasses and shrubs formed a barrier about the mudhole. But wide trails led to the spot, likely tromped by immense animals.

Five hippos languished in the mucky water. Only a few inches of their backs and heads lay exposed above the surface. One enormous beast lurked in the shallows among a crop of leafy plants.

Milo pointed at it. "Turtles."

"Hippos." I countered.

"Turtles," Milo insisted.

On closer inspection, the animal's back was covered with a bunch of turtles.

"Must be new imaging." I turned to Briana. "We've never seen that in this video before."

"It's incredible." Briana adjusted Adam. "Any idea how often they send drones to capture new footage?"

"Not a clue. It could come from research drones or satellites." When an elephant trudged across the path, I turned to Latrice. "Want to touch the elephant?"

"Yes." She pulled at her restraints. "Out."

Milo sat back, waiting to see if his sister's demands were met before expending energy.

"Let's go for a walk." I nodded at Briana. "Want to come along, or would you rather stay inside?"

"I'll go."

"Freeze zoo viewing program and transition to interactive mode for five players."

Our scene morphed from the hover saucer to a grassy opening near the bank. A breeze ruffled my hair, carrying fragrances from dung and vegetation rotting at the water's edge.

"This heat's suffocating me." Briana rolled her eyes. "Can we make it cooler?"

"We can, but it wouldn't be authentic." I chuckled. "Anyway, the heat never bothered you before."

"After being indoors for a year, I'm used to constant temps in the Merlin Building." She shrugged. "Nothing to be concerned about."

"Once the babies are older, you should join me outside."

"I can't make decisions for the other boys, but Adam's not breathing the outside air until I'm convinced he has full immunity."

"But I go outside."

"You're not nursing the babies." Briana cuddled Adam closer. "He's mine until Nanny Tori takes over when he turns one, but not a minute before."

At the mention of her name, Nanny Tori materialized from where she'd stood outside the program marker.

"You look out of place in sub-Saharan Gulf-Africa." I patted the top section of her hourglass form.

"Not at all. Humans can visit via holo-programs. But robots are the only non-natural visitors permitted in these places. The HCC allows me to roam anywhere in Gulf-Africa in silent observation mode." Her sighting ports flashed blue to let us know she wasn't finished speaking. "Humans are only allowed to tour in population centers."

"You got me there." I scooped up Latrice, swung her onto my shoulders, and reached to take Milo's hand. "We're going to feel elephant skin. Why don't you join us and teach the youngsters about them?"

Before I could step toward the elephant, a penetrating tone sounded, followed by, "Urgent in-coming Holo-link call from Jayla Memphis6. Family members are allowed, but ARP Simon Merlin must not attend. Will you accept the call?"

While I wanted to reject the call, Briana jumped in to respond. "Mother wouldn't interrupt us unless it was important." She raised her face toward the ceiling. "Bifurcate interactive zoo program and incoming call."

"Okay." I heaved a heavy sigh and turned to Nanny Tori. "Please bring Latrice and Milo to the elephant while Briana and I take this call."

Nanny Tori and the children moved to the room's far side, where Latrice touched the elephant's hide, and the nanny robot spewed statistics about elephant populations and feeding habits.

Briana and I moved to a corner where the program carved out a space. We settled onto a comfy sofa in a living room setting, waiting for the connection.

"Why do you think your mother's blocking Simon?" I stroked Adam's balding head. "He looks so different from when he was born. Where did all his hair go?"

"Into his blanket. It'll grow back." Briana adjusted his sling. "I don't know about Simon. Makes me think this is serious. My mother includes him in everything."

Jayla's holographic image appeared, but she'd masked her surroundings with a gray blur. Based on how Jayla's saffron-colored shawl moved in the wind, she likely sat on a balcony at the Capitol Complex Guesthouse.

"We're in the middle of the zoo program with Latrice, Milo, and Adam." I moved my thigh next to Briana's. "What's so urgent, and why did you ask us to ban Simon from this call?"

"My work at the capital is on a need-to-know basis, and Simon isn't currently on the list."

"He's not, and we are?"

"Neither of you is on the list either." She glared at me, and I figured she wanted to say, "Especially not Sofia." But she continued without the jab. "You should understand what we're dealing with here. I would have arranged this call with Briana, but she'll tell you anyway."

I moved closer to Briana to emphasize our solidarity.

Jayla clasped her hands in her lap. Her lips narrowed into a fine line. Whatever came next would be serious or devastating.

"What's happening with Brad?" Briana tensed, and I reached for her hand. "Last night you told me he was fine, and your trip was for a routine checkup."

Jayla stopped Briana with a raised palm. "That's the HCC company line right now. A handful of people at the top know the truth. CYR leadership, the other presidents, and representatives from the press don't know what's happened. And you mustn't tell anyone."

My heart raced. *What's going on?*

"You're scaring me." Briana pressed a fist against her thigh. "Is Brad dead?"

"No." Jayla crossed her arms in front of her chest. "He's showing early signs of HAV infection. But we're fighting the virus, and it hasn't yet advanced to TWS."

"How did this happen?" Briana sunk against me, and I slipped an arm across her shoulders. "You supervised building Brad's living quarters. They were identical to our setup here."

"They're still investigating how the virus could have infiltrated the building. There may have been sabotage."

"Why didn't Brad's vaccinations protect him?" I leaned forward, wanting answers. "With all the filters in place, no saboteur could have brought in enough HAV to contaminate him."

"You have to realize this only happened in the past few days. Security is checking how the virus got in Brad's space, and the medical staff is working on why the vaccine didn't protect him."

Jayla stood and moved toward her daughter with her arms extended. Burdened with Adam in front of her, Briana rocked forward a few times before she could rise to accept her mother's hug. Briana wouldn't have felt the warmth from her mother's body, but the virtual hug would have been a start. My wife loved me but still needed her mother.

"How is Brad doing?" Briana mumbled into Jayla's image. "Is he in pain?"

"We've induced a coma. Based on Brad's brain patterns, we believe he isn't suffering. But the virus is ravaging his body." Jayla stepped back and stared at her hands. "I'm not sure we'll ever wake him."

"Don't say that!" Briana patted Adams's back harder than usual.

"Do you want me to take Adam?" I jumped up and offered my hands if she were willing to let him go.

"No." Briana held him closer and shifted her weight to rock him.

"You need to be realistic about Brad's condition." Jayla shoved her hands into her pockets. "While he doesn't have TWS, the damage is severe. We can use him to test treatments for the other boys if they contract the virus."

"You're making him an in vivo study subject?" Briana snapped at her mother.

I stroked Briana's arm to calm her and considered the medical terminology. I wasn't familiar with in vivo, but *study subject* seemed clear. Nausea bubbled from my stomach. I swallowed hard to suppress anything from coming up.

"You need to listen to everything I'm telling you." Jayla shifted her weight. "His damage is extensive, and we'll probably never revive him from the coma. The best we can do is ensure his continued contribution to Mission Y."

"Does Celine Ottawa7 know what's happening?"

"Of course she does. Brad's her son." Jayla grasped something behind her—maybe a balcony railing. The ends of her scarf fluttered in the wind. "Ottawa7 hasn't left Brad since his symptoms started a few days ago. She's beside herself with grief and believes his situation is her fault for moving him to the capital too quickly."

"Don't forget that Brad is my son, too. I carried him for eight months, and he started with my eggs." Briana took a breath. "When are you planning to tell the other presidents? They won't take kindly to being left out of this discussion."

"As I told you at the beginning of this call, there's a short list of people who need to know. The HCC doesn't want Brad's situation announced to the public. So the fewer people who know, the better."

"Thank you for telling us." Briana stared at the floor.

"Of course." Jayla's eyes narrowed as they drifted toward me. "Based on how Sofia reacted to that rumor about how the babies might be distributed, I don't know if she can keep this to herself."

"Please don't talk about me like I'm not here." I stepped forward.

"The last thing we need is for you to send missives to the HCC or alert the press about Brad's treatment." Jayla scrutinized Briana. "Do you think she can be discreet?"

"Sofia will have to be." Briana reached out to take my hand. "She will—for me."

I'd do my part, but did the HCC believe they could keep Brad's condition a secret from the world? "You know this office sends daily broadcast videos of the three boys still in CYR headquarters. Ottawa7 streams at the same time."

"The boys enchant the public," Briana added. "HCC's marketing arm wants to put a live cam in the nursery."

"Live feeds? I'll make sure that idea goes on hold." Jayla nodded as if making a mental note. "Your team should keep uploading videos. The ones from Panama City will continue as well. But they'll be computer-generated imagery. Engineers are creating an ARP for Brad. He'll age and play like the other boys. Anyone watching will be none the wiser."

"Sounds like you've got this all figured out." I sighed.

The HCC would be fooling the public while Brad became their test specimen.

"I've been in meetings day and night since Brad's condition worsened."

"I assume Celine Ottawa7 will hold a private ceremony for Brad." Briana brought up the subject but wouldn't travel to the capital while the other three boys were still nursing and vulnerable. She and I could join via Holo-link.

"He's not dead." Jayla scoffed.

"A permanent coma doesn't sound like living," Briana retorted. "Just let Ottawa7 know our hearts are with her. If she'd like to talk with me, I can arrange a private, encrypted line. If you hear anything about a ceremony for Brad, I expect you to let me know."

"Fine." Jayla tapped her foot. "Since the boys were born, you've become very assertive."

I grinned. Jayla had noticed it, too.

"Get used to it, Mother. I've spent all my adult life trying to keep the peace with you and letting you run over me. Let's agree to be honest with each other for the time we have left."

"I'm not dying anytime soon." Jayla lifted her chin in defiance.

I took a step back to give mother and daughter room to spar.

"I wasn't implying you would." Briana softened. "You're in fine health, and I hope you're around to celebrate lots of birthdays with your grandchildren. Latrice and Adam miss you while you're in the capital."

But not Milo. Jayla barely gave him the time of day.

"I doubt that." Jayla crossed her arms. "You and Nanny Tori keep my grandchildren engaged. I hope I'll return for a break in a few weeks."

"That'll be nice. Until then, we can arrange a few Holo-calls for you to talk with them."

Unable to stop myself, I barged in. "Hey, speaking of calls, why did you exempt Simon from this one? Why can't he know about Brad?" While time travel concepts were his forte, his processing power could help mitigate Brad's decline.

"Simon is resident in Denver. Now that he's disclosed himself, I'm in an ongoing battle with HCC leadership—they want to grant him powers to leave CYR headquarters. If they have their way, he could materialize and have system access in all the HCC locations with connections to CYR or Mission Y."

"Does he want to go outside the Merlin Building?" He'd hinted at greater access before my clandestine jump but not since.

"Of course he does." Jayla straightened. "He's been asking me for more geographic fluidity since my mother introduced me to him nearly forty years ago. The original Simon Merlin made it clear ARP Simon wasn't to materialize beyond the building. Once we allow Simon to transfer his program outside his current security barriers, we lose control over him. You forget that I was eleven when the original Simon died. I was there when my mother spoke with him about his creation."

"I've known Simon for a few months. But for you two, he's always been there."

"I can definitively say the original Simon never intended his ARP to leave CYR headquarters." Jayla glanced over her shoulder. Without seeing her setting, I had no idea what drew her attention. "Be assured—the ARP Simon won't gain greater proximity freedom while I'm still alive."

"Who are you expecting to carry on with this edict after we're gone?" Briana reached into Adam's sling, giving him her attention.

"You first and then Latrice." Jayla scoffed.

"I'll present him to Latrice soon." Briana stroked Adam's head.

When Briana met ARP Simon, she was five years old. Latrice was barely two. What was the hurry?

Lisa and I huddled inside the time capsule to prepare with only three days left until two doctors traveled to what used to be Francistown, Botswana to fertilize their eggs. Each computer program, hardware system, and safety feature needed testing.

"Thanks for coming in today to run these protocols with me." Lisa inserted a bypass circuit to measure response times. "I know the HCC is pushing to monopolize your days through January. But Mission Y needs you, too. You've managed more jumps than anyone in Mission Y. We can't afford to lose your experience."

"They're pressuring me to ignore what's happening at the lab. But I keep pushing back." I levered off a bolt and set a loosened panel on the floor. "They don't know what they want. First the HCC asked me to be their spy, and now they want me to go back in time to harvest data on male behaviors. Briana and I decided not to ask why. If they clear my record of past indiscretions, I'm happy to do whatever they ask."

"Spying?" Lisa set down her tools and moved to sit cross-legged, giving me her full attention. "You didn't mention this before. Who were you supposed to spy on?"

"Relax." I'd already said too much. "I'm not qualified to work in espionage, and they changed their minds. I'm too old to start training in a new field."

"You're twenty-four." Lisa snorted. "How is that too old?"

"I've trained and worked as an engineer for ten years." I waved a coolant flow meter at Lisa. "We're close to the same age. Tell me whether you're keen to switch jobs at this stage in your life."

"Thanks for the compliment, but I turned thirty-three last month." Lisa turned back to her work. "There aren't enough credits in the world to get me to change jobs—even if at times I wonder whether we're on the right side of this mission."

"What are you talking about?" I gripped my continuity tester.

"I have a balanced view about reintroducing men." Lisa shrugged. "Don't get me wrong. I love our team, and time travel is an important field. I wish we'd worked harder on finding a way to bring back sperm without needing to reintroduce men."

"You've looked at the science and all the early results. Retrieved sperm doesn't survive—only male zygotes inside a live uterus make it." I gave her shoulder a shove. "If you discover a way to do it, you'd be famous."

"It's a bit late to rework Mission Y's core objectives, and who's got the time to do their job and more research?" Lisa grinned. "I'd rather lose to you in tennis on my off-hours."

"Are we playing this afternoon during break?"

"When'll you finish your HCC conference call?"

"We're meeting soon. I can send you a message after we're through."

"No." Lisa fidgeted with her Holo-meter. "This afternoon I'm working with procurement. There's a delay in the boron supply chain from EuroRosse."

"No problem. I'll go for a run instead." I turned to my panel. "Our boron reserves are critical. Can't we buy it locally?" California's boron supplies weren't depleted.

"It's cheaper and easier to use EuroRosse's suppliers. They're pushing back to negotiate a better price."

"Their delay could affect the January jump. You'd think they'd be more amenable since a EuroRosse doctor is scheduled to travel in January."

The countries needed to pull together for Mission Y since they all had much to gain from cultivating a new group of men.

Dr. Atacama6 folded her hands on the polished mahogany conference table and glared at me. Our meeting was well into the second hour, and with each passing minute, her animosity escalated from 5,800 kilometers away in the capital.

"Why did you decide to leave 2025 after only twelve of their hours?" Atacama6 tucked a strand of ebony hair behind an ear.

"I contacted Luis Pierce twice during the mission, and he'd be suspicious if I orchestrated a third. Plus, it was too soon in our association to show up at his home. There was a title for individuals who followed people—they were called stalkers. If I approached him again, Mr. Pierce might have responded with a police order for me to stay away."

"I see." Atacama6 nodded and tapped on her Holo-tablet, noting something I'd likely regret later. "We've discussed your six log entries, and I appreciate your thoughts on what Mr. Pierce might have meant. I have a few follow-up questions."

I stood to retrieve a water softpack from the chiller, hoping she wouldn't ask if I had a physical reaction to him. While I'd try to misdirect my response, these proceedings were recorded. Simon had warned me the HCC would run the footage through a lie-detection program.

"You mentioned Mr. Pierce seemed open to meeting you when you returned to Denver."

"Yes."

"Do you believe he'll want to have intercourse with you next time?"

"What?" My breath caught, and I nearly dropped my water pack. "None of my log entries suggested he wants to have sex with me, and I certainly didn't give him the impression I was available."

"I'm not suggesting you did." Atacama6 cleared her throat before continuing. "We believe many men at that time chased sexual relationships. Historical records indicate that about 25 percent of married men had intercourse outside their marriages. However, these studies relied on data supplied by the participants, and other studies estimated the average person lied a minimum of once to twice per day. We hope your research will help us support or refute these historical findings."

"Based on a sample of one?"

"Of course not." Atacama6 rested her elbows on the table and stared at me. "Your experiences will form a basis for future studies."

"Be sure to write down that I haven't done or said anything he could construe as an overture." I squeezed the softpack so hard that water leaked from the ecostraw.

"I will. But would you consider his demeanor flirtatious?"

"Based on what criteria?" Simon would be pleased with my deflection.

"Think back on when you met Dr. Briana Memphis7. How did she let you know she was interested?"

Briana and I met during the 2236 Olympics. I was competing in tennis, and she was with the American volunteer medical staff. Briana had taken three precious weeks off from work to join us in Singapore.

Before the competition started, I appeared on an athlete panel for an interview, and she sat in the front row. Every time I looked into the audience, I saw her staring at me. When the interview ended, she approached.

After that, Briana managed to find her way to the front row of my tennis matches, including my final loss. She was tender, supportive, and adoring. I felt safe and protected with her.

"Well?" Atacama6 leaned forward and tapped a finger on her lips.

"She listened and was there when I needed her. Plus, she's charming."

"What physical attributes do you find attractive in your wife?" Atacama6 touched her Holo-tablet.

"Is this relevant?" I could talk about Briana's height or smooth skin or the little bit of belly fat that felt sexy under my touch. But none of that was Atacama6's business.

"Yes." Her smirk belayed her insistence. "We need to know if attributes for attraction are consistent with males and females."

"I never said I was attracted to Mr. Pierce, and I don't know if he finds me attractive."

"Yet he's planning to see you again."

"For a scheduled workout and coffee when he's off work."

"An after-hours meeting could be construed as an invitation to a sexual encounter."

"Hardly. I even asked if he wanted to bring along his wife." That should let Atacama6 know I tried to force a platonic meeting. I sucked the softpack dry.

"I see." She pressed her lips together as she formulated her next question. "So do you think he might want you to have intercourse with both him and his wife? Three-way engagements might have been popular."

"You're way off target." I tossed the empty pack across the room and fist pumped when it landed in the trash can. "Mr. Pierce gave me no indication that he wanted to arrange a sexual encounter—with him alone or with him and his wife. He seemed friendly and sexually disinterested."

"I'll make a note of your observations in this area." Atacama6 abandoned her Holo-tablet and placed her palms flat on the table. "You'll tell us if his ambitions change?"

"I'd be surprised if they did."

Again, Simon would be pleased with my response. I breathed a sigh of relief. Atacama6 never asked whether I felt attracted to Luis. I planned to spend time with my ARP Luis later that day—not the same as the real one, but a good substitute in my circumstances.

Long afternoon shadows fell across the path when I jogged into Survivors Park. Following my routine, I slowed after reaching the park and walked around the twelve monuments.

I swiped the back of my hand across my brow. Dried sweat had crusted along my hairline, leaving a gritty salt ring. Denver's dry air absorbed my perspiration before it had time to drip down my neck and into my new Hipposkin running suit.

I paused in front of Simon Merlin's obelisk, silently thanking him for his life-long research and advancements in time travel and temporal engineering studies.

And for creating ARP Simon, who despite lots of grumbling splits his time between my engineering team and Briana.

Without looking, I backed up to sit on a bench within the circle surrounding the monuments. Two benches away a woman coughed and caught my attention.

Mia. She had the advantage of seeing me first and scowled when I glanced her way.

She stood with a huff and yanked a leash connected to her scruffy little dog, encouraging him to leave the park with her. "Come, Shampoo."

I should have let her leave, but I couldn't help myself. "I'm sorry I haven't returned your calls."

"You're sorry?" Mia snapped around to face me. "You have a lot of nerve snubbing me again. Last spring I thought we were friends, and you disappeared. Then a month ago, you called to apologize. You said you wanted to make up for lost time." She stabbed a finger toward me. "I haven't heard from you since that call. What am I supposed to believe?"

She had every right to be angry.

Unbeknownst to her, my first disappearance was in response to demands from the HCC. I'd reconnected in September because the HCC demanded I spy on Mia to gain intel about the Front.

Days after I'd called Mia, the HCC changed my mission to travel back to 2025 and accumulate data about men through a liaison with Luis Pierce. Embarrassed about the call, I'd never circled around to tell Mia I'd changed my mind.

"It's not a good excuse, but work's been crazy busy." I crossed to where she stood and knelt to scratch behind Shampoo's ear. "Anyway, I felt guilty about seeing you. I get the impression you want more from our relationship than I can give you. You know I'm in love with my wife."

"Then why did you call me?" She eyed her shoes. "I've been clear about my intentions."

"Not exactly." I stood and tipped her chin with a knuckle to stare her in the eyes. "We did research together last spring. I didn't mean to lead you on, and you never told me you wanted something more than friendship."

"We spent hours alone together. I knew you were married, but you didn't talk about Briana. You never offered to introduce us. What was I supposed to think?"

Mia had a point. I'd used her prohibited websites access to investigate the Cursed Decades and Luis Pierce's history. I could tell she was flirting but chose to ignore the signs. "I enjoyed our time together and am truly sorry if I gave you the wrong idea."

"Sorry worked for the first time but not for the second."

Mia gave the leash a swift jerk. Before I could stop myself, I said, "Please don't take out your frustration with me on Shampoo."

She turned in a huff before calling over her shoulder. "Do *not* contact me again."

I'd burned a bridge the HCC might later ask me to mend. Mia had powerful friends. Hopefully, she wasn't vengeful.

Chapter 26

OCTOBER 15, 2241

Briana and Simon leaned over the transparent isolation chamber. She manipulated a tissue sample with Holo-tweezers while laser beams scanned inside.

"Whose tissue are you messing with?" My question from the entryway made Briana's hands jump.

"Don't startle me like that!" Briana clapped her hands to dissolve the protective gloves and any potentially hazardous materials clinging to them before withdrawing her arms from the box. "It's a low-level project—on the fringe of Mission Y's program. Looking for signs of blebs or necrosis."

"Looks like dinner before it's cooked." I peered into the box. "What is it?"

They responded simultaneously. But Briana said, "kidney," and Simon, "lungs."

"Can't be both." I sniffed.

"Actually, it can." Briana glared at Simon. "We've evaluated two samples. They're both in the chamber."

Briana took me by the arm and walked me to the other side of the lab—far from the isolation box.

I can't believe she's running a low-priority job with Drs. Meru7 and Lascar7 leaving for 2026 Botswana this afternoon.

"The results should process quickly." Briana nodded toward Simon. "He's helping me."

"Seems like you're expanding your repertoire." I teased Simon. "When did medical research take priority over your work in temporal engineering?"

"The Memphis women have always benefited from my help with medical conundrums." Simon straightened and tugged at the lapels on his wrinkled raincoat. "I'm no one-trick pony."

"I've not heard that one before. But I get your gist." I shook my head after taking in his costume. "I'm sure you've already explained it to Briana, but what's with the outfit?"

Simon's raincoat hung loosely over a taupe antique business suit. A stained navy necktie draped from his neck.

"His name was Columbo, one of the best twentieth-century police detectives."

"Real or imaginary?" I raised a brow.

"Good question." Simon's mouth turned into the grin he used when mocking me. "While fictional, he always solved crimes through unrelenting pursuit and finely tuned intuition." Simon disappeared and reappeared uncomfortably close. I felt his engineered breath against my hair. "His character was based on a similar detective in a nineteenth-century book by an author from a country called Russia."

Was Simon trying to distract me?

"The former country of Russia represented 31.277 percent of the combined European and Asian landmasses in the mid-twenty first century." Simon leaned over me and continued. "However, the figure varied depending on which countries were occupied by the Russians at any given timeframe. But I believe the number is close enough for our purposes."

"I'd have said it was about a third. But I appreciate your precision."

"Why did you stop by?" Briana placed a hand on her hip.

"I planned to ask you for a date night. Want to carve out some you-and-me time tonight?"

Briana blinked without responding. She'd never passed up alone time before.

"Let's wait until Meru7 and Lascar7 come back, and we're sure they're safe."

Briana's hand trembled as she wiped her brow. She glanced at her fingers as if they didn't belong to her. After a moment, Briana shoved her hands into her jacket pockets.

"What's going on?" I stepped forward and tipped Briana's chin with a finger.

"She's nervous." Simon dematerialized and reappeared next to Briana.

I peered into her eyes, waiting for her to respond.

She stared at the floor.

"Don't be concerned." Simon placed a hand on Briana's shoulder. "Before you came in, we were talking about the last jump—when the police shot Torne7."

"Don't worry about today's jump." I elbowed Simon out of the way and drew Briana into my arms. "The capsule's in top shape, and the Docs are fully prepared. Nothing bad is going to happen to them."

"It's not only the jump." Briana pulled away and studied me with red-rimmed eyes. "I can't stop thinking about Brad."

What could I say to ease her anxiety? "We have to believe the medical staff in Panama City is doing everything to keep him comfortable." I pulled Briana close and rubbed her back. She tensed. "Hey. Am I hurting you?"

"No."

"Really?" Remnants of a wince lingered on Briana's face. "Don't lie to me."

"You're too observant." Briana's smile seemed forced. "I've been doing double workouts in the gym—taking off my baby weight. I probably overworked my lats the other day."

"I thought you looked slimmer." I patted her rear. "Don't lose too much. I like you with meat on your bones."

"Don't worry about that. I'm still snacking on nut butters." Briana nodded toward Simon. "He's got me under constant surveillance. Probably under orders from my mother."

"What makes you think Jayla's the only one around here interested in your health?" Simon peered at Briana over the top of his faux glasses. "You're stuck with me."

"Be sure to get our girl in positive spirits." I winked at Simon. "Stop dwelling on what can go wrong—here *and* in Panama City." To Briana, I said, "Let's help Nanny Tori with the kiddos for their dinner and have a late meal for the two of us."

"I'd like that." A weary smile crossed Briana's face. "Why don't you make a reservation and message me the time?"

"Perfect." I hoped I wasn't pushing Briana to stay up later than she wanted. "I'll leave you two with your low-priority project."

By the time I paused at the entrance, Briana and Simon were already back at the isolation box.

The pair seemed excessively absorbed in a task unrelated to Mission Y or helping Brad.

In the control room, a holographic clock hovered over the space where the time capsule once stood. To my surprise, the tone signaling our travelers' return sounded when the clock read thirteen minutes. A second timepiece appeared below the first and counted down from ninety seconds.

"That's good news," I said, turning to Lisa. "Out of our three sperm harvests, this is the shortest yet."

"I can't imagine Meru7 and Lascar7 are intentionally trying to beat your fifteen-minute record." Lisa chuckled.

"I'm just pleased they aren't delayed like the last jump." The image of Torne7's sheet-covered body still haunted me.

"With the donor living on Francistown's outskirts, our calibration included a greater margin for error—both for the landing site and interference from 2026 inhabitants." Lisa nudged my arm. "Look at the VSE figures—both doctors have readings close to 1.0."

I released a slow breath. Healthy returning travelers meant the cargo and capsule would reappear without damage, virtually assuring my return to 2025 in twelve days.

"When is your next jump?" Lisa asked as she tapped the control console and manipulated several Holo-screens.

She was likely curious about the timetable. But Lisa knew the engineering team would ready the capsule immediately after these travelers returned—despite my schedule.

My jumps were classified, and the only women at CYR headquarters with that information were myself and top leadership—except for Briana, who knew more than most. While I'd told Briana I'd go twice a month for four months, even she didn't know the dates or times until shortly before

I left.

"Our team needs to make sure I can go tomorrow if the HCC tells me to." I smiled, hoping she didn't take my ambiguity personally. "They've got me on a short leash, and I go when they signal me."

"But they wouldn't schedule you to leave on the same date the capsule returns, right?"

"Why not?" I should have changed the subject, but Lisa's curiosity derailed me.

Lisa stared at the return clock as it clicked from four to three, and the landing pad oozed icy smoke. A cloud blossomed and nearly obscured the capsule as it materialized, covered with vapor and ice.

"I don't see you preparing to zip out of here anytime soon. So I assume you aren't leaving today or tomorrow."

"As soon as the doctors are out, we'll prep the capsule—whether my flight's this afternoon or in two weeks or a month."

"I don't know what all the secrecy is about." Lisa shrugged. "We know the dates for the next half-dozen sperm harvest missions. What's different about your trips back to 2025?"

After our date-night dinner, Briana and I languished in bed in her studio. I brushed Briana's belly with the back of my finger and traced the fading stretch marks until she laughed and rolled onto her front. "Don't remind me the scars still show." She chastened me into her pillow.

"Your body is stunning, and the resurfacing treatments have mostly erased the stretch marks." I pinched the skin over her ribs, prompting a giggle. "But is it safe for you to lose weight so quickly? You're skin and bones. I liked you better when you had more to hold on to."

"You should put on 60 extra pounds in a few months and be happy about it." Briana pulled the pillow from under her head and shoved it at me. Her playful smile told me she wasn't angry.

I snuggled beside her, shifting my body to spoon hers. She smelled of her favorite soap with hints of sandalwood and musk. I slipped an arm around her body to pull her close. The ribs in her back felt like rungs from a ladder.

"Please don't lose too fast."

"Can we drop this conversation?" Briana flipped around and brushed a stray lock away from my face. She kissed me deeply, sending a pleasant shudder across my skin.

As her lips left mine, I stared into her dreamy eyes. "I worry about you. Is that wrong?"

"No. But you'll be doing another jump soon." She sighed. "When you're in that capsule, I'd like you to remember something other than a fight about diets."

"I'll be thinking of you—and Latrice, Adam, and Milo." I stroked her cheek. "But not Jayla."

"That's understood." Briana chuckled and rolled onto her back. "You must be happy to have her stationed in the capital."

"I'm not missing her if that's what you mean." I mirrored her position and stared at the blank ceiling. "Invoke constellation program," I called to the room. It responded by dimming the lights and transitioning the ceiling into a dark sky dotted with bright specks and occasional flashes to mimic shooting stars. I had a similar program in my studio. "I'm glad she's with Brad."

"Me, too."

Briana's heavy sigh made my chest tighten. Had I brought up another subject she'd rather avoid? "We don't have to talk about Brad if you don't want to."

"It's okay. Brad's on my mind all the time. The news keeps showing videos with computer-generated imagery of him playing with President Ottawa7. He kicks and pushes her hands. Yesterday, they posted one where he rolled from his tummy onto his back."

"I watched that one, too." I tracked a blinking satellite across the ceiling. "You'd never believe the images weren't real."

"Adam hasn't gotten that far yet." Briana's voice was soft as a whisper. "Maybe the HCC wants the world to believe Brad's an overachiever."

"Let them believe the best about him." I'd seen Brad for occasional visits in the isolation ward in the three short months before an AereoPod whisked him to Panama City. But Briana had carried him for eight months. He was our Adam's twin brother. Even though Latrice was 100 percent Briana, Brad was her half-brother. Come to think of it, since Brad came from Luis' sperm, he was Milo's half-brother, too. "He's serving humankind differently, and the public doesn't know it."

"You always know how to find something positive in a bad situation." Briana pulled the cover over her body.

"Increase room temperature to 21 Celsius," I called out to address her chill.

First the zoo program was too hot, and now she's cold.

"I'm fine." Briana tightened the fabric across her chest.

"Usually you like it colder than I do." Perhaps pregnancy had changed her tolerance for cooler temps. Briana's lips pressed tight, and I knew I'd struck another nerve—time to redirect. "I watched a vid with President Ottawa7. They used a beach setting for the background. I can't imagine anyone believes she took Brad outside."

"They'd use a faux background whether he was healthy or not. They do it for sequences with Adam, Kifle, and Issey, too. The HCC videographers say the local backgrounds make citizens feel the babies are part of everyday life—nothing to be worshiped." Briana drummed her fingers on the cover. "I wish Brad was the baby in the videos instead of being trapped in a lab under my mother's care."

"Let's hope Jayla can muster some tenderness for him," I mused.

"You know my mother's not the cuddly type." Briana scoffed. "But I can suggest it on our next call with her."

"Even if I could live without her jabs and how she pushes your buttons, our kids probably miss her." A brilliant moon rose in the eastern sky, and the distant stars dimmed in response. "Since Jayla turned 56, they may not have her for long."

"I guess that's a good reason to make the most out of every minute we have with her." Briana took my hand.

Chapter 27

Lisa adjusted my restraints inside the time capsule and tugged on each strap. Our pre-flight stress tests measured the fabric's failure potential, and acoustic wave tests did the same for connectors. Still, our safety protocols required her to evaluate each clasp manually.

Simon materialized on the arm of my zero-gravity recliner. "All systems are GO." He stood about six inches tall, wearing a CYR lab coat and holding a Holo-tablet.

"I've never seen you so small." I chided him. "Or looking like a company lackey."

When Lisa cocked her head as if wondering what I'd meant, I realized Simon must have materialized through my optical implant, tricking my brain's occipital and parietal lobes into believing he stood inside the capsule.

To Lisa, I said, "Simon's here, double-checking the programs."

She nodded and continued with her pre-flight checklist.

"Don't let my dimensions and garb fool you." Simon peered at me over the top of his dark-rimmed glasses. "I'm still larger than life. There's barely enough room in here for you and Lisa Chicago6. I can be considerate when I want to."

Tempted to return his sarcasm, I ignored him. Bantering with Simon would be rude to Lisa.

Simon turned his back and tapped his Holo-tablet.

"Are you ready for the ride of your life?" Lisa placed both hands on my thighs and squeezed the Hipposkin enviro-suit. I could feel her touch as if I wore nothing at all.

"This is my fifth trip, and it never gets old." Adrenaline quickened my heart rate in anticipation. The VSE readout ratcheted from 1.0 to 1.2.

"I wish they'd let me try." Lisa clasped my shoulder. "You're lucky to go back again and again."

"Briana would disagree with you. One time was plenty for her." I poked her arm. "You've ridden in the simulator. What did you think?"

"Is it the same?"

Lisa would expect an honest answer, not one to placate her. "No. It's not even close. The simulator shakes the crap out of you, but time travel pounds you like putting your forehead under a percussion drill. When I travel, I can almost feel my cells getting ready to explode."

"Now I'm jealous." Lisa ran a hand over the console as she backed out, leaving me snug inside a recliner. Before she hefted the door closed, she paused. "I still think they should give us your schedule. If I'd known you were traveling today, I'd have uploaded our latest vibration control patch. You might have a smoother ride."

Simon gave her a sideways glance and a look that told me he'd uploaded the program enhancement without her knowledge. If so, she would discover the change after I left for 2025 and give him a hard time for tinkering with the programs without the requisite signoffs and logbook entries. But that was a fight for Lisa and Simon.

"Meru7 and Lascar7 made it back twelve days ago, each carrying five new zygotes embedded in their uteruses." I tried to appeal to Lisa's concerns. "I'm sure I can handle the program's last build."

"Despite that, consider asking HCC to release the schedule." The door closed with a thud. Air whooshed as the capsule's compartment flooded with supplemental oxygen to increase the internal pressure.

"What's with Lisa Chicago6's ceaseless pestering about your timetable?" Simon dissolved and rematerialized next to my chair.

"Why are you wearing a CYR uniform?"

"I've added an immutable object to my functional programming. I dress to fit in whenever I'm in the control room. I want colleagues to treat me as an equal."

"You're far from equal. You can program circles around all of us."

"True." Simon's mouth spread into a wide grin. "You always know the right thing to say."

"I'm speaking the truth." Four months ago, when I returned after giving Luis Pierce his TWS vaccine, Simon told me he'd have my back. We both hoped Luis would connect with Simon's original in 2060 and mentor him. For the time being, Simon was on my side.

"I expect you to give me a full description of your time in 2025 when you return." Simon's voice construction was both demanding and suggesting.

"I'm available to talk, but don't you have access to Dr. Atacama6's official transcripts?"

"Seriously? I can tell by your micro facial expressions you didn't tell her everything." Simon sneered. "Anyway, she's not smart enough to ask the right questions. I want all the salacious details."

"There's nothing to tell. They told me to develop a friendship and list any inherently masculine traits, and that's what I've done." I recalled the homeless man I'd seen on my last trip to 2025. "Wait. Before you leave, do you think homelessness was a male or female condition?"

"In 2025, 71.038 percent of the recorded homeless population in the former United States of America were males." Simon examined me over the top of his fake glasses. "Why do you ask?"

"I forgot to mention it during my last debrief with Atacama6. Maybe extra details about other males in 2025 will make her happy. She's always disappointed with how little I know about Luis." My suit started to compensate for a temperature decline. The capsule's thirty-second countdown had begun.

"We can talk more about this when you return. I need to transfer into the control room before you leave." Simon rolled his eyes. "The last thing I want is to spend half a day fixing broken code if part of my program leaves the Merlin building."

Hmm. Had Simon already tried and failed to escape the building's confines?

2025

When Luis motioned toward a table in the coffee shop, I stood, unmoving, unsure of what he expected.

"Go ahead and save us a table." Luis placed his palm on my back and gently pushed me toward an open spot near the window. "I'll bring the coffees when they're ready."

At his touch, warmth spread across my chest like a syrupy wave. I cleared my throat and walked on wobbly legs toward the table.

If Briana and I left the CYR complex—to share a meal or stop for refreshment—we would find a table and ask a holographic attendant to bring us our order.

We minimized interaction with servers and order takers because they were not humans—only machines designed to remove undue burdens on other humans.

Did the people in 2025 imagine human service providers would disappear? It shouldn't surprise them. In the 1900s, air conditioning units took the place of domestics fanning their masters. Computer programs replaced rooms full of scribes. But people living in 2025 might anthropomorphize service robots, especially ones designed with human features.

Before I could pull a chair away from the table, a sandy-haired man stepped in front of me and set down his drink. "Care to join me?" he asked.

"Oh." I jerked back in response. "I didn't know this table was taken." Without signaling through my ocular implant, how would people know my intentions?

"I don't mind sharing." His eyes scanned my face and briefly dropped lower. Clearly, he was evaluating my physique. In my time, mothers counseled children to keep their gaze above the neck. Any deviation was rude and could be perceived as body judging.

"I'm here with someone else," I stammered.

"There's four seats and plenty of room for three." He settled into a chair and pulled a slim computer from his satchel. "Maybe you misunderstood. I'm here to work. I won't bother you and your friend."

Had I misread his overture and wandering eyes? Atacama6 assumed all males were after sex. Was I falling into her mindset?

"Sorry." I cleared my throat. "We have a private conversation planned. I'll find another table."

The man was already tapping on his keyboard. Perhaps his friendly demeanor was designed to snatch the table from me.

Well, it worked.

I bumped the table before I moved on and gave him my sweetest smile as he snatched his coffee to keep it from spilling.

Patrons occupied all the other tables. Most were single customers tapping or talking into devices. A few couches and overstuffed chairs sat in the room's darker recesses—many unoccupied except for a couple snuggled in an oversized chair. They whispered and snickered with first-date mannerisms.

Luis waited near the counter for our drinks. Would he mind talking while sitting on a sofa, or would my choice seem too intimate?

Like my assumptions about the man who took my table, I was probably overthinking Luis' potential reaction.

Time to decide.

After striding away from the windows, I plopped onto an armchair beside a roomy sofa. I bent to sniff the fabric and guessed it was genuine leather—the skin of an unfortunate animal.

When Luis approached with our drinks, he found me flipping pages of a magazine. He set down the cups and pulled the publication from my hands. "You didn't strike me as the type to read *Vanity Fair*. Not that there's anything wrong with it. But you haven't seen any recent movies, you don't watch TV, and you don't follow sports. So I figured you're not interested in pop culture."

"I found it on this table and was looking at the advertisements." Telling the truth would be easier than remembering a pile of fabricated lies.

"A computer engineer who follows marketing trends?"

"Something like that." I picked up the drink with my name on it and took a sip. Maybe it was my imagination, but the latte seemed less creamy than the ones I drank in 2241. Luis' time couldn't compete with the future's manufactured milk products—rich flavor, enhanced nutrients, and no abused animals.

"Thanks for another great workout today." After slipping off my athletic shoe, I leaned back into the chair and pulled a leg underneath. "I was sore for two days after our last session."

"I find that hard to believe. You must work out all the time to stay in shape." Luis blushed. "One of these days, I'll stop tripping over my tongue. I wasn't trying to flatter you—it's just that I can tell by the weights you use you're not new to lifting."

"You're right. I work out every day—when I'm not playing tennis. Do you play?"

"I was on my high school team."

"Not only the football team?" The words left my mouth before I could stop them. Nearly a year had passed since I'd seen the media photo on Mia's computer. That image was the first time I'd seen his cocky smile. The same grin emerged when he tilted his head, no doubt considering my question.

"Did I mention playing football?"

"No." I cleared my throat. "You seem athletic, and I assumed you might have played. Did I guess wrong?"

"I was on both the football and tennis teams in high school. Tennis paid for my Health Fitness Specialist degree in college."

What could he mean? In the future, education was accessible to anyone. How could playing tennis convert into upper-level training?

To avoid admitting my ignorance, I dropped the subject. Conversations with my ARP Luis were more straightforward—if I said something he couldn't process, I asked his program to delete it.

For the next hour, I steered the conversation into areas he might be inclined to discuss. Besides sharing his philosophy about fitness, he told me about his two children, six-month-old Milo and three-year-old Olivia. While he went on and on about his progeny, he never talked about Megan.

Perhaps he assumed I, as a female, would be interested in hearing about his children. I'd make a note of his topical focus for Atacama6.

"You and your wife must be proud of your children. Especially Olivia. It sounds like she's already mastered the alphabet." His description of her achievements seemed rudimentary for my time. With only half the life expectancy in 2241, we made the most of our lives and taught our young early. Many toddlers spoke several languages and understood coding concepts long before their fourth birthday.

"She surprises me every day." Laugh lines creased the corners of Luis' eyes. "Last night, Olivia insisted she wouldn't recite the alphabet anymore. It was too easy. Once they added new letters, she'd start doing it again."

"She's clever." Latrice was cheeky enough to say something similar.

"Megan must have enjoyed hearing that story as well."

"I haven't had a chance to tell her." Luis ran a thumb along the seam in his cup. "She doesn't always spend the night at home."

How should I respond? Instead of changing the subject, I devised an excuse. "Does she work evenings?"

"No." Luis scanned my face as if trying to decide how much to disclose. "I barely know you, but you're a great listener, and I haven't been able to confide in anyone. I don't want my folks to know about it."

Briana might be surprised to hear someone say I was an accomplished listener. She'd likely suggest I constantly blurted out the wrong words. I pressed my lips together, hoping to avoid my verbal diarrhea.

"A few weeks ago, Megan told me she was having an affair with a guy she met at the police department. Her mother's the Chief of Police in Denver, and Megan spends a lot of time in the stations."

"I'm sorry to hear that." I pushed myself into the soft cushions to distance myself from his story but desperately wanted to hear more.

"Megan told me she won't give the guy up."

"Does she want a divorce?"

"That's the crazy thing." Luis leaned forward and rested his arms on his thighs. "He's married, too, and neither wants to divorce. They want this affair, and his wife and I should play along. Megan doesn't plan to tell Milo and Olivia about him. She says this arrangement will keep our family together. Megan would live a lie in our home and see him whenever she feels like it."

"All on her terms?" I squirmed in my seat.

"Megan says I'll get used to it."

"That's a lot to ask. How do you feel about it?"

"What choice do I have?" Luis hung his head. "I can't make her stop seeing him."

"Do you think she'll eventually come back to you if you go along with her?"

"Part of me hopes that can happen. But every time she goes off to meet him, another piece of my love for her fades. How can someone who swore to love and respect you change like this?"

I knew full well that relationships were complicated. Briana took me back after learning I'd designed a fantasy lover to imitate Luis, made a repeat visit to see him in 2026, and brought his son to the future.

While Luis was unaware of my circumstances, Briana knew about *him*. She believed my infatuation was over, and I was time-traveling to see Luis at the HCC's insistence.

Even though I'd promised to erase my ARP lover, the program remained intact.

The difference between Megan and me was that she was honest about her affair. Would I want Briana to experience the pain Luis expressed?

For the moment, Briana was blissfully ignorant of my selfishness.

Chapter 28

OCTOBER 30, 2241

The annual call with my sister Phen happened on a rainy day last year. But on this lunch hour in October, the sun shone brightly, leaving long autumn shadows on the fitness path. The wind ripped crisp brown leaves from desiccated tree branches and skittered them across the track into a concrete ditch border.

The ditch would be flowing or at least wet from Cherry Creek in spring. But in the fall, the bed was bone dry. I drew parched air into my lungs on my run to Confluence Park, where the creek met the South Platte River. The sweet, musky scent of rotting aspen leaves tickled my nose.

When I reached the tables, I found them occupied and searched for a place to make my call. At the park's far edge, a flat boulder sat under two white androgynous dancing figures. They were twenty meters tall and towered over the trees. The plaque underneath said Borofsky created the piece more than two centuries ago.

The sign didn't indicate whether the sculptor was a man or a woman—either was possible that long ago. Had the city's curators intentionally decided to keep those specifics a secret? If so, I suspected the artist was male.

I scrambled to the boulder's top and pulled a light jacket from my waist pouch. After deciding whether to cover my shoulders or behind, I smoothed it over the knobby surface and scooted on top. The sun's rays warmed my dark jogging shirt, and I pushed my sleeves past my elbows. My Hipposkin running suit would have been more comfortable, but I'd left it behind because the weather seemed mild when I left the Merlin Building.

Before I could unwrap a protein bar, my com-card vibrated. As I thumbed the card's connection button, my ocular implant activated the encryption program to block others from accessing the call.

Phen's image materialized in front of me, a duplicate of my features but with longer hair tied into two braids. She'd woven bright blue ribbons into her hair.

Would Briana like a similar look for me?

No. The contrast against Phen's dark hair seemed a bit non-conformist. Briana was too conservative to appreciate an avant-garde style.

Since I was sitting on a rock instead of a table, Phen's chair looked like it was floating in midair. Beyond her, boxy agri-robots crept along the evenly spaced rows at her reformatory farm.

"What are those white pillars?" Phen squinted at me.

"I'm at the bottom of an enormous sculpture in this park. Let me move the card so you can see the dancers." I tilted the card to scan the structures.

"What the hell?" Phen laughed. "Somebody stole their genitals."

"Who knows what they were thinking?" I joined her chuckle. "The artist didn't think it was important for us to know whether the figures were male or female, and the name plaque doesn't give a clue about the artist's sex either. It makes me think both say *gender is irrelevant*."

"Is that the sculpture's name?"

"No. But maybe it should be. It's called Dancers."

"It's nice to laugh with you." Phen took a sip from a wine glass—something red—I guessed a merlot. Her part of southern America was known for the red wines they recultivated. "Frankly, it's nice to laugh with anyone. Being around robots for the past couple of years is pretty boring."

"What about your ARP lover?"

"Yeah." Phen sighed. "He's still around and continues to evolve. But it's not the same as having a flesh and blood companion. He's too amenable."

"I forgot to ask you last year. Does your ARP have a name?"

"ERAC."

"Eric?" I leaned forward to hear her better. "I guess that sounds romantic."

"His name isn't spelled the way you think. It's E-R-A-C for ERgonomically and Anatomically Correct. He's designed for my comfort and pleasure."

My laugh jerked me so hard that I nearly lost my balance on the boulder.

"It's not that funny." Phen lifted her chin as if offended.

"You've spent too much time alone," I chided. "My ARP has a name, too. It's Luis—the same as the guy the HCC wants me to keep visiting in the past. He's the man I met a year ago."

"What?" She tipped her glass at me. "The all-powerful HCC authorized you to time travel beyond when you went with the high and mighty Briana?"

"Stop calling her that." Phen had never met Briana and likely coined the name when I'd talked about Briana coming from the world-renowned Memphis lineage. "I'm scheduled to go back eight times to early 2025 and form a friendship with Luis Pierce *before* we take his sperm. He's the guy we used to impregnate Briana when we traveled back last year."

"Let me get this straight." Phen wriggled in her chair, ostensibly to find a comfortable position for my story. "A year ago, you went back to October 2026 and nicked some guy's jizz. You fell madly in lust with him and created an ARP in his image. Now the HCC is sending you back again—earlier than your first encounter—so you can become his pal before you steal his seed?" Phen shook her head. "This is too much. What does the HCC have to gain from your trips?"

"They want to know about inherently male characteristics."

"Why you?"

"I assume it's because they suspect Luis and I can forge a connection. It's less efficient to send someone who might fail to interact with a man." Unless Phen asked, I had no plans to tell her about my clandestine trip to see Luis the previous summer after Briana birthed Adam and his three brothers. I didn't want to hear her judgment about how I broke laws and suffered negligible consequences. Phen was serving a five-year sentence for illegal debt, and I'd hijacked a priceless time machine.

"Seems pretty suspicious to me and frankly too decent for the HCC. Are you sure about their motives?"

"That's what they've told me." Phen's question made me wonder—

was Atacama6's badgering intended to distract me from considering whether the HCC had ulterior motives?

"Well, I don't believe it." Phen raised a brow. "Seems like lots of resources and wear and tear on the time capsule. Are they planning to assess male characteristics on your experience alone? They're smarter than that."

She had a point. At our next meeting, I'd try to squeeze Atacama6 about the HCC's plans. In the meantime, Simon might help me figure out their real purpose.

"Are you pleased with the ARP lover program I sent?" Phen asked.

"My ARP Luis is fun to talk with and knows how to pleasure me. But he's not like the real thing. My heart pounds when I'm near the real Luis, and I trip over my words. It's disarming."

"So you get what I said about ERAC." Phen crossed one leg over the other and snuggled into her chair.

"Yeah. Maybe that's why being with ARP Luis doesn't feel like cheating. I don't love him the way I do Briana."

"Are you in love with the real Luis?"

"No." My response came out quickly—maybe a bit defensive. "I wouldn't call it love. Maybe infatuation. Briana made me feel this way at first, too. I couldn't stop thinking about her. But after four years together, we feel more comfortable and less passionate."

"Uh-huh." Phen ran a hand down her thigh. After another sip of wine, she gazed out into the farm fields and away from my image. "I've heard from my captors. My penalty officer asked if you might want to visit my farm."

"I'd love to come." I hadn't seen her face-to-face in years.

Phen gawked at me, her eyes wide with surprise. "Why would you want to travel all this way to see me?"

"For one thing, Mom died since you've been trapped there." I ran a nail alongside the card's edge. "We talk once a year, but I look forward to it."

I stared hard at Phen's face and noticed lines deepening at the sides of her mouth. At twenty-five, we might have twenty more years to live. But Phen lived life to the fullest and befriended women who survived on the other side of the law. Who knew how long she'd be around? "Seeing you in person would be better than a short call once a year. You're the only family I have left."

"What about your family in Denver?"

"Just because I love them doesn't mean I don't love you. We're from the same flesh." I stood to stretch. "Are you trying to talk me out of coming?"

"Not at all. When my farm had bumper yields this year, my officer said I deserved a bonus. She suggested a family visit. Honestly, I prepared for you to turn me down."

"You're an accomplished farmer?" I laughed.

"It's not hard for an engineer to keep a few hundred agri-robots in top condition. They do all the work—not me."

"Well, it's nice for them to offer you a bonus." My ocular timepiece warned our call would end soon. "Will the central government contact me or someone from the Judicial Division?"

"Not sure."

"Well, whoever calls, I'll pretend you haven't warned me."

"Good idea. Someone will send you a missive asking whether you want to visit." She stared into the distance. "When I last spoke to my penalty officer, she asked if you might be inclined to bring your son. I can't imagine Briana would let you bring Adam with you."

Hmm. I stroked my chin, giving myself time. "I'm guessing she meant Milo. He's two and a half."

"What?" Phen jerked upright in her chair and almost knocked over her wine. "Who's Milo?"

"Milo is Luis' son. I brought him forward from 2027. He's my son now."

"You brought a boy forward from the past?" Phen's jaw dropped. "Why hasn't he contracted the HAV?"

"I gave him a huge dose of vaccine before we traveled through time, and our medical staff's been dosing him for the four months he's been in CYR headquarters."

"Are you comfortable bringing him here?"

"That's a great question. I'll talk with the doctors who monitor his resilience. If they think he'll be safe, I'll bring him. If not, I'll come alone." I chuckled. "I assume you don't want me to bring Briana?"

"You've got that right." Phen chortled. "But be sure to download ARP

Luis for the trip. Maybe he and ERAC can interact and expand their repertoires about how to please the Andes7 women."

"Sounds like a plan. I'll wait until your handler contacts me. What's her name?"

"Whitney7"

"First name?"

"I've never asked." Phen grinned. "I call her Whitney7 to her face and Half-Wit when I talk about her with ERAC."

Phen's earlier comments about the HCC's ulterior motives niggled in the recesses of my mind. "Did you know about rewards for crop yields before they gave you this benefit?"

"No. But I'm not complaining."

"You're more suspicious than I am. So why aren't you wondering why the justice system is granting my visit?"

Phen grasped her glass, twisting it at the stem. "Maybe we should be."

A chill swept across my exposed arms. Were Phen and I pawns in a government scheme?

Briana and I leaned over the desk in her office, sharing a virtual jigsaw puzzle offered through the CYR's enhanced visual-spatial reasoning program. Since the babies had been born, we habitually took a twice-a-week afternoon break in her office.

I tapped in a piece and stroked the back of my fingers over Briana's forearm. When a shiver shook her body, she pulled down the edge of her sleeve.

"You need to check the environmental settings in here." My implant's atmospheric moisture reading displayed 27 percent humidity. "You're shedding dry skin like crazy. Can I add more humidity to your airflow?"

Briana gave a slow nod and didn't respond. Her attention never left the puzzle.

"Don't worry about it." I stroked Briana's hand. "With more moisture in the air and a good lotion, your skin will be as smooth as Latrice's."

"You're right." Briana glanced at me before resuming her search for puzzle pieces. "I've been busy with work and ignored my daily rituals. I'll order a cream with extra collagen. That should make a difference."

"I need to talk with you about something." I drew a breath, unsure of how to proceed.

"Yes?" Briana leaned back into her chair.

"Right before I came to your office, I received a missive from the Justice Center in the capital."

"What?" Briana returned to the puzzle. "Why are they after you now?"

"It's not about me." *Thank goodness for that.* "They've invited me to visit Phen at her reformatory farm. It's in southern America, about two hours by AereoPod."

"That's pretty far." She tapped the puzzle to insert a piece. "How long will you be gone?"

"Only for a couple of days."

"A couple, as in two, or more like a week?"

Fair question.

My time was stretched thin between the missions, spending time with the children, and my team's work schedule for the sperm collections.

"Two nights at the max." I took Briana's hand. "I could ask them if you might join me."

"No way."

The last thing Briana would want was to visit a prison farm. But I had to ask.

She continued. "I'm overloaded here at the lab, and the little boys can't manage without me yet. Anyway, I don't know your sister."

"Okay. But you might like to meet Phen at some point."

"You haven't seen her in years. You'd have a better time without me hanging around." Despite Briana's newfound family assertiveness, she was still a master at passive aggression. She'd build a case for not going without saying she didn't want to come.

"You're right." I took her cue. "I can go alone if you can't come."

"Why are they asking you to see her now? Are they considering extending her sentence? Or maybe she's done something to damage the farm?"

"It's not like that." There was no need to compromise Briana with my illegal calls to Phen. "I've always painted Phen as a troublemaker to you, and we never got along as kids. But if the Judicial Division suggests I visit her, she must have asked." I squeezed Briana's hand. "If Phen wants to see me, I don't want to turn her down. This visit might be what we need for a fresh start."

"You're already leaving twice a month for the HCC's time travel missions." She stared at my hand on hers. "I know each jump only takes a few hours. But the prep and your Atacama6 debriefings take time, too. Now you're planning to leave again?"

"Phen's not asking me to move to the farm. It's a couple of days." I moved around the desk and draped my arms around Briana's neck. "I'll be back before you know it."

Briana relaxed into my embrace with a heavy sigh.

"One more thing." I leaned close. "They've asked whether I wanted to bring Milo with me."

"Is that safe? Not that I have any say in the matter." Briana raised both hands in surrender. "Milo's your son, and you need to decide on your own."

"I messaged Milo's medical team right after the Justice Center called me. They'll have an answer in a couple of days."

"It seems like a big risk to take him into the atmosphere at this point. He's only been here for four months."

"I'll let the team weigh in and then decide."

"Good idea." Briana cocked her head. "I've seen Milo's medical charts. He's responded well to the HAV vaccine. Maybe better than the other boys."

Before Milo and I left 2027, I injected him with the vaccine laced with Simon's long-lived nanobots. I'd never mentioned the bots to the medical staff and assumed Simon had told them. Could those bots have anything to do with Milo's exceptional resistance?

Chapter 29

My heart pounded as I tried to keep up with Luis' pace. He led us along Wynkoop Street until we reached a small truss bridge over Cherry Creek. In his time, the creek was a stormwater drainage ditch with high cement walls sheltering the waterway and a fitness path. While Cherry Creek existed in 2241, durable, natural-looking materials reinforced the banks.

Luis hooked to the right and accessed an entry ramp to a concrete running trail that bordered the creek bed. I paused at the ramp's summit to read a plaque about the bridge constructed in 1908 for railroad use.

What am I thinking? This isn't the time to play tourist.

Before Luis disappeared, I looped down the ramp and sprinted until I caught him.

"I thought I'd lost you for a minute," Luis called. His voice showed no trace of being winded.

"I stopped to read about that bridge." Gulping air, I caught my breath.

"Why?" He chuckled. "You can read it another day. The bridge and the sign will be there forever."

Luis would never comprehend that railroad relics hadn't been preserved in my time. Our bridges were constructed from more environmentally sensitive materials than steel or concrete.

"It caught my attention."

Once I fell into an even rhythm next to him, my heart rate stabilized. I struggled for a breath. The thin atmosphere hadn't changed in 215 years, but the air in 2025 tasted dirty, embedded with grit from vehicle exhaust and uncovered fields.

"How far do you want to go today?" Luis asked.

"I'm willing to go with the current. I don't need to get back to my office right away. You decide."

"With the current?" Simon raised a brow. "I get your meaning, but I've not heard that one before."

"It must be something they say on the west coast." I pushed past him to hide my blush. Avoiding colloquialisms would be trickier than I'd assumed.

"Hey, slow down. If we're going to make it to the Cherry Creek mall, I'd like to keep a breathable pace."

"Okay." My training covered shopping malls—a setting where people came together to evaluate goods and socialize. "How far away is the mall?"

"Just over three miles. It'll be about 6.4 round trip.

My implant translated the length into 10.3 kilometers. In four decades, the entire world would abandon his archaic measurement system.

As we ran along the path, passing walkers and women pushing baby carts, I kept my attention squarely on Luis. He rarely talked, but I homed in on his breathing and the sound of his rubbery shoes slapping against the pathway. My sight drifted to his rhythmically pumping legs. His defined muscles coiled and uncoiled like thick ribbons of rope. The circumference of one of his thighs likely exceeded the girth of both of mine.

"You better watch where you're going." Luis laughed.

Had he noticed where my eyes had wandered or that I was looking down instead of forward? I shook my head and glanced beyond the walls bordering the path.

"Do you see that?" I skidded to a stop and asked before I could harness my excitement.

"What?" Luis slowed and turned to look over the embankment. "What did you see?"

"It's that statue with the enormous dancers."

"Yeah. What about it? It's been here for close to twenty-five years."

"Here?" I figured it had always been in Confluence Park, where I'd called Phen.

"Yes." Luis ran in place. "In front of the Performing Arts Complex. Don't tell me this is the first time you've seen it. You've been working right across Speer Boulevard at the Auraria Campus."

How am I getting out of this one?

"Forgive me." I cleared my throat. "I've gotten my directions turned around on the fitness path. I thought we were running west."

"At this point, we're headed south. But our route is mostly southeast. As an engineer, I never imagined you were directionally challenged." Luis gave me his disarming smile. "Don't tell me you're one of those women who's always losing her way?"

"You believe men perform better at orienting and cardinal directions?" My mouth dropped at the revelation.

"I didn't say that." Luis laughed and placed a hand on my shoulder. "Some women have a reputation for being bad at directions. But all the ones I know are better than me. Talk to some fitness instructors at the gym—Holly is a board member for the Denver Orienteering Club, and Kris teaches map and compass for the Colorado Mountain Club."

Luis squeezed my shoulder before turning back to the path and starting slowly. "If we keep stopping, this jog will take all day."

I looked at where he'd touched me. Luis' fingers were strong, and he'd gripped me with confidence. My ARP Luis had identical dimensions, but the copy seemed small and frail compared to the real Luis. I sighed and leaned into a run to catch up.

After nearly a half-hour on the path and another ten minutes along a wide sidewalk next to clanking, gasoline engine vehicles, Luis abruptly turned into a small park. He approached a stone obelisk with a metal figure emerging through a curtain. Luis placed his toes on a step and shifted his weight to stretch his calves.

"What was the Hungarian Uprising?" I asked after reading the plaque.

"Not sure. But I assume it had something to do with bad politics in the former Soviet Union."

I bit my lip to keep from asking more about history so familiar to him and utterly foreign to me. I chose a different side of the monument and mimicked his stretching routine.

"It's been a couple of weeks." I started my practiced lines. "Are things at home getting better?"

"Nope." Luis sighed as he switched legs and stretched. "Megan spends more nights with him than at home."

"I'm sorry to hear that."

"In some strange way, I'm getting used to it. She waits until I come home from work and has dinner with the family like nothing's happening. After Milo and Olivia are asleep, she leaves the house and comes back early in the morning before they get up."

"What if they wake up in the night?"

"Both of them have. They crawl in with me for a few hours and go back to their beds before Megan comes home. They've never asked why she's not there." Luis stared at his feet. "Maybe somehow they know."

Children understand more than they admit. Were they coming to comfort themselves or him? "Do they treat Megan differently than before she started her affair?"

Luis cocked his head as if rifling through memories. Simon made that gesture when he was searching through databases or calculating. The original Simon Merlin must have assumed it made ARP Simon seem more human.

"Milo's pretty oblivious, but Olivia seems guarded. She's spending more time alone in her room. It could be a normal phase or something related to what's happening with Megan." He stretched his arms over his head. Luis' thick muscles creased his thin shirt across his shoulders. "Last night, Megan told me she's taking the kids away for Thanksgiving."

"She's taking them on a trip with *him*?" After the words came out, I knew they were laced with judgment.

"Good God, no." Luis twisted at the waist, stretching his obliques. "Her folks live in Nebraska. They'll drive out there for the long weekend. I'm not invited."

Holidays still existed in the future, but women chose which days to celebrate and followed family traditions—sometimes based on heritage or spiritual occasions. "My work schedule has me in Denver for loads of holidays. I can't keep them all straight. What day does Thanksgiving fall on this year?"

"Thursday." I'd grown accustomed to knowing when Luis was teasing me and rolled my eyes in response.

"Date?"

"The 27th."

"I don't want to be presumptuous, but I'll be in Denver on the 27th." Would offering to make plans with Luis seem too forward? If he were a female friend in 2241, a similar invitation would seem normal and innocuous. But male/female interactions were a bit of a mystery. "Are you opposed to having company for Thanksgiving?"

"Wow." Luis stopped to round the statue's edge and stood before me. "I'd love company. Not only to keep my mind off not being with my kids, but it would be a great way to spend the day."

"Perfect. You'll need to give me directions. I look forward to a traditional meal."

"Whoa. Who said I'm cooking dinner?"

I sputtered, searching for a way to respond.

Luis placed his now familiar hand on my shoulder. "I'm giving you a hard time. I'm a great cook, and having you over for Thanksgiving dinner would make my day." He squeezed, and my knees went weak. "I have to warn you. We'll be watching the game."

I nodded but had no idea what he meant. When I was back in 2241, I'd research what type of *game* he could possibly mean.

Chapter 30

**REFORMATORY FARM, CENTRAL SOUTHERN AMERICA—
NOVEMBER 17, 2241**

After putting Milo to bed in the second-story loft, I came downstairs and found Phen sitting on the deck, watching dozens of cube robots roam among the plant rows.

I stopped at her bar service to pour myself a glass of southern America's finest red wine and crossed to the railing. Once I leaned a hip against the transparent fencing, I inhaled the wine's complex fragrance with hints of raspberry and plum before taking a slow sip.

When we arrived hours ago, Phen gave us a tour. She described both her work and what she expected from the machinery. The farm was eerily quiet compared to Denver's constant background sounds. The city reverberated with voices, the whine from electric motors, and clanging robots keeping the streets and walkways detritus-free.

Besides a faint hum from the agri-robots, the only other sound came from drones. Like bees returning to a hive, drones flitted in and out of squatty warehouses where they recharged and received software updates from the collective and Phen.

I recalled Phen's name for the robots—FART. When Milo repeated the word, Phen and I laughed uncontrollably. Much to my dismay, he'd adopted the acronym as his new favorite word. I'd need to figure out a way to convince him to stop before we returned to Denver in three days. Briana and Jayla would be less than pleased if he encouraged Latrice to repeat it. Of late, she'd started to mimic her older brother's every word and action. They were adorable together.

"Care to call up our ARPs?" Phen asked from her lounge chair. "I assume you brought Luis with you?"

"I did." I fingered the data card in my pocket and scanned the roofline covering the deck. "Are you sure the Justice Center or the HCC isn't watching?" The HCC had never confirmed knowledge of my ARP Luis. While it wasn't illegal to create an ARP for personal use, Luis' core programming came from Phen, and I had no idea whether she procured it lawfully.

"I'm confident they can't listen in."

"Always confident, but sometimes wrong?" I didn't want to insult my host. But from an early age, Phen played in the gray margins of the law.

"Not this time." Phen continued with her defense. "I'm the best programmer you'll ever meet. Besides, with all the efficiencies I've installed for the agri-bots, I've got loads of free time to evaluate the systems here. I've swept every line of code controlling this place and installed added encryption for my bedroom and out on this deck, where I meet with ERAC. The blocker makes any ARP's image and voice invisible to surveillance devices."

"Okay." I withdrew the card and placed it next to Phen's chair on an end table before retreating to the deck edge. "But first, I'd like to talk with you about the real Luis."

"How often has the HCC let you see him so far?"

"I've seen him three times. The next time is in about a week. He's going to fix me dinner for a holiday they celebrate in 2025 called Thanksgiving."

"What planet are you from?" Phen huffed. "Everyone in America has heard of Thanksgiving. Just because our roots are from southern America and it was a northern tradition doesn't mean I don't know about it."

"We grew up in the same household, and Mom never talked about it. How could you know?"

"The ARP arcades include old holiday themes. The programs create elaborate costumes and food, all related to the traditions. You ought to try it sometime."

"I can't believe you'd encourage anyone to visit the independent arcades, especially after what your ARP addiction did to you." Behind my back, I gripped the transparent barrier's top rail.

"Not everyone is as susceptible as I was. I didn't become an addict until

I started the erotica ARPs. The holiday routines are cheap and might be fun to do as a family—or on a date night with Briana."

"Still, I'd rather not start down that path." I took a sip of wine. "We're off track. I wanted to talk about Luis."

"Okay. You've seen Luis three out of eight visits and already convinced him to have dinner with you."

"He's *making* dinner."

"Without robots?" Phen grinned. "You'll need to give me the details so I can program ERAC to cook a meal for me. It sounds romantic."

"Besides dinner, we'll watch a football game on a broadcast device."

"I'm not familiar."

"It never regained popularity after 2060. Football was a male-dominated sport with two teams pushing and shoving each other while trying to carry or toss a ball into the other team's goal."

"Like a more physical version of soccer?"

"Something like that, but you can move the ball with your hands, and it's shaped differently. To help me prepare for this next jump, Simon found antique game footage. More than a few players got hurt, and there was a lot of grunting and posturing."

"Yum." Phen rubbed her crotch. "I could watch a few rounds of that. Sounds positively delightful."

"Great segue for my questions." Holding my wine glass with both hands, I pressed my back against the cool, clear fencing. "Whenever I'm near the real Luis, I feel like my world is spinning out of control. It takes all my concentration to maintain a normal conversation. If he comes close or touches me, I can barely stand. Every one of my erogenous zones is on high alert."

"Is there a question in there somewhere? Sounds pretty normal to me. Those feelings are what hooked me into daily visits to the arcade."

"And you've never had those same feelings when you dated women?"

"Never." Phen set down her glass and leaned toward me. "What about you?"

"I can't remember whether the intensity was the same, but I've always been attracted to Briana. Even now, our lovemaking is tender and satisfying."

"You're not pretending to be with Luis when you're with Briana?"

"Sometimes." I drew a breath. "I can't help but feel if I'd met Briana after being with Luis for four years, maybe my emotions and attractions would be similar." I turned to stare at the sunset as slashes of orange and pink lit the clouds from underneath. "Luis is suffering because his wife is having an affair."

"Well, that's rich." Phen laughed.

"What do you mean?" I spoke over my shoulder, unwilling for Phen to see my face.

"It sounds like you feel sorry for him because his wife is stepping out. All while you're trying to worm your way into his bed. Do you see the irony?"

"Who says I want to have sex with him?"

"You've been infatuated with him since you and Briana stole his sperm over a year ago."

I slouched against the fence.

The last sun rays disappeared, and with them the vibrant red tones on the cloud's underbellies. The clouds turned gray and dull.

Phen still knew little about my illegal trip to see Luis. She'd never asked about how Milo came to live with me. She must have been waiting until I told her the truth. Or perhaps she wasn't entirely confident about whether someone was surveilling us.

"Last summer, I stole the time capsule to visit Luis."

"Why?"

"I gave him a vaccine to prevent him from getting TWS and left a booster for him to take in five years."

"That was very noble of you." Phen chuckled. "Did you fuck him?"

"Let's not talk about that here." I turned toward Phen and nodded at the eaves, hoping she understood I was nervous about listening devices.

"Okay. Then tell me why you brought Milo to our time."

"Let's leave that to a later time as well."

"You brought up the subject. What do you want to ask me?"

"I first met Luis in October 2026, but he was asleep. The next time I saw him was in 2027 in his time. That's when I took Milo. My HCC trips are all before those trips. So Luis doesn't recognize me. The HCC wants me to interact with him without any influence from taking his sperm or his son."

"I'd love to know why you took Milo." Phen wriggled deeper in her chair. "He seems comfortable being with you and doesn't treat you like a kidnapper."

"Another time," I insisted. "I haven't told the HCC about what happened on that trip. After you and I spoke a few weeks ago, I've started thinking about the HCC's motives for sending me back to see Luis."

"You don't believe their line about being the best candidate to talk with a man? And not any man but Luis Pierce specifically?"

"I bought the HCC's rationale when they told me. But when you say it aloud, their story sounds like propaganda. What do you think they're after?"

"Finally, I get to hear your question." Phen reached for the wine flask and stood. She poured a generous portion into our glasses. After curling into an overstuffed chair, Phen motioned for me to sit in the adjacent lounger. "I have absolutely no idea. But let's have our wine and talk about the possibilities. The HCC isn't known for philanthropy. They've never done anything without an angle."

Even if Phen and I figured out what the HCC had in mind, what could I do to keep them from hurting those I cared about?

Chapter 31

After two days back home, the calming pace on Phen's farm started to wear off. We'd spent hours wandering the fields with Milo, letting him clamber over equipment that was three times his size.

Phen had played the role of doting auntie, encouraging his curiosity and tempting him to explore. In the evenings, Milo could barely stay awake past our dinners of fresh vegetables and meat substitutes designed and fabricated at the farm. I swore he'd grown inches throughout the trip—both in height and his belly.

Once back home, I'd spent the two days catching up with my family and work backlogs. On the second night, I stopped at Briana's office to confirm our planned evening alone and headed to my studio.

After a quick shower, I wrapped my hair with a towel and left the lav. I pushed a pile of laundry off a comfy Olympic green faux leather armchair and sat—time to gain another perspective on the HCC.

"Simon. I need to speak with you."

No response.

"Please, Simon. I'll tell you all about the prison farm."

"You're a fast learner." Simon appeared. "Why haven't the Memphis women figured out how to tempt me?" He wore wrinkled, black- and gray-striped pants and a matching top. A similarly colored cap fit snuggly on his head, and gold-colored wire-rim glasses perched on his nose. Simon sat on the floor with crossed legs. His chin rested on steepled fingers, and he stared at me like a pet dog waiting for a treat.

"I can't speak to how Briana and Jayla communicate with you." I shrugged. "Maybe they don't appreciate how you're drawn to scandals."

"Indeed." Simon glanced at me over the top of his glasses. "Briana and her mother are always playing by the rules. They're rather boring. While you, on the other hand, can be quite surprising."

"I'll take that as a compliment." I waved a finger at Simon's outfit. "I assume you're wearing prison garb from some long-ago era?"

"Memorializing the Congregate system from Auburn, New York in the 19th century. They had strange ideas about how to rehabilitate prisoners."

"Phen didn't seem particularly repentant or remorseful. Maybe they still don't have it right." I drummed my fingers on the chair's arm. "I'd like to talk with you about why the HCC is sending me back to spend time with Luis."

"To research inherently male characteristics?"

"That's the company line. But Phen believes the HCC wouldn't spend resources on educational pursuits. She believes they have an ulterior motive."

"That hypothesis has merit." Simon gave his processing data head tilt. "Did you come up with alternate objectives?"

"Nothing definitive." I rose and gave a thought directive to change a wall into a window with an early evening Denver skyline view. "But we came up with two plausible ideas."

"Only two?" Simon smirked.

"We thought up plenty of ridiculous opinions, usually after several glasses of wine. But two seemed reasonable."

"Tell me."

"The first is that the HCC wants to chart Luis' predilections and anomalous character traits as a baseline." After turning from the view, I pulled the towel from my head. My damp locks cascaded around my shoulders. "They could test Briana's babies to see if they develop similar traits. This research might address the nature versus nurture conflicting theories about male behaviors."

"Okay." Simon nodded. "That seems feasible. Still a bit altruistic for the HCC, but a possibility."

"Agreed. On a more devious note, they could decide whether Luis' temperament is sufficiently desirable to become the sole male influence for the 12 infant boys who survived TWS in 2060. After all, I gave him a vaccine in 2027 filled with the nanobots you enhanced. That dose plus the booster he'll take in 2032 should keep him alive through the epidemic. It seems logical for the government to scoop him up with the 12 infants and bring them to Panama City."

"That included me."

"Sort of—it included your original."

"I have yet to detect any changes in my programming to evidence Luis Pierce lived past 2060 and influenced the other boys or me."

"Maybe the HCC intends for me to do something in the past to negate what we put in place." I raked my fingers through my tangled, wet hair. "Their actions would irrefutably prove the Tobar Principle."

"Just because the HCC tries to undo what we put in motion doesn't mean the future will revert to the original timeline." Simon tapped a finger on his chin.

"You sound optimistic."

"I prefer to believe Luis will be around for me in my youth." Simon's lips formed a tight line. He emulated anger well. "Why would the HCC want to negate our efforts? I don't understand how that benefits them."

"What if they decide Luis isn't the best influencer for male behaviors? They could arrange for him to die of the virus."

"And not allow any adult male to live past 2060?" Simon seethed.

"The HCC has a time machine. They could spend a decade evaluating candidates and pick one more suited to their ideal of maleness."

"Actually, they can't." A smile spread across Simon's face. "They don't have my nanobot enhancement."

"The one you added to Luis and Milo's vaccine?"

"That's the one."

"So once you gave it to me, you never uploaded the revised formula into CYR's medical database?"

"Nope." Simon raised the back of his hand to gaze at his fingernails.

If the HCC decided to replace Luis as the sole representative of adult men, they'd have to extract the formula from Simon.

Simon had leverage over the most powerful organization on Earth. But if our assumptions were accurate, the HCC was one step ahead and already working on getting what they needed from Simon.

Chapter 32

Meat, meat, and more meat. A roasted turkey lay on a platter in the table's center. Next to the bird sat a bowl of caramel-colored bread cubes interspersed with pieces of cooked celery and hunks of sausage. Pink ham slices piled on an adjacent plate alongside a tray with green beans topped with bacon bits. Smashed potatoes seemed to be the only item without a meat element.

"Looks delicious." The aromas made my mouth water. But how would my digestive tract handle the highly caloric and fat-laden 2025 foods?

Luis grinned at my praise as he took the seat next to me. Not facing me like Briana would have done, but right next to me. We both had a view out the front window of leafless aspen trees and the house across the street. His neighbor had decorated the front yard with an enormous cartoon-like, inflated turkey. What a spectacle—Jayla would have been appalled, and Latrice would have loved it.

I mentally noted Luis' seating choice for my debrief with Atacama6. She'd suggest he chose the chair in the closest proximity in case he could tempt me into his lap for a quick tryst between courses. I regretted conjuring the idea as soon as it came to me. My nipples grew hard, and I twisted my napkin to tamp down my desire.

"Are you ready for the big game?" Luis spooned potatoes onto his plate.

Unable to control myself, I laughed when he covered them with brown gravy. My olfactory sensor implant suggested the sauce was swimming with turkey innards and grease.

"What?" he asked. "Don't you like gravy? It's a family recipe. I couldn't get enough of it when I was a kid."

"The gravy looks delicious." I placed a hand over his. "It's only that I haven't had a traditional family feast like this."

"Ever?"

I cleared my throat to give myself a second to correct my statement. "It seems like forever. Because I don't have family here, I work a lot on the holidays and don't get a chance to celebrate in the usual ways."

"I'm glad you had time to celebrate with me. When Megan left yesterday with the kids, I came back in the house and channel-surfed for hours until I finally fell asleep on the couch."

What could *channel-surf* mean? Both words had ties to water, but how could Luis bring water or waves into his home without Holo-programs? The main point of his message sounded like he was despondent and found a mindless activity to occupy time until he fell asleep. I nodded and intently listened in case he provided clues with context.

"When I woke up in the living room, I thought about you coming for dinner." He wrapped my hand in both of his, and a flutter filled my chest. "You kept me in a good mood all day. I'm grateful you're here."

Slowly, I slipped my hand from under his, attempting to suppress my attraction. "I've been looking forward to dinner with you, too. I'm not a cook. Tell me how you prepared all these."

While I stuffed myself with foods I'd never had an opportunity to taste, Luis bantered about his past. He told me about his upbringing in a home a few hours away from Denver. When he talked about buying the house he shared with Megan and their children, he pointed to his enhancements.

Recently built bookshelves lined the walls in his combination living and dining room. I admired his craftsmanship, wondering how Luis would feel if he knew décor in the future could be reconfigured daily with a simple command.

"Olivia's room is next on my list." Luis broke my thoughts.

"What are your plans?" I rested my chin on a fist, thinking about how Olivia's room looked on my first visit, with the walls covered in posters of superheroes and manga.

"Olivia told me she's outgrown the leaping lambs I painted for her before she was born."

I nodded in understanding. Latrice had outgrown the baby-appropriate styles we picked for her as well. Even at two, she knew how to change the wall art to suit herself.

"Are you going to keep her constellation lamp?" *What did I say?* After the words left my lips, I clamped my mouth shut.

"How did you know about that?" Luis cocked his head. He scanned my face for clues.

Did she already have one, or would they buy it for her in the coming months? When I walked into Olivia's room in October 2026, the lamp shot tiny flecks of light onto her ceiling, forming the familiar outlines from both our night skies.

"It's all Olivia talks about." Luis gazed into the distance. "Ever since I took her to the Gates Planetarium by City Park, she's been bugging me to buy her a star projector."

"You must have mentioned it when we took that jog along Cherry Creek." I stood and crossed the room to stare out the front window. I clenched a fist and rubbed it with the other hand, trying to stop my nervous tremble.

"I don't remember talking about it."

I took a long breath and stood tall.

Think. I can work through this mistake.

As I turned back toward the table, I straightened my shoulders and slipped my hands into the waistband behind my back.

Staring directly at Luis, I asked, "I'm not a mind-reader. How else would I know?"

"Good point." Luis laughed and stood.

When he started to stack the dishes, I joined him and mimicked his unfamiliar actions. We piled the dirty dishes onto trays and brought them to the kitchen.

After glancing around for an open spot, I placed the turkey platter on the center island. The counter appeared different from when Briana and I broke into Luis' house. That night, the polished surface was devoid of clutter.

I placed a palm on the cold, stone countertop. On this spot, Briana prepared CVIs of sleep serum for Megan and Luis. A short while later, we crept into their bedroom and stole Luis' sperm. Despite being unconscious, he'd awakened long-dormant feelings in me.

Luis' pull unceasingly overpowered me. While Atacama6's leading questions were biased toward uncovering a predatory Luis, she had no idea I was drawn to him far more than he was to me.

Oblivious to my wandering mind, Luis stacked dishes in the sink. After rinsing, he organized them into a box with racks inside. Could this machine be an early version of the dishwashing robots installed on the food prep floor in the Merlin Building? Without AI to guide the device, how effective would it be?

With minimal help from me, Luis loaded the last pan into the machine and shut the door. After several finger stabs on a command panel, the device chugged to life with a whir and a thump.

"Are you ready to watch the game? The kick-off should be in about fifteen minutes. So we're right on time."

"Looking forward to it. Will you be rooting for your favorite team?"

"The Broncos aren't playing, but Denver will improve in the standings if the Lions win today."

The names rolled off me like caramel sauce on ice cream.

I nodded and hoped he didn't ask me something I couldn't answer.

He placed a hand on the small of my back as we started toward the living room. He likely would have made a similar gesture to any guest— male or female. But it made me feel protected. I'd be sure to mention his action to Atacama6 and hope she wouldn't assume he only touched me to initiate greater intimacy.

"Sit wherever you'd like." He released my back with a gentle push.

I scrutinized the two side chairs, separated by a large sofa. All were situated to take advantage of a solid video screen.

Luis beelined to a chair. When he leaned back, it tilted, and a footrest emerged. He crossed his legs and waved a hand at the remaining seats. "It's your choice."

I snuggled into the sofa's corner on the side nearest him, figuring the proximity might help keep our conversation going even during the sporting event. He picked up a small handheld device and switched on the screen. How long would it take for the world to change to voice or brain-activated commands?

While the offensive and defensive possessions were brutal and initially tricky to understand, I appreciated the rivalry. Despite the men's size, they moved like nimble Olympic athletes I'd known, cutting between other players and snatching the odd-shaped ball from the air when I was sure it was uncatchable.

I'd drank my fair share of Luis' beer by the second half and found myself leaping to my feet when his team intercepted a throw, forced a fumble, or kicked a field goal. The lead bounced back and forth, with both teams positioned to triumph. In the last few minutes, my heart raced, and I sat glued to the action.

Each team fought with all its might and strategy.

In the final seconds, the opposing team threw the ball far down the field in a desperate attempt to steal the win.

When the ball struck the ground before reaching the waiting receiver, Luis and I leaped from our seats.

Luis released a 130 decibel whoop that made me cover both ears.

My reaction prompted Luis to double over laughing. An instant later, he rushed forward and drew me into an embrace. He lifted me from the floor and swung me in a circle.

Luis must have realized I'd gone stiff, unsure how to react to his physical closeness.

He set me down without taking his eyes from mine.

"I'm sorry. That was completely inappropriate." Luis stepped back, his chest heaving as he caught his breath. "Why is it so easy to be with you? Are you sure we haven't met before? I feel like I've known you all my life."

Atacama6 had warned me about men using time-honored dialogue to trick women into intimacy. Were his questions part of the common language of men, or was he being honest? Whether or not he intended it, Luis had charged my body with energy. My heart pounded so hard I could feel it in my ears.

"What are you doing to me?" was my simple response.

Still facing me, Luis took another step back. "I need to call you a taxi before I cross a line."

I understood what he meant about lines. Besides both being married, the situation was more complicated than he could ever conceive.

A taxi would take me to the safety of my time capsule. I'd be back in 2241 with my family before Luis had a chance to unload the dishwashing machine.

It was the right thing to do.

His face reflected a mixture of confusion, passion, and profound sadness.

"Yes." I lowered my eyes. "A taxi would be great."

I moved in a foggy trance, gathering my purse and letting Luis help me put on my coat. We stepped outside onto the front porch and along the walkway to the street.

"I'll hang here until the taxi comes." Luis stared at the house across the street, his hands shoved deep into his pockets. "He should be here in a few minutes. I don't want you waiting in the dark alone."

"Thank you." I pulled my collar tight to ward off the chilly breeze.

"You're shivering." Luis stepped closer. "Let me warm you up."

I stepped into his arms, and he ran his hands over my back, not with a lover's slow, exploring movements but with the firm strokes of friendship.

A vehicle's headlights appeared at the block's end, and the car approached slowly as if the driver was unsure of their destination.

Luis released his embrace and nuzzled my neck. "I had an amazing time today. Thank you for making it special."

"I'll never forget this Thanksgiving your cooking, the game. Everything's been perfect. Thank you."

Luis glanced down the street toward the approaching taxi.

I reached up to hold his head in my hands and stood on tiptoe to reach him.

Arching my back and stretching tall, I kissed his lips.

Luis slowly leaned away. His eyes were full of questions.

He weaved his fingers into my hair and pulled me close.

Luis' lips crushed mine.

I forgot about the approaching car.

Chapter 33

DECEMBER 2, 2241

Each time Atacama6 glared at me from across the table, my fear of her diminished. Her badgering never wavered—always looking for evidence that Luis was a predatory seducer. She'd become a repeating loop.

"Maybe we should've met right after I got back." I deflected. "At this point, my memories are fading."

"I had other priorities." Atacama6 straightened. "You should take more comprehensive notes. These assignments are your top priority. Your revelations should be increasing each time you go back." She picked up a Holo-tablet and waved it toward me. "These transcripts are the scantiest I've seen from you. What happened during your last visit that you're not telling me?"

My logbooks were filled with details about the meal Luis prepared—about how he held spatulas with a firm grip and muscled overflowing spoonfuls of food from pots into serving dishes. I'd filled pages with minute observations from the football game.

Players had crashed into one another and fought to recover stolen balls. They were penalized for unsportsmanlike conduct, yet they openly taunted their opponents. Besides reams of data, Atacama6 was rightfully disappointed. Few references dealt with my direct interactions with Luis Pierce.

"I've summarized our entire evening together." I shrugged. "What are you looking for?"

Atacama6 laid the Holo-tablet on the table. She fiddled with the device until it sat perfectly parallel to the edge. After drawing a breath, she asked, "How did he react to you being with him on an auspicious day rather than spending time with his family?"

While I'd reported that Megan and the children were away for a weekend trip, I'd never mentioned the holiday in my reports. How did she know the day would be significant to him? Phen and I had talked at length about Thanksgiving when Milo and I visited her. Had the Judicial Division surveilled our conversations and transmitted transcripts to Atacama6 and the HCC?

"Interesting that you mention the holiday." Could I entice her into divulging her source? "I didn't know about it until after I arrived in 2025. While Luis prepared traditional foods and neighbors decorated their yards, I didn't think it was relevant."

I wanted to understand how she knew. But I'd asked Atacama6 questions before. She never answered, and I had little hope that she would during this interrogation.

"I'll ask you again." She placed her folded hands on the tablet as if guarding her resources. "What are you holding back from this report?"

"What makes you believe Thanksgiving was important to the Pierce family?"

"In 2025 northern America, that holiday was the most important nonsecular celebration. We included the date in your scheduled jumps to see if you could arrange a rendezvous with Luis Pierce on a day he'd normally spend with his family. You convinced him to send his family elsewhere, and we'd like to hear more about why he chose to be with you instead of them."

The HCC had access to historical calendars. It would be simple to identify holidays. Maybe I was overly suspicious about surveillance at Phen's farm. I gripped my chair to keep from fidgeting. "I didn't convince him to send his family away so he could spend time with me."

"Did *he* suggest sending them away?" Atacama6 opened her Holo-tablet and touched the screen.

"No." I considered each word before speaking. "For personal reasons, Megan Pierce needed to go to Nebraska. That's where her parents lived. They wanted to see her. Luis' work schedule is demanding, and he stayed in Denver."

Both statements about Luis' situation were factual, even if they were unrelated facts. I hoped Atacama6 decided he couldn't travel because of work obligations. Simon would have approved of my deflection. "Luis invited me for dinner when I told him I'd be in town with nothing else to do."

"That was an interesting ploy to get you alone in his home."

"Women ask other women to dinner all the time—sometimes as potential dating partners but more often as friends or because it's more fun than dining alone. Why do you think it was different in 2025? Just because the people have different genitalia doesn't make the word *dinner* translate to romance or a sexual encounter." I leaned back. "Luis may be less interested in sharing a bed with me than you've assumed."

"Do you believe he trusts you?"

"We're still in an early stage of friendship. Luis trusts me like anyone he recently met. Is that what you mean?" What was she getting at now?

"The HCC will have you bring a CVI to 2025. Can you get close enough to dose him without him becoming suspicious?"

"What?" Her request made me laugh out loud. "How do you think Luis Pierce would respond if I pulled out a 2241 medical device and shot him in the arm?"

"We could manufacture a CVI to replicate something from his time. You only need to place it next to his bare skin—anywhere on his body. Like the standard CVI, the injection would be painless."

"What do you want me to give him?" A knot formed in my belly at the thought of giving him anything at the HCC's whim. "Are you planning to hurt him?"

"I don't have the freedom to give you more information on this topic."

"Unless you tell me what you're giving him, I refuse to inject it."

"I expected you to comply." Atacama6 tapped the table with a finger. "You realize the HCC is sending you on these jumps at their discretion—not yours."

"I agreed to observe him and gain intelligence on male characteristics—not to give him injections. If you don't tell me what's in the CVI, I won't do it."

"I'll talk with my superiors about your demands." She cleared her throat. "Let's talk more about the sports game."

"They called it football." I snapped, still angry about the HCC's request.

"Right." She swiped the screen, and I imagined her scrolling through my statements. "You said the game was excessively physical."

"Excessively compared to sports today, yes." I stood and rounded my seat to grip the back and face her. "I can't speak to whether it was more or less brutal than other games of that time."

"How did Luis Pierce respond to the violence you were watching?"

"If the other team was overly aggressive—like they committed a foul— he became animated." How much did Atacama6 know about games of sport and their rules? I understood the basics of any game from my tennis experience, but not all women engaged in sports. "A foul is when a player commits a rule infraction."

"Thank you." Atacama6 rolled her eyes. "I'm fully aware of what a sporting foul entails."

"Sorry, I wasn't trying to be disrespectful. You've asked me to be thorough, and I don't know your sports background."

"I played on the HCC's virtual golf team for years."

"Wow. I'm impressed. They have a great reputation." Was Atacama6 finally warming to me? She'd never disclosed personal information during our sessions. Perhaps this debriefing would be a turning point for us.

"We won several international championships while I was on the team." She glanced back at her tablet and cleared her throat. "Let's continue about Luis Pierce's responses to watching aggressive sports."

"Okay."

"Did his penis gain an erection during the entire game or only when the action was particularly intense?"

So much for developing rapport.

I stormed into my studio and directed the entrance to shut.

"Simon!" I called to the ceiling. "I don't care what you're doing. I need to talk with you right now."

No response. Why had I bothered with a direct approach? It never worked in the past. But I was in no mood to come up with something to tempt him into my space.

Ugh. I sat on the bed and pounded my fists against my thighs. What was the HCC planning? Did they want to help Luis survive the virus or want to neutralize Simon's bots?

"Simon." I gripped the bed covering and squeezed. "I need to speak with you about the HCC's plans to neutralize your self-charging nanobots and kill Luis Pierce before he can become your mentor."

He materialized immediately, sitting beside me on the bed. My request must have surprised him as he wasn't wearing anything sensational—only a male version of the CYR medical garb.

"What did you say?" Simon grabbed my arm and shook it. "Those nanobots are cutting-edge technology. For the first time in history, I've developed bots that don't need recharging with a 2241 power source. The HCC should rally around me and explore how to expand my discovery into further uses. But instead, they want to dismantle my bots and force Luis Pierce to fend for himself against HAV?"

"Settle down." I jerked my arm free. "That's one possible theory."

"You'd better fill me in." Simon glared at me. "Don't skip any details."

I told Simon about my discussion with Atacama6, including her deferment to speak with HCC leadership about whether I needed to know the injection's purpose.

"There could be dozens of reasons for the HCC to inoculate Luis Pierce." Simon tapped his chin with a finger.

"Benevolent and otherwise?"

"True." Simon stood and straightened one of the antique rackets on my wall. "Your theory about neutralizing my nanobots is one idea. If they've decided he's not a good representative of male characteristics, they'd want him to die alongside all the other men."

"Based on the crazy questions Atacama6 asks me—all laced with innuendo about Luis' persistent libido—I don't know if the HCC has enough information to make a reasonable decision about him." What if the injection wasn't about letting Luis contract TWS but about Simon's nanobots? "Has anyone from CYR or the HCC asked how you programmed your long-lived nanobots?"

"Never." He stared at the wall. "But if they can access records showing Luis Pierce lived past TWS, they'd know I solved the re-charging problem."

"Can you access those data?" My pulse quickened. Imagine if they had proof our plans worked and Luis lived past the disease.

"Wait." Simon's head tilted—the telltale sign when he simultaneously accessed hundreds of files. "I can't find anything conclusive."

"What about something borderline irrefutable?"

"Please." Simon shook his head. "Sometimes you push my limits."

"Did you find anything that shows Luis lived past 2060?"

"No."

"I assume you've planted routines to notify you if evidence pops up. Please let me know if an alert comes in." I struggled to find an alternate objective for dosing Luis. "Do you think they're angry about us leaving 2241 technology in 2027?"

"Perhaps. But no medical screening could have detected the bots at that time. Even decades later, when TWS killed nearly all the men, my bots would have been invisible on any existing scans, blood tests, or micro-imaging screens." Simon sat and crossed his legs, swinging one back and forth like a pendulum. "Did Atacama6 give hints about the serum's purpose?"

"No. I figured killing Luis or your bots were likely reasons."

"Any chance they're giving you something to help Luis live rather than trying to kill him?"

Simon's face held no trace of sarcasm. "While that's possible, I think Atacama6 would have told me. If she had, I'd have agreed right away."

"Her caginess makes it seem like they're up to no good."

"Precisely." I flopped on the bed and stared at the ceiling.

"What if they come back with a lie to persuade your cooperation?"

"We need to be prepared for that." I sat up with a jerk. "Atacama6 told me they'd load the dose into something that looks like a 2025 device." My thoughts raced into overdrive. "If they give me the CVI before my next jump in two days, I can hand it over to you. Would you be able to figure out what's in the device before I leave?"

"That depends on how much time I have." Simon took a breath. "If you could find a way to remove some of my access restrictions, I might analyze the drug more quickly and determine if the HCC has better data about what happened to Luis."

"Let's talk about greater access later. Getting the HCC's drug to you is the pressing issue." Jayla had warned us about Simon looking for expanded access. "Let's plan for me to give the CVI to you before I leave. If you tell me what it does before I go, I can decide whether to inject Luis."

"And if I can't confirm it before you go?"

"I'll have to figure out a good reason for not injecting him while I'm there. Atacama6 didn't say when I'd receive the CVI. But the minute she hands it off, I'll call you."

I pressed the access button to Briana's studio again—this time with force. Weeks ago, we'd reserved a time to review Nanny Tori's curriculum, and I was only fifteen minutes late. Was she paying me back for being late, or had she forgotten our appointment?

"Access denied."

"Why denied?" I thumped a fist against the entrance.

No response.

"Can you tell me if she's inside?" I paced before the access panel, steaming.

"Briana Memphis7 is unavailable at this time."

"Unavailable?" I huffed. "Locate Briana Memphis7."

"Briana Memphis7 is inside her studio."

"Then open the door." I kicked the panel.

Miraculously, the door dissolved. Briana stood inside, her face an ashen shade of gray. She reached up and grasped the doorframe.

"What's happened?" Afraid she'd fall, I rushed forward, and Briana collapsed in my arms.

"Do I need to call the medical staff?" She'd appreciate my asking before I alerted them.

"No. Help me get settled. I'll be fine."

"Bed or chair?"

"Chair." Her voice came out in barely a whisper.

We shuffled across the room to her most comfortable armchair. Once I helped her sit, I grabbed a blanket from her meticulously made bed and pulled it across her legs.

Sitting on the floor in front of her, I rubbed her thighs and felt her tremble.

"If you don't tell me what's happening, I'm alerting the medical center." While the air felt stifling to me, Briana's comfort was primary. "Increase room temperature by two degrees."

"It's not necessary. I need a few hours to recuperate, and I'll be good as new." Her brow wrinkled. "Please don't tell anyone about this. I don't want anyone to know—not my colleagues and certainly not my mother."

"What happened?" I tensed. How bad was it?

"It's fairly routine in my lineage. My kidneys gave out, and I've given myself a new one."

I tried to respond, but my lips were frozen.

"Sofia?" Briana reached to touch my face with a shaky finger. "Don't look so shocked. I didn't do it alone. Simon helped me. We used a 3D epithelial and connective tissue printer and a surgical robot."

"You did a surgical procedure in your studio, and you're telling me I shouldn't be surprised? It's routine?"

"Everything worked out fine. As I said, Simon was here in case anything went wrong."

"Where is he now?"

"He dematerialized when you wouldn't leave. Simon thought we should have time alone so I could tell you about the transplant. I haven't restricted him from appearing. So he's likely around."

"You and I had a meeting scheduled. You're never late. I was worried."

"Sorry about not canceling. I must have forgotten when my creatinine level maxed out this morning. I didn't have much time."

"Simon was here with you the whole time?" He'd been with me an hour earlier. His ability to appear in more than one place simultaneously still confounded me.

"Yes. Simon doesn't have an extensive medical background, but he designed a masking program to hide my equipment requisitions. I don't want anyone to know about this procedure."

"Including me?"

"You know now."

"What if something happened during the surgery?" If she had to fight for her life and I was away, I'd never forgive myself. "What's your VSE reading now?"

"It's hovering around 3.0 and peaked at 3.1. But it'll keep dropping over the next hour or two."

"I'm not happy about Simon being here, and I wasn't." I stood and called to the ceiling. "Simon, if you're around, please materialize."

When he didn't respond, Briana released a low chuckle. She knew him better than I did.

"Simon, I'd like to speak with you about Briana's recovery time."

Again, no response from Simon.

"He'll assume you should ask me," Briana offered.

"Simon, I'm scheduled to time jump in a week, and you need to convince me that Briana is well." I balled my fists on my hips. "If you don't appear right now, I'm contacting the HCC and canceling the jump."

"There's no need for idle threats." Simon materialized and waggled an antique stethoscope's chestpiece toward me.

"About time." I stepped to him and flicked his name tag. "Who is Dr. James Kildare?"

"Dr. Kildare was a highly respected medical professional in the 1960s. Over five years, he won the admiration of senior doctors in his internal medicine specialty."

"I've never read any of his research." Mirth peppered Briana's soft voice.

"You've read every piece of research in the past 281 years?" Simon peered at Briana over the top of his faux spectacles. "I'll let you in on a secret—I dress conventionally in front of CYR colleagues because I want to fit in. I reserve my more expressive outfits for the Memphis women." He glanced at me. "And occasionally for Sofia."

"Is Briana telling me the whole story?" I needed answers.

"I already told you what happened." Briana started to lift from the chair. "It's routine."

"Stay where you are." I rushed to her and pressed her shoulder to keep her in place. "You need to relax. I'm asking Simon to confirm."

"Yes." Simon held out a hand and examined his fingernails. "Mostly everything that Briana said is true. The transplant was a success, her VSE reading continues to improve, and she'll be ready to resume her workload tomorrow."

"Why mostly?"

"She said her VSE peaked at 3.1, but the real value is 3.148."

"Plus about a dozen more digits?" I gave him an eye roll.

"I find you humans grow weary if I calibrate beyond the thousandths."

"Close enough." I searched his facial expression to detect any anomalies but saw nothing unusual. "If this is routine for the Memphis women, why aren't we telling Jayla?"

Briana started to say something, but I shushed her with an open palm. "I want to hear this from Simon."

"You have to ask? Jayla's dealing with Brad's condition. She's working to keep the same condition from happening to the other boys. Jayla doesn't need Briana's procedure to distract her." Simon huffed. "Are you suggesting you'd like her to abandon her work in the capital and come home?"

He was programmed not to lie, but what about hiding the entire truth?

"I don't want Jayla to rush back for no reason." I knelt by Briana and took her hand. "Promise you'll tell me if you need more surgical procedures."

"I will." Briana looked at me with half-closed eyes. "I need rest. Would you please give me some time alone?"

"Well?" Simon indicated toward the room portal. "Briana is asking for you to leave."

"Actually," Briana snuggled into the chair, "I'd like you both to leave."

Why did I feel like we couldn't afford to spend time apart?

Chapter 34

DECEMBER 10, 2241

When the real Atacama6 walked through the control room doorway, I jolted in shock. Since becoming my liaison, our meetings were conducted via com-cards. I'd not seen her in person since the HCC tribunal months earlier.

Lisa glared from her to me, ostensibly for an explanation of why someone she didn't know had the audacity to enter the launch site less than an hour before my time jump.

After my introductions, Atacama6 moved her purse strap higher on her shoulder and turned to Lisa. "You need to leave the room until I instruct you to return."

"I will not." Lisa crossed her arms over her chest. "You might have clout with the HCC, but you're on CYR property, and the engineering team is in charge of the control room."

"We can take time for you to check my status, but Sofia Andes7's jump will be delayed. I assume you'd like to stay on schedule?"

"I'm not leaving until I see something authorizing you to be here and recognizing your authority."

"Very well." Atacama6 drew out a Holo-tablet. After a few taps and blinks, she handed the tablet to Lisa. "This won't take long. Please go out until I tell you to return."

While Atacama6 and Lisa postured, I hoped Simon watched the events from wherever he lived in the Merlin Building cyberspace.

With a huff, Lisa balled her fists and marched from the room, rematerializing the entrance door behind her as she left.

"We have a ton of last-minute details to work out before my jump to 2025." I tightened the waist strap on my enviro-suit. "Can this wait until after I'm back? I doubt I'll be away for more than a few hours."

Atacama6 removed a smooth black medical case from her shoulder bag, and my heart sank. I hadn't received any deliveries with the CVI Atacama6 had spoken about and assumed the HCC wouldn't send one on this jump. I was wrong.

She slowly opened the case to reveal a CVI, similar to the ones I used when I borrowed the capsule and brought Milo to the future.

"What's in it?" Like I'd practiced, my question was succinct, and my tone was all business.

"That's not your concern." Atacama6 snapped the case closed and held it forward as if she expected me to take it.

"I'm not taking it with me until you tell me what it is and what it'll do to Luis."

"What makes you think you have the right to ask?" She shoved the case at me, and I stepped backward toward the capsule. "You're on a research mission for the HCC, and what we ask you to do is solely at our discretion. If we asked you to incapacitate Luis Pierce, we expect you to comply."

"Is that what you plan to do to him? Incapacitate?" My face radiated heat. She had to know I was angry.

"Of course not." With a flick of her wrist, Atacama6 snapped the box at me. "My superiors tell me the vaccine you gave Luis Pierce contained a new generation of nanobots. Our research department has discovered the enhancement will fail, and the bots won't self-charge. This vaccine has an update to keep them charged until Mr. Pierce takes the booster in five years."

"Why didn't you tell me that in the first place?" Something about her approach set off warning bells. I snatched the box from her outstretched hand and pried open the lid. The CVI lay nestled inside a shock-absorbing gel, probably to keep it safe during my jarring voyage back in time.

"It's not your place to ask questions." Atacama6 forced a smile. "I supervise over a dozen women on probation. You're the only one who questions my authority and directions."

"I'm on probation?" I drew a quick breath. "I thought the HCC chose me to conduct this mission for research, and you're my liaison at the HCC."

"That's another way to look at it." Atacama6 waved a dismissive hand. "Did you think there would be no consequences for taking the time capsule last summer?"

"I cut a deal with the HCC. They wouldn't press charges if I agreed to spy on the Front for them. Before I could reestablish my relationship with the Front activist, the HCC changed my objective to time travel and to feed you findings about male characteristics."

"I'm familiar with the details." Atacama6 pointed at the capsule. "You'd better secure that CVI in your suit and call your colleague back inside. If you don't leave shortly, you'll need to restart the countdown clock."

"Fine." I examined the bulky case. "You said you'd disguise the CVI."

"There wasn't time. You'll find a way to dose him without his knowledge."

"Thanks." I rolled my eyes and slipped the medical case into an interior pocket in my waistband. To the ceiling, I called, "Open entrance to the control room."

When the entry dematerialized, Lisa rushed in. "Get out now!" Lisa blurted at Atacama6, nudging her with an elbow.

"Have a safe flight." Atacama6 nodded before she strolled to the door.

"Go ahead and start strapping in," Lisa commanded. "I'll finish the final settings and be inside to check your straps in a sec."

I slipped into the capsule and sat in the zero-gravity recliner.

When Simon materialized dressed in all-black Ninja attire, I froze. Hopefully, he'd watched the entire performance by Atacama6 and was coming to my rescue.

Simon glanced over his shoulder, ostensibly to see if Lisa could see him from her console.

With a look of satisfaction on his face, he whispered, "Give me your case and take this one with you."

He handed me a box, identical to the one Atacama6 brought with her.

"What's the plan?" I stammered, ready to implement whatever he suggested.

"This box has an empty CVI. You can hand it to Atacama6 when you return." Simon winked at me. "I'll evaluate what they put inside the real one while you're gone."

"Did you believe what she said about the bots you programmed?" I pulled the authentic case from the back of my suit and exchanged it for Simon's fake one. Even the heft and colors seemed identical. The trick would be to ensure the CVI was alike, too. If Atacama6's CVI was a standard issue, Simon's stand-in would be a sufficient replacement.

"I don't trust her for an instant." Simon gave an authoritative head wobble. "My tech was foolproof."

"But what if she's right?" I stared at the replacement box, running a thumb across the top.

What if, by failing to give Luis the vaccine, I was dooming him to die from TWS?

Simon's ego could jeopardize Luis' life.

2025

I hesitated at the bottom of the escalator before placing a firm foot on the step. The clunky, moving metal stairs with marred handrails and scratched, oil-based plastic sidewalls seemed unfathomably dangerous. We had similar mechanisms in my time, but the grips were virtual to avoid germ transmission, and the solid-state holographic steps and sides allowed for maximum views with complete protection for riders.

Yet dozens of school-age children clambered onto the moving steps, giggling and shoving their comrades while traveling from the first to the second floor at the Denver Museum of Nature and Science.

One or two adults—primarily women—escorted groups of young boys and girls. While the children displayed varying assertiveness, the girls tended to the shy side. The rogue element was typically male if one child moved beyond the *front* of the pack. When a youngster fell behind to look at a display or tend to a personal matter, like inspecting their image in a mirror or tying a shoe, the lagger was more often female. Atacama6 would likely conclude the boys behaved more aggressively to assert their dominance in the group.

As I mused, a young girl rushed past me, with an adult following close behind. "Britney, if you don't stay with the class, I'm walking you to the bus. You can sit there for the rest of the day for all I care." The adult gave me an apologetic nod as she passed.

If I had more time, I'd find a seat and collect more data. A longer-term study might yield different results than my initial conclusions about which sex pushed limits.

I checked my optical implant for the time. Ten more minutes to find Luis at the moose and caribou diorama in the North American Gallery.

According to my map, the room was on the second floor at the building's north end. The rooms were dimly lit to accent the dioramas filled with stuffed animals. Fake shrubbery and detailed paintings lined the interior walls. As I moved farther into the space, the crowds thinned and the children's chatter faded.

Behind a wall of glass, an enormous animal towered over low shrubs. A man sat on a bench in front of the scene with his back toward me. I recognized his broad shoulders immediately.

"Luis?" I hadn't intended to whisper, but my voice caught in my throat.

He turned. When he recognized me, a deep smile spread across his face. My hands trembled in response.

"I was afraid you wouldn't come." Luis stood and scrutinized the room, likely to be sure we were alone before he approached and circled me in his arms.

I relaxed into his chest and took in his scent, a mixture of soap and something earthy.

In 2241, my daytime hours passed quickly with family and work obligations. But at night, Luis filled my thoughts. Activating my ARP Luis hadn't helped. While he could physically please me, I found his reactions uninspiring. Maybe I would deactivate him, as I'd promised Briana months ago.

"Why can't we talk on the phone when you're in California?" Luis tipped my chin with a finger and softly kissed me. "Seeing you every two weeks is making me crazy."

"You have a life that doesn't include me when I'm gone." I pulled away to round the bench and sit facing the diorama. Without encouraging him, Luis followed and sat with the side of his thigh pressed next to mine. "You need to let me have a life, too."

"Do you think of me?" Luis placed a tentative hand on my leg.

"More than you could imagine." I traced his fingers before putting my hand over his. "Meeting like this isn't fair to Megan or your kids."

"Megan checked out months ago." Luis turned to face me. "Maybe she never planned to be exclusive."

"Did she give you any reason to doubt her?"

"From the beginning, there were times when she'd get home late or tell me she was going away with friends for a weekend. I never questioned her." Luis shrugged. "I filled in the gaps with excuses for her."

"Not all relationships are based on lies." The irony of my statement wasn't lost on me. Briana deserved better. But I'd come too far with Luis to turn back, and the HCC would force me to meet with him no matter what.

"Sometimes I wonder if Olivia and Milo are mine."

"Milo looks so much like you." Not only his looks but his mannerisms as well. In my future, every time Milo cocked his head, I saw Luis. Confusion swept across Luis' face, and I recognized my mistake.

My heart raced as I grasped for a plausible story. "At least that's from what I've seen in Milo's photos in your home."

"Of course." Luis chuckled. "Sometimes I forget you don't know them."

"You've shared so much about what they're doing and how you've raised them. You must be insanely proud."

"I am." Luis nodded. "They're the reason I stay with Megan. I'd do anything to keep them safe."

I stared at my hand over his. Did he believe his children were unaware of his failed relationship with Megan? Olivia and Milo were likely more intelligent than he gave them credit. But at that moment, Luis didn't need my advice. I held my tongue.

A cluster of school children swept between our bench and the diorama. They jostled one another and bantered, some with asexual friendship and others laced with flirtatious touching. I grinned, watching the mixture of boys and girls.

Behavior clues for attraction hadn't changed much over the centuries. People still gave intimacy signals with a lingering touch or a breathy, whispered secret. In my time, groups of young girls acted similarly.

Luis squeezed my hand and brought me back. "I know we've only met.

But your friendship means everything to me."

His eyes spoke of honesty and trust. I'd left a CVI for him in the time capsule. How could I blindly follow Atacama6's instructions without being sure the HCC's dose would prolong his life?

Simon would uncover what was inside, and I'd inject Luis on my next mission *if* it could save his life.

As another group of children passed, Luis pulled me closer. "Can we go somewhere that's not so public?"

Our last encounter ended with a kiss that still burned my lips. If that taxi hadn't beeped its horn and forced us out of our private world, I might have already given way to my hunger for him.

How long could I go on fooling myself that having an affair in the past wasn't cheating on Briana because Luis was long dead?

I stroked Luis' cheek with the back of my fingers. His hand moved to my thigh, and tingles radiated through my body.

There was no denying my attraction. Whether I stood and returned to the capsule right then or agreed to find a more secluded place, I was already faithless to Briana.

At that point, my only decision was whether to carry through with my infidelity—again. I'd already had sex with Luis when I visited him in June of 2026. But in November 2025, he was oblivious to our coupling. That day was eight months in his future.

My dreams were peppered with anxiety and lies. When I pried open my eyes, I saw the view from the hotel room window had changed from bright daylight to darkness.

A glance at my optical implant told me I'd been with Luis for eight hours in his time, nearly two hours in mine. I could spend another sixteen with him in 2025, and no one in the control room would be concerned.

Initially, the HCC directed me to spend up to twenty-four hours in 2025 with less than five hours passing in my time. Time spent in 2025 was exponentially longer than what elapsed in 2241—a full day in 2241 would give me nearly two weeks in Luis' time.

If this trip came close to the HCC's suggestion, Atacama6 would be ecstatic, salivating for any new details I could share. She'd be sorely disappointed with my results. I'd never tell her the truth about how I'd spent the afternoon.

Mmm. Luis mumbled as he pulled me closer.

I pressed my back into his chest, and he wrapped his arms around my bare middle.

Keeping my breathing shallow, I didn't want to wake him and start a conversation. Would he be embarrassed about what we'd done, or would he pressure me to stay longer in Denver?

I felt his steady exhalations against my hair and relaxed. No wonder he was exhausted.

After an uncomfortable encounter with the hotel clerk, we'd arrived at the room. I still felt the sting of her judging eyes.

Once inside, I hesitated for barely a second.

When Luis rushed to me and crushed me into a kiss, my fate was sealed.

Lust seeped through my every pore. I wanted him more than anything I'd ever desired—more than Olympic medals or the first passionate evenings with my wife. My body ached for him to consume me.

Our first time went fast and furious. Clothes hit the floor, bedding flew off the mattress, and I wrapped my legs around Luis before we could think about the implications of our actions.

My body exploded with pleasure each time he surged into me. Before I climaxed, he moaned, and his body tremored. While I wanted more, his full weight collapsed on top of me.

Luis buried his face into my hair, panting and moaning.

As I struggled to dampen my desire, he propped on an elbow and smiled at me with his cocky, self-assured grin.

Why did he stop? Wasn't my satisfaction as important as his?

I gasped for air, disappointed for myself and all the women who had sex with selfish men. Briana and I talked during lovemaking. We made sure each of us was satisfied.

How could I have been so attracted to Luis and so ignorant about a man's attention to giving satisfaction?

Luis rolled to his side, and I half expected him to rise and start to dress. Tears formed in my eyes. When I blinked, one escaped to track down my cheek.

When he saw my expression, Luis' smile fell. He brushed the tear with a finger and cupped my face with a hand.

"Why are you sad?"

Struggling to keep my disappointment at bay, I sat up and drew the sheets around my body. The words tumbled out before I could stop them. "That's it? You're satisfied, and now we're done?"

When Luis flopped onto his back and laughed, I tightened the covers with a sharp tug.

What an insensitive ass. How could I have been attracted to him?

He slipped his hands under his head with his elbows splayed to the sides. Staring. Smiling. His eyes never left mine. "Has anyone told you that you're gorgeous when you're angry?"

What does that mean?

I huffed and turned to look at the wall.

The sheets tugged as Luis shifted toward me. He lifted my chin with a finger and moved my face so I looked directly at him.

All his laughter was gone. His chest moved up and down as his breath came in deep waves.

My pulse quickened.

"My sweet Sofie, I'm sorry I satisfied myself first. This time is all about you."

Luis' fingers threaded into the hair at the back of my head. He pulled me closer and pressed my lips with his kiss.

My body went limp, accepting his advance without protest.

That was hours ago, and as promised, Luis ensured my satisfaction.

I sighed and relaxed in his arms.

Confident I could deflect Atacama6's prying questions, I struggled with how to face Briana. Should I come clean and tell her what I'd done or hide the truth and pretend my mission for the HCC was progressing according to their expectations?

How were my actions different from Megan Pierce's?

Megan took what she wanted and told Luis what she expected of him. While I hated her for hurting Luis, I admired her honesty. The decision to stay with her was 100 percent up to him.

Would our tryst change his mind about leaving her? If I summoned the courage to tell Briana, she might abandon our marriage and break up our family.

Chapter 35

Deep into my thoughts, I moved through the yoga poses with minimal attention to Briana as she progressed from cat to cow to child's pose.

"Oof," Briana grunted as she raised onto her knees.

"Have you missed a few sessions?" I asked as I stood to start my balance work. "You're so graceful, but this morning you seem stiff."

"It's nothing," Briana countered. "I had a tough workout the other day, and I'm still sore."

"Don't overdo it. Your transplant was ten days ago." I focused on a spot on the wall while I moved into tree pose. "Besides your weight loss and aggressive workouts, is there something else you're struggling with?"

The previous evening, I started to tell her about what happened with Luis. When I got serious, she told me not to burden her with anything too gloomy. She was dealing with stressful work matters and wanted to keep our private life on a lighter note—at least for the time being.

While I'd mustered the courage to tell her the truth, Briana's request derailed me. I kept my mouth shut, knowing the longer I kept my affair from her, the more difficult it would be to confess.

Instead of standing and starting the balance positions, Briana lay on the floor in corpse pose and stretched her arms over her head. She must have been hurting to revert to relaxation mode before finishing the routine.

"Simon told me the CYR medical staff has increased routine testing for Milo since you've been back from visiting Phen." Briana lowered her arms and lay still.

"He didn't mention it to me." Most of my conversations with Simon had centered on the CVI serum the HCC wanted me to inject into Luis. Milo's testing may have fallen into a lower tier of his attention. "I'm glad they're monitoring him. He's been so healthy. I almost forget he's at risk."

"Jayla was the adult of record who ordered more tests." Briana glanced at me but otherwise didn't move. "Did she ask you about it?"

"Your mother is authorizing medical procedures for Milo?" I nearly toppled over when I switched my gaze from the wall to Briana. "What are they testing for?"

"Simon said they're routine assessments for traces of HAV in his system—the normal stuff they've done since you brought him here last June."

"Then what's new?"

"Over the past five months, they've checked less frequently and less invasively—like doing more with blood work and almost nothing with biopsies or other tissue work."

"But they're more intense lately?"

"You visited Phen about three and a half weeks ago. Since you've been back, they've tested Milo nearly every day—including muscle biopsies and one cerebrospinal fluid collection."

"That sounds serious." I sat in front of her and rested my hands on her knees. "Where do they get the fluid?"

"They did a lumbar puncture."

"There must be a reason for all these. The staff hasn't told me anything." I slumped. "Have you spoken with Jayla about this?"

"Simon mentioned it the day before yesterday—while you were gone on your last jump. I know you've been consumed with your HCC mission and preparing for the ongoing sperm harvests. So I didn't tell you right away. I started sleuthing yesterday and confirmed the spinal tap results and authorization before we met for this yoga session."

I squeezed Briana's knee. Despite my gentle grasp, she winced. I rubbed the place where I'd pressed.

"Why are your joints sore?" Briana had never complained about distress after a workout, and her pain seemed to be in her knee and not in an overworked muscle. "Don't tell me this is from your weight training."

"It's nothing." Briana placed a palm against my cheek. "I turned up the weight specs. I overdid it on squats for my flabby butt.”

“You have a great-looking ass.” I shook my head. “It’s getting a bit scrawny lately, but it’s still sexy.”

“The higher weights will help me put on more muscle.” Her eyes twinkled. “Maybe I’ll advance my programs to the body-builder settings.”

“You know I’ll support any decision you make—as long as you’re safe.”

Briana kissed me, and guilt over my affair flooded over me.

“I don’t deserve you.” My words felt forced as my throat thickened.

“Keep thinking that way.” Her brow furrowed as she grew serious. “Let’s make the most of all the time we’re together.”

“Every minute.” I raised to my knees to hug her.

When I released Briana, she smiled. But her eyes told a different story. Tiny creases in the corners reflected her pain.

Did she suspect I’d been unfaithful?

Perhaps she wasn’t ready to confirm her doubts, so she’d asked me to keep our conversations light. Uncertain of how long I could hide my secret, I turned the conversation back to Milo. “One or both of us need to confront Jayla about Milo’s tests. Do you want to bring it up with her, or should I?”

“I know she’s crazy busy with work at the capital, and we can’t bother her during the day. How about I send Mother a call request for this evening? We can both talk with her and get to the bottom of this.”

“I’ve got a meeting with Atacama6 this afternoon and a full schedule before and after. We could have dinner with the kids and meet with Jayla afterward in your studio.”

“Only if you promise not to go back to work after the call. I’d like to have you to myself this evening.”

“I promise.”

Briana’s trusting smile prompted another flood of remorse for how I’d betrayed her and our entire family.

Simon materialized at my office’s entrance moments after Lisa left with a Holo-tablet holding my recent programming updates.

“It’s nearly time for you humans to stop for the day. I thought Chicago6 would never go back to her office," Simon said, rolling his eyes.

"We have regular work to do—it's not all about you."

"You're suggesting my evaluation of the CVI contents is all about me?" Simon thrust out his chin. "While I'd like Luis to live long enough to meet my original in the 2060s, I suspect I'm not the only one who wants to keep him alive."

"You've got me there." I leaned back in my office chair. "Tell me what you've found."

"I'm not sure." Simon smoothed the front of his shirt and tucked the slack into the waistband of his antique business suit. He snapped the lapels of his wrinkled raincoat as if readying himself for a big announcement. But nothing further came.

"If you don't know, then why are you here?" I ignored his outfit.

"The serum includes complex compounds with innovative strains and a horde of state-of-the-art nanobots. There's nothing in the CYR's medical databases that match it."

"What do you suggest we do? When I met with Atacama6, she took my empty CVI and told me she'd give me an empty one to draw a sample from Luis on my next trip on December 27. That's about two weeks from now. Once the HCC analyzes the draw, they'll know I didn't inject their sauce into him."

"I understand your conundrum."

"If it's designed to counteract the vaccine you enhanced, can't you test it against a sample of your vaccine?"

"Duh." Simon glared at me over his fake glasses. "Don't you think I already tried that?"

"Well?"

"It did nothing to countermand the actual HAV vaccine, and the self-charging nanobots weren't compromised."

"Doesn't that mean their stuff won't impact your vaccine?"

"On the surface, your logic is sound." Simon grew a few inches and tapped his chin. "Because my tests are taking place in 2241, I'm not able to evaluate whether it deactivates the nanobots in 2025."

My blank stare prompted him to continue. "I made the bots self-charging because they don't have access to the 2241 technology that allows all bots to recharge and stay long-lived. When I add their serum to my bots in 2241, I don't know if the nanobots are recharging because they have access to 2241 tech or because their self-recharging programs are still effective."

"If you've never been able to prove their ability to recharge in the twenty-first century, how did you decide the ones I originally gave Luis were effective?"

"Simulations."

"You were never certain?"

"Confident enough." Simon huffed.

I moved my hands under the desk and laid them on my thighs. Squeeze, release, squeeze, release. "So it's possible your enhancement didn't work, and the HCC is attempting to fix them?"

"That's doubtful."

"Their vaccine must be designed to do something. Why else would the HCC make such a big deal about me injecting Luis? If you don't believe it fixes a problem and can't figure out if it compromises your enhancement, give me a clue about what you think."

"Maybe they gave you a benign solution to test your loyalty to the HCC?"

"If it's benign, why is it full of complex strains and state-of-the-art nanobots?"

"I can't be sure. They could be markers that will show up in the sample Atacama6 is asking for."

The HCC had painted me into a corner. If I didn't give Luis their serum, they'd know I disobeyed their orders. But Simon and I still didn't know whether they designed it to test my loyalty or affect his enhanced bots— either in a good or bad way.

"What now?" I asked.

"I used a small portion of their dose for my tests. What's left might still do whatever the HCC had planned." Simon adjusted his position, likely to stop towering over me and deliver his message like a conspirator.

"Go on." My shoulders tensed. No option seemed optimal.

"I think you should inject Luis."

"And possibly compromise his immunity to HAV?"

"That might happen." Simon nodded. "But you have three more trips to meet him. Give him the HCC's serum as soon as you see him in 15 days.

Before you return, take two blood samples—one for the HCC and one for me. I can test it to see how their stuff affected my bots in 2025."

"Without testing it there, what can your evaluation tell you?"

"Okay." Simon cocked his head. "How about you loosen my proximity parameters so you can take me with you? I can test it there."

"That makes sense." Simon could definitively prove the HCC's intent—all with added flexibility to address any improper changes. While I could make the draws, I'd have no idea how to evaluate what the serum did to Luis' immune system.

Simon's face remained motionless, with nothing to evidence whether my acquiescence might please or displease him.

That's not typical.

Simon should have been overjoyed at the mere mention of giving him greater access. He must have been worried about overplaying his hand. Why was he forcing his facial programming to look neutral?

I stared at him for a full thirty seconds—no response. Was Simon's goal to expand his access?

"I'm not changing your programming to expand your reach." I placed a closed fist on my desktop. "If you want greater access, you'll need to arrange that through Briana or Jayla."

"Fine." Simon's demeanor unstuck, and he shrugged his shoulders. "Bring a sample back, and I'll test it here. But it won't be as conclusive as if I could check it back then."

"I understand." Once we figured out the HCC's objective, we could undo anything they put into motion. We still had two more jumps after this one.

After dinner, Briana suggested we make the call to Jayla. We decided to initiate the call from Briana's studio because Jayla might take offense if we chose a more intimidating venue like a conference room.

Jayla's holographic image stood in the center of Briana's room. Her robes and the ends of her turban flowed with the blowing wind—like a goddess standing watch on the prow of a ship. But more likely, she was standing on the balcony of her hotel suite.

We hadn't told Jayla that Simon planned to sit in on our meeting.

While Simon could conceal himself in a holographic piece of furniture, like a chair or table, that wasn't Simon's style. In a far corner, behind Jayla's image, he'd fashioned a tiny shelf that held a fifteen-centimeter-tall lounge chair.

I tried not to laugh when I spotted him reclining as if he were watching video entertainment. He'd see Jayla's back from his perch, but Simon added a wall mirror in front of her, undoubtedly scrutinizing her expressions and looking for any trace of a lie.

Briana and I sat next to each other on a leatherette sofa. To confirm our united front, I draped an arm across the couch's back and around Briana.

"Well?" I gently squeezed Briana's shoulder. "Do you want to start?"

"Mother," she cleared her throat. "We understand you've authorized extensive tests for Milo in the past couple of weeks."

"Is this what all the fuss is about?" Jayla straightened. "I've got two centrifuges running in the lab—one to precipitate DNA and the other to purify virus particles. My experiments are time-sensitive, and I must return to them. Please get to the point."

"Did you authorize Milo's tests without consulting with us?" I jumped in without waiting for Briana.

"Do you have a problem with ensuring Milo is well?" Jayla snarled.

Briana placed a palm on my thigh, signaling me to stop talking. "Of course we appreciate your input to keep our children safe. May we ask why you've increased his testing regimen?"

As Briana finished her question, Jayla's aggressiveness deflated like a balloon with a slow but steady leak. I leaned back into the sofa and pressed my lips together, letting Briana take the lead. After twenty-seven years of managing her mother, Briana knew precisely how to de-escalate a tense situation.

"Since he arrived, Milo has shown remarkable resilience to HAV. We wanted to check his antibodies and their reactions to any virus exposure he might have had in the reformatory farm."

"Excuse me?" My gut clenched. "The CYR medical staff said there was no risk of exposure to HAV at the farm or while we were transiting from Denver to southern America."

When Jayla's lips formed a firm line, Briana patted my leg. We wouldn't squeeze any details from Jayla if I kept interrupting. I took a breath and nodded at Briana to fix any damage.

"Mother," Briana started, "when we agreed for Milo to join Sofia at the farm, CYR staff assured us he was in no danger. I assumed that meant air filters kept the farm HAV-free. After all, except for Phen Andes7, there aren't humans or animals for the virus to feed on. Without any hosts, how could the virus survive?"

"The environment where Celine Ottawa7 lives should also be HAV-free. But her son contracted the virus."

"Her residence is in a city, and I assume there were dozens of staff passing through their home. While I believe our filtration systems in the Merlin Building can keep the other boys safe, I was never certain about rooms in the capital."

"The systems here mirror what we have in Denver." Jayla tightened the belt securing her robes.

"Then how did Brad become infected?" Luckily, Briana asked the question before I could blurt it out.

"While there's been no arrests, we suspect a terrorist act." Jayla spoke as if she were reporting the scores from a low-ranked tennis match.

I tensed and felt Briana's fingers drumming on my thigh. She knew I was about to say something I'd regret. I stuffed a hand under my leg and kept silent.

"In the capital?" Briana's nonjudgmental tone matched her mother's.

"Because the public doesn't know about Brad's condition, there's no reason to announce anything about the ongoing investigation. My sources tell me the HCC suspects the Front, but it could have been a less notorious group."

"Let's circle back to Milo." Briana masterfully redirected. "Is there reason to believe a radical group planted HAV on Phen's reformatory farm? I can't imagine why the Front would make the farm a target. Milo isn't a state secret. But only a handful of staff knew he was joining Sofia on her trip."

"Don't be so naive, Briana. The Front has tentacles in every city. I guarantee they know all about Milo and would do anything to eliminate him."

"He's a little boy." I jumped from the couch to stand in front of Jayla's image. My hands balled into fists with my chin inches from hers.

"Calm your wife." Jayla stared at me but directed her command at Briana.

Briana's hand circled my arm near the elbow.

I allowed her to pull me to the sofa. When she tugged at me to sit, I shook free and stayed standing.

"These boys aren't simply children." Jayla's commanding voice rolled over us as if she spoke from a podium, not through a com-card. "By providing original genetic material, they'll save all of humanity. You need to stop thinking about them as your progeny. They belong to everyone. If one stops contributing as a member of society, then the HCC will decide how he can best promote the cause."

"Is that what you think of Brad?" Briana's outburst wouldn't calm Jayla. "Now that he can't grow up to learn, play sports, and become a normal citizen, he's relegated to live out his life under your microscope?"

Jayla didn't respond but stared at the sofa where Briana sat. Jayla's head tilted as if evaluating what she saw.

I turned to see what caught Jayla's attention.

Briana's mouth moved like an automaton, but no sound came out. I slipped next to her and took her hand.

"Simon, what's happening?" I asked as my gut clenched.

In an instant, Simon grew to full size.

He knelt before Briana and manipulated her lids to peer into her eyes. "I think it's a stroke."

Jayla rubbed her hands together and squinted as if trying to focus her vision. "We need to hurry. Simon, call for a medical team."

My heart raced.

Jayla was a doctor, and Simon had instant access to emergency procedures. Feeling powerless, I surrendered the lead but stayed at Briana's side.

"The medics are on their way." Simon put a hand on Briana's forehead. "Can you speak to me?"

Briana's voice came out in a garbled mess of syllables.

Moments later, the entry portal evaporated. Two medical staff members rushed into Briana's studio, followed by a boxy robot, undoubtedly filled with all the equipment they'd need to help Briana.

I stood to give them room, and Simon appeared next to me. He took my arm while we both watched the medics work.

"Simon, tell me what's happening." My voice caught in my throat.

"Leave this to the experts. They know how to care for her." Simon patted my arm and glanced at Jayla's image, stoically watching the medical team working on her daughter.

"But what's happening?" I searched Simon's face for clues. He must have an answer.

"I still think it's a stroke." He smiled at me. "Don't worry. We can stop the bleeding before it causes any significant damage. In a couple of days, she'll be fine."

"Do you think she's been overdoing it?" I glanced at Jayla before lowering my voice. "Could there be a complication from the transplant?"

"Absolutely not." We both turned to Jayla, but she seemed oblivious about our discussion.

"Thank goodness for that."

"She's been under a lot of pressure at work and with the boys. You know how driven Briana can be. They'll know how to minimize damage and advise her about lifestyle changes." Simon gave me a nod. "When she's fully recovered, let's give her hell for scaring us."

I gripped Simon's arm to keep myself upright.

Thankfully, I hadn't added to her stress by confessing my infidelity. I'd wait until she was stronger before I came clean.

In the meantime, I'd fulfill my HCC obligations without further indiscretions with Luis.

Chapter 36

Briana gritted her teeth, and I willed her arm to move higher than the last repetition.

"Nearly there," I coaxed her.

"If you can't raise it beyond the marker, I'll start designing you an exoskeleton." Simon goaded Briana from the corner of her studio—behind the Uni-fit machines we'd installed for Briana's physical therapy.

"Not going to happen." Briana strained. She leaned to the side.

"That's cheating." I grasped Briana's shoulder and moved her to the original position.

"Hey. You're supposed to watch and encourage me—not make it harder."

"Admonish me if you need to." I chuckled.

"Listen to Sofia," Simon piped in. "She won't let you hit the goals through chicanery."

Simon's image morphed into a chubby man with long curly locks framing his receding hairline. His flouncy, velvety outfit ended at his knees, exposing saggy gray socks and shoes topped with rosettes.

Laughing, Briana stepped away from the machine. "Are you here to offer support or make me want to stop?"

"Simon, don't force me to make you leave the room." My tone would have told Simon I was half-joking.

"As you were." Simon materialized next to the machine. "Chicanery evolved from a French word in the 17th century."

"You're planning to tell us whose costume you're copying, right?" For Briana, I pointed at the hovering holographic markers with the session's range of motion objectives.

"Blaise Pascal. He was a great mid-century French mathematician." Simon drew a breath and fluffed his cloak. "There's lots to tell. I'd like to believe his most impressive invention was the digital calculator. It took him three years to invent it, from 1642 to 1645."

"Was he responsible for the world adopting your chicanery word?"

"No." Simon pursed his lips as if disturbed by my interruption. "But I believe he spoke both French and English." In a lighter volume, he added, "Probably Latin as well."

"Are we going to finish my therapy?" Briana rested her hands on her hips. "Once we're done, I'll work at my office. I'm still researching the latest developments for artery micro-bots."

"If we resume immediately, you'll finish in the next 14.629 minutes."

"Thanks for your precision." I reached for Briana's hand and assisted with the initial lift, releasing as she closed in on the mark. "That's only if Briana goes through the routine once."

Briana grunted, and I said, "Again."

"Simon, can I rely on you to search the other countries' databases for the latest nanobot advancements?" Briana asked with a grimace.

I watched her form with a hand near her elbow.

"I'm available to assist." Simon replaced his costume with the standard CYR attire. "Do you want me to limit my search to medical resources?"

"I hadn't thought about looking in other sectors. What are you considering?"

"Switch sides," I directed, and Briana complied.

"Industrial microbots reinforce leaky pipes in buildings and find fractures within coolant systems." Simon brought up a Holo-tablet and tapped. "If we use industrial bots to detect arterial weaknesses and early-stage aneurysms, we can use medical bots to fortify the weak spots with stents, grafts, or sleeves."

"Sounds logical, but I haven't heard about those techniques used for medical procedures."

"We use them to test the time capsule," I offered.

"It seems like all today's advancements sit squarely with nanobots. But they have limitations." Simon bowed his head. "I'm not sure nanobots could handle the sophistication we're discussing. They're too small, and the processing power would overburden them. Microbots might work."

"Simon Merlin, I appreciate your logic and programming skills." Briana stepped away from the machine and stared at the structure.

"Even though you're likely referring to my original, I'll take that as a compliment." Simon held out a hand, encouraging her to stand. With a nod and a blink, he materialized a solid-state, holographic band to constrain her weak leg. "You're not finished. Sofia asked me to design this band for you."

"Looks like what she needs." I patted Briana on the back. "Do twenty raises in each direction, starting to the front."

Briana sat on a bench and started the repetitions. "EuroRosse has a reputation for their ground-breaking industrial technology. Why don't you start with their resources?"

"Certainly." Simon paused. "If you authorize a higher clearance for a bilateral investigation, I could pierce their corporate databanks. I'd gain immediate access to microbot schematics, which might take me weeks through the official channels." Simon gave Briana a deadpan stare. "Weeks we may not have."

"Draw up the paperwork and forward it to my Holo-tablet when we finish here."

"Uh." I'd stayed out of their medical discussion until it sounded like Briana would expand Simon's access. "Do you think that's wise?"

Simon shot me a stern look.

"If Simon can replicate microbots and modify them for medical use, it'll be worth giving a modicum of added freedom." Briana swiped her brow with a cloth.

Was Simon's microbot project related to something he was working on with Briana or Luis' vaccine? Or was his request designed to augment his reach?

During my mid-day break, I defeated Lisa handily in three sets.

"Congratulations." She shook my hand, catching her breath. Years ago,

I'd let her beat me to ensure she'd keep playing with me. But she was furious, and I'd never faked a loss again.

"You're getting better. I used to limit you to two sets. You'll kick my butt one of these days," I chided her.

"I'm not getting better. You're losing your edge." Lisa slapped my arm. "If the HCC keeps filling your schedule with assignments, I'll have a shot at beating you. When do you head out again?"

"Late this afternoon. You'll get the notification to meet me in the control room at about 3:00, and I leave at 5:00." Lisa wasn't supposed to hear for a few more hours, but what was the harm?

"What if I'd booked court time with your Serena Williams program this afternoon?"

"You're practicing with the programs I developed?"

"Maybe." Lisa's grin spread wide across her face. "Sometimes, when I know you're headed for practice, I schedule time with the program and let it run without me—just so you can't use it."

"You're vicious." I rolled my eyes. "And deviously competitive."

"One of these days, I'm going to beat you."

"I have no doubt."

"I'm serious about giving us notice before you jump." Lisa placed a hand on her hip. "You may have agreed to be at the HCC's beck and call, but assuming the engineering staff is always available isn't fair."

"I hadn't thought of it that way. My handler is emphatic about keeping my schedule a secret." I shrugged. "Maybe the Front or another extremist group made a threat. Or maybe she's a control freak."

"Why would the Front care if you traveled back in time to gather research? They're only interested in not reintroducing men. They'd be fine with you digging up dirt on bad male behaviors."

"Men aren't all evil." I sniffed. "Frankly, the more time I spend with them, the more I see they're complex and not very different from women. They can be sensitive, curious, and loyal. They're not solely motivated by power and greed like some believe."

"We haven't had a war in over 200 years." Lisa started toward the showers, and I followed. "Based on what I've heard, there was always some aggressive conflict going on when the men were alive."

"But we survived and continue to evolve. If they were around after

2060, they'd see the benefits of peaceful collaboration. Women were forced to face the future without men, and the only way to survive was to consolidate resources and find ways to all get along."

"You have a generous view of what happened and how we arrived here." Despite owning a holographic self-straightening racquet, Lisa stopped to fiddle with the strings.

"Men all died during the Cursed Decades chaos. We never had a chance to see how they'd react during a catastrophic event."

"They didn't simply die during those awful years. Their deaths are what ended the Cursed Decades." The muscles in Lisa's jaw tightened.

Until that moment, I had no idea she felt strongly about the topic. Should I change the subject? Aside from Briana, Lisa was my closest friend, and I wanted to keep it that way.

"Do you have time to join us for lunch?" When she didn't answer immediately, I added, "I'm meeting Briana and the whole crew—Latrice, Milo, Adam, and Nanny Tori. I could message the dining system and add you to the table. It's been a while since you've seen the little guys. You'll be shocked at how much they've grown." I leaned toward her. "Adam's not in that meatball stage where all he did was eat, poop, and sleep. He responds to voices and smiles a lot."

"I'll have to pass." Lisa motioned for me to enter the shower rooms ahead of her. "Now that I know you're planning to jump today, I have work to do. Plus, the next sperm harvest is in three weeks. Each time you leave, I have extra structural evaluations on the capsule's seams and connectors. We don't want something to crack or come loose from all that shaking."

"Thanks for making the capsule's integrity a priority." I drew a long breath of moist air in the shower room and recognized a eucalyptus scent. "We haven't lost any travelers from engineering malfunctions or miscalculations. I want to keep it that way."

"We all do. Mission Y ensures our future." Lisa grinned. "We agree that the only way to save the cloning process is to introduce original cells. That said, you and I can disagree about what role men should have once they're here to produce sperm for us. We might be grateful, but we don't have to reintroduce them into society."

"I assume we'd both want to give them the same rights and privileges we have." As soon as I said the words, I regretted them. Why should I assume anything? I'd reintroduced the subject, and she might have opposite views.

"We need their seed, but that doesn't mean we should risk having them take over." Lisa's eyes glinted with anger or spite—I wasn't sure which. "Once they're old enough to want more freedom, we'll have to decide how much to grant them."

Maybe I'd arrange for Lisa to play tennis with Milo. If she spent time with my son, she'd see Milo was nothing to be feared.

2025

"I preordered everything with some vegetarian dishes and others with meat." Luis' downcast eyes spoke of bashfulness and a desire to please.

Our server was dressed in a colorful costume, likely related to the cuisine called *Indian*. She held open the alcove's curtain and beamed as I mounted the platform supporting the low table.

I kept one hand firmly on my heavy opal amulet to keep it from banging my chest as I bent to slide onto the cushions lining the table. The HCC's necklace felt bulky and wasn't to my taste, but it held their blood draw mechanism. They'd taken my advice and created a medical device that didn't look like 2241 tech.

I'd unloaded the CVI with their serum into Luis while we wrestled in the back of the taxi. Simon had assured me their vaccine and requisite nanobots would trigger Luis' immune system to create measurable antibodies in less than an hour. Sometime after dinner, I'd find a way to press the amulet next to Luis' skin and take the blood sample to prove I'd given Luis the HCC's inoculation.

We relaxed onto cushions as the server pulled the curtain across the front of our cubicle.

After a quick, confident breath, I stared Luis straight in the eye.
Time to tell him our affair was over.
Before I could speak, Luis drew me into his arms.
I wilted.
Straining, I pressed both hands on his chest to push him away. But once my palms connected, they refused to respond and slid around his body to

pull him closer.

How did he do this to me?

"I missed you." Luis' husky voice echoed in my ear as he kissed my neck. Tingles started there and spread down my body.

"We need to talk." Not sure where I found the strength—but I pulled away. My hands felt glued to his chest.

Stop touching him.

I slipped both fists under my legs, forcing my hands to behave.

"What do you want to talk about?" That irresistible smile crept across his face.

I shook my head to clear it.

"Give me a minute." I stared at the table. The back of his fingers stroked my arm.

Ignore it. Get your mind together.

"Okay." I took a long breath. "We need to antipole what's going on."

"Huh?" Luis cocked his head. "What's antipole?"

"Sorry," I stuttered. What would people say in 2026? "Put things in reverse?"

"Sofie," Luis covered my hands with his, "I can't do that. Even if you refuse to sleep with me, I can't give you up. I think about you all the time."

Luis was focusing on what he could accept rather than understanding my rationale. Was this another male/female difference? After changing the subject, I'd add my observations to Atacama6's list.

"How is what we're doing different from Megan and her lover?" I focused on my lap, unable to look at him.

"Megan bailed on our marriage and forced me into a corner. The only thing wrong with my relationship with you is timing."

Time? You don't know the half of it.

"They're cheating, and so are we." How could he see it differently?

"My relationship with Megan is over. She didn't give me a choice. At this point, dissolving our marriage is about paperwork." Luis squeezed my hand. "I wish we'd met after my divorce. But we can't change that now. Give me a chance to do right by you."

"I'm not sure we can make it right. How can you change the past?"

"We don't need to change the past." Luis leaned toward me. "I wasn't planning to bring this up until after dinner. But last night, I told Megan about you."

"You what?" Every muscle in my body tensed.

With a mighty whoosh, the privacy curtain scraped across the rod.

"Here's your appetizers." The server balanced three dishes along an arm.

If she weren't staring at the plates, she'd see shock across my face. No amount of control could have kept my feelings concealed. I needed to get ahead of this situation and pressed my lips together to keep from asking Luis a torrent of questions.

The server recited the names of each dish while placing them on our table—something about samosas and chutney. The details were lost inside my swirling thoughts.

With the pace of a garden snail, she straightened the tablecloth and refilled our wine glasses.

Water came next, with the server taking great care that ice from the pitcher didn't splash into our glasses.

"Your main dishes will be ready soon. May I bring you anything else while you wait?"

I wanted to scratch the courteous grin from her face. *Just leave!*

When she finally closed the curtain, I snapped. "Why did you tell Megan?"

"Whoa." Luis rolled his shoulders as if preparing for a brawl. "You didn't want me to tell her?"

"I never suggested you should confess." I wriggled sideways in the seat, giving myself space.

Luis slid to follow me and slipped a hand behind my neck. My head wanted to pull away, but my heart drew me toward him.

Luis massaged my taut muscles and stared into my eyes. The longer he watched me, the weaker my resolve. Anger turned to frustration and morphed into helplessness—about his future and ours.

"What did Megan say?" The question caught in my throat.

"She threw a fit." Luis scoffed. "Can you believe it? After all her cheating and demands, she's mad at me?"

"Megan wants to preserve her family." When the words left my lips, his mouth fell open. Slowly, he turned to stare at the dishes on the table. He picked up a fried dough ball and moved it to his plate before resting his closed fists on the table's edge.

I'd sided with Luis' wife because I walked in her footsteps. I'd cordoned off walls to separate my affair from my family back home. Luis despised Megan for her selfishness—how was I different?

"It's too late for her to save our home." Luis never lifted his gaze from his plate. "Megan's affair killed our family long before I met you. Kids aren't stupid. I try to keep things normal. But they hear us fight and know she's not around." Luis gulped a swallow of wine. When he put the glass back on the table, he swiped his lips with the back of his hand.

"Don't get me wrong." I placed my tiny hand over his. "I'm not defending her. You're perfect, and she doesn't deserve you."

"Perfect?" Luis gave me the smile I didn't deserve. "Then you agree to stick with me until Megan and I work out all the divorce details?"

Luis didn't know, but they couldn't separate now. When Briana and I jumped to October 2026, they were both in bed. Luis and Megan need to stay together for at least another ten months.

Chapter 37

DECEMBER 31, 2241

When the siren blasted into my studio, I jumped out of my seat, nearly dropping the Holo-tablet with notes for my next meeting with Atacama6.

"Cease notification!" The sound came from everywhere and nowhere. I covered my ears to block out the worst of it. "Computer, stop warning."

"There are no warnings issued in your proximity."

Ugh. "Stop message alert!"

"There are no messages in your mailbox."

"Tell me what's causing this horrific noise."

"Question unclear. Please clarify."

An oversized Simon appeared in the center of my studio, dressed in a rubberized suit and an orange hat, flat in the front with a longer brim at the back. He carried a thick black hose under one arm.

"Computer, stop the fire alarm." Simon snapped his fingers. The sound ceased, and the hose disappeared.

Simon lifted a mud-covered boot to rest on the arm of a chair.

"I'm guessing you've decided to play firefighter today." I folded my arms across my chest. "Want to tell me what the drama is about?"

"You should know that I'm the hero of the day."

"Because?"

"I have irrefutable proof." Simon removed his thick gloves, pulling each finger with a languishing flourish. "Based on Luis' blood sample, the HCC's serum destroys my self-charging nanobots."

I plopped onto my desk chair.

"What a bunch of liars!"

"I told you they might arrange to let Luis die."

"Right before you told me to dose him." How could I be so blind? "Why are you celebrating?" I gestured to his outfit. "Two days ago, I gave Luis a death sentence."

"Would I give you bad news without having a solution?"

"The jury's out on that."

"When I picked apart their serum—one molecule at a time—I designed an antidote."

"If I give this to him on the tenth, can we save his life?"

"It's not as simple as that. Their drug is time-activated and will erode the nanobots' ability to self-charge over time. I know how to counteract what they created, but manufacturing the antidote will take time. I can have it ready before your eighth jump on January 27th."

"Isn't that cutting our timing a bit short?" I rolled my shoulders. "What if you can't finish it before I leave for my last jump?"

"Why do you continue to doubt me?" Simon's supersized body grew taller, and I trembled. "If I say it'll be ready before your eighth jump, it *will* be ready."

"Okay." I drew a long breath and relaxed into the chair. "Why would the HCC want Luis to die?"

"Could be several reasons—maybe they're concerned about any anomalies in the timeline." Simon glanced at me over the top of his fake glasses. "Don't start quoting the Tobar Principle at me. I assume they question its validity."

"That's possible. But the HCC is committed to bringing men back. Why kill the one man who could help the infant survivors adopt male characteristics?"

"You've already answered your question." Simon shrank to human size and commandeered a chair from my desk. "They want men to return on the HCC's terms."

"What right do they have to develop men in the HCC's image? Adam and his brothers should choose their paths. We shouldn't keep them from knowing about their past." I straightened the clutter on my desk, wondering how much to share. "Luis took me to a theater to watch a 2025 movie."

"Of course it was a 2025 movie." He rolled his eyes. "Did you think Luis might take you to see something you've watched with Briana and your children?"

"You don't understand." I shook my head. "I'm oversimplifying, but my family watches vids about nature or ones where people get rewarded for moral behavior. The movie with Luis showed a range of people."

"You mean both men and women?"

"Not only that. Some people were rich and others poor. While everything worked out in the end, the plot questioned politics and society's norms." I rapped my knuckles on the desk. "We don't have vids like that today."

"I've extracted clips of old movies from illegal sources but never a full-length film." Simon tapped a finger to his chin. "Do you plan to expose the HCC's censor policies?"

"Before Briana and I took our first jump, I never questioned the HCC's motives or control. Luis' time was violent, but people had more freedom."

"Are you planning to join a protest group?" A slight smile formed on Simon's lips.

"Right now, we need to save Luis—not just because I care about him."

"No?" Simon raised a brow.

"He's the right man to guide your original and the other eleven boys." I nodded to confirm. "On a completely different subject—do you know where Briana is?"

"She's with Dr. Le7 in the arcade. They're walking the Singapore Botanic Gardens simulation."

"That's the one we created for Le7's mother." The program could relieve Briana's stress—she'd been fragile. "Briana's been spending a lot of time with Le7 lately."

"They commiserate about pregnancy, and Briana gives her tips on the birthing process. Dr. Le7's scheduled to have her five sons on February 10th."

"Udzungwa7 eventually took Torne7's boys. It seems like Briana spends more time with Le7 than her."

"Actually, in the past month, Briana spent 31.526 hours with Dr. Udzungwa7 and 30.782 with Le7."

"I stand corrected."

The doctors wouldn't give birth for another month and a half. Why was Briana spending inordinate amounts of time with them?

Atacama6 slammed shut her Holo-tablet and gave it a disgusted shove. "What do you mean you didn't have time to gather a sample of Luis Pierce's blood?"

"I didn't say I didn't have time." With both hands held up in surrender, I forced my voice to stay unemotional. "I said I didn't have the opportunity."

"Same. Same." She snarled.

"No, it's not. When I saw him two jumps ago, I barely got close enough to jab Luis with a CVI. Sidling up to him to press a necklace against him isn't as easy as you think."

"He's a man. You must have had dozens of chances to get close to him."

"When I go on January 10th, you should give me a ring or something connected to my hand to stick him." I slid the bulky necklace across the table, knowing her holographic image couldn't retrieve it. "It's empty. The amulet didn't work out."

"I'll send a messenger bot to retrieve it and send you a new device." Atacama6 shook her head. "Your failure is disappointing."

"Let's not call this a failure in your report. How about saying something more like an *unsuitable appliance* decision on your part?"

"I'll handle my reports in my fashion." She retrieved her tablet and shot me a smug look. "Let's get back to your most recent experience."

"You have my list." I adjusted myself in the chair, preparing for more of her inane questions. "What else do you need to know?"

"You've included another set of minor traits." She wiped the screen with a fingertip. "Females demonstrate many of these actions. I see nothing unique or significant."

"Did you ever think the differences might be small but significant in their entirety?"

"That's not consistent with our hypotheses."

"Which is?" *This'll be good to hear.*

"I can't tell you, or our findings will be biased."

"Isn't harassing me into saying what you want biased?" I slid a hand across the table. "He's not the brutal rapist you think he is."

"Tell me more about his behavior when you sat in the darkened theater with him." Atacama6 flicked the Holo-tablet screen as if looking for a specific entry. "You said he sat quietly for approximately two hours and watched the screen. What aren't you telling me?"

She'd love to hear that Luis put his arm around my shoulder, held me tighter when something on the screen made me tense, and drew me into a long kiss at the movie's end. But I didn't divulge those details.

"There's not much to tell about his actions. We both found the content interesting." I was getting good at half-truths.

"Your notes indicated that he chose the video. Did it include salacious or violent scenes?"

"Somewhat more than what we see today. I'd call the experience provocative. But not because of explicit sex or violence. The characters questioned society's norms and ultimately were rewarded for pushing boundaries." After I said it, I wished I hadn't. What would Atacama6 make of my borderline subversive sentiments?

Oddly, Atacama6 didn't take any notes. She stared at me. Had my statement about questioning the status quo intrigued her?

"So," she cleared her throat, "Luis Pierce didn't take advantage of the darkened room to touch you?"

While Atacama6 reverted to her typical probing questions about Luis' intentions, something in her voice seemed different. The forcefulness I'd grown accustomed to had diminished.

As an HCC arbitrator, she'd spent her career interrogating women who may have violated HCC directives. Her view of right and wrong sat firmly within the HCC's prescribed boundaries. Had my experience with a two-centuries-old film tempted her to question whether citizens had rights beyond what was allowed by the HCC?

"Are you doing anything special to celebrate New Year's Eve?" Lisa asked over her shoulder as I walked past her desk on my way out.

"Two dinners tonight." I paused and turned to face her. "The first is with Milo, Latrice, and Adam. There'll be sparkling grape juice and a trip to the atrium to watch the 7:00 fireworks."

"Sounds like fun."

"Once the kids are exhausted, Nanny Tori takes over so Briana and I can dress in fancy clothes before our adults-only dinner. If Briana's up for it, we'll join the crowd for dancing and late-night fireworks at midnight."

"Where are you headed now?" Lisa tapped her screens closed.

"With two meals in my future, I decided to go for a run."

"May I join you?" She nodded toward the exit and fell into step with me.

"When did you take up jogging?" I chuckled.

"It's a resolution for 2242. But I know it'll never happen without peer pressure. You'll need to keep your pace slow, but do you mind?"

I ran to keep fit and clear my head. The last thing I wanted that afternoon was a conversation with Lisa. But her pleading eyes said she needed something. Whatever it was, Lisa wasn't comfortable talking about it inside the Merlin Building.

"Sure. I'll meet you in the lobby in fifteen minutes. Don't dress too warm—it's cold outside, but you'll heat up quickly."

When the elevator doors opened into the atrium, Lisa was waiting for me. I checked the time—only five minutes past when we'd agreed to meet.

"Sorry, I'm late." I shrugged.

"You're blameless." Lisa spread her arms wide. "Am I dressed appropriately?"

I studied her attire and nodded. "Let's get outside and stretch for a few minutes before I take you on my favorite route."

We passed through the access control vestibule and walked to the concrete steps near the hologram fountain. If it were real, the water would have frozen into a solid mass. But the spurts gurgled and bounced in winter the same way they did in summer.

A few Front members stood on the sidewalk, stamping their feet and thrusting blinking signs into the air.

It's a holiday, can't they take a day off?

Among the group stood Charlotte Danube9—or maybe her sister Mia—I could never be sure. When I spotted her, she glanced past me to take in Lisa. After giving a slow nod to my colleague, she looked away and turned her back toward us.

I grabbed Lisa by the arm and hurried down the stairs.

"I thought we were going to stretch." Lisa hustled along with me, but her voice betrayed her confusion about the change in plans.

Once we rounded the corner and were out of sight of the demonstration, I planted both feet and poked a finger into Lisa's shoulder.

"What was that about?"

"What?" Lisa took a step back.

"Do you know those women?"

"The demonstrators?" Lisa waved a dismissive hand. "How would I know them?"

"One of them looked at you like she knows you." I stared at Lisa, willing her to tell me the truth—whatever it was.

"Why are you all worked up?" Lisa snugged the cuffs on her gloves. "Let go run before the cold sets in."

Charlotte could have given Lisa a nod to make me suspicious. But the recognition seemed real. "Do you talk with them?"

"They're always outside our building. Whenever I leave, I give the demonstrators a nod. I like to encourage different views. They have a right to be there. If one of them acted like she knew me, it's because I don't snub them."

"You've never talked with them?"

"Why would I? Just because I admire their courage to go against the system doesn't mean I want to join their ranks."

Lisa turned and headed to the fitness path at a slow jog.

Hmm. I'd asked Lisa if she knew them—not whether she'd consider joining their movement.

Music floated across the atrium, alternating between modern electronic tunes filled with ear-pounding energy and slow songs drawing couples to the dance floor.

In years past, Briana humored me by gyrating to the fast songs. After her recent medical struggles, I didn't encourage her to overdo it. When the hard-hitting songs played, we huddled at the atrium recesses to share memories and discuss our children's futures.

"Anything new from Jayla about Milo's testing regime?" I swirled a neon stick in my drink.

"Not since we called her a couple of weeks ago." Briana tightened the clasp on the copper lamé wrap, covering her faux leather gown. "His charts show they're still looking for any trace of the virus. But there's no evidence he picked up anything on your trip to see Phen or since then."

"Do you think the HCC treats Milo differently than the other boys?"

"It's basically the same, but Milo *is* different. He's 100 percent original, and the other boys are 50 percent clones."

"I've reviewed his records. They include his vitals, cognitive development, and growth. He's behind on a few educational aspects—probably because in the twenty-first century, they didn't educate kids like we do. But Nanny Tori'll help him catch up." I leaned in to reduce the risk of being overheard. "The HCC's research data is missing."

"I can download those data and findings and give you a copy. I check Milo's records every time I review the babies'. Everything looks normal." Briana gave me a thin smile. "But what concerns me is what we don't know."

"What does that mean?" I pushed my drink aside.

"I don't want to make you worry."

"Too late—give it to me." I reached forward to nestle her wrap higher on her shoulders. "I'd rather know than be surprised."

"What if Milo has the same condition as Simon Merlin and the other eleven immune boys? They lived through HAV but couldn't reproduce."

"Can they test for that?" My heart started to race. I never considered that Milo might not join the other boys to provide for humanity's future.

"Even though research continues, we never could isolate the factors keeping them immune."

"But all grown men died in 2060, and Milo would have been in his thirties."

"Did the records say he died before you brought him to the future?"

"No." I stared at my hand on the table. Briana had never asked for details about last summer's jump. I hoped she wouldn't now. Let our evening be about us.

"Maybe it was the vaccine you gave him before you jumped or the jump itself. We're fairly certain it's not in his DNA or other markers."

Briana sighed. "It'll be years before we can test Milo's fertility."

"So what can we do?"

"Be patient and wait." Briana glanced up when flecks of light fell from the ceiling like iridescent snowflakes. "We'll learn more from him and the other boys over time."

I brushed chartreuse holographic specks from her cheek. When they disappeared at my touch, I cradled Briana's face. Her skin felt like porcelain, cold and slick.

"Is that wrap keeping you warm?"

"After designing my outfit, Simon reprogrammed the specs to include some Hipposkin fibers." Briana reached out to give my hand a reassuring pat. "I'm looking chic and feeling great."

"I'll say." I indicated to my violet gown. "It's not from last year, but maybe the year before. These clothes come with memories—ones I never want to forget. I think we did the New Year's Eve on a cruise ship program at the CYR arcade that year."

"It was three years ago—before I cloned Latrice."

We'd spent the whole night swaying under a Caribbean moon. Briana and I could recapture the romance. I needed us to try.

"Let's dance." I stood and held a hand out to Briana.

After a micro-grimace, she pressed her palms against the table and pushed upright. I moved in close to take her in my arms. As we rocked to the music, I tucked a hand under her wrap to slip it around her back.

Instead of the soft flesh I'd expected, my fingers crossed rows of bumpy ribs.

"Are you still losing weight?"

Instead of answering, Briana raised a finger to her lips.

She closed her eyes and moved to the music.

"I'm serious. Why are you so thin?"

Briana sighed, shifting closer.

What wasn't she telling me?

Maybe I should cancel my next jump.

Would the HCC revoke all my future jumps if I didn't go?

Without Simon's antidote, Luis would undoubtedly die.

Chapter 38

My workout with Luis was nearing the end. The weight machine plate hit the stack with a clank, and Luis pulled the pin to increase the weight.

"Again." His voice came out all business.

Ever since I'd offered him friendship instead of a romantic relationship, Luis had erected a solid wall between us. At first, I thought his coldness would make my last visits easier, but every word in his new tone stabbed my heart.

When my hour finished, I draped a fresh towel across my sweaty neck. "Do you have time to get away from the gym this afternoon?"

"Maybe. Megan took Olivia and Milo away for the weekend. Even though it's Saturday night, I don't have any big plans." Luis tilted his head as if weighing options. "What do you have in mind?"

"Coffee would be fine." He was home *alone* for the weekend? I balled my hands into fists, looking for strength. I'd committed to disentangle from Luis. My future lay with Briana and our family. "Yes—coffee sounds perfect."

"Dinner would be better." Luis smiled.

Stop doing that!

If I joined him for dinner, I'd be away from 2242 for slightly more than an hour. Flex. Unflex. We could go somewhere well-lit. I could add more characteristics to my list for Atacama6. She'd be thrilled.

"I know a great French restaurant." The twinkle in Luis' eyes told me the place wasn't what I needed. I suspected dark corners and romantic table settings.

"I'm hoping for something lively."

"Like Mexican with a mariachi band?"

I searched my woefully inadequate cortical implant for his words. Nothing. Ugh. "Sure."

"Okay. I'll ask around." Luis snugged my towel against my neck. No gym member would have seen his finger casually stroke under my hair. I trembled at his touch.

"Let's meet at 6:30 at Skyline Park. Make sure you wear warm clothes."

I had assumed a mariachi band was a group of musicians, but maybe they were a band of athletes? After my shower, I'd head back to the capsule to fabricate something I could wear outside for an extended time. Denver in January was cold in my time and his.

Maybe I'd wear my Hipposkin enviro-suit under my clothes.

I'd played tennis at the Olympic level and traveled through time—but nothing prepared me for skating on natural ice at Skyline Park in Denver. In my time, the Merlin Building arcade simulated rock climbing, sky diving, and base jumping. All death-defying acts for adrenaline junkies like me. But those programs had fail-safes to prevent injuries.

While Luis rented our skates, I stood at the rink's edge staring at the crowd. Couples locked arms and glided around the rink. Dozens of children scooted across the ice with minute steps, gripping an adult or a moveable frame barrier to keep them upright. Why was I terrified if they were brave enough to balance on the ice on a thin shiny blade?

"Are you ready?" Luis nudged my elbow and nodded toward a row of benches. "Let's gear up."

I followed him, and we sat on the frigid boards. Luis slipped off his shoes and stuffed them under the seat. Once he'd laced his skates, he tapped my shoulder. "Are you okay?"

Luis knew I played competitive tennis, ran miles each week, and worked out with weights. How could I tell him that ice skating was beyond my comfort level? If I were injured, I might need medical assistance in

2026, where I didn't exist.

"Well," a direct approach might work, "I've never skated before."

"Surely they have indoor rinks in California." Luis placed both fists on his denim-covered thighs. "You must have roller-skated. It's not that different."

"I've done neither."

"No problem." He slipped from the bench to kneel in front of me. Luis took my foot in his hands. "You're such an athlete. I'll show you. You'll be a natural."

I stared at the rink while Luis changed my shoes for the skates. Once he snugged the laces tight, he stood and took me by the hands.

"You can hold onto the wall if you feel like you're going to fall." He grinned. "Or I can grab a kiddie helper for you?"

"No." I straightened. "Just hold on to me and make sure I don't fall."

"Not a problem."

Luis placed an arm around my waist and gripped my hand.

My heart throbbed. Was it my fear of falling or being in Luis' arms again?

I glanced up at him. While he focused on the rink ahead, I knew he was enjoying my fragility and dependence. This was precisely the type of interaction Atacama6 would drool over—him taking charge and my relief at giving up control. These give-and-take exchanges occurred between women as well. But why did it seem different when the other person was twice my size?

Luis guarded me as we moved around the circle. He never released my hand—even when he spun to skate backward and pull me along. With each rotation, the laughter from other skaters muddled into the background. People standing beyond the barrier became a blur.

When Luis told me our hour was finished, I couldn't believe the time had passed. After another turn around the rink, he guided me to a break in the partial wall, marked *exit*.

Before we reached the safety of the rubberized walkway beyond the walls, I maneuvered to face him. "Thank you. This was fun."

Luis stopped short of the exit and moved us to the side, allowing others to enter and leave. He pressed his hands on the wall, pinning me in front of him.

His eyes locked onto mine, and breath escaped his lips in misty clouds.

I wanted to look away and gain composure but couldn't.

Briana—my wife, the mother of my children—was in Denver but a million miles away from where Luis and I stood. Or, more precisely, nearly two million hours from me.

A flush swept across my body.

"I'm not hungry." My words spilled out. "Let's go to your place."

Luis drew me into an embrace, and my battle to stay loyal to Briana was lost.

Chapter 39

Twelve hours had passed in 2026—but only three would have elapsed for Briana in 2241. For Luis and me, it was two in the morning. When I arrived home, Briana would do the math and wonder why I'd stayed so long.

I rose on an elbow and watched Luis as he slept. In ten months, he'd be in the same spot. And Briana and I would break into his home to steal his sperm. But Megan Pierce would be lying by his side. Unbeknownst to them, I'd stand at the side of their bed and shoot a sleep serum into Luis' neck before Briana bore him four sons he'd never know or see.

My stomach churned until I could taste the bile bubbling at the back of my throat.

Guilt over our affair, stealing his seed, and taking his son. How could I do it to him?

With a low grunt, Luis rolled onto his side.

I slipped under the sheet and curled next to him. He moaned and nuzzled his face into my hair.

"Sofie," he muttered, still half asleep. "I love you."

My eyes filled with tears. Drops trickled onto the pillow and moistened the fabric under my cheek.

I love you, too. But that doesn't matter.

"Stay with me."

"I'm here now."

I fell into a fitful sleep—dreaming of coming ill-prepared to meetings and running through the Merlin Building, trying to find my studio but not knowing how to find it.

At daybreak I woke, barely able to catch my breath—my chest weighed down from a mountain of deceit.

With my eyes still closed tight, I slipped a hand toward Luis. His space was empty.

"Where on earth did you get this?" Luis' accusatory voice from across the room snapped me fully awake.

I flew off the bed to find Luis standing in the middle of his bedroom. His contorted face spoke of confusion and concern.

In his outstretched hands, my Hipposkin suit stuck out at all angles.

2242

"I've been at the control console for four full hours." Lisa shook her head as she unclasped my restraints. "That put you in 2026 for close to twenty hours. This is a record—even for you."

"Atacama6 will be thrilled." But Briana will grill me about being away for so long. I dreaded leaving the safety of the capsule's recliner. "I've got gigs of data for the HCC. Or at least I will once I take a few hours to consolidate my notes."

"I'm glad you're back." Lisa didn't look me in the eyes. "Simon Merlin's been waiting for you."

"Simon?" I took Lisa's arm to steady myself getting out. "Why is he here?"

"I need to finish the post-jump checklist. Simon'll finalize your medical scans for me. Shouldn't take long—your VSE never made it to 2.0."

Lisa's never coy. What's going on?

Simon stood next to one of the surgery beds. He wore the standard-issue CYR medical uniform. No antiquated costumes—probably because Lisa was there.

With help from Lisa, I crossed the room to sit on the bed, facing Simon. His snarky grin was missing. Had they detected something amiss in my readings?

Simon laid a hand on my shoulder.

"She's gone."

"Who? What do you mean *gone*?"

Simon placed a hand over his heart. "Briana."

"Where did she go?" Had she found out about my affair? Did she flee Denver and run off to be with Jayla in the capital?

"About two hours ago." Simon bowed his head. "Everything shut down at once—her kidneys, heart, and lungs. There was nothing we could do."

The room started to spin.

Simon's face faded, and everything went black.

Chapter 40

JANUARY 15, 2242

When the arrival tone sounded in the control room, a second timepiece appeared below the one tracking how long the doctors were away.

"Please let me handle this one on my own." Lisa nudged me aside as I stared at the control panel. "You look like a walking coma. If you're ever going to let me handle the return procedure, this is the time."

I glanced at the VSE readers. Both doctors registered under 2.0. They'd be fine.

Long before Briana's memorial services and evenings spent with my children to explain why their mother would never hold them again, I'd promised Lisa she could manage this sperm recovery jump. Despite my pledge, I'd wheedled my way into the mission's every aspect. I second-guessed her calculations and hovered over her like she'd never stepped foot near a launch pad.

"You're right." I gave her the most reassuring smile I could muster. "Are you ready?"

"I am." Lisa nodded toward the entrance portal. "Leave before I lose my nerve and beg you to stay."

The countdown clock ticked down to sixty seconds.

"If I go to the engineering floor, you know I'll watch on the vid."

"Then go somewhere else." Lisa pointed to the exit. "Go."

I left and closed the portal behind me.

Lisa knew how to bring them home. As second in command, she'd worked on two sperm collection jumps since I went with Briana and served as primary for all seven of my trips to visit Luis.

Lisa's a professional. Don't micro-manage her.

I wished her well and left. With a tone, the portal door reconsolidated behind me.

The hall between the control room and the elevator was empty. I'd left the arrivals medical staff in the room with Lisa, where they'd ensure the returning travelers and their cargo were safe.

Aside from Lisa, my engineering team would be huddled over their desks on the fifth floor, monitoring entry protocols.

A faint hum from the overhead lights rang in my ears as my shoes squeaked against the polished floor.

When I waved my hand to call the elevator, the holographic door opened immediately, and I stepped inside.

What command should I give? Tempted to stop and watch the return with the other engineers, I knew Lisa would prefer my absence. If I went to my studio, Lisa would have complete autonomy.

"Floor seventeen, please." After a relaxing shower, I could pick up the children and spend a few hours at the arcade. We were helping each other to carve a life without Briana. But the wound was still fresh.

The elevator shuddered and started to lift.

Before the floor indicator changed, a blast threw me against the back wall. I hung, suspended from the wall, before I slammed to the floor. Pain radiated from my back.

The door flickered, then faded altogether.

Smoke flooded the elevator, and I hugged the floor, coughing.

"Stay down." Simon's voice penetrated the fog. Someone slipped a ventilator mask over my mouth and nose.

Hunks of building material filled the once pristine hallway.

Twisted ventilation shafts and wiring snaked along the corridor.

Sparks shot in all directions, illuminating smoke plumes from the hall's far end.

"What's happening?" I grabbed Simon's arm and yanked him toward me.

"Someone set off a bomb in the control room." I could barely hear him over the hum in my ears.

"We have to go help." I pushed off the floor, determined to stand.

"I've checked for signs of life. There are no survivors." Simon slid his arm under mine. "The elevator is out of commission. But the emergency stairs are clear. Can you walk up four flights with my assistance, or shall I carry you?"

"What about Lisa? The medical staff? The returning doctors?"

"No life signs." Simon snugged his arm around my waist. "We need to get you upstairs and to the medical team on the sixth floor."

"All dead?"

How could this happen?

"Yes. And keep your mask on until we're away from the dust."

"It couldn't have been a bomb." I clutched his sleeve. "Maybe it was equipment failure."

"I can assure you, a bomb caused the explosion." Simon pulled me toward the emergency stairs.

"No." I dragged my heels with little effect against Simon's solid-state body. "We need to check."

"There's nothing we can do for them." Simon tightened his grip on my waist and drew me to the first step. "I'm not letting your children lose another parent. If you don't start moving right now, I'm carrying you."

Determined to make it upstairs at least partially on my power, I forced my feet to move.

"She saved my life." I lifted the mask off my face but snapped it back when grit filled my mouth. Airborne debris made my tongue stick to the roof of my mouth. I swallowed hard, trying to work up saliva.

"Who?" Simon tugged me up the first flight.

"Lisa. She wanted to handle the capsule's return. Told me to leave."

"She may have spared you. But don't make her out as a saint."

I grabbed the handrail and came to a complete stop. There would be a full investigation, but Simon would've already penetrated the control logs and reviewed the room's video streams.

"Tell me this was an accident."

"I can't. Lisa Chicago6 blew up the time capsule."

"What?" My legs buckled. "Are you sure?"

"I've already penetrated the Denver security company's footage for the past six months. Chicago6 has met with the Danube9 sisters since

October."

Lisa started meeting them after I last saw Mia in Survivors Park. Mia must have gone after Lisa in retaliation for my rebuff. Or Mia recruited Lisa when she'd failed with me.

I leaned against Simon, making slow progress. "The capsule's designed to take a beating. What's its status?"

"Their sabotage was effective. It'll take years before we can jump again."

"But I'm scheduled to jump in twelve days." I gripped his arm. "I need to give Luis your antidote, or he'll die."

Much later, I'd realize how irrational my statement sounded to Simon.

Chapter 41

Phen and I sat in adjacent lounge chairs on the lawn below the balcony. Since my visit to her farm three months prior, Phen avoided the balcony—unwilling to risk whether her blocking programs could fully secure the airspace.

Latrice and Milo hopped on the grass, with Nanny Tori directing them in a game with continually changing rules. Latrice's enthusiasm taught Milo to embrace the modifications. His 2027 learning may have focused squarely on do's and don't's rather than maybes.

I adjusted my feet on the footstool, taking in the backdrop of crop rows and the setting sun.

"I'm sorry that Half-Wit refused to grant me a hardship furlough to come to Briana's services." Phen's voice cracked when she said Briana's name.

She'd never liked Briana—barely knew her. Phen's emotions likely stemmed from empathy for me or Latrice and Adam.

"The ceremony was jammed with Briana's colleagues from around the world. Some came virtually, but most showed up in person." I took a sip of wine. "Jayla knew them all—they came for her."

"Jayla must be beside herself."

"All the more so because she spent the last few months away in the capital." I ran a thumb around the glass's rim. "No one expects their clone to die before them."

"Are you warming up to the old gal?" Phen set her glass on an adjacent table and stood. She faced the kids with her back toward me.

"We'll probably be at each other's throats in another month. But for now, we have an undeclared detente." I joined Phen and linked an arm with hers. "Jayla agreed to stay in Denver until we're back. Since we brought Nanny Tori, Jayla is in charge of Adam. Issey and Kifle are with her, too."

"She's into babies?" Phen could read people like no one else I knew.

"Nope. Jayla isn't the cuddling type, but the medical staff will fill in the gaps."

When Milo tripped and tumbled to the grass, Latrice dashed for a holographic post and declared victory. Milo rose and approached her with an extended hand. He'd adopted our twenty-third-century gaming traditions—everyone wants to win, but arrogance benefits no one.

"Was it tough to leave Adam?" Phen broke my thoughts.

"It's crazy, but part of me thought of Adam as Briana's boy and Milo as mine. Maybe because Briana always carried him—like he was still a part of her. Since Briana died, I've been the one holding him. I see Briana's personality and expressions in his face."

"Do you see Luis, too?"

Was I ready to talk about him?

"I do." I let the next sip of wine rest on my tongue before swallowing.

"I've avoided asking how Milo came to live with you." Phen gave me a soft hip bump. "Being on this farm has taught me patience. If no one's around to complain to, you learn to let things go."

"Are you saying you don't jump to conclusions or bolt into action anymore?"

"Not completely." Phen laughed. "But I'm getting better at taking the long view."

We stood in silence, watching Tori give instructions and taking in the sun's last rays.

"Well?" Phen asked.

"That's your take on patience?" I rolled my eyes. "You want to hear about Milo?"

"If not now, then when?"

She was right. I would never share the details with Atacama6 or anyone else in CYR or the HCC. Why hold back with my sister?

"When I jumped to October 2026, my main goal was to give Milo and Luis the vaccine with Simon's long-lived nanobots. But when I arrived, nothing seemed right. First off, Megan and their daughter Olivia were missing, and the place was a mess."

Phen held up a finger and pulled me back to the chairs. She curled her legs underneath and tucked a comforter over her thighs as if preparing for a long and detailed account.

"When I saw Luis alone in bed, I couldn't resist."

"What?" Phen straightened. "You drugged him and jumped on?"

"No." I glanced at Latrice and Milo to ensure they weren't within hearing range. "I didn't drug him. I stripped and climbed into bed with him—like I was in a trance. Maybe it was because I'd fantasized about him for so long or because it didn't seem real to cheat 200 years in the past. I wanted him more than anything."

"More than Olympic gold?"

I nodded.

"I'd give up my freedom for good to spend an hour with a real man." Phen wriggled in her seat.

"He called me Sofie."

"Nobody calls you Sofie except me." Phen cocked her head. "You must have been shocked."

"I was." I nodded. "But Luis told me the whole story. For him, I'd visited a bunch of times. He knew Briana and I had taken his sperm and that she had four sons with him. The boys would live in the future and help humankind survive. At that point, I'd seen Luis once. But for him, we were in love."

"Love?" Phen's eyes glued to mine.

"It was hard to understand when Luis told me. But now that I've gone back, I know he told the truth."

"When do you get to the part about Milo?"

"That was tough." I drew a long breath. "I told Luis about the Cursed Decades and TWS. He knew they'd die and asked me to save Milo."

"Couldn't you save them both?"

"We talked for hours. Luis wanted to stay and try to change history— to stop the Cursed Decades, warn people about the virus, and, most of all, keep Megan from being blamed for Milo's disappearance." I shook my head. "From what I can tell, nothing he did worked."

"The Tobar Principle."

"How do you know about that?"

"Just because I'm not an engineer doesn't mean I'm stupid."

"I never said you were." I reached to squeeze her arm. "Well, you asked, and that's the story."

"Does Milo know everything?"

"As much as he can understand at his age." I turned to watch him. Nanny Tori had illuminated a wide swath in the lawn to lengthen their playtime after the sun had set. Milo tagged Latrice and ran as she shrieked and giggled.

"Will you introduce Milo to your ARP Luis?"

"No. I labeled his program as offline after Briana died. He brings up too many memories."

"And guilt?"

She knows me too well.

I nodded. "It's getting cool. Should we go inside?"

"Sure. ERAC can have an appetizer ready in minutes. The kids will want to eat early. But we'll have a late dinner."

"Perfect." I craned my neck to speak toward the balcony. "Simon, we'll be inside in a few. If you're not busy elsewhere, I'd love for you to join us for dinner."

Simon materialized on the deck, leaning over the rail and wearing a gaucho's homespun poncho and a wide-brimmed hat. "You should know I'm currently problem-solving with colleagues in all four countries."

"Are you bragging or making excuses for not joining us?"

Take it down a notch, would you, Simon?

"I'll sit with you and the family at dinner if you send Nanny Tori to her room. I don't feel comfortable making small talk with machines."

For Book Club questions see: www.LVDitchkus.com/book-clubs

Glossary

3D epithelial and connective tissue printer: A bioprinter used to reconstruct tissue from various body regions.

AereoPod: A sleek, narrow, sixteen-passenger airplane that travels at Mach speeds and is the most common equipment for long-distance travel in 2240. Manufactured in EuroRosse.

AI or Artificial Intelligence: Computer systems that can perform tasks typically requiring human intelligence or simulating human behavior. This can include machine learning, which allows a machine to learn from data without explicit programming.

An-mother: The noncloned parent in a family. A cloned child would have a mother and an-mother if her parents were married. Grandmothers follow the same tradition—grandmothers on the cloned mother's side are called grandmothers, but grandmothers through marriage are called an-grandmothers.

ARP or Augmented Reality Program: A computer program similar to virtual reality, but the objects and people feel natural to the touch.

Com-card or communication card: A small, thin bioplastic card used for voice calls, signaling, or basic holographic calls without holomatter technology.

CVI or Compressed Vaccine Injectors: A jet injection device to administer medicines and vaccines. It replaced needles and syringes in the late 2000s.

CYR or Chromosome Y Reestablishment: A division of the HCC where both Briana Memphis7 and Sofia Andes7 work.

Defense 43 pistol: An electrically charged firearm used primarily for self-protection to subdue an attacker without causing permanent physical harm.

EBAS or Experimental Birthing Android Simulator: A pregnant-looking humanoid robot designed to simulate an expectant woman's responses during the birthing process.

ERAC: Phen Andes7's acronym name for her ARP Lover—stands for ERgonomically and Anatomically Correct

FART or Fully Automated Robotic Team: Phen's made-up acronym for the system of robots attending to the nationally owned reformatory farm where Phen is completing a five-year sentence.

Holo-tablet: A semi-transparent holographic computer screen that can be called up and sized by anyone within a work team for either collaborative or solo use. It includes the same programs and data viewing capabilities as the ocular implant version, but it looks like a handheld device and is viewable by others besides the user.

HAV or Human Androgen Virus: A virus that surfaced in 2060 and attacks only men. When it spread, there was no cure, and nearly every man exposed to the virus died.

HCC or Humanity Continuance Coalition: An organization adopted by the remaining four countries (America, EuroRosse, Asia, and Gulf-Africa) to promote cooperation and collaboration and ensure the continuation of the human race.

Levi-plate: A loaner hoverboard used to hasten travel—typically available at busy intersections or near transportation stations.

Mission Y: A time travel reliant project by CYR to rejuvenate the reproduction process by replacing cloning techniques with inseminated clone eggs.

Ocular implant: A minuscule computer processor embedded within the eye that holds routine programs (e.g., time and calendar) but can connect to more sophisticated computer systems and create virtual semi-transparent computer screens visible to the user but not to others.

Tobar Principle: If you go back in time and change something, events will fill in so that the future comes out the same. That is: the events "will always adjust themselves" to avoid any inconsistency in the Universe. Thus the grandfather paradox (a person travels to a time before their grandfather had children and kills him, it would make their own birth impossible) is irrelevant.

TWS or Testicular Wasting Syndrome, commonly referred to as TWS or twas: The deadly syndrome is caused by the human androgen virus and can kill the victim within hours or days.

VSE or Vital Signs Elucidator: A medical device that compiles and displays a person's vital signs and creates a composite death probability score. A reading of 10 means the patient is deceased, but a score above 9.0 compels a doctor to cease treatment.

READ ON FOR AN EXCERPT FROM

PRIMOGENITUS:

FIRST BORN

Book II of The Chrom Y Series

BY L.V. DITCHKUS

Available soon on Amazon

For information on the release date, follow at:

LVDitchkus.com

Chapter 1

COLORADO TRAIL—OCTOBER 11, 2260
ASSISTANT ENGINEER LATRICE MEMPHIS8

From inside our hover tent, my cousin Gael and I gaped at the 300-plus kilogram creature pummeling its paws against my brothers' refuge. If our flexi-pane dome shelters were bear-proof, why was a grizzly fracturing the sides? The animal already took out their propulsion unit. Fleeing wasn't an option.

"According to my wildlife database, the grizzly's night vision is like ours," Gael called to the men over the comm system. "If we turn on our proximity lights, it might get distracted and leave."

Gael pressed her face so close to the side that her breath fogged the flexi-pane wall. Her gaze never left the beast. I could almost hear her brain evaluating and discarding strategies to save the guys—ideas leaking like sweat from her pores.

Shuddering, I took another step back into our tent's recesses. I could run calculus and trig equations in circles around my sixteen-year-old cousin. Despite being five years her senior, when *she* stepped up in a crisis, I stayed out of her way.

"Don't do anything to make it come after you." My brother Milo's voice came across the comm with the composure of ordering appetizers for dinner. Regardless of the danger, he'd stay calm. He always did.

At the attack's start, the guys turned their tent's transparency setting to blackout mode, hoping the animal would lose interest.

Great idea—too bad it didn't work.

Something attracted this animal, and it wasn't giving up.

The bear stood on his hind legs and stretched, its full three-and-a-half-meter height towering above their tent. The creature raised its snout. With nostrils flared, it took in all the invasive scents we'd left in his territory. After nearly a week on the trail, our camping protocols had become routine. We'd stowed dinner remnants in odor-proof containers and extinguished our holographic campfire that emitted a realistic smoke aroma.

What unnatural fragrance could it smell?

It must be after something.

Or maybe we'd invaded the creature's domain, and it was angry.

I clasped my hands and squeezed, waiting for it to strike their tent again.

When it plunged, dropping the full force of its weight on their tent, their dome shuddered under its powerful paws. The grizzly's dagger claws screeched against the polymer until its forefeet hit the ground with a reverberating thud.

"Ugh." Gael pounded a fist against the wall.

If the bear heard her in our tent, its attention didn't falter. It slouched, slithering to the ground with fat rolls rippling like a water-filled balloon. The creature stuffed its nose under the edge of the guys' dome and scooped the ground under the rim. Dirt and pebbles flew to either side, spraying our tent with debris.

"It's digging underneath," I called to the comm but couldn't imagine what Milo or Issey could do about that.

"Really?" I winced at Issey's sarcasm. "We can hear it."

With a thought directive, I accessed a Colorado wildlife guide I'd downloaded before the trip. "There hasn't been a grizzly sighting in Colorado in hundreds of years."

"Says who?" Issey responded before I could go on with more specifics about the HCC's wildlife surveillance cameras.

"I looked it up." Any details could be helpful. "The last sighting was in the mid-twentieth century."

"I don't know how that's relevant," Issey snapped. "They're here now."

"I'm just saying, the bear couldn't possibly know the dome's underside is more vulnerable than the walls."

My brothers mumbled in the background momentarily before Milo said, "We appreciate your research, Latrice. And we've got a plan. Can you maneuver your shelter so our tent is between you and the bear?"

"We're not using your dome as a shield." I grasped the back of a camp chair.

We were all adults, and they didn't need to come to our defense.

"That's where your mind went?" Milo's chuckle made me bristle. "We're going to distract it at the front and escape through the back. But you'll need to move close to get us all to safety."

"Latrice, really?" Gael scoffed. "What makes you think they need to protect *us*?"

Before I could respond, Gael plopped cross-legged at the sealed front entrance and took control of our dome's propulsion system.

Gael directed our hover tent to lift. It swayed and drifted away from the animal, circling behind the men's dome.

I dropped to the floor and braced a leg against a cot to keep from toppling. Low grasses and brush scraped the underside as Gael edged us into place.

They'd designed our tents to carry equipment and food between campsites or emergency evac an injured hiker. "Do you think one hover-dome can carry all four of us?" I asked.

"Got a better idea?" Gael smirked over her shoulder.

I pressed my lips together, forcing further questions to be left unasked.

"I've scored the back wall," Milo said over the comm. "In a sec, I'll start cutting a hole with a laser saw. When I'm about three-quarters finished, Issey's going to open the front door and kick out some food. That'll keep the bear distracted until we jump into your dome."

As I crawled to the front, Gael activated the controls and nestled the two tents together. Once we were firmly on the ground, I initiated the opening. Cold, dry air rushed through the doorway, carrying rotting aspen leaves' bitter scent into our space.

A laser beam flashed through the side of Milo and Issey's tent, sending smoke and a sickeningly sweet smell into the night breeze.

When the bear's frantic digging stopped, I froze.

Did it hear us? Would it come around the back of the guy's dome to investigate?

Gael would know the answers and how to prepare for an encounter, but I dared not ask.

I held my breath, straining to hear movement over the throbbing of my heartbeats. Nothing. Just the slow hiss from Milo's laser as it tracked a line from inside his dome.

"Done," Milo called.

Before I could scoot to make room, a panel from their tent exploded open.

Milo tumbled through our door, careening past Gael and whamming into me. In an instant, Milo was on his knees and leaning through the opening. His hand stretched toward Issey and motioned for our brother to join us.

"No!" Issey screamed.

I raised to see past Gael and Milo. Kicking, Issey crab-walked to escape from the bear's reach. But the beast had pinned his leg against the floor near the opening.

As I stepped back in horror, Gael pushed Milo aside and dove into their adjacent tent.

"No, Gael." She wouldn't have heard my pleading whisper until I added, "Stay with me."

She ignored me.

"You're not taking Issey on my watch." Gael thrust her hands under Issey's arms and closed them across his chest to yank him backward and away from the bear. "Milo, give me a hand."

The grizzly lifted its head and roared. My breath hitched when the animal's shoulders pressed through the opening. It was coming for all of us.

My feet froze on the tent floor, legs filled with lead.

Then the beast made a mistake. Its massive paw on Issey's leg lifted, maybe to regain purchase. But Gael and Milo's tug-of-war prevailed. As Issey pulled his mauled leg free, they yanked him across the floor and through the nested opening.

"Close entrance," Gael called to the ceiling. To us, she said, "Grab ahold of something. We're outta here."

The entrance sealed.

I dove for the floor next to the equipment chest and hugged it as Gael steered our dome upward to clear the trees. Electric fans whined, compensating for the excess load. The tent vibrated. The subtle tremor grew into an all-out thrashing.

I checked the specs. "We need to slow down, decrease pitch, or toss out equipment."

"Stopping to throw away gear will take time we don't have. We need to get Issey to the med center right away. I'll reduce speed." Gael closed her eyes, and the dome slowed. "Prevailing winds are from the west. That'll help us get to Denver before we run out of power. But keep monitoring our power levels."

"Will do." I modified the dome's modest propulsion system to optimize performance and responsiveness.

Milo held Issey's head in his lap. He stroked our brother's hair and leaned near an ear—no doubt whispering encouraging words.

After opening a Holo-screen to keep monitoring our progress, I pressed a finger against the equipment locker, and the lid flipped open to reveal our camping kits. I rummaged through dehydrated meal packets and parts from our water-making hydrogen/oxygen burner until I found the med-kit.

Once situated next to Issey, I rolled up his pant leg. His calf was a mass of gouges and shredded skin.

"I'll do the best I can." I pulled an antiseptic lamp and wound sealant from the kit. "But you're going to wish I kept the family tradition and trained in medicine like you."

"Maybe I should stabilize the wound." Issey tried to sit up, but Milo kept him restrained.

"Let Latrice do this." Milo gave me a cocky smile. "Let her feel like she's contributing."

"Thanks." I rolled my eyes at Milo and opened a packet marked *Penetrating Wounds*.

"Despite being a geeky engineer, you'll do fine." Issey tensed as I gently opened the skin flaps. "My HAV drug regimen helps with hemostasis. To stop infection from whatever lives on that bear's claws, you'll need to clean and close the wounds before we get to the medical center at CRY headquarters."

"Tell me if I'm doing anything wrong." I swept the germicidal ultraviolet excimer lamp over his leg to kill offending bacteria and viruses. Issey gritted his teeth but didn't tell me to stop.

"Latrice," Milo glanced up at me, "your mother fixed me up a few times when I was little. You remind me of those days when I see you like that."

"I'm glad you remember her." The lamp's finishing tone sounded, and I stowed it in a sleeve. "We were almost three when she died. My memories of her are murky."

"You look exactly like her." Milo placed a friendly hand on my shoulder.

"Not surprising. I'm 100 percent her clone." I shrugged and reached for the adhesive applicator to seal Issey's wounds. I smiled at my patient. "Unlike Issey, who's only 50 percent from my mom."

"I think of you as 100 percent my sister." Issey drew a sharp breath when I sealed one of the largest gouges. "Unlike Gael, who's 100 percent instigator."

"Don't blame me for what happened with that bear." Gael tapped the air in front of her, adjusting the dome's course on Holo-tablets that—as the driver— only she could see. "It was my idea to hike sections of the Colorado Trail. But you all agreed to come along."

"I'm not sure what the HCC will do to us when we get back." I coated another deep cut and moved on to the smaller ones. "Gael and I were the only ones authorized to take this trip. You guys left without permission."

"They can't force me to stay at headquarters." Milo jabbed a finger toward me. "As long as I'm around for testing and sperm donations, the HCC shouldn't care how I spend my free time."

"Settle down." Issey wriggled his head deeper into Milo's lap, and his eyes drooped from the sedative bots infused in the adhesive. "I wouldn't have missed this trip for the world. Adam covered for us, and he'll know how to smooth any ruffled egos when they find out we left without authorization."

Our brother Adam—ever the peacemaker and politician in our family— helped Gael and me garner a few days off work. But based on his short tenure at the capital, he may not have enough clout to keep us out of trouble.

ACKNOWLEDGMENTS

I must start by thanking my writing partner Susan Bavaria. From reading early drafts to giving me suggestions on character development and scene-setting, she was vital in my journey to complete this book.

Four special beta readers, my sister Tina Pickell, brother-in-law Bruce Iannuzzi, and friends Matt Cushing, Cam Torrens, Greg Pickens, Rich Barclay, and Samone Yuen provided in-depth comments that resulted in this book's complexity and consistency. Sherry Richardson, Mary Craig, Laurel McHargue, Kayelle Allen, Zoe Katsulos, and other beta readers spent countless hours reviewing drafts and providing helpful comments.

Feedback from the Rocky Mountain Fiction Writers' Spec Fiction and the Chaffee County Writers Exchange critique groups also helped me fill plot holes and deepen my characters.

I value and appreciate my editor, Anita Mumm, owner of Mumm's the Word Editorial Services, for her time and attention to timing, pace, tension, and those pesky words that crop into my work. Her suggestions helped my storylines blend.

My final thanks are to my loving husband, David. For all the times we've been hiking, and I've asked you to remove my phone from my pack so I could record an idea and took hours away from our vacations to write and edit—I give you my sincere thanks.

L.V. DITCHKUS is the author of the award-winning *The Sasquatch Series*, which includes *Crimes of the Sasquatch, Mission of the Sasquatch, Legacy of the Sasquatch,* and *Passage of the Sasquatch.* While writing her new Sci-fi series and the soon to be released second book in the *Chrom Y* series, she's led adventure travel trips, hiked and snowshoed hundreds of miles, and volunteered for wilderness advocacy and writing organizations. She and her husband live in a rural mountain community in central Colorado, where she gains inspiration from the five 14,000+ foot tall peaks viewable from her window.

Check out her blog at LVDitchkus.com